The Rescuists

Geoffrey Fitchett

Published by Clink Street Publishing 2022

Copyright © 2022

First edition.

ISBNs:
978-1-914498-53-4 paperback
978-1-914498-54-1 ebook

Chapters

Introduction

While my wife and I were visiting a neighbour, her six-year old daughter told me she wanted to read me a story and promptly fetched a handwritten booklet of eight small pages.

"It's called, The Princess and the Knight!" she said and so commenced the tale. The essence was a Princess in great danger being saved by the Knight mainly by him slaying the dragon. And so it followed a traditional path for these things, and yet was very sweet.

Two things stood out about the story though. One was that her booklet read right-hand page before left-hand page, rather in the way that newspapers sell their advertising space while the other was that she had spelled Knight, 'Nit' the way you would prior to the confusion and enlightenment that follows learning how to spell more conventionally.

As lovely as the story itself was and as charming as its author made it by personally reading it to lucky me, I was left chuckling about the idea of a Princess being saved by a Nit rather than a Knight.

That the Nit managed to slay a dragon might be to his credit but chewing it over I became increasingly bothered by the image of David Attenborough explaining that the dragon population has never been smaller than it is today and unless we allow them some habitat (a few castles, caves and hilltops perhaps), we may be the last generation of human beings with whom they will share this plastic-speckled planet. Slaying such a rare and endangered animal, even for the love of a Princess might turn out to be very unecological.

Life experience suggests it could well be waste of effort too since it's almost certain that the Princess will thank Nit profusely but announce she's always had a soft spot for Tarquin instead. "Oh my Tarquin!" she wails, sniffing his rugger socks. The same Tarquin who keeps dumping her and kissing Cassandra instead, but always comes back eventually, saying, "I'm so sorry my snuggle-muffin, I'm just a cad aren't I? Will you ever forgive me?" and then they hook-up again until his next little real ale-fuelled error of judgement. It's a cycle, like a vicious cycle or a virtuous cycle, but this blitheringly idiotic one is a cycle for blithering idiots.

And perhaps the biggest idiot was Nit, who should have checked his passport and/or traced the origins of his honorary title; 'Nit'. Open-mouthed, he could have come to the painful realisation, "I'm a what? I always thought I was a Knight…" and though temporarily crestfallen, might have embarked on a new path that did not include killing rare and exotic creatures, nor rescuing ungrateful, fickle rich girls. Come on Nit, sort yerself out!

The day after Mila read me her little booklet I woke up with the idea for the story that follows. Some of the wording in it was there, tumbling around, echoing, reforming, written across synaptic connections while unconscious or at best semi-conscious. It happens to me a lot and I find it's best to get typing pronto. In this case I started and couldn't stop. I expected to finish the original short story in a day, but the next day I carried on with no loss of pace and continued for six weeks until it wrapped itself up. I now better understand the claim of some musicians that the hit in question came from somewhere else because for whatever reason, it flowed faster than anything I've ever written before. Mila's wonderful little story of *The Princess and the Nit* unlocked the tale you are about to read.

Chapter the First.
Vienna

With so many present, it might seem odd that one absentee should be so sorely missed. Not so, for she would be like the last piece of a colourful jigsaw, in essence just one of so very many rich and gilt-backed works of art, tipped onto the plush velvet in an untidy pile and waiting for the process of sorting, grouping, aligning and conjoining. Now look more closely and notice they are all unique in shape, with their outies and innies, their holes, slots, tabs and knobs, the occasional straight edge and the wonderful hues they cast under party lighting. She may be just one of many hundreds but here she was made crucially important by virtue of not being where she ought.

There they were gathered, the others. All the kings, all the queens, all the princes, all the princesses, a great many barons and baronesses, lords and ladies, counts and viscounts, knights of great gallantry, poets of great notoriety, composers and designers, artists and musicians and indeed anyone who had done anything of sufficient note to make them famous beyond their own city walls.

Also gathered, but not as guests, were the hundreds more people whose task it was to ensure all went smoothly. These were the cooks and waiters, porters and cleaners, bakers and butlers, chauffeurs for the many carriages and grooms for the countless horses, stern looking ladies and gentlemen directing events, ladies-in-waiting who were indeed waiting on their mistresses and a few others who just appeared to be waiting, for what precisely? For money of course, but in the meantime, they would wait for the next request to do some little thing for their master or mistress which any normal person would happily do for themselves. Mostly they were being busy bees grumbling about what time it was and how much they still had to do and how they wished they could sit down with a nice cup of tea but in between, they stood about looking like disdainfully snooty statues. Their location was carefully chosen, not close enough to immediately offer assistance but not far enough away to be accused of desertion.

And what was all this society doing gathered here in Vienna, having travelled from the ends of the Earth, namely Lisbon and London, Naples and Edinburgh, Budapest and Brussels, Copenhagen and Istanbul, Paris and Barcelona, Helsinki and Hamburg, Saint Petersburg and Stockholm, Seville and Oslo? Why, for the wedding of Princess Isabella and Prince Rupert of course, he soon to be King, she soon to be Queen and if all goes as expected, the bride and groom's departure for their honeymoon would promptly follow the funeral of the groom's father and old King Johan (those two people being one and the same) and who was particularly ill with quinsy and dark fevers of the furrowed and feverish brow. The coincidence of his death and their union would swell the list of attendees to his send off and save another long journey for all those annoyingly obliged to return should he selfishly linger longer.

But linger he would not, for no amount of cormorant's blood, hedgehog fat or snail slime seemed to help and various poultices applied by hopeful apothecaries did little to alleviate his symptoms. Yet they did make his bedchamber stink of their ingredients, too many of which were based on the hoped-for benefits of goose-poop and the like. Some things are simply too unpleasant to mention so let us not mention them here.

You might wonder if the death of a parent might put a dampener on celebrations. Let us say that in regular families it would, in others it should but does not and they take pains to hide the fact while in some families it simply does not. At all. When it comes to heads of state where a prince or princess face the interminable wait for their forebear to expire before taking the reins (and the reigns), some have been known to let their impatience show. Patricide isn't unheard of and sometimes, to allay fears of it, infanticide precedes the possibility.

King Johan was at death's door courtesy entirely of natural causes and not hastened in the slightest by Prince Rupert and so, while facing the abyss gave him cause to shudder, he did at least have those facts he could be grateful about. Rupert marrying Isabella was not coincidental however, since King Johan had invited her to court some months before with ambitions his lively mind had envisioned without due diligence. He had forgotten his age, his portliness and general lack of vigour. With selfish myopia, he had omitted to consider she might prefer his youthful son and heir and having never witnessed it before, entirely underestimated Rupert's determination to win her once his heart was hers. You might say bringing them together was his last act of kingly generosity, though whenever they presented themselves to him, arms tightly wrapped around each other and grins as wide as their youthful faces allowed, he grimaced like a man who'd bitten into a sour apple and staring at it in disgust, had seen half a worm. Just yesterday, he had waved them in and rasped his wisdom to their turned ears, "Be there balance in the world, it is because we lead, they follow, because we collect the taxes while they toil to pay them and thus we have wealth and they, some measure of poverty. It is the way of things." They nodded, turning towards him, peering into his dull and opaque eyes and offering their most sincere expressions of gratitude for his words – though wishing his breath was more posies and less poopies. "Forbearing the great responsibilities thrust upon us, we benefit in countless ways and I'll admit, that while the burden can sometimes be great, the benefits are often taken for granted. Having anything… everything we want," he regarded Isabella and grimacing, coughed unpleasantly causing her to recoil and him to be disgusted that nature should be so cruel, "I've realised that for two people to be so very happy, one must be doubly unhappy." He laid back with a sigh. These last words confused them, making no sense they could deduce and while they looked at each other for an explanation, they found only a mirrored frown and shrugging simultaneously, smiled in amusement at their never-ending synchronicity. "Now bugger off and be stupidly happy somewhere else!" he rasped, coughing again with the effort.

"Thank you, father!" said Rupert gratefully.

"Oh, thank you dear Papa!" said Isabella with tears of even greater gratitude welling up as she leaned in to kiss his forehead. Grinding his teeth, the old King moved a free arm to push her away but instead found his hand on her hip and misunderstanding this as a hug, leaned in closer herself, inadvertently squishing the old King's face into the very cleavage which had earned her a place in court all those months ago.

He stifled a cough and muttered, "And now I can die," surprising himself at how little it took to provide a moment's delight at this critical juncture. They reversed out of his vast bedchamber, the Prince bowing, the Princess blowing kisses like a thespian.

On the Saturday was the tremendous wedding where a great many people drank much too much champagne and fine wine and in between feasted on far, far too much rich food and, having eaten and drunk themselves into a staggering, clumsy crowd of boisterously noisy nitwits, they earnestly blabbered utter nonsense about nothing of any real importance and generally embarrassed themselves in a manner that only the servants would remember. The most sensible ones and those with more fragile constitutions retired around midnight, apologising profusely for their inability to make fools of themselves further to all those remaining who preferred company for their nonsense and feared being left alone to finish off the many part-drunk carafes and bottles. The hardy revellers determined to extract extra value from the event, stayed up later and didn't make for their beds – or any bed they could find – until around three o'clock in the morning, while a few, mostly men it has to be said, stayed talking around messy tables littered with food and drink, their clothes and hair telling the story of their long drinking session until dawn broke and the appearance of nature's alarm clock became their cue to retire.

"Why do they stay up so late? It's nearly half-past five and I have to be up by... five!" asked one maid.

"Well done my dear, you've managed your first task of the day," answered an elderly butler standing nearby.

"Yeah but only cus I never went to bed in the first place! When am I gonna get some shut-eye, that's what I wanna know?"

The butler shrugged the shrug of a man who had been in service a long time and for whom very little mattered very much. "They will all be unconscious soon, your chap too... and you can join him."

"Ere! I'll 'ave none of that thank you very much!"

"I mean in slumber my dear girl, nothing more!" but his expressionless face exhibited a small twitch in one corner of his mouth and this did indeed suggest something more. The twitch faded and his blank expression returned and though he didn't look at her she wondered if he knew and blushed just in case. She started humming the tune to All Things Bright and Beautiful which gave cause to the butler to adopt a puzzled frown and squint at her out of the corner of his eye. Upon sensing his awareness, she stopped humming, gave a little cough and glowed a bright red. It was one of those moments when she didn't know what to do with her hands.

"They don't think of us at all, keeping us up til this hour!" she moaned after collecting herself.

"They don't think at all you mean," he said with school-master-like authority. "I believe you can measure the emptiness of human existence by the individual's reluctance to retire to bed." He swept his arm about the vast patio as if gently slapping all the important people still seated, gossiping loudly, laughing at their own bad jokes and yelching, that being a belch combined with a yawn, or vice-versa, depending what started it.

"Eh?" said the maid obligingly.

"People with things to do, full lives, a purpose in their tomorrows go to bed in readiness." The butler didn't look at the maid, only at the revellers and it would have taken an observer with a particularly acute eye to see the note of scorn in his expression, because it was almost entirely professionally respectful. The note was not tiny because he had practiced hiding it but because his scorn was tiny too. It existed, but barely.

"Well I wouldn't behave like them if I had their... means!" said the maid, a tad exasperated with impatience.

"You say that only because you are you. If you... any

of us… were unfortunate enough to be them, we would all behave just like that." He gave a nod in their direction and winced as a young gentleman, leaning too far back on his chair, fell and did a backward roll, yet via a deft revolution of the wrist, managed to retain all the wine in his glass. Amazed and staring at the wine retained and rocking within its vessel, his friends cheered and hammered the table like jungle drums. "You would only be compassionate to the likes of us if you had some memory of this life." She gaped at him but he remained fixed on the revellers. "How often do you contemplate life on the moon?"

"Wot?" she wrinkled her nose.

"Because you have no knowledge of it." The wrinkle spread to her brow. "Which one's yours?"

She indicated with her head, "That lanky streak of nonsense Prince Adalbert."

"Ah, I know him, he visits mine; Prince Charles the diminutive one in garish colours."

"Oh him who don't never shut up?" she said, latching her eyes on Charles.

"Hmm," he agreed. "He's never quite sure when to be quiet, so doesn't risk it." He couldn't help smiling when her reaction to his prince was a disrespectful tut and for the first time turned to look at her properly. "Born to a different house you yourself would be a good princess young lady. That's the irony of the lottery of birth. If only the stork had flown a few more hundred metres and dropped you down a grander chimney."

"Wot?"

She met his eye wondering what the dry old fellow wanted by flattering her. He turned away and said, "Life is a lottery of mostly booby prizes where everyone thinks theirs is bad until they walk in someone else's shoes." She frowned as she processed the butler's latest snippet of wisdom, the pair watching their employers and wondering *why*. Just *why*.

Gradually the boisterousness faded until it finally abated. After so many hours of drinking and eating and drinking (with a bit more eating in between, but also a lot more drinking) they had become oddly quiet and reflective and as they shuffled towards where they vaguely remembered their bedrooms to be, they passed by the wreckage of party-goers who had neither managed to retire when constitutions dictated that they should, nor had they been able to meet the dawn still conscious, but instead slept, crumpled and ungainly, tongues lolling from their mouths as they snored loudly. Everything about them an absolute mess.

One particular fair maiden (it should be noted, very fair indeed) had stayed up especially late but remained only a little bit tiddly herself because she had drunk much less than the others, stopped at each and mused over how much fun it would be if someone would invent a machine that could instantly paint their image, for what discomfort and embarrassment would arise by showing them a visual account of their self-destruction the day after? They would wince and laugh, then complain of their headache and laugh again and ask whether they really had looked that bad, or had the artist exaggerated the scene?

She had spent her evening passing from throng to throng, eavesdropping and observing and avoiding being dragged into their twaddle. She never stayed long, generally slipping away when some bore attempted to refill her glass, "No thank you, anyway what is that?"

"Wine!" they would say, baffled.

"Of course, but which particular wine?"

"Red!" they would say after looking at it, delighted with themselves.

"That much I can see. Which red wine? For it may not be the one I am drinking."

"Oh…" they would squint at the label, wondering why

the words were blurring, jerking and dancing around in front of their glazed and sozzled eyes, pass it around the table until someone announced it to be a Syrah, at which point she would say she was on the Cabernet. Or Merlot, or Rioja or any wine they didn't offer, at which point she would be off for she was on a little quest all of her own, preoccupied by a kind of curiosity. It had given her a purpose, a mission of sorts, but she had failed, and failure wasn't something that sat comfortably with her at all.

Sunday consisted mostly of hundreds of servants doing all the clearing up, a huge chore that took all day. In between, their various masters and mistresses were either sleeping the entire time or waking and calling for water, breakfast, more wine, a fresh chamber pot or their mummies. Some behaved as it was their servants' fault that they felt so ill.

None were quite so ill as King Johan though, who chose today to finally (and conveniently) die. He'd been wheeled to the wedding in a chair built for the purpose and updated as to events through the course of the day by his favourite steward. His son and brand-new daughter-in-law had attended him at one point in the afternoon and were warned by the most eminent physician that his pallor did not auger well. He had leaned in to plant his face in its happy place, but Isabella had pushed him back into his chair, telling him he should not strain himself and so his last act of any worth was frustrated – and rightly so, some might say. Nodding and thanking the man, the couple returned to the ballroom, for music and dancing were soon to commence. It was this very Sunday then that the Prince was crowned King and his bride became Queen.

To avoid delays and all the ghastly smells that accompany them, the grossly ceremonial laying to rest of one-time King Johan took place first thing in the morning the very next day and his royal grumpiness was celebrated in song, verse and soliloquy, none of which mentioned his many faults, and the sum of which caused the impatient and still slightly nauseous attendees to think they were written for someone else entirely. In a matter of days, King Moody-Snarly-Grumpy the Umpteenth had gone from looking very pale on a vast throne, to paler still but with an ominous greyness about him as he lay in his bed, to lavishly boxed and wrapped and installed with his ancestors in the vast and dusty royal mausoleum.

Immediately after the hugs, handshakes and triple-cheek-kissing that mark the end of a funeral, the delirious newlyweds set off for three months of travel – for royalty could afford to have three honeymoons instead of just one – with all manner of things tied to the back of their carriage clattering along and frightening the horses up front so that they went faster. The large white carriage was decorated with ribbons and scrawled with slogans painted in bright pink such as 'Royal Marriage Carriage' and 'Betrothed this Saturday last' and a rather cheeky, 'Too busy to wave!'

After waving off the happy couple, bags were packed and the gathered throng began their long journeys home to the far-flung corners of the world from whence they came, meeting again only when such occasions might arise sufficient in import and grandeur to deserve their patronage. Yet a small group remained on the wide pavement outside the Gross Teuer Hotel.

"No sir, I did not!" said one, shaking his head and frowning deeply, "How about you? Did you fare better?"

"Not I, though I spent all my time on the quest. You sir?" He had turned to the third man. He too shook his head.

"Then I suppose we have failed, each of us, but not for want of trying."

"Ahem!" said a fourth person, the aforementioned fair maiden (very fair indeed). They all turned towards her. "Sirs, you neglected to enquire as to my efforts in this matter. For

I too searched, enquired, spared no energy in pursuing all avenues of possibility, and what's more I did so as one of the Princess's own feminine variety, thinking as she would think, not a clod-hooved hunter, but a will-o-the-wisp with guile, greatly used to the ways of avoiding unwanted attention." Indeed, as we know, she spent much of the party, a glass of fine red wine in her hand, moving from throng to throng, discreetly seeking their quarry.

"And?" they all gaped. "You found her? You have her?"

"I do not." Her head dropped. "I conclude she is not here. She did not come."

"Nonsense!" cried the first man, himself a prince of course.

"She was invited!" said the second prince.

"She accepted the invitation!" said the third.

"She would not break her word!" said the second.

"Unless..." said the fair maiden, herself a Princess as it happens.

"Yes?" the Princes leaned in closer to the Princess. "Well... I mean, unless..."

"Unless what, Princess Shoshama? You say unless. Unless what, unless what?"

The Princess put on her best conspiratorial face, "Unless she was... unable."

"How so, unable?" said the first Prince, his name Charles, abbreviated to 'Chatty' among friends, the same one of whom two nights before, one of the other two's maids had said, *Oh him who don't never shut up,* and here, like pretty much everywhere else, he was clearly the most inclined to do most of the talking.

"Detained?" the Princess ventured, "Restrained?"

"Contained!" barked Prince two, Adalbert being his name and him being the one the maid had referred to as *That lanky streak of nonsense.*

"Enchained! Perhaps restrained with the help of chains, hence – enchained…" cried Prince Darius, his hands clasping his own face. Darius was the third of the group and the only one we haven't met before.

"Then it is we who must unchain her, de-contain her, un-restrain her, un-detain, um… de-detain…" Charles stumbled in his speech, he looked confused.

"Tain?" ventured Princess Shoshama.

"Say what?" asked Prince Chatty, a fellow who liked to dress in bright colours to go with his surprisingly straw-coloured hair (an unkind person might say it was yellow – unkind and yet chromatically accurate). Chatty and Adalbert had met before, Darius and Shoshama were new acquaintances to the pair, and to each other come to that.

"You can't say, *dedetain*, surely two de's cancel each other out and the word meaning, to release from detention is, *tain*!" explained Shoshama. Seeing her you might wonder which was more dazzling, her sapphires and emeralds which flashed in the morning sunshine, or her sparkly blue eyes. Shoshama's dark, dark brown hair cascaded onto the shoulders of her perfectly fitted dress, a single item made of a sturdy wool-mix in three distinct shades of ochre.

"I'm going with, *release from detention*," said Prince Darius, athletic yet compact with jet black hair contrasting with his preference for a suit of all white.

"Would the opposite of *contain* be *sintain*?" asked Prince Adalbert. They stared in silence. "I'm thinking Spanish. *Con* is *with*, *sin* is *without*." Adalbert was tall, plump and traditionally dressed in maroon and purple, the colours of Princes and Kings for as long as anyone could remember.

They still stared, but Princess Shoshama, not always known for being nice, chose to be just this once and said, "We believe Princess Petra to be without *tain* and it is up to we four to make her situation much more with freedom to er… *tain*."

"Why just we four? Won't some others join us? Are we the only ones who care?" asked Chatty, exasperated.

"I could barely find anyone who knew her," said Shoshama, "When asking around I found myself having I had to explain who she is."

"Two of my brothers attended her fourteenth birthday bash," said Adalbert, "They got totally blanked by her and said she was a proper minx, had a full-on tantrum apparently...

"I like a girl with a bit of spunk!" said Shoshama. The Princes looked at her like she'd said something surprising. "You know, why should a girl be meek, quiet, seen and not heard? Give me someone with spirit and vigour any day!" To the Princes, this seemed to explain her sentiments better.

"My brothers also said that she was incredibly beautiful. Either way, I don't know her personally, but *you* do, don't you?" he said, asking Shoshama.

"Actually, I've never met her either, but my mother has and she charged me with inviting her to our palace. I think they met a few years back and she feared the poor thing might be at a loose end," Shoshama answered. Her mother had also said she believed the Princess to be a fine horsewoman and good with a sword and a bow, all things Shoshama shared. She had made a great many plans in her head and hadn't for one moment, expected to be thwarted by her absence from the wedding.

"I had fun plans for the two of us," Shoshama continued. Darius winked at her. "No, fun that did not include any boys, sorry!" which made Darius smile at her a little more. "Aww, girls like girl company sometimes. You boys can be mightily tiresome don't you know! Like now for instance!" she fixed him a little stare, so Darius held his hands up in surrender. "I've been banned from complaining that I'm bored," she added confidingly. "The King and Queen just

17

say, *go and find someone to play with*, like I'm ten years old." She looked sulky.

"So you've come all this way to find someone to play with and she's not even here," said Darius, unnecessarily. Shoshama looked at him wondering if he was teasing, but as usual, he just smiled warmly, so she frowned even more sullenly.

Darius turned to the others. "I asked Prince Donald because I was told he knows <u>all</u> the Princesses, but he mistook my interest to be romantic and advised I look elsewhere for a match." The other three waited for an explanation. "He said her grandfather was so generous, he had given away their fortune and she was subsequently worthless." They gasped. "I explained I was purely enquiring for the sake of interest, not romance, but he just punched me on the arm and winked at me like some blinking idiot."

"The rake!" said Adalbert and now they looked at him instead. "Who cares if the poor thing has money? Anyway, I did ask a few people," he said sheepishly, "but then the food came out and I rather forgot all else."

"So what's your interest Prince Adalbert?" asked Shoshama.

"I overheard Chatty asking about her at the do on Saturday and then heard all this hullaballoo about how ravishing she is and thought, *golly how thrilling!* And set off to find her! Then in came the little chipolatas wrapped in bacon and all other thoughts were instantly and permanently banished!" He was lost, deep in his thoughts, then re-emerged to say, "Sorry!" They all looked at Chatty.

"My mother the Queen told me she was the most beautiful of creatures and that I should seek to woo her," he said somewhat quietly and deep in thought. "Mummy didn't mention the Princess was a pauper, but she did tell me I should make it clear I must move into her palace and not she into ours."

"How strange!" they said, "And *you* the Prince and *she* the Princess."

"I think it is on account of all my older brothers and them being the proper Princes. You see it would be too crowded if we all lived in our palace forever. My mother keeps sending me hither and thither to find this Princess or that one and always adds that I must live with them."

"Sounds like she wants rid of you!" said Adalbert, then "Ow! That really hurt!" as Shoshama kicked him hard.

"What's your interest Prince Darius? Is yours romantic too?" asked Shoshama, with just a hint of tease about it.

Darius's easy smile faded and a bleaker expression took its place. Adalbert opened his mouth to speak but a look from Shoshama and the fear of a second bruise on his shin stopped him. Missing the incident, Chatty took a breath in readiness to say something and met the same fate from the Princess. She might well be a fair maiden, but she had a way of looking rather fierce when her mood dictated. Now two of the Princes looked hurt and a third more like he was somewhere else and wherever it was, that it hurt too. After what seemed to her like long enough, Shoshama made to break the silence herself but Darius spoke without looking up. "I have a message for her, that's all. I was hoping to deliver it early so that I could just relax and enjoy myself. Having failed weighs heavily on me and I don't want to go home and say that I didn't even see her to talk to." Now he looked up to see three blank faces, waiting. He smiled kindly. "It is for her ears alone. I will not share it with anyone, no matter how dear they might be," and he smiled again, more warmly this time because they were the dear ones to whom he referred.

"Anyway, she's not here," said Shoshama, "it's certain she didn't attend," returning the atmosphere to its former nature.

"So where is she?" whined Chatty.

"She is withheld and needs to be *tained*," *said Darius.*

"But why? Why de*tain* her?" cried Prince Chatty.

"For her great beauty of course!" sputtered Princess Shoshama, as if it was obvious.

"Obviously!" said Prince Darius, barely hiding his tut.

"You tutted!" whined Prince Chatty.

"I did not." Said Prince Darius calmly, "Though I'll admit I was inclined to and for that I apologise." He half bowed, half curtsied and Prince Chatty wondering whether he was being mocked appeared to be ready to complain once more, but the Princess interrupted.

"Tuts have been known to start wars between principalities." They turned and stared again. Darius looked uncomfortable. "Insults, rebuffs, affronts, slurs and slights. As often as anything else, a lack of due respect can start a war between principalities such as ours."

"Yes, and small armies of untrained poor folk fight with pitchforks, clubs, daggers and long spikey poles for the honour of their Princes!" said Prince Chatty, showing he knew something of world affairs.

"Or because they've been told to and if they don't their fate will be still worse," explained Princess Shoshama who seemed to know a thing or two and have unladylike opinions. The Princes squirmed, Chatty coughed to attract the others' attention and did something with his eyes as if to indicate the Princess was a bit... bossy.

"Their fate is to be very poor and do as they are jolly-well told!" said Prince Adalbert most emphatically, the way men speak when showing they are more important than women.

"Even if it is utterly pointless and it kills them!" said Princess Shoshama.

"Precisely!" agreed Prince Chatty.

"While the Prince of their principality sits sulking in

his castle…" said Shoshama. Prince Chatty made to agree once more but hesitated, confused. "After all, the Prince has had his feelings hurt and we can't have that can we?!" she continued. Prince Chatty frowned. Princes Adalbert and Darius copied him, frowning in numbers increased the frown factor. They watched the surprisingly outspoken Princess, for who knew where her line of thinking might lead? "Someone must die!"

"Absolutely!" agreed Chatty and Adalbert simultaneously and smiling at each other because *great minds think alike* while Darius smiled because he recognised Shoshama was having some sport with the other two. "Someone must die… er, for the cause," said Chatty with Adalbert nodding such that his head might fall off at any moment. This was a sentiment that suited their elevated and all-powerful station. *Someone*, as in; faceless, unknown and entirely other (than themselves) must die. It's what Kings were inclined to say when angered or affronted by rumours of distant events, even if entirely made up, or at least, exaggerated.

"Off with his head!" cried Prince Adalbert.

"Off with his head!" shouted Chatty.

"Off with some poor fellow's head!" laughed Darius winking at Shoshama.

"Off with *whose* head?" enquired Princess Shoshama, more quietly.

"Well, whomever, er, is the one who, you know…" Prince Chatty was thinking it through as he spoke, "er, is the villain of the peace, in whatever, you know," his thoughts came out slowly, as befitted the modest power of his brain, "… the particular circumstances of the event um, in question might happen to be. That's who!" he shouted that last bit with triumph as if he'd solved the mystery.

"And who is that?" asked the Princess.

"It doesn't matter!" whined Prince Chatty.

"Don't worry your pretty little head about it," said Prince Adalbert. "Princes and Kings decide such things. When did you last hear a Queen say, *Off with his head!*?"

"My own Queen, my mother, when referring to my father the King, most days." She was joking of course, but the Princes didn't know that.

"That doesn't count," said Prince Adalbert, looking sulky.

"Anyhoo, way?" interjected Prince Chatty-Charles.

"Say what?" asked Prince Darius.

"I mean, anyway, who?" confirmed Prince Chatty.

"Anyway who what?" asked Prince Adalbert.

"That's simple. Guess who else wasn't here," said the Princess.

"I'm sorry, I'm still saying, who what?" said Prince Adalbert.

"And so am I," agreed Prince Adalbert, "Hoo way? Hey woo? What ho?"

"Whoooo…" Prince Chatty dragged it out, "has con-*tained* the unfeasibly, immeasurably beautiful Princess Petra?"

"Like I said, *that's simple…*" There was silence. She repeated her words slowly, "*Guess, who, else, wasn't, here.*"

"Lots of people wasn't here! Weren't not here. Were not here!" Prince Chatty nodded with emphasis, satisfied with his last version.

"I know people who weren't here and I don't think it was them," said Prince Adalbert, a bit grumpily.

Darius joined in, "Everyone who wasn't supposed to be here, wasn't here. I'm afraid it's quite a list, dear Princess."

"Exactly, so narrow it down to who else should have been here and wasn't," said Shoshama. Confusion and silence reigned supreme. "Who would you expect to see here with Princess Petra and didn't?"

"I didn't see Princess Petra, so I certainly didn't see who wasn't with her!" said Prince Chatty.

Princess Shoshama sighed, "Did anyone see her father, King Wenceslas?"

"Good King Wenceslas? I haven't seen him since the feast of, um, what was it?" pondered Prince Darius.

"It doesn't matter, that's the wrong King Wenceslas, this is *Bad* King Wenceslas, someone else altogether. *Good* King Wenceslas would be an unlikely tainer of an incredibly, unbearably beautiful Princess daughter, whereas Bad King Wenceslas might very well do all manner of mean things."

"Such as re-*tain* his own extraordinarily, unbelievably beautiful Princess-daughter in a dark and dingy tower of immense height."

"A dink and dargy tower!" cried Prince Adalbert, "However will we rescue her from there?"

"She might plat her hair so I could climb up!" cried Prince Chatty.

Princess Shoshama winced, "I'd recommend the stairs," but no one was listening. She spoke louder, "Did anyone see Bad King Wenceslas?" They shook their heads. "Then it is settled. We must formulate a plan to visit the ridiculously and annoyingly beautiful Princess Petra and if necessary, somehow bring her away from her father the bad King.

"Stephen!" shouted Prince Darius.

"Who is Stephen?" asked Prince Adalbert.

"The feast of Stephen, December 27th, the day after Boxing Day 17 years ago, when I was six years old. That's the last time I saw Good King Wenceslas!"

"Good. It's not him," said Princess Shoshama. "Come Princes, we have a task, a mission, a duty of great import and we must make a plan."

"My dad the King doesn't agree with import duty," muttered Prince Adalbert, but they all ignored him.

And with this new vigour and determination, they returned into the Gross Teuer Hotel in the grandest part of the grand city of Vienna. Leaving their carriages, footmen, horses, coach drivers and a solitary lady in waiting, waiting. Hats were removed, sighs were heard, cheeks puffed and one horse did a poo. Noses were fanned with hats while the offending horse waved its tail and the one shackled next to it gave him one of those looks, as if to say, 'You just did a poo!' to which the much-relieved horse seemed to laugh while shaking his head and the other lifted his hooves as if out of concern for getting something icky on them. He shuffled left and right, forward and back on tippy-hoof, which of course was the worst thing to do and he would have been better to stand still with the carriage presently static and sure enough, on his umpteenth nervous step (one too many as it transpired) he planted a hoof centre-pile. Now finally he stood still, afraid to lift his hoof from its soft warmth lest he make things worse. Somewhat depressed, he shook his head slowly while wearing the most contemptuous face a horse knows.

Chapter the Second.
A Right-Royal Elevenses at
The Gross Teuer Hotel

Inside the Vienna Gross Teuer Hotel, the party of four young royals ordered tea and a great many cakes, pastries and fancies. Prince Darius asked for cocoa and Prince Adalbert, fascinated asked what it was and changed his order to the same. The very snooty waiter sighed quietly and modified his long list of their requirements. Prince Chatty, feeling left out said he might like cowcoh too, pronouncing it entirely wrongly and so the waiter scratched his paper more loudly, licking his pencil tip as if to make it write better and repeated, *cowcoh* as he wrote it down firmly. "Your Highness?" the waiter looked at Shoshama expectantly.

"Pardon me?" she asked him.

"Would your Royal Highness like me to obliterate the final order for tea and change it to cocoa, thus making a complete set of tea drinkers switching post-order and post-scribing to cocoa instead."

"No. Like I said, I'll have tea please, thank you." The waiter looked surprised. Disappointed even and licking the tip of his pencil once more, appeared to add a tick to her tea order to confirm that her request for tea, meant tea and was not changed after all. He left with an odd gait to his step where he lifted his feet higher than necessary, as if walking through snow.

"A plan!" said Prince Chatty.

"Super! What is it?" said Prince Adalbert.

"No, I mean we need a plan," said Prince Chatty.

"Oh, I thought you already had one because you just said, *a plan*, rather than the complete communication of *Princes and Princesses, we need a plan,* which would have been clearer," Adalbert said, leaning back in his comfortable winged chair and crossing his long legs, long arms and disappearing into its vast softness.

"We should go to her castle, announce ourselves and demand to see her!" said Prince Chatty. "That ought to do it." The other Princes nodded.

"But if Bad King Wenceslas has locked her away, as we suspect, what do you suppose he'll say?" asked the Princess, sweeping a strand of her long brown hair away from her mouth.

"No!" shouted Prince Adalbert, pleased with himself.

"And then what?" she asked.

"Oh!" Adalbert's face dropped. "I see what you mean."

"If he's genuinely bad and really clever about it, he might make up a story," offered Prince Darius.

"Such as?" asked Prince Chatty, smoothing his multicoloured waistcoat, his yellow hair looking like it might be on fire with the bright sunshine on it.

"Well…" continued Prince Darius, thinking hard, "like, she has gone to the seaside in order to take the sea air because the dusty, smoky atmosphere of the old castle has proved bad for her lungs. And, the invitation to the wedding arrived too late so she was already on her travels and unable to attend in any case due to her ill health!" He finished, pleased and excited.

"Yes. Except she accepted the invitation," said Princess Shoshama, but no one was listening.

"Poor thing!" said Prince Adalbert, genuinely concerned.

"But it does make things easier, does it not?" They looked at him. "I mean, we just go directly to the seaside and while politely enquiring as to her health, also surreptitiously make sure she isn't being held against her will." There was some silence and frowning again, but Prince Adalbert was personally delighted with his plan.

"Certainly Prince Adalbert. A fine plan *in that specific situation* yet we must still enquire and then deduce what might be truth or what might be lies. For what if the bad King tells us she is at the seaside but all the while, she is actually in the tower, locked away, trapped?"

Adalbert pouted, "And she so delicate, with her fragile lungs and no sea air!"

Cocoa arrived along with several trollies of delectable goodies. The very snooty waiter poured tea for the Princess and cocoa for the Princes while waitresses sliced cakes and laid out all manner of pastries and biscuits, jams and butter, whipped cream and jugs of milk and bowls of sugar. Princess Shoshama chose an iced bun and a chocolate Hobnob while the Princes sliced off giant wedges of chocolate cake and jammy sponges. Darius arranged about six large napkins over himself to protect his white suit while Adalbert and Chatty began to look distinctly as if they had been in a very violent chocolate cake fight, and both lost. Noises of pleasure erupted all around while the snooty waiter stepped back and twitched his nose, looking down it somewhat disgusted.

The conversation turned to cake and who had tasted the best one, when and where.

"Is that it?" asked the Princess.

Prince Chatty waved his arm at the immense array of food, "You want more? Of course! Simply order more!" he turned to the snooty waiter who was looking mightily concerned at this turn of events.

"No!" called Princess Shoshama, "I refer to our plan. Is that it? Is that all there is to it?" Prince Chatty went to speak but the Princess put her finger to her lips and glanced towards the staff. "I feel we need more…. detail. To be prepared for more eventualities. I'd go so far as to suggest we don't really have a plan as such at this point, but we should discuss it… privately lest word reach the wrong ears before we have made our move."

"That will be all! Thank you!" Prince Darius waved away the loitering staff. The waitresses curtsied, the snooty waiter bowed so far forward he looked as if he might topple, but still retained that look of deep disdain when he rose and walked off, his knees rising much too far and his feet lifting off the ground by at least a metre. They watched, baffled, then leaned in to talk, all except for Adalbert who appeared trapped in the back of his voluminous winged chair, panting and puffing and waving his legs to come forward. Prince Darius pulled him in and received a nod of sincere thanks.

Prince Chatty spoke. "People like Bad King Wenceslas know only one thing; force. He must be met with force, so I propose he is spoken to firmly and issued an ultimatum to release the irresistibly lovely Princess Petra!" Princess Shoshama raised an eyebrow and mouthed the word *irresistible* to herself.

"You speak as if you know him well. Do you?" she asked.

"His type!" Chatty prodded the table firmly, "I know his type and I know what his type responds to."

"And how would his type respond to that demand? Might his type simply say, *she's not here, she is vacationing at the seaside for her good health* when actually she is locked in the dark and dingy tower?" asked the Princess methodically while stirring her tea with the most delicate of silver spoons.

"I would demand to see in the tower!"

"So he obliges, but by the time you see it, she has been

removed to another place. In any castle, such a game of cat and mouse might go on indefinitely." The Princess spoke kindly, avoiding any appearance of smugness, but Prince Chatty had lost some of his confidence and spoke more quietly as he picked the currents from a creamy bun.

"I think you underestimate my force and what it can achieve…"

"With that type," they both said it together and "Yes, I see," concluded the Princess. "Listen gentlemen, I believe we should each think of a plan and reconvene over lunch to share our ideas."

"Excellent!" cried Chatty, "And may the best man win!"

"Or woman," said the Princess, more quietly.

"What?" asked Chatty but was waved away with a smile from the Princess and with that the group disbanded to various corners of the many lavish reception rooms offered by the Gross Teuer Hotel. Princess Shoshama took her tea and seeing her doing so, Prince Adalbert collected several plates of cake and finding he was unable to carry all he wanted, began to stuff more into his mouth. Sensing the dilemma, the snooty waiter approached and gently unburdened him of the plates and placing them on one of the wheeled, wooden trollies, offered to bring them to his chosen location. The Prince pointed to a chair by the window so close it required the trolly to be pushed no more than two metres. From there, Prince Adalbert set to work demolishing the various cakes and to an onlooker, was not in the least distracted by formulating a plan.

Chapter the Third.
A Very Portentous Luncheon
At the Gross Teuer Hotel

At noon, the four reconvened in the glitzy restaurant, seated by a waiter behind each high-backed chair and with a voluminous embroidered napkin delicately flapped so that it floated into its respective lap. Their chairs were pulled in, aided by the expert push of the same snooty waiter who'd attended them earlier in the day and as champagne was poured, Prince Chatty took the role of chairman. "Princess Shoshama, gentlemen," he nodded at each recognising them in turn, "we have a duty thrust upon us by fate and we must now elect how to execute it. I shall go first." The waiter was still present pouring the champagne and Princess Shoshama made to speak, but Chatty, having learned discretion in the earlier meeting, jumped in with, "but first we will wait for privacy." The waiter, hearing his cue to depart, bowed out backwards and as he did so once gain lifted his feet far higher than was necessary or normal. Chatty, whose face hid nothing ever, frowned deeply as he stared at the man's curious perambulation. Catching Chatty's gaze, the waiter looked at them too and apparently confused by the Prince's interest, frowned back in equal measure. The waiter's face said, *What?* as if what he saw of himself was entirely normal. The frown-off continued until Darius rapped Chatty on the arm to draw his attention back to the table.

"And now we may speak," said Prince Darius looking intently at Prince Chatty.

"Ah yes!" he coughed, "Yes let's! Prince Adalbert, your plan, what is it?"

"Me?"

"You sir, yes."

"Oh, well, I just thought that caution and a degree of *expionage* might be in order. I propose approaching under a pseudonym and enquiring about the village as to the where-abouts of the immeasurably and unequal...ably beautiful Princess Petrol and also as to the state of mind of Mad King Westenplatz." Darius interrupted him throughout, correcting him with, "'*He means eSpionage, Petra, Bad King Wenceslas.*'

"The village?" asked the Princess. Do you know where Princess Petra is from?"

"Norricum? Pannonia?" offered Chatty, who knew some geography, but wasn't quite right.

"Prague," said Shoshama, "She is the Princess of Praha Castle. It's a city, not a village. A large and prosperous place on busy trading routes. You won't be mingling with the vil-lagers there."

"I will use *expionage* to mingle with the cityers. A minor tweak in my otherwise clever plan."

Prince Chatty seemed to mull the idea over for a second or two and then said, "And you Prince Darius?"

"No espionage for me. To my mind, a direct approach is required..."

"Agreed!" barked Chatty.

Darius held a hand up, "But direct in appealing to the King's better nature, his responsibilities as a father, as a King and as one of the elite of the known world."

"Meaning what exactly?" asked Prince Chatty, who looked visibly unimpressed.

"That we are concerned for her well-being, her safety, concerned because she missed such an occasion in Vienna. She accepted the invitation. Her attendance was anticipated. She was missed and many were disappointed not to meet the incredibly, insurmountably beautiful Princess Petra."

"She's at the seaside!" barked Princess Shoshama in a bored voice.

"She is? Really?" asked Adalbert.

"No! But what's to stop the King lying as blatantly to a polite enquiry as he might to a bold one?" she asked.

"*Expionage*!" said Adalbert. "That's why my way is right." Chatty shook his head. They all looked at him.

"So what's your plan Prince Chatty?" asked Shoshama.

"People like Bad King Wenceslas know only one thing; force. He must be met with force, so I propose he is spoken to firmly and issued an ultimatum to release the boundlessly beautiful Princess Petra!"

"That's exactly what you said this morning!" exclaimed the Princess.

"It isn't!" cried Chatty, indignant.

"It is so!" she replied.

"It is not so, I said. '*irresistibly lovely*', not, '*boundlessly beautiful*.'"

"Oh well then, it's an entirely new plan after all, I do beg your pardon!" she said gruffly and then they all fell silent as soup was brought to the table and served to each of them.

"Cream of...." The next word was unintelligible.

"I'm sorry?" said the Princess.

"Princess?" said the waiter.

"Cream of...?"

"Yes that's right," he confirmed.

"Cream of what man, cream of what?" she asked again.

The waiter muttered the unintelligible word.

"Pistachio?" asked Prince Darius.

"Mushroomio?" asked Prince Adalbert.

"Mushroomio!" barked Chatty.

"No, that's my guess," said Adalbert.

"Yes, I'm talking to you. What's mushroomio?"

Adalbert turned to the waiter, "Good question Chatty. What exactly is mushroomio?"

"I have no idea your Highness," said the waiter.

"Waiter!" Princess Shoshama jumped in with force. He looked at her, "What is this soup?" Again came the unintelligible word. "Say it again." There was utter silence now so the waiter said the whispered the strange word even more quietly still. "Louder please, we cannot hear you." He hung his head and muttered. "Still no good. Look at me, speak clearly."

The waiter slowly raised his head. "I am sorry I do not know. The chef refuses to speak to me. I gave a little waft and a little sniff and I think, tomato, yet it is not orange, it looks mushroom, yet smells of pepper, no, maybe truffle, or perhaps nutmeg and so…"

At this point he was interrupted by a loud and extended belch from Prince Adalbert. They turned, he had his napkin thrust in his collar, soup around his mouth and was holding an empty bowl up at a jaunty angle, "Marvellous! Don't care what it was, it tasted lovely. More please!" The waiter opened his mouth to speak, "Don't delay dear chap, get me more!" and with that the waiter turned and strode off in search of more soup. They all tucked in and agreed it was delicious.

"It's official. I love mushroomio soup."

"It's not *mushroom*!" said Darius.

"Quite right old bean!" said Adalbert, "Mushroomio he said. Not the same thing at all, like fennel and flannel, different! Potato and tomato. Spinach and rubbish. Beef and beak. Lamb and jam, not the same. Custard and mustard.

You see, just because they sound similar, doesn't mean they are. Some aren't even edible. "Scone and stone for instance! See?"

"It's not mushroomio either," said Darius, but he was ignored because the waiter had returned with an urn of soup, its lid trapping a giant ladle used to serve up lashings more of the aromatic goo for Prince Adalbert.

"Go on," he kept saying as each ladleful was poured in, the waiter hesitating as first, it reached the polite depth, then as he received further encouragement to continue pouring, again as the bowl was so full, one more ladle would see it overflowing. He paused, "More!" cried Adalbert, dipping his spoon in and slurping it down. "You ladle in, I'll spoon out, let's see who is the faster!" and so they continued, with the waiter taking care not to win lest what was already becoming quite a mess, be made yet worse. Adalbert paused to belch several times but saved the loudest for the point at which the bowl and urn were both entirely empty. The belch was so loud it echoed about the illustrious dining hall and caused loose windowpanes to rattle in their lead frames. On their table, all the candles blew out and Princess Shoshama clutched her lacy handkerchief to her fair (very fair) nose.

"Haha!" bellowed Adalbert, delighted with himself."

"Goodness me!" said Prince Darius quietly. Silence followed.

Prince Chatty broke it. "I believe it's obvious my plan is the better and we should all follow it. Agreed?"

"Not agreed!" called Darius.

"*Ex ------ peonage!*" said Adalbert, but with another giant belch in the middle.

"Then we are no further forward," said Chatty, shaking his head despairingly.

"And we haven't even heard all the plans," added Princess Shoshama.

"Indeed we have," said Chatty. "One good one, and two which will surely fail for want of bravery."

"Mine. I mean mine," she said.

"Oh right! Well which one do you favour? Don't tell me it's one of theirs!" said Chatty indignant at the very idea.

"No dear Prince Chatty, I have my own plan."

"Oh good grief, what for?" he replied.

"Let's have it," said Darius.

"I say, dear Princess," said Adalbert, "if you don't intend to finish your mushroomio, do you mind awfully if I…?" and without waiting for an answer, he leaned in and swooped it up, spooning the remaining soup into his mouth with some very appreciative noises.

"My plan," she said, very business-like and confident, "is to mingle in the community and gain myself work in the castle. That way, learning from the inside, the truth of the famously beautiful Princess Petra."

"Employment?" the Princes called out together, following it with much laughter.

"Perhaps you might darn the King's socks and ask him the whereabouts of his incredibly, stunningly beautiful daughter," joked Chatty.

"Perhaps I might," she said, but they weren't listening, Adalbert was already laughing and suggesting she might like to empty his chamber pot and enquire where the old brute was hiding her.

Darius paused in his mirth and commented with a shrug that, "Women have their ways," then wrinkled his nose and finished with a sniff.

"Having added naught to the sum of suggestions, it's clear we must join in my approach!" said Prince Chatty.

"Not at all, I am convinced mine is the way to go," said Darius.

"I think I've forgotten mine for the moment," said

Adalbert, "but I remember feeling it was good and I wish to pursue it and none other."

"Espionage," offered Darius.

"No, expionage is mine!" said Adalbert.

"Yes, that's yours," confirmed Darius, "You said you had forgotten."

"Or was I just been expionagatious? It is the way of we purveyors of expionage, to be mysterious and appear to have forgotten a thing when all along we know it infintimately well. Inside up, front to back, upside out and never a twixt shall twoxt the um… twain, I think."

"Well, we are stuck until you realise mine is the best way, no the _only_ way," said Prince Chatty.

"Or…" offered Princess Shoshama with a fair (a very fair) finger in the air.

"Or?" they replied together.

"Or, we each carry out our plan. Carefully so as to avoid giving each other away, but all aiming to locate and aid the ravishing…"

"Bewitching!" offered Chatty.

"Beguiling!" suggested Darius.

"Predispossessifying!" spouted Adalbert with great enthusiasm.

"… Princess Petra." She paused. They thought deeply, except Adalbert who had found he could wipe up the dregs of soup with leftover cake. "One of us ought surely to succeed with each of us approaching the matter from a unique angle."

"Just one thing though," said Chatty more seriously. They waited expectantly. "Should we do this? I mean it's a bit of a trek and everything. We could all just go home." Adalbert frowned as if thinking, but not being very good at it, pulled a variety of faces hoping one would convey the impression of deep thought. Meanwhile, he kept one eye on his friends waiting for one of them to say something. When they did, he'd know what to say.

Darius was first, "Look, some people would say we shouldn't meddle…"

"That's exactly what I was thinking!" said Adalbert, jumping in and looking delighted about it.

Darius made to speak again but was beaten to it by the Princess Shoshama, "Fine! Boys!" she added a little deprecating emphasis to the last word, "Do as you wish, but I am going. I feel it is my destiny to find her, with or without your help." Adalbert looked confused while Darius was if anything, a little annoyed.

"Ahem!" said Darius, "I was going to say, before I was interrupted…" he looked at Adalbert, who made a load of mouth shapes like he was talking silently, "That we surely must go. I have a message to deliver, Chatty is supposed to woo her, the Princess is charged with inviting her home to Persia and Adalbert seeks excitement. Of course we should go!"

"That's exactly what I was thinking!" Adalbert said for the second time in a few moments, every bit as delighted as the first and not at all perturbed about contradicting himself.

"Really?" asked Darius rhetorically, "But Princess Shoshama, would you truly have gone alone?"

"Uh-huh," she said shrugging like it was nothing. "I just feel like I have to. It's not a question for me, it's fate."

Chatty stood solemnly. "I feel we should pledge." They stared at him. "By standing."

"Oh!" they each said and stood.

"And um, raise our right hands…"

"But I'm left-handed!" said Darius.

Princess Shoshama leaned toward him and whispered, "Me too, but I find it is best kept a secret!"

"And clap them to each other, so all hands clap, like so. Our four fingers and thumb raised high together!" Palms clapped.

"Our four fingers like we four heroes!" said Adalbert.

"High clapping!" said Chatty.

"We are high-fouring!" said Adalbert. "It is a thing. We have invented a thing, high-fouring!"

"It'll never catch on," said Darius.

"But it is pledged. Our fate is joined. We will travel to Prague to free the heavenly Princess Petra from Bad King Wenceslas!" announced Chatty.

"The ravishing Princess Petra!" cried Adalbert, high-fouring Chatty for the umpteenth time.

"The arresting Princess Petra!" called Darius, high-fouring Adalbert, the only other remaining high-fourer still playing.

"The pulchritudinous Princess Petra!" said Princess Shoshama with a wink. The three Princes stared at her in silence. Adalbert gaped, Chatty screwed up his expressive face, Darius smirked… very slightly.

Chapter the Fourth.
Prague

Prince Chatty arrived first, his three horse-drawn carriages taking a particularly direct route and covering the 310 kilometres in a mere five days. Being the end of the fifth day though he checked himself and his entourage into a fine hotel and had a slap-up meal for all 18, he at one table, his coachmen at another and various servants and so on seated in order of importance.

Buoyed with bravado, but tinged with just a soupçon of nervousness, he talked brashly to his servants, saying again how he would make his demands of Bad King Wenceslas and bully the truth out of him, though at this point he added, "and insist on her hand in marriage!" Food was spat out lest his servants choke.

"Marriage?" they muttered, and hotel employees ducked away into the shadows, carrying away this great piece of gossip.

The next morning, after a prolonged breakfast, where additional kippers, toast with lemon curd, and shapes made from baked sugary-starch soaked in chocolate flavoured milk were consumed in vast quantities until the Prince's eyes were wild and his hair stood on end, he ordered his carriages up the long steep hill towards the castle. The castle gates were shut and so Chatty had one of his footmen (the left one) ring the doorbell, a lengthy knotted rope plaited red and white in the style of those street barbers who improve the health of the poor by slicing them to let blood.

Two bells rang in a distinct 'ding-dong' sound, oddly jolly for such a vast and imposing castle. It was followed by silence.

"Ring it again!" called Chatty.

"Again?" called back his leftfootman, "I already rang it just a moment ago."

"Again! Again!" bellowed Prince Chatty. The leftfootman pulled on the stripey rope and the cheery ding-dong rang out for all to hear. Nothing happened.

"Again! And this time keep pulling until someone answers the door!" The poor man did as he was told and a few minutes later a man in uniform with a shiny steel helmet on, appeared way above on the battlements.

"Alright, alright!" He shouted down, "Who are you? What do you want?"

Chatty leaned out of his carriage, the last of the three, "I am Prince Charles…"

"What? I can't hear you!" shouted the soldier.

"I am Prince…"

"Nope! It's no use, you have to come closer!" Prince Chatty climbed out of his carriage and approached the walls.

"I am Prince Charles of Wolverhampton and I demand to see the King!"

"Who of where?"

"Prince Charles of Wolverhampton. I demand to see the King. Open this door."

"Just a minute!" the man called down.

"There. You see?" Chatty said to his leftfootman, "He'll respond to an order from a Prince like that. The door will open now." And he took steps towards the tall, half-arched structures of oak and black iron, placing himself immediately in front of them in readiness. They waited. They looked up. A few minutes passed. Then the man reappeared on the battlements.

"The King says he's never heard of you and where the… um, where is Woollyhampton?"

"Wolverhampton is the Kingdom of the Angles, Saxons and Celts across the sea from Frankia! Now open this door!" The man gave a shrug and vanished. They waited, alternately looking up and staring at the big doors and waiting for them to open. Once again, the man appeared at the battlements.

"The King says he's out."

"Then he clearly isn't! Let me in!"

"Nope. He's out!"

"I insist you let me in. I have travelled a great distance to demand the release of his divine daughter, Princess Petra."

"Divine eh? Hang on!" This time they stood waiting and looking up. The door might not open until the King realised just who he was dealing with. "The King says…"

"This is the King who is out?"

"Yes. The King who is out says, Princess Petra is at the seaside on account of a nasty cough brought on by a long winter in a dark and dusty castle." Prince Chatty frowned deeply. This was all so unexpected, unless your name was Darius, or maybe Shoshama.

"Are you sure?"

"About what?"

"That the King who isn't here, isn't here and that the Princess who isn't here is actually at the seaside?"

"And dingy."

"What?"

"He said, dark, dusty and dingy castle. I forgot dingy."

"But, in spite of all that you maintain all this is true."

"Yes, utterly. The Princess you seek is at the seaside."

"Where?"

"Where what?"

"Which seaside?" The soldier threw his hands up, returning a few minutes later. "Split!"

"What's that you say?"

"Split!"

"Not before you tell me where the Princess is having her holidays."

"She's having them in Split. It's a place by the sea." Prince Chatty looked confused so the soldier pointed south. "That way. A thousand kilometres or so. Bye, bye!" The soldier left and while Prince Chatty stood staring at the rope for the doorbell, it was pulled up from inside, vanishing over the top of the giant oak doors. Chatty sighed deeply and dejected, climbed back into his carriage. The lead driver followed him to his carriage door and knocked.

"Yes?" the driver opened the door. "What?" asked Chatty glumly.

"To Split sir?"

"Do you honestly think she's there?"

"But your Highness, to quote you directly if I may…" Chatty nodded, "…not paid to think your Highness, just to do as I'm told. Split?"

"Alright, Split it is." And a shimmer of glee and excitement ran through the 17 staff, they were off to the seaside. The reputedly fetching Princess Petra was unlikely to be there, but what did that matter? Chatty would cheer up, buy everyone an ice cream and they could build sandcastles. If they were lucky, there might even be fish and chips for supper, donkey rides, trampolines and a Punch & Judy show.

The driver whipped off his hat and detaching the flat brim from the tall bit that housed his head waved the flat

O-shaped piece at his companion on the high driving seat, "You should see this fly! I spin it with a flick of the wrist and it sails a great distance on the air! Amazing it is! I call is a frizdee!"

"Frisbee?"

"No, watch my lips, *frizz…*"

"Friz."

"…dee!"

"…dee."

"Correct, frizdee."

"I'll give it a go if it will amuse you, but I doubt it will ever catch on." They laughed and attempted to high-four but missed through lack of practise.

Chapter the Fifth.
Still Prague

Next to arrive was Prince Adalbert, who checked directly into the same hotel with just one footman (responsible for both left and right), a coachman also employed to look after the horses and carriage itself, a butler with by far the least to do and a handmaid-stroke-companion. When initially employed this latter young woman had asked whether she had been mistaken in thinking she would be working for a Princess rather than a Prince.

"Why so?"

"Because Princesses have handmaids, Princes generally do not."

"But you're not being employed as a handmaid, you're being employed as a handmaid-stroke-companion."

"So I am to be a companion to your Highness?"

"Well, a stroke-companion."

"A handmaid and companion?"

"No, you're forgetting the stroke. The stroke is crucial. Handmaid… stroke…companion. Hand…maid…. stroke…companion." He gestured very slightly, she went pale, he instantly doubled her salary to eight farthings and a mite per 13 weeks with one afternoon off each month and some colour returned to her cheeks, then too much colour returned as she turned a bright shade of red and her eyes bulged a little, so he added a sixpence for Christmas and thruppence for easter and her face finally went back to its original shade.

"You are employing me, in part, to stroke you?"

"Yes. In part."

"You like being…. Stroked."

"Doesn't everybody? And I am fortunate in having sufficient wealth to employ a companion for that purpose… in part."

"So I am to be part stroker and part companion?"

"Let's just leave it at part stroker shall we?"

And while it was not quite the work she had imagined as a youngster while so utterly bored singing in the church choir and hoping for a way out of her village of Whetstone Blaby, she soon became used to it and found herself thinking back to those dull times and, in her mind, thanking the vicar for all the endless hours he had made her ring a pair of handbells in the 16-peal choir. Oh, how heavy they were and how they made her wrists ache! But now, without difficulty, she could recite every hymn, every carol and all the other respectable, popular tunes they had learned and so her mind might wander to 'Oh Come All Ye Faithful', followed by 'Be Still My Soul' and her absolute favourite 'All Things Bright And Beautiful' which she liked for its quicker pace.

The journey to Prague had caused Prince Adalbert, first, to worry, then to plunge deep in thought, then to fall even more deeply asleep (because that was the effect of deep thought on Adalbert) then to wake up having entirely forgotten what was troubling him so, then to remember, which caused him to worry, think deeply, fall asleep and so on, all the way to his destination. Having arrived, he sat motionless in the carriage while servants unloaded baggage and came to the following conclusion, "I'll be no good at *expionage!*" he cried in realisation. "There is some doubt as to whether I can even pronounce it properly. Let alone do it, so…" he put a finger in the air, "I intend to be direct and appeal to the King's good nature!" He stared into space reciting the notion inside his mostly hollow but well-meaning head and could be seen muttering and nodding with increasing satisfaction. This fresh approach brightened him up immensely and he hopped down from the carriage with a weight lifted from his shoulders and was soon humming one of his maid's jolly stroking tunes. Thinking of these ditties always made him feel better.

In effect though, he had simply stolen Prince Darius's plan entirely, meaning there was a distinct possibility that two Princes would each approach the castle in precisely the same manner. That fact that that made things pretty pointless for whoever tried the approach second passed him by. This was not something Prince Adalbert concerned himself with, his brain being barely big enough for one thought at a time.

The Prince had a light lunch, well, for him it was, for any normal person it would be the equivalent of several mighty feasts, and then was attended to for a while by his hand-maid-stroke-companion, while the horses were fed, watered and groomed by the coachman. Afterwards, the footman laid out some fresh clothes for the Prince and the butler directed as to what order the Prince should put them on, lazily pointing and saying, "That one," while barely taking his nose out of the local paper. Adalbert was almost dressed when the butler started choking.

"I say! Are you alright or what?" enquired Adalbert annoyed by the hullabaloo. Purple and still unable to breathe, the butler stabbed a finger at an article in the paper. The headline caught the Prince's attention instantly and he read loudly, "Three children eaten by castle dragon," he said matter-of-factly, followed by a bellowed, "WHAAAT?"

Then, "A dragon?" sounding incredulous, "A dragon?" more stupefied than anything, and finally "A dragon!" somewhere between impressed and frightened. He shuddered and made a loud noise of someone shuddering because it was important for people to know what a Prince was doing whenever he was doing it. Meanwhile, the footman was pounding on the butler's chest and the handmaid was loosening his clothing, her first response in any situation.

Prince Adalbert continued to read out loud. "Mumble, mumble, the dragon of Praha Castle, mumble, mumble, three MORE children disappeared, presumed eaten, mumble, mumble, bringing the total to 17, mumble, THIS YEAR ALONE! Good grief! A dragon that eats children!" he shrugged, "Rather him than me!" and looked lost in thought. Meanwhile, the footman gave up on his pounding as it had been to no avail, but the handmaid-stroke-companion continued her loosening until there was nothing left to loosen.

"You can stop now, it's no use," said the footman.

"Yes, I see," she said.

"I have to go alone," announced Prince Adalbert. "I cannot risk any of you coming to harm!" The footman pointed at the dead body of the butler. The handmaid-stroke-companion, tidied up some clothing realising she may have over-loosened unnecessarily.

"What's up with him?"

"Dead your Highness. Choked on a carrot."

"Idiot thing to do! Well it's a lesson isn't it and I dare say he won't do that again. Right, fetch the coachman, he can run me up to the castle and drop me off. I am doing this thing ALONE!"

A while later he stood outside the gates and knocked, his carriage already out of sight and sound. He regarded those same gates which had confounded Prince Chatty a mere three hours after that particular Prince had been on the same spot, foiled and frustrated and despatched to Split.

He knocked. "Ouch!" his fist had clattered a black iron stud making little noise but bruising his Princely hand. He knocked again with the knuckles of the other hand, carefully selecting bare wood. A shuffling noise from above caught his attention and he looked up to see a fat, plaited rope, red and white being slowly lowered down the vast oak door. "Hello?" he called out.

"Doorbell pull," came back the voice from inside.

"Hello? What?" Adalbert called again.

"It is the doorbell pull. You pull it, the doorbell rings," came the muffled voice. It swung slightly in front of him. He pulled on it and a jolly ding-dong sounded from within. "Yes, who's there?" The voice now had a face, a soldier with shiny helmet was above at the battlements.

"Oh hello, so nice to see you! My name is Prince Adalbert of Egham, England."

"The Kingdom of the Angles, Saxons and Celts, across the sea from Frankia?"

"Yes, that's the place, how clever of you!"

"It's nothing. I have a memory for such things. What can I do for you Prince Adalbert?"

"I come seeking news concerning the health of King Wenceslas who was greatly missed at the wedding of Isabella and Rupert in Vienna. Many people asked of his whereabouts and health and I volunteered to come in search of news. News we all hope is good in spite of his absence." The soldier mused over it for a moment.

"People were asking about the King, were they?"

"Oh yes. Many. And all those who knew him spoke highly of him."

"Did they indeed? And what did they call him?"

"Call him? Why King Wenceslas of course!"

"Yes but what King Wenceslas?"

"What?"

"What King Wenceslas? As in *Something* King Wenceslas." There was silence from below, Adalbert wasn't sure how to proceed. The soldier guided him, "Did they call him *Proud* King Wenceslas or *Handsome* King Wenceslas, or maybe not being quite so polite, they called him *Old* King Wenceslas perhaps?"

"Oh. I think they called him *Good* King Wenceslas."

"Then they were talking about his father, long dead, not him. The present King Wenceslas is a different man entirely. The news is *Good* King Wenceslas is long dead. Now you have the news you came for, you may leave. Goodbye!"

"No, no, that's my mistake. They called him um… *Mysterious* King Wenceslas, son of *Good* King Wenceslas. I was confused there for a minute. Phew, thank goodness we cleared that one up eh?"

"*Mysterious* King Wenceslas?"

"Yes, *son of Good* King Wenceslas," confirmed Adalbert. The soldier pondered.

"And what do you want again?"

"To pay *Mysterious* King Wenceslas a courteous visit and to enquire about his health."

"Are you alone?"

"Yes."

"You, a Prince, alone?"

"Well no, but my servants are staying at the hotel, including the dead one. I came alone out of politeness and courtesy."

"Yes, it is very discourteous to bring a dead person to visit a King. Just a minute." A while later there was a loud clattering from behind the door, the sound of many bolts and chains being slid and jangled. "You must wait there for five minutes and then you can enter."

"Wait?"

"Yes, five minutes.

"How will I know when five minutes has passed?"

"Um, you can count to 500."

"Is that five minutes?"

"Well, maybe more but the main thing is five minutes is a sort of minimum. You are not required to enter after exactly five minutes, that is not the requirement. The requirement is to not enter before five minutes. Approximately."

"Oh I see."

"But nor must you wait some other, longer length of time like ten hours or something because the King will be waiting. Five hundred give or take, then close the door behind you and walk to the large door in the far-right hand corner which is up three steps. Enter that door, then the one in front, the up a few more steps and…"

"How many?"

"What?"

"How many steps?"

"Oh, three, four, maybe five?"

"Maybe?"

"Yes, well, all of them! If you climb three steps and there are two left, climb them too or you won't be at the top. Then through a wide pair of doors which will be already open and you will find King Wenceslas there in front of you."

"Got it. Shall I start counting?"

"Yes. And remember, shut this door firmly behind you. Whatever you do, don't leave it open or… well don't leave it open. And don't open any other doors except the ones I have told you to. Is that clear?"

"Yes, perfectly. Can I ask, is all this caution to do with the dragon?" There was silence from behind the door. "Hello?"

"Dragon?"

"Yes. Pardon my caution but there was some talk of a dragon."

"Who said this?"

"It's in the local paper."

"Well, don't believe everything you read in the newspapers, most of it is made up. They say nice lies if they like you and evil lies if they don't like you. How many guests attended the wedding?"

"How many?"

"Yes. Was it twelve? Ninety-two? Five hundred and seven? The answer to a question like, how many, is generally a number."

"I think it was about 507…"

"Well if 100 of them were newspaper reporters instead of lazy, spoiled, good-for-nothing aristocrats and royalty, they would write 100 different accounts of the wedding so that when you read them you'd be hard pushed to believe it was one and the same event. It's human nature – which isn't always nice – mixed with politics – which isn't always straight-forward and a need to make money – which is generally the fastest way to pervert anything. Do you get my point Prince Adalbert?"

"Yes! Absolutely! What was it again?"

"Don't believe everything you read in the paper!"

"So there's no child-eating dragon?"

"Oh no, no, no."

"As in, what's referred to as The Dragon of Praha Castle. Which is here I believe, unless there's another one."

"No, this is it, but also no, no child-eating dragon, definitely not. Not as such. Not in the way they mean anyway. Bah, it's complicated! Are you still counting? How far are you? Not past 100 I hope or we'll need to add some on."

"No, I stopped. I don't think I can count and talk at the same time."

"Right well resume then." He could be heard scurrying away, then he called from some distance, "And close the door when you come in! Make sure you do!"

This insistence made Adalbert nervous, but he continued to recite successive numbers in his head but because he was unsure exactly how to count to 500, he just did from one to 100 five times and hoped it would do. At the end he took a deep breath and pushed on the big door, it creaked and swung open. He peered inside and saw a gravelled court-yard of considerable size and still on the outside of the door and it being ajar, he scanned the entire space looking for anywhere a dragon might be lurking. "What does *not as such* mean?" he muttered grumpily. He took a short and hesitant step inside, "And what does, n*ot in the way* _they_ *mean* mean?" he added, a bit sulkily. "And what about, *it's complicated*? Either there's a dragon or there isn't a dragon! That is <u>not</u> complicated!" He looked everywhere at once with his eyes as wide open as they could go. He definitely couldn't see a dragon. This was a good thing. "Dragon?" he called quietly, as if one might attract a sleeping housecat if one was clutching a cat treat. Then realising the nature of dragons, he began to look upwards to greater heights, the tall towers in each corner and the one on the far left, the tallest of them all and surely the one where the delectable Princess Petra would be held captive. He stared at it won-dering. There were no windows at the top, just a few arrow slits lower down. If she was there she could not see down into the courtyard and he could not see in her quarters. *If...* she was there at all.

And now he had searched all the high walls bar one, the one above his head and as he slowly began to crane his neck up, a certainty swept over him that sent a chill through his spine, that he would look up into the red eyes of a monstrous scaly dragon and once their eyes met, he would be instantly consumed in a blast of its fiery breath. If he was right, this was his last moment of life. He suddenly felt something for his dead butler.

He craned his neck, twisting as he did so in order to see clearly, not just in the periphery of his vision and having done so, he could see… an entirely empty wall. He breathed out, gasping now that he realised he had held his breath this entire time. His heart raced and his lungs strained. He felt cold with sweat but knew he must go on. Stepping completely inside, Adalbert obediently closed the door behind him, once again certain that this would be the cue for the dragon to commit murder. But no, it shut with a loud creak and the Prince set off across the courtyard to the far-right corner. Was this gravel specially imported from somewhere to be particularly noisy? He was certain he would not hear the throbbing wings of a giant dragon because his own footsteps were so loud. Crunch, crunch, crunch as he crossed the yard to the steps. Up three and in the door which he closed behind him, another door in front. In part he felt safer now, but somehow worried that he was increasingly trapped with each step, each door. Through the next door he faced five steps (five!) which he climbed with wobbly legs and across a short stone landing to two more doors, swung wide open into a grand room with dark oak beams, dark oak furniture, flags and tapestries and a roaring fire. It was large and impressive in a castle-like way, but otherwise homely to a Prince. "Hello?" he called.

"Enter Prince Adalbert and welcome!" The King stood, not a big man but robust looking, robed in maroon and purple and so very similarly attired to Adalbert. The Prince gestured between them, "What?" said the King.

"Look! Same clothes! How about that?"

"Not the same at all! Those are yours and these are mine. It would be jolly tricky two chaps trying to share the same set of clothes! Wouldn't fit and we would be squished together!" the King brought his palms together to demonstrate, then wiggled them, pulled a face and wrenched them apart, "No, no, no, wouldn't do at all!"

"Oh, well I rather meant to point out not that we shared a single outfit, more that we are both wearing similar outfits of very similar colours." Adalbert had lost some of his enthusiasm for the coincidence, "that's all, nothing more than that really."

"Ah I see. So you wanted to alert me to the fact that two members of different royal families had both chosen the same colours, specifically maroon and purple, the two colours worn most often by royalty everywhere for the last who-knows-how-many centuries?" Adalbert nodded humbly and squirmed a little, the way he tended to when his stupidity was brought to his attention. Adalbert had squirmed his way through life and was quite expert at its smaller intricacies. The King stared at him while Adalbert glanced embarrassed and obliquely at the older man, surprised to realise he looked and sounded exactly like the soldier on the wall. "Adalbert, let me ask you something," Adalbert looked at him and waited. "Do _little_ things amuse you? Are you excited by _little_ things like the colour of our clothes? Does frippery occupy your mind such that the big issues of court sail over your head?" This was accompanied by another gesture.

Prince Adalbert was aghast at the King's insight into him, "Why yes! That's right! That's exactly how I am."

"Well good for you young man!" laughed the King, "I imagine that has kept you much happier than most people born into royalty, burdened with a brain and forced to be educated in its full employment!" The King seemed genuinely pleased for him. Adalbert glanced around. There was no one else here, was the King entirely alone? "Sit, please.

Pour yourself some wine. Eat. There is pheasant, carrots, potato."

"Thank you. I am avoiding carrots for now, dangerous things apparently! Potato?" Adalbert could not see potatoes.

"There. I have them shaped into portcullis-like grids and fried. They are wonderfully, awfully good, taste one!" Adalbert did as requested and agreed, telling the King they were indeed wonderfully, awfully good. "Wonderfully, awfully good!" the King repeated. "I have a name for them, *wawfulls!* Haha, it is a portmanteau of wonderful and awful you see? Potato wawfulls, what do you think?

"A bit of a mouthful!"

"Oh how splendid! A fine pun my lad, potato wawfulls are a bit of a mouthful! I am enjoying your company!" Have some more wine, I have lots, more than I could ever drink and cases of the stuff arriving all the time." Prince Adalbert washed down the tasty potato wawfull with the drink and belched loudly in his customary fashion. The King's face changed to a sudden ashen and Adalbert realised what he had done. He wasn't at home now. He wasn't among friends. He was in a stranger's house, eating a stranger's strange and exotic food and he'd been unspeakably rude. What's more this stranger was famed for being a bad King and also for owning (or at least giving refuge to) a dragon which (according to the unreliable press) ate bite-size human beings. A cold chill ran through Adalbert. But then, suddenly, Bad King Wenceslas let out a bellow of a laugh and seemed to explode with good humour, his eyes watered, he clutched his belly and droplets of spittle sprayed in all directions. Adalbert covered his glass and allowed a smile, hoping this deafening laughter wouldn't be followed by another mercurial change in mood and mark Adalbert's end. It didn't. The King clapped him on the back and attempted a belch of his own but managed only a pathetic little burp.

They sat in happy silence for a while eating. "You enquire as to my health boy well, how do you find me?"

"Vigorous and quite jolly," answered Adalbert honestly.

"And who were all these people asking after me in Vienna? Tell me their names."

"Oh well there was King John of Belgium and Queen Rosemary of Sweden…" and so Adalbert went on recounting all the names he could think of, none of whom had actually asked about the King of Prague, while the King muttered things like, *really?* and *him?* and *who?* and *who's she?* and *well I'll be blowed, I was sure he hated my guts*".

"And of course," Adalbert went on, "people also asked about Princess Petra." Adalbert had asked THE question. He knew he must and he'd done it as casually and as innocently as he could and while the question stopped the King in his tracks, Adalbert maintained his innocent smile and continued, "And it was a wonderful wedding and if I may say so, a fine funeral and then of course…"

"They asked what?" asked the King, clenching his fat fists and vibrating ominously, his purple-faced fieriness back again, but doubled, no, tripled.

"Um, about your health your majesty," Adalbert ventured cautiously, "And generally about the health of any of the unfortunate few invitees who we had all been hoping to meet, but who had seemed not to arrive, including, well you… and…" The King was waving his hand in a revolving fashion as if to say, *get on with it.* "And I believe I faintly recall someone or other, not sure who, no one of any significance probably, just one of those inconsequential enquiries out of nowhere, sort-of asking about the strikingly lovely Princess Petra, though I may have been mistaken come to think of it."

"Who?" bellowed the King at his most bellowy, a rather incredible volume which bounced around the castle walls,

echoing into *WHO? WHO? WHO? WHO? WHO? WHO?*
until it finally faded.

"Um…. let me think now, who asked me that? Who
wanted to know, in all politeness and innocence, who… can
I remember I wonder?" Prince Adalbert tapped his head as
if to aid his thinking. The tapping didn't achieve anything
useful, he didn't know what to say, so he just said, "Um…"

The King vibrated through purple and into beetroot and
black, then seemed to steady himself sufficiently to speak.
But his words hissed out, calmly and quietly, but sinister
too. Each syllable pronounced distinctly, "Oh I know who
wanted to know!" Adalbert regarded him hoping the King
was less angry than he appeared, but the next sentence
exploded from the King, confirming his worst fears about
the King's rage, "Apart from YOU that is!" a jabbing finger
stabbed into Adalbert's flabby, weak chest, "It was that
unbearable oinky twit Prince Chatty of Woollymammoth!"
Well he's gone! I doubt you'll see him again." The King's
eyes flashed victory. "So, do you want to know about her
health, her situation, her whereabouts? This *is* why you are
here is it not?"

"No, no. It was really all about you dear King Wenceslas.
I'm just passing on the small talk and gentle enquiries of
the good people who missed you so and having done so,
I am perfectly content to bid you good day, thank you for
the awfully wonderful wawfulls, gamebird and wine and be
on my way. I have the funeral of a dear butler to arrange.
Passed just this morning don't you know! Killed by a carrot
of all things…"

There was a long pause while the King looked him up
and down as if he were a painting or a piece of furniture.
The shaking stopped and the King's mood appeared to
soften, helped perhaps by emptying his tankard of wine,
refilling it and emptying it once again. He let out a little

belch which seemed to amuse him slightly and then he spoke more genially once again. "No, I wouldn't dream of it. You'll stay." The volume rose slightly, "Your journey will not go unrewarded," and louder, "Your enquiry will not pass unanswered." Then louder still, "You will get the just desserts of your meddling intrusion!" This last statement bothered Adalbert deeply and now he knew he was in trouble. He hoped to be helped by his servants for they knew he was here in the castle, but then imagined the King, dressed as the soldier on the wall, shouting down, "Who? Prince Albert? Prince Adalbert? No, not here, never heard of him. Bye!" and them all scuttling away. He gulped.

"Allow me to show you to your room." King Wenceslas drew a long sword from the wall and Adalbert, lazy, fat from overeating and weak from a lack of any exercise or any outdoor pursuits, noticed that the King may be old, and not nearly as tall as he was, but that he was muscular and strong.

Five minutes later he had crossed the yard, a frightening experience in itself, for as they passed one particularly large and thrice-bolted door, an inhuman noise, deep and grumbling began to arise from inside and the King, to Adalbert's horror, hissed, "Quiet Dragon!" and it stopped instantly. Adalbert went to speak but feared his interest might be rewarded with an introduction, so stayed silent. They entered the tallest tower and climbed hundreds of steps with the point of a sword keeping him on his toes and speeding along. He was told which door to open, requiring the turning of big keys, top and bottom and was prodded into a room with only narrow arrow-slits for windows, a single bed with straw mattress, a stool, small low table and a single candle, as yet unlit. In a recess sat a large chamber pot. The room was very dark, with even darker corners which seemed to tremble as if alive. Corners of dark, unoccupied castle rooms were the homes of rodents and arachnids. Adalbert whimpered, he liked neither rats nor spiders. "Make yourself comfortable. I am delighted to know you have eaten and I'm sure you must be tired."

"But…"

"Yes?"

"You can't keep me here?"

"Whyever not? Of course I can! Your next thought ought to be how you can make yourself more useful alive than dead."

"Oh well that's simple, my parents will pay for my release! There, let me send word, or better still let me go and I'll arrange payment as soon as I am home."

"Money? Gold? What for? No, no. I have no use for any more wealth. Local taxes provide much more than I can ever spend and releasing you would bring me trouble." At that point a cockroach ran across Adalbert's boot and he whimpered again. "The question is are you less trouble dead than sharing this little room with nature's hardy survivors?"

"No, I'm more trouble dead! I'll be less trouble here, honestly."

"Well, I don't see how, but I'll ponder on it. Meanwhile, you can ponder on it and we'll talk again in a few days perhaps."

"A few days?" Adalbert went to the window and peered out the slit, angled so that from inside a wide vista could be spied by looking this way and that but from outside the gap was so narrow as to be able to see very little looking in, even when close. No one would ever be close to this tower. From out there, no one would ever see him in here.

"Would you like to call out?"

"I suppose no one would hear me."

"Oh not true! They would indeed hear you, but only those already behind locked doors up here in the tower. No one in any position, or with any reason to help you. And perhaps you might hear them call out in return. One prisoner calling out to the other prisoners. Pathetic really but feel free." He then left, locking the door top and bottom with two large keys and as he went down the stone stairs, his footsteps echoing, the King himself called out in a whiney nasal voice, "Help me, help me please, I am locked up by Bad King Wenceslas!" then roared with laughter.

Adalbert strained his ears to listen for the other voices. They would be distant and weak, forlorn and feeble. "Hello!" "Hello, who's there? Is someone there?" they would call out, "Can you let us out please!" "Please let us go!" Adalbert shook his head, was this his imagination or could he actually hear something? He strained all the harder and fancied he heard one feminine voice say, "Father, father!"

"Oh zooks! I'm hearing things! I'm losing my mind I've been locked up so long!" then realised that it was really only a few minutes. "I'm already losing track of time! My grip on reality is shaky!" but this admission didn't sit well, because his mother had long suggested it to be the case. He slumped and slid down the wall and being tall with long legs it was an especially long slide ending in a soft plop at the bottom.

He remembered his jolly friends and their enthusiastic high-fouring and said quietly to himself, "So Prince Chatty has been and gone. I must hope that Prince Darius can save me," and as his mind lingered on that thought, Prince Darius alone and in disguise was checking in to a simple hostelry in a poorer part of the city. Once in his basic, cold and draughty room, Darius opened a dirty window and gazed up at the distant castle. One tower rose higher than the others. That's where she must be locked away, she, the unfathomably beautiful Princess Petra.

Chapter the Sixth.
A Poor Bit of Prague

Darius left his little hostelry that evening and walked the streets. In a city of this size it is easy to be anonymous, but Darius became aware that he was arousing interest. He'd felt that way on the final leg of the journey, a day's ride in a coach seating six and pulled by four horses. The other passengers, one young family of three and an elderly couple regarded him and whispered, making him wonder whether they might possibly recognise him from some portrait in spite of his disguise. He looked casually at his shoes, mid-priced and practical, dark brown and so very new he had deliberately given them some mild abuse over the last few days to make them look more worn-in. His jacket, mid-priced and tweed, inconspicuous in its ordinariness. His trousers, striped as was the fashion, but not garishly so. His cravat, considerably more subdued than he would otherwise have chosen, just maroon with a paisley pattern in gold, printed, not embroidered and nothing special. His hat was equally unremarkable, he wore no jewellery, had added no scent beyond soap, carried only a plain bag and practical walking stick, had the most popular newspaper and nothing else about his person which might mark him out. Yet still they stared and still they whispered. Unused to mixing with common folks on carriages, he concluded this was the etiquette of the masses, smiled at each of them when the opportunity arose and otherwise did his best to ignore it.

Upon arrival though, he was sure others were staring and pointing him out to their companions but glancing around he consoled himself that there was sufficient pointing, waving and embracing for this to be a consequence of families and friends meeting others at the coach station. They were mostly likely pointing at someone behind him.

At the hostelry, the landlady hesitated as he approached her and to ensure they started on the right foot, Prince Darius had slapped onto the bar top a whole month's worth of payment for the room; bed, breakfast but no board. She had counted the money greedily and thrust it into her ample cleavage, then fetched her husband from the kitchen to look him over. He raised an eyebrow upon seeing Prince Darius for the first time, followed by a brief and private exchange with his wife from which Darius could only deduce that whatever question the man of the house had asked, his wife had answered in the affirmative and so, with what looked like a modicum of resignation, she showed him up to his room on the top floor.

Darius concluded the woman was a business proprietor well used to people trying to trick her out of payment, so he put her odd behaviour down to commercial caution, but why was he even now attracting attention on his evening stroll? He ducked into a saloon, the drinkers' raucous laughter and squeals of bawdy women giving him hope of a draft of ale and some quiet anonymity, but the noise faded as he entered, and the locals stared at him. In silence he ordered his ale and found a corner of a table. Men nodded a greeting but kept up with their unapologetic staring and more than one bawd winked a promise to seek out his company as soon as their present benefactor had finished spending whatever pittance he could ill-afford.

Something about Prague was making Darius doubt the sense in his original plan. Somehow, the idea of marching up to the castle and appealing to King Wenceslas' better nature seemed doomed to failure and he found himself being drawn to Prince Adalbert's more cautious approach.

"*Expionage!*" he said to himself, then chuckled. There could be little harm in keeping a low profile and asking a few questions of the right people here and there. With information gathered, he could then determine his approach, direct or otherwise. "Espionage it is then! *Expionage*, espionage, *espionage*, espionage! Adalbert, you can do *expionage* and I'll do espionage!" he said to himself and pleased with his new plan, supped ale.

A voice interrupted his thinking. "Where are you from stranger?" said a big, scruffy man uninhibited on account of a now-empty, gallon barrel of ale adjacent to him on the table. The woman with the drunk man, looking as if she'd tumbled down a steep hill and through a great many hedges, pulled faces of intrigue and expectancy.

"A place far south, many days travel." Darius now wanted to gather information, not give away personal facts.

"And are they all like you down there?" He seemed friendly enough, even if there was an impertinence to the question.

"I'd say there was as much variety of peoples as anywhere else, and I am just one of many souls making my way in the world."

"Or maybe a greater variety. And what brings you here, stranger in a strange land?"

Darius hesitated, the fellow was mightily coherent for someone who had sunk a gallon of ale.

"Oh, my dear uncle passed away some months back and word took time to reach me, so now and I am en route to Copenhagen to see my aunt and cousins."

"Oh, they got your sort in Copenhagen have they?" Darius frowned slightly, clever enough to know this man was impolite and perhaps too easily steered into trouble.

"You are a resident of this fine city I presume dear sir?" The man nodded and the woman added that she too was one.

"I am intrigued by the that fine castle yonder. Is it your King and Queen who live there?"

"Yeah, King. Don't go there!"

"No don't go there!" echoed the woman resting her arms on the table underneath her bosom and doing a great deal to draw attention to herself. Darius's attention was drawn to her for a moment. "You can go *there* if you like though," she giggled.

"It's not open to the public then? No visitors?" asked Darius.

"Not on your nelly, not unless you want trouble," answered the man.

"Might be, depends who's asking, buy a girl a drink and who knows where you can go?" said the girl.

"I can go to the castle?" asked Darius of the woman. She looked confused. Darius spoke directly again, "Did you just say I might be able to go to the castle if I bought a girl a drink?"

The man laughed and shouted for more ale while the woman looked sheepish and twiddled with her hair, "No, I weren't talking about the stupid castle. Why's everyone so fascinated about the castle?"

"Who's everyone? Have other people been asking?"

"Yeah, two lots been up there today! One lot left with a flea in their ear and another nutter went up alone-like, so 'e'll never be seen again will 'e?"

"Why ever not?" asked Darius, but both the locals just laughed raucously. The bartender delivered a barrel of ale and put his hand out for payment at which the local man indicated towards Darius.

Darius looked at the bartender confused, the latter pointed at Darius with a grubby finger, "He says you're paying. Think of it as a custom, a kindness for letting you drink with them." Darius paid two shillings which was more than enough and the bartender left them, biting the coin to check its integrity.

"They friends of yours then, these idiots visiting Bad King Wenceslas?" This was the woman speaking, revolving her tankard between the palms of her hands, her elbows pressing inward on her bulging bosom.

"I have absolutely no idea who they were. It seems a coincidence that my solitary passing through and mild interest in ancient castles has coincided with others. I would be equally happy to visit any other buildings of note, a cathedral, the old town hall…"

"Good idea, just don't go up there," said the man seriously as he wiped froth from his lips, but leaving a great deal in his moustache, "The King is a mean old nutcase who will trick you, trap you, eat you for breakfast!"

"Eat me?"

"Well, no not literally, I just ran out of impressive things to say after *trick you* and *trap you*."

"Trip you?" offered the woman.

"Why would he *trip* you?" asked the man in an exasperated voice.

"I dunno, in order to trap you. You were the one who said trap you, I just thought it was better than *eat you for breakfast!*" this last bit she did in a mocking deep voice, then amused with herself, did it again, "*Eat you for breaaaaaak-faaaaahst!*" She paused, "I know, trop you!"

"No such word as *trop*," said the man, still exasperated.

"There is!"

"There absolutely is not!"

"What did I say then?"

"You said *trop* and I'm telling you there is no such word."

"Well there is such a word," she said indignant (and it has to be said, mildly amused), "… because *I* said it, *that* word that doesn't exist, then *you* said it, that same word that doesn't exist, so it's obviously a word because we both said it!" she made a gesture of something coming out of her mouth, "Trop! There, that's a word, see?"

"It has no meaning! It might be a word in the literal sense but without a meaning it's pointless!" his voice was raised and he was doing a kind of karate chop gesture for emphasis.

"Still a word though …" she muttered, "Not a word!" she then said to herself in her mock deep voice, then chuckled because she found her impression amusing, "Eat you for braaahhhkkkfffaaaahhhsstt!" but she put so much effort into the last word and saying it really deep that she began a coughing fit and the man took the opportunity to slap her on the back much too hard. She coughed with her cheeks puffed like a trumpeter in a brass band, her eyes bulged and she went bright red, as did her chest, noted Darius. The man slapped harder until she fell off her chair, after which she was silent. Darius leaned back to peer under the table, from whence came a little voice, "I'm alright! Thanks a lot, I'm fine. Don't worry about me!" then, "Eat you for braaahhh-kfaahhsstt!" followed by more laughter, coughing and then silence under the table. The man kicked out and she yelped, "Yeah, still here, not dead nor nothin', no thanks to you. Braaaaaaahhhhkkkkfffaaaaasssssssttt!"

"There's talk of a dragon." Asked Darius of the man.

"Yes…"

"Legend has it, it eats children, least ways that's what I read in the paper."

"Yes…" said the man.

"Lives at the castle?"

"Yes…"

"Well, what do you know? Is any of that nonsense true?"

"I told you, yes! You asked me question, I answered! Yes, yes and yes. What else do you want to know?"

"Yes, there's a dragon? Yes, it eats children? There's an actual child-eating dragon at that very castle up there?" Darius was keeping his voice down, but it was strained with amazement. Darius was pointing, and the man pulled Darius's arm down.

"It's rude to point. People can see what you're pointing at. Yes, there's a dragon, though I've never seen it myself, many others say they have, apparently it eats children, they certainly go missing often enough, and the castle is its reputed home. I wouldn't put anything past that bad old King."

"What about his daughter?"

"Not been seen for years."

"Is she locked away up there?" asked Darius.

"Some say, but like I said, no one's seen her for years."

"How long exactly?"

"I keep telling you, four years, FOUR YEARS! How many more times? Are they all stupid like you down south? She was 14, coincided with her 14th birthday party, a celebration across the city with eligible bachelors invited to attend, but…"

"Yes?" asked Darius impatiently.

"Something went wrong. The King wasn't satisfied with the bachelors or the Princess herself didn't take a fancy to them, but that was it, party over, King and Princess back in the castle never to be seen again. So, now you know, she ain't been seen four years."

Darius jumped up from the table, banging his knees hard on the underside and tipping his chair over, a shocked look on his face. From underneath came the woman's voice, "Oh. Bit ticklish in't 'e!"

He walked back to the hostelry and up five flights of stairs plus two half-flights to the top of the building and his room. On the way he sustained the intrigued looks and titters of amusement of the residents of Prague and suddenly feeling a slight draught, realised his fly was unbuttoned. "How embarrassing! That's what you get when you buy cheap clothes!" he grumbled as he closed his bedroom door.

He hung his jacket and placed his shoes tidily in the bottom of the wardrobe, then sitting on the bed, stared up at the castle. "But what am I to do, Princess Petra? My inquiries have provided hearsay but no answers. I have speculation but not certainty, a problem but no solution." He lay back, eyes open and unable to sleep.

Also unable to sleep lay Adalbert, cold in his dark, stone room, alone except for the variety of scuttling and scampering noises around him and a certainty that he was providing body heat for all manner of passing traffic. Every itch on his face felt like it might be a spider, every imagined sensation anywhere about his clothing, surely an inquisitive rat and those nocturnal itches in the inky blackness of the cold night – well they were scurrying cockroaches.

Laying in his bed in an inn at the roadside, denied sleep by his sadness and confusion, not to mention the raucous din from downstairs in the bar, was Prince Chatty. He deeply regretted his ill prepared assault on Bad King Wenceslas and his feeble lack of a back-up plan when thwarted by the soldier posted on guard duty. He now felt certain the mind-bendingly, bone-achingly beautiful Princess Petra was not in Split and that the suggestion that she was, was no more than a ruse to misdirect him. Persuaded to head south by his servants whose interest lay more in seaside frolics than rescuing a damsel in distress, he wondered what to do. He too thought of his high-fouring comrades, missed them, wished they were here. Downstairs, he could hear his own servants singing a jolly ditty along the lines of *going on a summer holiday for a week or two*, recognising that cheery scamp Clifford's voice above all others while his chief costumier, Elton pounded the piano. They were all looking forward to Split. All except him. He felt he was being pulled in two directions and as the party broke into another song, Chatty mused over *the story of his life* and said quietly to himself, not two directions, *One Direction*.

Chapter the Seventh.
Still the Poor Bit of Prague

With her valise in one hand and umbrella in the other, Princess Shoshama mingled with the throngs and mentally mapped the streets of Prague as she walked. She searched for lodgings within sight of the castle and while dressed like a servant, albeit a reasonably successful and proper one, she understood what she might, and might not, afford. All hotels were out of her reach in this role. A hostelry might do for a night or two, but a week's wages would vanish in a matter of a few days and no servant would willingly throw her money away so readily. She took to knocking on doors and asking for a room. The first two apologised that they had none to offer, the third recommended a fourth, but the fourth said she was full with family from Dresden, all of who she sincerely hoped would be gone soon, then added, "The sooner the better!" then as Shoshama walked away, called after her, "Can I come with you?" The fifth door was opened by a man with a long-stemmed pipe clasped by thin lips under a long, thin nose. His hair was slicked back in a sinister fashion and long, sinister slippers adorned long and sinister feet. His voice sounded the way it would if a snake could talk, with one word running into another and each sentence joined to the next by noises from his throat. As he spoke, his housecoat twitched disconcertingly and something about him caused

Shoshama to reject his invitation to inspect any of the seven empty bedrooms he said had been waiting for her.

"One shilling?" he said, almost desperately. This was more than she could afford.

"No thank you," she said stepping down from his doorstep and on to the pavement.

"One and six?" he offered imploringly.

"No!" that was even worse. She'd be notionally broke (but not actually broke) within days. She thanked him politely and began walking off.

"Two shillings!" he called after her. This was ridiculous, she could have a nice hotel room for not much more. Then as she was almost out of earshot he shouted, "Alright I'll give you half a crown, how's that?"

'Give you? Give YOU? Oh my goodness,' she thought, realising these were not room prices, but offers of cash for her to take up residency in his house. She shuddered at the thought and strode on.

Her walk took her closer and closer to the castle and seeing it was atop a substantial rock the size of a large hill, found herself in a narrow street of cottages built into the side of the rock itself. "Castlerock Street," Shoshama said to herself reading the sign on the rough stone wall of the first house on the left, "Sounds promising." Houses often used castle walls as their backs, but this row of dwellings on her left were built right into solid rock with no sides or roof. In fact, if it weren't for their little doors and windows, the houses on the left side of the street would simply appear to be part of the rock itself. The row of houses opposite and to her right were built from the same big grey rocks fashioned into manageable lumpy shapes but stood apart from the big castle-rock and had proper roofs. Regarding the more interesting properties on the left side of Castlerock Street she mused that they were virtually caves.

As the little street progressed, it followed the contour of the ground upwards which coincided with the rockface getting steeper, and as the rockface got steeper, so the houses got taller until she stood outside one which was obviously only one room wide, but by counting the windows vertically and positioned directly one above another, she could tell it rose to a total of seven floors. If any house might have an empty room, surely one with the most rooms and floors would be that one, thought Shoshama. She recognised this kind of logic might be flawed, but it was time to knock and something about this house made it feel like a reasonable place to restart her search for accommodation. She used the decorative knocker, styled like a dragon to alert the occupants. A chilly breeze swept up the street and Shoshama shivered. The light was fading, faster now that a dark cloud obscured the evening sun.

She heard footsteps from within and with a turn of the latch the door opened to reveal a small man, rounded and jolly. "Oh!" he said, and took out his pocket-watch, "Twenty-two of six of the clock!" then looked back at her. "Yes?"

"Um, I'm sorry to trouble you..."

"No trouble my dear," he interjected.

"I was wondering..."

"Who lives here? Just my dear wife of 39 years and my own self. Thirty-nine years married that is, she's not 39 years old! No, no, 34 I think, or thereabouts. Anything else?" Shoshama was lost by the impossible mathematics and made to speak, then didn't on account of not knowing quite how to ask the obvious question and amidst her confusion her hesitation prompted a "Goodbye then!" from the gentleman, so she quickly asked if he and his wife might have a room to let. "Oh dear, oh dear!" he said. "Well, it's a matter of space you see, I don't really think..."

"But…"

"Yes?" he enquired.

"Is all this your house?" she swept her hand up to the very top, seven stories above.

"Yes!"

"Well then surely you have space!" she said gently, imploringly.

He stepped into the street to see things from her perspective. "Oh goodness! Yes, I see what you mean. But the thing is those are our children's bedrooms."

"You have children? I thought it was just you and Mrs… er, Mrs…"

"Wife!" he answered pleased.

"Yes, just you and your wife, but I don't know your name, you are Mr…?"

"Mr Wife and my wife is Mrs Wife."

"Goodness! So she really is Mrs. Wife?"

"Yes and I really am Mister Wife. My first name you see." Shoshama appeared puzzled. "Mister. My first name is Mister so I am properly entitled Mr Mister Wife." Shoshama gasped slightly, trying not to laugh. The man smiled. "Want to know something else? My wife's maiden name was Husband. By marrying me she became Wife and my wife all in one go."

"Does your wife have an interesting first name? Something surprising and unusual?"

"Not at all, it's House." Shoshama gasped.

"So she's…"

"Mrs House Wife, yes. She used to be Miss House Husband of course, terribly silly name when you think about it! How about you?"

"Oh, my name is…

" And then she thought, wondered whether she should take on a different name, but figured she was far enough from home, home being a very distant Persia, to not be known hereabouts and for there to be no chance of it at all.

"Yes?"

"Oh sorry, I was deep in thought. My name is Shoshama, pleased to meet you Mr Mister Wife."

"Now _that_ IS an unusual name. Wait there, Miss Shoshama." And with that he shut the door and climbed the stairs. She waited as instructed and a minute or so passed. Then another, then another and she was just about to give up altogether and try another door, albeit reluctantly, when a sash window opened one floor above and Mr Wife leaned out and said, "Almost ready! Wait there!" and vanished again, the window slamming down shut.

Five more minutes past and she began to notice the cold. It was almost completely dark now though there was light in the sky beyond the steep walls of the rock behind the houses. This hill, this rocky outcrop closed off the light so this street was especially dark. There was a noise from above and the window slid open again, "Unexpected complications, please be patient! Five more minutes please! Thirty at most!" and down went the window.

"Thirty?" she said to herself wondering what on earth it was all about, but realised she was obliged to wait. This constant address that she should wait and that her call would be answered soon, had the effect of forcing her to wait far longer than a single entreaty at the outset. There was something clever about it, yet it was also a kind of torture. She was entirely free to leave and yet felt she absolutely could not.

"Miss Shoshama?" a lady, rounder still than her husband and even shorter than his modest height had whipped open the door. Shoshama had heard no footsteps on the stairs this time. Shoshama confirmed it was she and Mrs Wife ushered her in, reaching for her valise, which Shoshama handed to her, but upon feeling its weight, she instantly dropped it again and reached out for Shoshama's umbrella instead. Once inside Mrs Wife shut the door and there they stood in the hallway, Shoshama towering over little dumpy House. The latter put the umbrella in an umbrella stand and said, "You're having Sammy's room. At first we thought Ozzy's room, but there is a spot of damp, then Bruce's but it's rather full of furniture, next Lemmy's but I'm afraid it would take too long to clean, next Jimi's but there's a kind of mustiness to it too which left only Sting's or Sammy's rooms and Sammy's is bigger because it's on the top floor and no space is lost to stairs to any further floors above."

"The top floor? Right then! Are those names all your sons?" Shoshama began climbing the stairs behind Mrs Wife who was waddling ahead of her. Every few steps a stair creaked, but only for Mrs Wife, not for Shoshama herself.

"Yes, all gone now, though we keep their rooms in case they return. The music business can be a fickle mistress, fame one day, fortune the next, rehab the day after, that difficult second album, the third one fans buy the day it is released but only ever play once with long-glum faces because it's absolute rubbish, then the fourth one the fans just leave in the music store because they don't even like the album cover, then a come-back tour, trouble with the nanny, a messy divorce and what then? Well home to mum and dad of course!" They turned a corner to the next flight, Shoshama following closely behind. More creaky stairs, though still not for Shoshama.

"No daughters?" It was getting creakier.

"Never once. It's a harder business for girls, impresarios are still nervous about booking girls for some reason, you rarely get two in a row on a playlist! So no, no daughters at all, so it will be lovely to have you about the place." Every step creaked up here as if Mrs Wife's considerable density put the stair-plank out of place as she stood upon it and then it already having been displaced, it didn't creak a second time for Shoshama.

"Sting? That's an unusual name isn't it? I haven't heard of a Sting before." Mrs Wife, slowed her pace climbing the stairs and Shoshama suddenly worried that saying one of their sons had an unusual name was not the best thing to a couple called Mister and House. House trod slowly for a few steps then picked up her pace again. The creaking continued.

"Not his real name, he changed it and we felt that if that's what someone wants to do then we shouldn't stand in their way. Lemmy wasn't actually named Lemmy either, but he's Lemmy to most people as is Sting to most people." They turned a corner to the last flight and what turned out to be the creakiest stairs of all. It occurred to Shoshama that creeping about this creaky house would probably be out of the question. At the top Mrs Wife rested, leaning forward with her chubby hands on her thighs and breathed deeply. In front of them lay a large open area with a comfortable looking bed, a writing desk and chair, a fireplace and a smallish sash-window with far reaching views of the city lights. Behind them, to the back of the house and deep into the rockface, a washing basin sat on a chest, there was a further chair and at the very back, the large doors of wall-to-wall wardrobes. It was a substantial enough room covering the whole floor with stairs emerging midway between the front and back. "Oh those stairs!" said Mrs Wife still catching her breath.

"Tremendous exercise though, I feel rather invigorated after the climb."

"Yes, but they do make me fart so. I'm sorry about that, it increases with effort, each flight more farty than the last." Shoshama fell silent. The stairs hadn't creaked at all. Only Mrs, Wife had creaked.

"Um… we haven't discussed the room rate, I do hope it's not too much now I'm in!"

"You'll pay for food at sixpence a day, less if you shop for it for me. Can you shop?" Shoshama said she could. "Good! I prefer not to venture out as farting loudly outdoors is rather frowned upon, I prefer to fart with free abandon in my own home! Can you sew?" Shoshama confirmed she could sew. "Can you cook?" She could. "Gosh, aren't you multifaceted! What else can you do?"

"I can play piano, is that any use?"

"Oh really?" she exclaimed excitedly, "That's absolutely marvellous! We'll have music about the house again! We've missed it so since the boys left. Wait until I tell Mister the good news! He'll be cock-o-hoop at the prospect!"

"Do you have a piano?" enquired Shoshama, wondering which room it would be in and on which floor it could be found and whether it might be a nice one, properly in tune and so on.

"No, don't you?" said House, a little surprised.

"Er, no. Not with me, no."

"Oh, how disappointing!" her voice tailed off sadly. "Now what am I to tell Mister? He'll be thoroughly disappointed after all the excitement of the prospect of hearing you play! Oh, I am so pained by that blow. Are you sure you don't have one?" Mrs Wife stared at Shoshama's valise. Shoshama followed her gaze.

"I have a few clothes, my makeup… but no piano at all I'm afraid."

"Your makeup. Yes dear we must talk. Whoever taught you to do it like that? And your hair! We will talk over dinner and fix you up in the morning. Dinner!" she exclaimed, "Dinner is at six precisely!"

Shoshama checked her watch, "It's just five minutes before six now."

"Yes hurry please. The parlour is on the second floor. Don't worry about changing, just come as you are. Delightful in spite of the make

up disaster and that hair, oh that hair!" She turned to leave.

"Mrs Wife! The room rate. How much?"

She was already down one flight of stairs, light-footed and not a creak to be heard. It was climbing stairs which troubled her system so. "I told you! Sixpence dear! Less if you shop, less if you sew, less if you clean or cook, or carry, and less still if you play the piano for us!"

Shoshama stood there bewildered and recited their names to herself, "Mr Mister Wife and Mrs House Wife? Sting, Lemmy, Sammy, Bruce, Jimi and Ozzy! Well I must say, *There's nothing as odd as people!* and felt as if she'd hit upon some kind of wise maxim or proverb and imagined how it might pass between the regular people of a kingdom, *There's nothing as odd as folk, there's nowt as utterly strange as everyday people, there's nothing as queer as the general population!* Then the right combination of words fell into a place, the purest arrangement of her various guesses and she said it out loud certain it would take root in popular language, "There is really absolutely nothing as utterly strange as the everyday people of... the general population!" and smiled, greatly pleased with herself.

Maybe there was something about the house which inspired clever words, maxims of truth, the lyrics which make up popular songs. She twirled in her room, content with her lodgings in spite of her odd landlady and landlord and thought, *There's something oddly intriguing about this delightful house of rock."*

She caught sight of herself in the large mirror and pulled a strand of her hair which tumbled down over her eyes. Mrs Wife had certainly rumbled her make-up and hair. As a fair (very fair some would say) Princess, she was used to the best make-up and hair dos and so, to support her disguise as someone more ordinary, she had cut her hair to shoulder length herself (and not very well it must be said), trimmed her long and lovely lashes, stained her dazzling white teeth a little by eating chocolate and not brushing, de-accented her prettier features and her eyes by carefully applying dark foundation where there should be light, light where there should be dark and dull shades of grey and brown where brighter colours might normally be applied. When she had finished, she laughed at her work and said, "Gosh!" then again, "Gosh!" There was nothing else to be said. She looked a little pale and unwell made-up so. Anyone who had seen an actual dead person would recognise the look for that what was what it was akin to. "I've invented a look!" she said, "And the only name for it is *Gosh!*" She laughed again, "I'm a Gosh!" Emerging into the crowd to find a coach to Prague those few days ago, her new Gosh makeup disguising her wealth and hiding her natural beauty, she caught sight of herself reflected in windows and thought, *'This Gosh-look, it's a bit ghastly. I'm pretty certain it'll never catch on!'*

"Well it won't now if Mrs Wife is determined to sort out my hair and make-up," she said to herself, still twirling the lock of hair. She smiled at her reflection, amused by the severity of her look yet finding it oddly intriguing. She pouted for a moment, then tilted her head and curtsied, "Pleased to meet you your Royal Highness!" and blew herself a kiss. Then checking her watch, realised she had just two minutes to run down to the parlour and blowing the Princess in the mirror a raspberry, waved at it and left, chuckling because the raspberry sounded like the creaky stairs.

Chapter the Eighth.
Shoshama In The House of Rock

At six on the dot Shoshama appeared at the parlour door to find Mr Wife serving dumplings and stew. She was seated and offered a glass of wine with her meal. Shoshama hesitated for a moment, noticing it was a bottle of '29 Chateau de Prétentieux, drunk in only the finest houses due to its scarcity and exorbitant price. It was a wine she knew well, but under the circumstances, she felt she ought not to reveal the fact. Instead, she took a sip and commented upon its magnificence.

"You can thank Mister for that, said Mrs Wife. Wine is his thing, always has been. He still dabbles, buys and sells."

Mr Wife smiled proudly, "I acquire some fine wine through, er, shall we say, my historical contacts and then sell door to door to a small group of monied enthusiasts. Keeps the door entirely unattended by the wicked wolf, wouldn't you say dear?"

"No dear, I'd probably say it keeps the wolf from the door, but you *are* quite the businessman, I'll say that for you!"

"I do my best to *preneur* the *entre*, wouldn't you say so dear?"

"No dear, I'd say you were an entrepreneur, or avoiding the need to speak French altogether I might say that you are an expert at taking between. Take from the supplier, sell to the buyer and you there you have it, simple yet marvellously profitable."

Dinner passed mainly in silence after that but once cutlery was down, Mrs Wife began her questioning. "Have you run away dear?"

"Run away?" Shoshama blurted, surprised by the suggestion.

"From a man? You're probably too old to run from your father, so it is your husband? How old are you dear?"

"I'm 22," she said, "and I've…." She was about to say she had run away from no one, but suddenly felt this might be turned to her advantage and help her maintain her disguise and anonymity. "How did you know?"

"You have taken great care to hide your beauty. This means you understand make up which itself means you are a young woman with some sense of fashion and expertise in the matter. Most girls can afford none and have little experience of how to use the little they get. Is that your natural hair colour?" Shoshama's hair was a very dark brown.

"Yes it is," she said puzzled, twirling a strand adjacent to her ear. Shoshama was unsettled. Her intention to have people think she was a maid had fallen apart at its first proper encounter.

Mrs Wife stared intently at Shoshama's hair with something akin to confusion on her face. "It is? Are you certain? I thought this too must be a disguise. Who do you run from, a husband I suppose?" Shoshama nodded. "He'll be a cruel brute of a man with a powerful family. You have come a long way no doubt, yet still you fear you might be discovered. But here in this house you are safe. Is Shoshama your real name?" Shoshama nodded. "We must not advertise the fact that we have a Shoshama living here and you must avoid using it as and when you venture out, for how easy it would be for someone sent to hunt you down to ask around for a Shoshama and you the only one in Prague for sure. I suggest you adopt the name Eliška if anyone asks, it is the commonest name hereabouts. So we must recut your hair and redo your makeup so you fit in and we must still hide your beauty but not in such a way that it looks as if that was the aim." Mister poured all three of them more Chateau de Prétentieux, from a second bottle, causing Shoshama to gape momentarily, she wondered how many families could afford just one bottle, let alone two! She sipped, Mrs Wife drank small mouthfuls, but Mr Wife glugged an entire glass down and immediately refilled to the absolute brim, his face a picture of the utmost glee.

Shoshama thought about Mrs Wife's notion of her having run away from a mean husband and smiled to herself. Her benefactors had created a cover story for her themselves with only her tacit agreement and no actual lies. While the effect was the same and she was deeply embroiled in a world of deceit, she took satisfaction from not having verbalised any of it, only acquiescing, agreeing, nodding with each suggestion. She stood from the table and pressing a hand on Mrs Wife's shoulder as she made to stand too, pushed her back into her seat, cleared the table and began washing up while the host and hostess sat comfortably with their wine.

"That's a penny Shoshama, tonight's fee is dropped to fivepence." Shoshama smiled to herself again, at some point when all this business was over she would pay this goodly couple in full for their kindness. "Have you run away without funds my dear?" asked Mrs Wife.

"No, I have some money." This was not a lie, just an understatement and she preferred to continue in such a manner as much as possible.

"Even so, we shall not take your last penny. We are not poor by any means. We raised six sons on the wages of a lowly cook and a vigneron, supplemented by Mister's business transactions. We can certainly manage to subsidise one temporary daughter in her moment of need."

"Even so, I should like to seek work," said Shoshama, turning from her washing up.

The couple looked at each other, "We can talk about it at breakfast. Breakfast is at seven sharp!"

When the washing up was done and everything tidied away, Shoshama bowed her thanks and searched in her purse for small change to pay for her first night with the Wifes. They laughed and waved her away, saying they would keep a tab and she could settle prior to moving on. "Have you thought about where you will go? No of course not," she continued when Shoshama hesitated. "Prague is by far the best place in the whole wide world you know. You could do much worse than make your new life right here." Mr Wife nodded enthusiastically at this and glugged wine all the faster as if happy thoughts must necessarily be matched by an equal number of happy slurps. Shoshama put on an expression of contemplation. Obviously she would be away home to Persia pretty soon, but she needed to behave as a runaway might.

"Maybe..." she mused. "I certainly like it so far!" and smiled to herself as she realised it was true. With a cheery goodnight, she skipped away up the stairs, tempted to blow raspberries as she went.

"Well it's 19 after 8 House," announced Mr Wife, taking a mouthful and emptying what remained of the second bottle into his glass.

"I'm sure it is Mister, I'm sure it is," she said, looking at the doorway Shoshama had passed through and then lingeringly at the chair she had sat it. "Delightful young lady, Mister."

"Delightful!" he agreed.

"Utterly charming," she said quietly, looking back towards the doorway.

"Utterly," echoed Mister. Then frowning at his empty glass said, "Another glass for you House?" with a hopeful tone.

"I fancy something sweet!" she said, slapping her thighs and Mister, announcing he had *just the thing*, set off to get it.

Next morning Shoshama arrived early and helped set the table. They had fried eggs, toast coated with a spread of yeast extract and curious biscuits of crunchy, dried wheat soaked to a soft consistency in milk and several cups of tea. Other than the tea and eggs, these were new culinary experiences for Shoshama and she felt certain she would be happy to adopt them permanently.

"You mentioned working," said Mrs Wife.

Shoshama spooned in some more of the delicious milky wheat biscuit mush and nodded, "I did. Mmm, what is this, I simply adore it!"

"My own invention. Something I created during my role as cook for all those years. Baked wheat, shaped in to these convenient biscuits, they stay fresh in the larder for a long time and then come alive with milk. Being biscuits of wheat I call them *Biscowheat*, but I don't suppose they'll catch on."

"Are you kidding?" erupted Shoshama, her mouth brimming with the wonderful Biscowheat, "Au contraire my dear Mrs Wife, I will entreat you for the recipe should I ever leave here!"

"How about my yeast extract spread?" asked Mr Wife, checking his watch and announcing the hour.

"Yes, I liked it a lot on toast. Quite zingy, a little salty perhaps, yet it has something almost addictive about it. I'm going to say yes for me, but I can imagine it's a bit of a love it or hate it kind of thing. Does it have a name?"

Mr Wife made to speak but Mrs Wife cut across

him, "I might." Mr Wife sighed but also chuckled good humouredly. Shoshama looked quizzical so Mrs Wife elaborated, "He keeps saying *I might* call it this or *I might* call it that, but he never settles on anything, so I have taken to calling it *I might.*"

"I might?" asked Shoshama a little confused.

"No dear, it's not a question, it's a spread for toast, or crumpets, or it can be used to add some zap to a sauce, *I might*, a statement pronounced more like *eyemite!*"

"Well you are both geniuses inventing such super breakfast marvels. Now, had you any thoughts as to where I might work?"

Mrs Wife looked perplexed. "The thing is dear, I believe you will find it impossible not to draw attention to yourself. Adopting a common name like Eliška is no use if people are still completely intrigued and fascinated by you everywhere you go. Did you find yourself the centre of attention between your arrival and finding us here?"

"Not really, a few people glanced at me, a few men mostly and one ghastly man whose door I chanced upon offered me money to reside with him, but I made a dash for it." Shoshama chuckled at her lucky escape, it seemed funnier now the danger had passed.

"Perhaps he was lonely and just wanted a friend, gentle female company, polite conversation?" offered Mr Wife rather generously.

"I think he was having trouble with a twitching housecoat!" guffawed Shoshama causing Mrs Wife to go cross-eyed and purse her lips like she'd just bitten a lemon. Such was her stress that her digestive system reacted as though she'd just mounted an extra-long flight of stairs.

Immediately, Mr Wife broke into a loud coughing fit, in Shoshama's mind, to cover his wife's inadvertent noise, causing her to think of him as a true gentleman, until he jumped up from his chair and shouted, "Good grief House! You'll kill us all with your abominable, abdominal farts!" At which, Mrs Wife laughed and farted and farted and laughed until the two were indistinguishable and Mr Wife laughed until tears came into his eyes, and Shoshama found herself laughing too, though what her parents, or her nanny, or her finishing schoolmistress, or anyone she had previously known might think of such a thing, she could not imagine.

Eventually things settled down with Mr Wife back in his seat and Mrs Wife maintaining her almost spherical shape and seemingly not in the least deflated for having expelled such a considerable quantity of gas. Mrs Wife picked up where she had left off as if the outrageous interlude had never occurred, "The thing is Shoshama, we fear that you will be noticed if you are unduly exposed to a great many people. Your work ought to be more private and time should pass before you can be considered safe to mix much."

"I don't think it's likely that..."

Mr Wife held his hand up, "You cannot be too careful. I am certain as certain can be that the man you have run away from..." Mrs Wife coughed forcibly and Mr Wife looked at her, "Sorry dear! Sentence construction is her thing, well one of her things, she has a lot of things! Anyway, The man from whom you have run... away..." she coughed again, "The man, away from whom you have er, run..." no cough, but she sighed deeply this time.

"Yes, yes, I understand," said Shoshama.

"Well, for one thing; pride. He has been outwitted, his property lost to him, to him lost, he'll take steps, a man of means he is and means will expended be! And for another thing, less practical, more heartfelt; you are a prize my dear, no man could see you go without longing for your return. A cad he may be, a bully, an arse!"

"Mister!" exclaimed House.

"Beg pardon House, over-excited! He may be, shall we say, an ass instead, but by golly he'll certainly promise anything possible, anything imaginable or impossible or unimaginable. To change himself all-recognition-beyond, a man-new to be, a limb to forfeit, or two, or all four if necessary it is! Or anything else you demand, in order to have you willingly return." Shoshama was taken aback. Of course, no one was actually looking for her, there was no husband and her family knew she was on a long jaunt around Europe with friends, and now it seemed this little convenient untruth might become her jailer. Or at least an inhibiter to her freedom. For now, she needed to play along in the hope that her original plan might still work.

"Which is why…" she said, pausing at this point while they regarded her intensely, "Which is why I thought it might be best to work at the castle." They gasped. Looked at each other, then back at her.

"No I don't think…" said Mr Wife but was interrupted by Mrs Wife.

"The King doesn't have staff."

"He doesn't?" That was a blow, what King doesn't have staff? "Surely he has some staff! That great big castle…!"

"Not anymore. He did. We two were among them, I in the kitchen and Mister his vigneron, taking care of his extensive collection of wine. In fact all the residents in this street worked in the castle, these houses were built right here for the very purpose of serving the castle behind us, up there, but things changed and the King decided he didn't want us around."

Shoshama looked puzzled, as she well might. Mister stepped in, "There was illness, the Queen herself, this coincided with their daughter, Princess Petra's 14th birthday celebration when she was due to be promised to a suitable young man, but that went awry …"

"Awry? How so?" asked Shoshama.

"Princess Petra didn't like the young men presented and her choice was not one her father could approve of..."

"Not one anyone would be likely to approve," corrected House.

"Did her mother, the Queen approve of her choice?" asked Shoshama.

Mrs Wife continued, "I think she was more willing to discuss it at least, she and Petra were close, as mothers and daughters are oft inclined to be, but she died before the matter was settled and that broke the family. The King never recovered, Petra's heart was broken and broken again, all within such a short space of time and she, no more than a child."

"So where is she? How old is she now? What happened to her?" Here was Shoshama's chance. Did they know? If anyone might know, surely two of the castle staff, there at the time, *they* would know!

They just shrugged. Mr Wife spoke first, "No one really knows. Some say she died of sadness and it was all hushed up, some say she was despatched to the seaside at Split, a lovely spot, have you been by chance?" Shoshama shook her head, but made a mental note of the place, "Some say she's locked in a tower. I ask you! Like some badly written fairy story! Haha!"

"What do you think?" Shoshama leaned in, her eyes squinting, her most serious interrogator's face on, something she had learned from her uncle Jeremy of Paxford.

"Tower!" buckled Mister.

"Yes, tower!" said House.

"Not Split and not dead?" asked Shoshama firmly.

"He'd never let her go and there's no reason for her to die and little chance that could happen without actual knowledge of it. It was just a rumour. When Princesses die, you hear of it properly, it's big news."

"And what about the dragon?" asked Shoshama.

Mister blew out a puff of air from bulging cheeks, leaned back and folded his arms, "Dragon? Oh, keep away from him! If he hasn't been fed, he'll have your head off!"

"Have your head off!" echoed House.

"So he does exist? There _is_ a dragon in the castle!" Shoshama could hardly believe what she was hearing and looked at the pair to check they weren't mad.

"All the staff were afraid of Dragon," said House. He's kept in a massive stable in the courtyard, no one's safe if he's let out, I've even seen the King afraid of him and he raised him from... this big." She held her hands 20 cm apart. "He was so lovely then, so playful, such a widdle, wubbly, widdle, kuddly, wuvly fing!" She had slipped into that ridiculous baby talk some people save for pets, or babies, or anything living that basically costs a small fortune and makes a terrible mess everywhere. Shoshama had little time for baby animals, especially baby humans. She appreciated horses and adults and if she had to have a pet, she always thought a tiger would be ideal.

"What happened, if he was so lovely as a little dragon?"

House answered, "Oh the usual. It's never the animal you know, it's the owner! The King wanted it to be vicious and he encouraged the soldiers to torment it, provoke it. He thought he could use Dragon to terrorise unwanted visitors, maybe to keep them away from the tower. It fits, do you see? It fits with the notion of Petra being locked away there."

"I do. Is it still up there? Do you hear it ever, roaring, shrieking, I mean, I don't even know, what noise does it make?"

"Oh a deep rumbling growl" said Mister.

"A terrible gnashing of teeth!" said House.

"And do you hear this? At night maybe, does the King let it out?"

"Never heard it. Not since we left four years ago. But it's rumoured to…" Mister paused, Shoshama looked expectant, nodding for him to continue. He looked across at House for help, she bit her lip and seemed hesitant.

"What? What is the dragon rumoured to do?" Shoshama asked.

"Well, it seems so unlikely," said Mister.

"Too far-fetched!" said House.

"Couldn't possibly be," said Mister.

"But still…" said House.

"Yes, but still…" said Mister.

"What? What? But still what?" begged Shoshama.

Mister sighed, regarded House with some resignation and both he and Shoshama saw her nod almost imperceptibly. "Children vanish and it is said they are eaten by Dragon."

Shoshama reflected on this piece of information for a moment and said, "Children vanish in every big city, it's not normally attributed to a dragon."

"These children are… selected. At least it appears that way. Orphans mainly, but occasionally children from families too. Very often the parents say they were bad children, not especially missed, not wanted back. It's like one of those terrible folklore things for children; *if you behave badly you'll be eaten by… by… Dragon!*"

"But the orphans? They haven't behaved badly, why would they be punished so?" House and Mister shrugged, shaking their heads sadly and looking at each other for an answer. Neither had one and Shoshama could tell they knew no more than they had already told. "Oh, that's terrible!" cried Shoshama. "How old are these children, are they babies or toddlers or what?"

"No babies as far as we know. All young though, three to six or seven in the main," said House.

"And how many?"

"Over the four years since it started? Forty, 45?" said Mister in a questioning voice.

"Forty, 45," echoed House, confirming his estimate.

"And why? Why would such a thing be happening?" begged Shoshama.

"All I can think," said Mister, "is that such a big beast has a big appetite!"

"Mister!" barked House.

"Well, what do you think? I mean, what do you feed an animal like that? Whole cows?"

"Yes!" agreed Shoshama and House in unison. "Anything but children!" added Shoshama.

"Do you like children?" asked Mister.

"I couldn't eat a whole one!" Shoshama said automatically, for it was an old joke. This time though her audience just stared at her, mouths gaping, brows became furrowed, confusion passed across Mister's face. "I mean, I do, sort-of, I haven't had that much to do with them."

"I was wondering if we might find work for you with children," he said.

"I was thinking sewing, in a backroom somewhere, not public-facing, industry not commerce, labour not service," said House.

"At the castle?" enquired Shoshama.

"Don't see how," answered House gruffly.

"No one works there, though the King does have deliveroos of food each day!" said Mister.

"Deliveries," corrected House.

"Oh yes, sorry, deliveries of feed."

"No, not deliveries of feed, not deliveroos of food, deliveries of food!"

Mister made the face shapes of eee and ooo, then had another go, "Deliveroos of feed."

House waved him down in exasperation, "It doesn't help

you if you want to go inside my dear because they don't, they just ring the doorbell and hand it over on hostess trollies. Not to worry, we will find something for you to in an office or the back of a shop or something." This didn't suit Shoshama one little bit. But she tried not to show it. "First, we must attend to this deathly look you have acquired. It is all artifice, for food and wine and amusing company have done nothing to bring colour to your chalky cheeks. And that hair, that hair!" she reached across and twirled it between her finger and thumb, "Beautifully silky, but it has no colour!" Shoshama regarded House's tight bun of silvery grey and wondered if that was what was considered a colour around here. "I'll fetch a big basin, towels and everything I need. Mister, make yourself scarce."

"Of course, House," he said without hesitation, but his eyes lingered a moment on Shoshama and there was just the tiniest sadness about him. Nevertheless, he bowed and left, shutting the parlour door behind him.

By lunchtime, a second transformation had taken place and when Shoshama was shown herself in a mirror, she gasped with surprise. Or perhaps it was more a gasp of utter shock.

Chapter the Ninth.
Prague Police Headquarters

''And your name again?'' asked the officious Sergeant at the desk. Darius passed him a handwritten note, which he then indiscreetly read aloud, "Police Inspector Purile." The Sergeant stared at him for an inordinately long time.

"It is pronounced, *Perr-eel,*" said Darius, correcting the man.

"Oh. Only it looks like Purile here."

"Yes, it is a matter of phonetics, spelling and actual, proper pronunciation."

"I see. Perr- eel. I'll see if the Chief is available to see you. Wait there please Inspector." And with that he left the desk. Darius obviously wasn't a police inspector, but he felt able to carry the pretence off for the purposes of his private enquiries. He needed information and he reasoned this would be a good place to start. The police ought to have answers to most of his questions, the problem was getting them to share intelligence and to that end, he hoped that posing as a visiting detective would open a few doors.

Looking around, Darius could see a number of Prague policemen. One was reading the current issue of *The Police Gazette*, something he approached in a fully reclined position with his feet on a desk. Another was eating nuts from a bowl, chewing one while cracking the next in a perpetual motion. A third had his cap over his face was clearly asleep, while the fourth and final policeman present was by far the busiest, occupied as he was by ironing his trousers. For this purpose he wasn't wearing them, nor any others. One thing which no one appeared to be doing, was police work.

The fourth policeman caught Darius's gaze and waving the iron said, "Need anything ironing while I'm at it?" Darius answered that didn't but thanked the kind policeman for his kind offer. The ironing policeman stared at Darius at length, appearing puzzled. Darius wondered if something about his appearance was undermining his story but could think of no reason for the policemen to be suspicious. One by one, the other three all gave Darius the once-over, the third policeman being nudged awake to do so, and all four giving each other surprised looks. Darius squirmed and felt the need to clear his throat. He stared at his pristine white shoes, his immaculately pressed white trousers, was it the white suit that was at fault now?

Convinced that his tweedy, bland disguise, his attempt to fit in had somehow caused the unintended and opposite effect of drawing peoples' attention, (though he could not begin to imagine what might be wrong with it) he'd resumed wearing his preferred all white as of this morning. "Back in my comfort zone!" he had said to himself as he smoothed the sleeves of his jacket in front of the tall mirror. He smoothed them again now, then looked at the four, all looking back at him as if he were a fascinating woman in her night things.

At this point, the desk Sergeant returned and bid Darius to follow him. They proceeded along a lengthy and echoey corridor to the left-hand end of the building and up several flights of stairs to the fourth floor. There, they walked the length of the corridor to the right-hand end of the building and down a flight to the third floor. Obviously then, there were stairs at either end of the building. Turning right, they passed through some swing doors into an entirely empty room, through which they passed into another room via a connecting door. That room was filled with filing cabinets arranged in a maze-like pattern that required some dexterity to get between until they reached more connecting doors into a third room in which was a desk and several chairs, the Sergeant muttering that it was the interview room over his shoulder. Turning left they exited by the main door into the third-floor corridor 20 metres of so from the staircase at either end of the building. Darius was about to ask what the Sergeant was doing going round in ridiculous circles but was beaten to it by the man swinging open a door midway down the corridor on the front side of the building, They were on the third floor directly above the entrance.

"Inspector Pair-ill Chief!" announced the Sergeant.

"Perr-eel" corrected Darius.

"Looks more like Purile!", said the Chief wafting the slip of paper and standing up to greet him. "Oh he is isn't he!" he said to the Sergeant. "You weren't exaggerating!"

"I beg your pardon?" said Darius.

"No need boy, no need, you're more than welcome here so sit yerself down! Where you from son? What brings you to good-old Praggy? How can I help a fellow officer of the lore?" As Darius began to sit, the Chief thrust his hand across the desk to shake hands and Darius was forced to abandon sitting to stand again and almost losing his balance, he caused a considerable amount of noise and disruption to the chair, the desk and things on it. After the handshake, the Chief examined his own hand, even giving it a sniff and looking surprised with what he found. Or didn't find.

"Did you?" the Chief addressed the Sergeant and whistled a strange little three note peep, while making a rapid stirring motion with his index finger.

"Totally Chief. He won't have a clue where he is." Darius frowned, he was supposed to be lost. Still straightening the desktop adornments, he found himself juggling them and trying not to drop anything.

"Sorry about the…" the Chief whistled the little tune again and waggled his finger exactly as before. "Can't be too careful. Security. Disorienting technique. Better than blindfolding everyone who wants to see me!"

"And I'm sorry about this, I seem to have…" said Darius, attempting to straighten the cluster of framed photos and pewter paperweights while struggling to keep up with the Chief's extraordinary behaviour. To Darius's surprise, the photos were not of the Chief with dignitaries, nor of family members, that is unless his family was made up of young female dancers in skimpy costumes. Darius looked awkwardly at the Chief while fumbling the picture frames, actually trying not to touch the ladies themselves. The Chief's response was to guffaw a little and wink, clearly delighted Darius had experienced them. The paperweights were hand-crafted pigs wearing police caps, belts with truncheons tucked in them and with whistles hanging around their necks and as Darius did his best to straighten them with a look of utter confusion on his face, the Chief laughed even louder.

"Marvellous aren't they?" said the Chief, rearranging the photo frames into an equidistant arc and then the pigs into an artistic cluster. He pointed at the pig-paperweights, "Splendidly oinky dontcha think? And these lovelies," sweeping his hand along the arc of framed dancing girls, "scrump-tious!" He made the two-syllable word in to two words, then picked up the picture to his far left and gave it an emphatic, noisy kiss. Then the next picture received the same treatment and all the way down the line until each had received the Chief's slobbery full-mouth treatment. "Lovely, lovely, lovely! Which one do you like best of all?"

"Oh well, they are all rather…" said Darius rather lamely.

"Go on! Which one's yer favourite?"

"Well I don't know, they all look…"

"Go on! Pick one? Which one eh? I think I know!" Darius felt cornered into playing the game and so leaning forward a little more, regarded them quickly and picked up the one second from the end. "That one? That one! Why that one?" The Chief grabbed it off the desk and looked closely at it through his monocle. "Well I never, you're a queer bird to pick her! Remind you of yer mother does she?"

"Well actually…"

"Right, chitchat over. To business, come on, what's what?" barked the Chief.

Darius composed himself, "The King."

"The King?"

"Is he alright?"

"Yes of course he's alright, why do you ask?"

"In my country we have difficulties policing the capital city and we heard you are the best here in Prague so I have come to see how you do what you do so well. This is all background stuff, I'm sure you understand." The Chief seemed to appreciate this, smiling a broad smile, shifting around in his chair and making funny little noises in the back of his throat.

"Right-ho! King's fine. Carry on," he barked, the words like bullets.

"The Princess Petra, and her whereabouts?"

"Strange question, watcha want to know that for?" the Chief threw himself back in his chair and put his hands on his hips.

"We have troubles keeping track of the whereabouts of our own Princess and wondered how you manage it here."

"I see. She went out of circulation four years ago, August 4th in the summer of '33. Vanished! Just like that!" he made a hand gesture like a puff of air.

"No idea where she is?"

"Told you! Vanished!" he did a less enthusiastic repeat of the gesture.

"Did you look for her?" asked Darius.

"Look for her? She'd vanished. Can't look for a vanished thing, it's not there! Don't you know what vanished means? Gone boy, gone!" He seemed a little agitated by the question but then brightened up and smiled, "Next question."

"The dragon."

"Yes, what of it?"

"You know about it?" asked Darius, incredulous.

"Know about it? Seen it with my own two eyes boy!" the Chief indicated his eyes, something Darius hadn't needed.

"Oh those eyes!" he said a tad sarcastically.

"The very peepers! Is that it? Glad to have had this conversation! Very impressive questioning technique! Good policemen where you come from obviously."

"No, I have more!" said Darius, desperate for the meeting not to end so soon.

"Incredible, absolutely incredible! Where do they train you? Some top interrogation school no doubt. Come on then, I can take it. Watcha got?" The Chief seemed delighted.

"Can you tell me about the missing children? The ones the dragon is reported to have, er… eaten."

The Chief stood up and looked darkly pensive. He moved to the place behind his chair and leaned heavily upon it, made to speak, then didn't. He paced to the corner where his Sergeant was still standing and although he stepped up to a point just a centimetre or so from him, didn't look at him, instead, turned to Darius and opened his mouth to speak. Then didn't. Instead, he paced back the length of the room, one fist pounding the palm of his other hand in a kind of tormented internal debate. Behind him, his Sergeant paced in time, mimicking the thinking behaviour of his Chief. In the other corner he stopped and turned, looking seriously at Darius. Finally, he spoke.

"They are all missing."

"How many?" asked Darius.

"Forty, 45?" he said glancing at the Sergeant.

"Forty, 45," confirmed the Sergeant.

"You don't know?"

"Forty we're pretty sure of, five we are less sure of, so, 40, 45 is the number we quote." The Sergeant nodded in agreement.

"Does the dragon... the dragon *you have seen with your own eyes...* eat the children?" Darius couldn't believe he was asking such an outrageous question.

"Well, no one's actually seen that. They normally get carried off by the keeper," said the Chief.

"Sorry? The what" blurted Darius, amazed at this turn of events.

"The dragon keeper. Dragon's on a lead. Keeper holds the lead. Keeper knocks the door and says Dragon's come for the child. Parents or whoever hand over said child. Keeper carries the child off." The Chief looked sad as he relayed each stage of the process factually and without embellishment for the purposes of court evidence. The Sergeant nodded, confirming each successive part.

"Why don't they say no? Why don't they refuse?" Darius's voice was raised in exasperation.

The Chief basically blew a raspberry in answer, the Sergeant copying with a less successful one. "You're joking right? Dragon!" he concluded with dramatic emphasis.

"These children. Badly behaved, orphans, not regular children, is that right?" asked Darius.

The Chief turned to his Sergeant, "Unrelenting, in't 'e? Marvellous technique!" then back to Darius, "Seems so. We've investigated all 45 cases and everyone is either a recent orphan, or there's something up with the family."

"What do you mean, something is up?"

"Ears like a bat! For instance, typical situation, subject Number 21, July two years ago, four-year old girl, mum a drunk, dad a wife-beater, Dragon takes the girl. Another one, subject Number 13, May three years ago, five-year-old boy, mum missing believed missing, dad working away, believed with another woman, boy alone at home, Dragon takes the boy. There's a pattern like this throughout."

"Missing believed missing. What's that?" asked Darius.

"Crikey, mind like a mouse trap!"

"Steel trap Chief!" interjected the Sergeant.

"Mind like a…"

"Steel trap Chief!" interjected the Sergeant, again.

"Mind like a steel mouse trap he's got, this bloke has! Missing believed missing is when we have a person who has gone missing and after looking into it, we conclude they aren't at home, or at work or at Auntie Susan's and so they are indeed, missing, believed missing" The Chief explained.

"Missing then." Said Darius.

"Well, we believe so. Hence the addendum, the modifier, *believed* missing. Things aren't always so straight-forward."

Darius moved on, realising something suddenly obvious, "Where do these kids go? The castle? I mean, that's where the Dragon is, right?"

"Who knows? Could be anywhere. Might eat them down by the river…"

The Sergeant jumped in, "Nice spot!"

"Nice spot!" confirmed the Chief, "Or on a hill, under a tall tree, bit of moonlight," continued the Chief.

"But you don't know the children are eaten at all! They are taken away alive! They might all still be alive!" burst Darius.

"Yeah, like Dragon wants a load of brat kids to look after!"

"And an empty belly when he's hungry!" said the Sergeant in a mocking tone.

Darius took a calming breath, "Have you investigated? Have you been to the castle? Have you asked the King?"

The two policemen whistled a serious, doubting kind of whistle. The kind given by dodgy builders asked for an estimate. "Can't do that! Can't *interrogate* the King!" said the Chief.

"He's the King!" said the Sergeant. "He's not just any Tom, Dick or Harry!"

"Or Jim," added the Chief.

"Or Jim?" ventured Darius.

"He forgot Jim", said the Chief, at which point the Sergeant said he *always* forgot Jim and the two of them laughed about it for a while.

"I don't understand," said Darius, bewildered again.

"Tom, Dick, Harry and Jim, all downstairs, that's the squad, sergeant here and me. Hello to Prague Police Force!" he held his hands aloft in victory.

"That's it? Six of you?" they nodded. "But everyone's in! No one's patrolling or actually policing."

"All doing vital police work!" the Sergeant looked affronted.

"Sleeping?"

"R&R. Everyone's entitled," confirmed the Sergeant.

"Ironing?" asked Darius.

"A police uniform, I think you'll find!" the Sergeant answered smugly, giving the Chief a cheery elbow in the ribs. Darius went to speak, but the Sergeant put his hand up to stop him, "Testing nuts and reading important police information material. You can't say we don't run a tight ship here!"

"Testing nuts? asked Darius, incredulous.

"Vital work!" they both confirmed.

"Look, have you thought of just going up to the castle and asking the King about these children? About the dragon, HIS dragon?" They puffed out their cheeks and looked at each other. The Sergeant thrust his hands in his pockets and shuffled his feet, after which they puffed out their cheeks again. "What? What's the harm? Just ask! Haven't you thought about it? They might not be dead! They might all be up at the castle, alive and well!"

The Chief looked glum. "What?" asked Darius.

The Chief hesitated. "He might not like it."

"What do you mean, he might not like it."

"I mean, the King might not like it." Said the Chief.

"I realise that, but so what?"

"So what? We are the police department, us six. Aside from missing children, there is no crime here in Prague. NO CRIME. Well, once in a blue moon we have to ship someone off for something or other, but basically Inspector, *we've cracked it!*"

"Almost cracked it," confirmed the Sergeant.

"Almost," said the Chief. Darius waited.

The Chief retook his seat, "Some crimes never reach our ears until they are solved, so to speak," he said nonchalantly, "Little bit of vigilantism going on out there. Happens in every Kingdom, yours?"

"I suppose so. Before we had an organised, tax-funded police force, it was pretty much all vigilantism. A sort of anarchy, mob-rule."

The inspector leaned forward on his elbows and looked intently at Darius, "And what's your view on vigilantes Inspector? For or against? Tolerate 'em or lock 'em up?"

Darius searched for the hidden meaning in the question. Had he been rumbled? Was he under suspicion? He tried to approach it from a police perspective. "We don't make the laws. The police are not the law and the law is not justice.

We simply enforce the laws of the land. If those laws are out of synch with the population, then the people restore the balance."

The Chief looked thoughtful but his expression maintained enough elements of confusion for Darius to feel obliged to elaborate. The Sergeant was more obviously lost and gazed into space while chewing the matter over. Darius continued, "When justice is considered too harsh and oppressive, the people join in opposing authority, criminals can become folk heroes and the weight of opinion is anti-authoritarian. When the population feels the system is too soft, when penalties aren't proportionately harsh enough, there is an emergence of vigilantism, in effect, the people become judge, jury and executioner. It's a matter of finding a balance for the time in which you live. These things tend to swing like pendulums. Like a lot of things, it's yin and yang."

"Hmm, sounds like you've got Triads," said the Chief. Now it was Darius's turn to look confused, "These Yingy-Yangy lot, Chinese I'll wager. We've had a little of that going on here. Our vigilante isn't Chinese though, pretty sure of that. Anyhoo, what with one thing and another and with a modest level of rather helpful vigilantism, we've pretty much got crime on the run, on the back foot, under control, down to a minimum."

"Swept under the carpet," added the Sergeant, swiping his hands across each other to signify a job completed and well done.

"Not swept under the carpet Sergeant! Swept into a dust-pan and carried carefully to the bin, out in the alley next to the recycling. Sorted! Done and dusted!"

"The dust of crime, the crime-dust, is done and dusted!" confirmed the Sergeant, happier than ever.

"Except for 45 very important and worrying, unsolved

cases of missing children!" said Darius. "Except for that, all the nut testing and ironing is completely under control!"

The Sergeant nodded enthusiastically and with obvious pride, but the Chief detected some implied criticism and pouted as he thought about it. Seeing him, the Sergeant quickly adopted a pouty face, but without knowing why, his heart wasn't in it. Finally, the Chief spoke, "I've got a department to run Inspector. I've got mouths to feed, not just mine, but five households. Big ones too. Policemen have a lot of children, don't ask me why, I've never understood it, something about the adrenaline rush, truncheons and handcuffs flapping on your belt all day..." he petered out, wondering.

"Maybe it's all the ironing," Darius offered sarcastically.

"Mm, could be," mused the Chief, "Has the opposite effect on my dear lady!" his contemplative expression was adopted by the Sergeant. "Anyway, I fancy you're missing my point. Let's say we ask the King and he takes us to the some picnic spot and shows us a lot of dragon footprints, scorched undergrowth and a massive pile of little kiddie-bones, what then? Solve the only outstanding mystery in Prague and where are we?" he indicated himself and the Sergeant

"Scrapheap!" said the Sergeant.

"Well not actually the scrapheap," said the Chief.

"Over, kaput, finished!" said the Sergeant, running a finger across his throat.

"Not that bad, obviously..." said the Chief, but the Sergeant was making a tongue lolling-out hanging kind of face, at which point the Chief snapped at him, "NOT. THAT. BAD. Fool!" and the Sergeant stopped, looking at his fingers as if his feelings were a bit hurt. "But, I might have a headcount issue with the Mayor. Do I need a team of six, she'd ask, budget cuts and austerity, could some of the current workload be undertaken by part-time civilian staff with less training and lower costs? Can you imagine, the department chopped in two, decimated, no, quinquaginta-mated that would be! And civilians, now then, untrained civilians I ask you, ironing uniforms… um… you know, testing nuts… and absolutely everything else. No, no, no, we need things to be precisely as they are. Natural order. Balanced, perfectly balanced!"

"On a knife-edge!" added the Sergeant.

"No, not on a knife-edge, on a nice thing, on a…" he wondered about it.

"On a kitten!" said the Sergeant with delight.

The Chief frowned again, "Yes that's it. Years of police-work, decades of experience and I've got the department perfectly balanced on a kitten!" He looked at his Sergeant with some disappointment, but it had no effect, only prompting some meows, paw-licking and face-washing from the man.

The Chief turned back to Darius and sighed, his forearms on his desk like a politician, "You think the children are alive, we hope they are alive, if they're not, asking questions won't make them alive instead of dead, but it might mean some of my team have to find new employment!" he turned and stared meaningfully at the Sergeant who immediately did a bit more paw-licking and face-washing. Turning back to Darius with his most serious face and tone yet, he said, "Everything's fine. Leave it alone." This sounded final.

Darius waited. His head shook from side to side almost imperceptibly. Then quietly, and suppressing a little anger he said, "Unless you're a missing Princess or a little kid."

"Inspector Purile. Our one and only jail cell is empty and has been for a long, long time. Please don't invite that to change. I would hate to think our only arrest is a police inspector from a foreign state. I would especially hate for anyone to think we were prejudiced."

"Prejudiced?" asked Darius? The Chief pointed at him, waggled his finger up and down a bit in his way and whistled a few random notes. The Sergeant nodded emphatically.

"I'm sure the whole city is delighted to have you and we are happy to assist you in your endeavours to learn anything which might help your troubled city and its wayward royals, but please don't cross the line between prosperous study and nosy-meddly-pokering!"

"Nosy-meddly…" responded Darius cooperatively.

"Nosy-meddly-pokering. It's one of the few laws punishable by bucketing these days."

"It's a law?" the Chief nodded, "Nosy-meddly-pokering is actually against the law?" The Chief nodded again, more emphatically, "And it's punishable by…?"

"Bucketing! Bucketing… *ON THE HEAD!*" The Sergeant wore a grim face as he patted his own head, to assist with his Chief's explanation. Darius was beginning to think that didn't sound too bad when the Chief added, "And it's full of dog poo and you wear it for a week! Or a month, or it could even be a life sentence. It's up to the King." Darius changed his mind, bucketing *did* sound quite bad after all.

They looked at each other, Darius had lost some of his bravado. He was satisfied the answers to their quest lay in the castle but frustrated that he was in such an odd place, with odd people and odd customs.

"Show him out Sergeant!" said the Chief, formally, but not unpleasantly, doing his little whistle and finger waggling, as if stirring tea.

"It's alright, I know the way," said Darius, absentmindedly. The other two looked speechless so Darius quickly added the simple directions to get out by the most direct route. The Chief's mouth dropped open while the Sergeant rubbed the back of his own neck, thoroughly confused.

"Special Ops training!" said the Chief. "My, my, where you come from the policeman have to be like, like… Commandos!" The Sergeant shook his head in wonder, "Navy Seals!" continued the Chief, "Guerrillas!"

The Sergeant continued to make impressed faces, then added one himself, "Orangutans!"

"No, that's not one," said the Chief, a hand up, waving negatively.

"Armadillos!" added the Sergeant.

"No. Another wrong one. That's just an interesting animal, not a name for special forces."

"Might be though!" said the Sergeant. "Inspector Purile…"

"Perr-eel," Darius said, correcting his pronunciation again.

The Sergeant pointed, "Are you actually, or also-ly, an armadillo?"

"No," said Darius, at which the Chief threw his hands up in a *I told you so* way. But the Sergeant put his hands on his hips and smiled broadly, nodding very emphatic nods.

Pointing at Darius the sergeant said, "You heard it from his own lips Chief, definitely Armadillo!"

"He's not!" said the Chief, "That's just an exotic animal and actually, he said he wasn't!"

"Aha! But he'd HAVE to deny it, don't you see? He can't walk in here and say, *Hello! I'm Armadillo!*" this last bit he did in exactly the same made-up voice as the dishevelled woman under-the-table in the bar. Darius frowned at the odd coincidence and the Sergeant continued with, "I know that look, it means *'you got me bang to rights but I can't comment to confirm or deny it because I'm Armadillo and if I said anything one way or another I'd have to kill you and bury the evidence so you'd never find it and don't try bucketing me either because I've been highly trained in the art of bucket-full-of-dog-poo resistance techniques and you're likely to find YOU'RE the ones with buck-ets full of dog poo on your own heads!'* That's what that look means Chief! Hundred per cent!"

The Chief stood up and extended a hand meekly, "You're welcome to Prague Mr Purile," he pronounced it carefully and properly, "If there's anything we can do to help you, please just ask. I would however appreciate it if you didn't leave a trail of destruction behind you here in the city." Darius looked puzzled, "You know, 50 carriage carriage-chases which scatter handcarts of fruit across the street and squash big empty cardboard boxes, you, leap-ing across narrow streets from the rooves of tall buildings, people kicked through high windows with Armadillo fight-ing techniques, buildings blown up, Prague's finest wom-enfolk behaving in an unladylike fashion and then your boss says that you broke every rule in the book, but you're a flippin' hero and your own King wants to give you a great big medal!" Darius couldn't help but smirk slightly at the absurdity of it all. The Chief smiled back broadly, "See! Got you! We know see!" he tapped the side of his nose with his index finger, "You might be Armadillo special agent number nought, nought and then an elaborate continental seven, but Prague's police department isn't fooled!" He chuckled, "And then the most glamorous of all the women… or… THAT ONE!" he grabbed the picture frame second from the end and turned it to face Darius, "She comes to the carriage sta-tion just as you're about to leave. You tell the driver to stop and for some reason he does so, making everyone else wait and causing a great big traffic jam and she says, *Oh darling! Will I ever see you again?* And you pull her door key out of your pocket and say, *What do you think I had this made for, at the cobblers, while you weren't looking, for sixpence, or two for a shilling with free coloured bits that go round the top so you don't mix them up.* Then you have a great big kiss and all the people who've been made to wait are pleased for you which they demonstrate with applause and long loving looks at each other. Then you leave."

"And he doesn't look round!" added the Sergeant.

"Oh, good one! You don't look round do you Mr Perr-eel, nought, nought and an exotic continental seven!" Darius gave a tiny little head-waggle, neither confirming nor denying whether he would look around or not.

"Crikey! He's amazing, isn't he Sergeant! This is between us right? Not a word to anyone Sergeant. Anything you want, anything at all, we're your Prague contacts!"

"I'd like to meet the Mayor," said Darius.

"Consider it done!" the Chief slapped the table. "The Mayor will expect you this afternoon. Town Hall, big office, third floor, directly above the entrance hall."

"Same as this office then," said Darius, the two exchanging impressed looks and making impressed *cor!* noises.

"I'd like to meet the head of the army," added Darius like it was just the second item on a long list.

"No can do," replied the Chief.

"Uh-uh," added the Sergeant shaking his head.

"There is no army!" said the Chief. "We don't have one. No war, no fighting, no army, no one dies in any wars because we don't have them, no high taxes to pay for soldiers or weapons, just peace."

"Oh, okay then, which means for now, the only other thing I need from you is a way into the castle."

"Blimey! You don't want much do you!" the pair looked flummoxed, brows were wiped and cheeks were puffed again. "That's a big one!"

"A great biggidi-biggi-boppy-biggi-one-y!" added the Sergeant, "None biggerer than that! They don't come bigger. It's the biggest of big. The biggerest of the biggerest in the history of all things big!"

The Chief sighed, opened a drawer and handed Darius a key. "What's this for?" Darius asked.

"Back door to the castle. Tradesman's entrance." Darius stared at him.

"It's a tricky one," warned the Sergeant, "None of my chaps like doing it."

He'll be alright," said the Chief to the Sergeant, "Easy as iced buns for an operator with his…" the Chief did some pathetic Kung-Fu style arm waving, then turned his attention back to Darius, "We have the key in case the royal family go on holiday. You know, sort out the post, take in the milk bottles, feed Dragon." Darius went to speak but the Chief put a hand up to stop him, "Course they haven't been for years, *FOUR* years. But… we keep the key for emergencies. Yeah, that'll get you in. After that, you're on your own!"

"You're on your own buddyboy!" echoed the Sergeant. "But you'll be fine with your Armadillo skills!"

Darius revolved the key in his hands. "You've fed the dragon?"

"Not me, wouldn't go near the thing, but Tom, Dick, Harry and Jim have," said the Chief.

"Tossed meat over the top of the door of his stable to the snarling beast!" said the Sergeant, making a snarling noise, "Then run like Husain Blot!" The two policemen laughed, "Very fast runner, Husain Blot. Stopped running, took up football instead."

"Rubbish at football!" said the Chief.

"Rubbish!" confirmed the Sergeant.

"I'll thank you for that back before you leave," said the Chief nodding towards the key. "You can mysteriously return it to this locked drawer without anyone ever seeing you enter the highly guarded police headquarters!"

"Like an armadillo in the night!" said the Sergeant in a

wistful voice and sweeping his hand across the imaginary sky.

"Or I'll just pop it into him at the front desk," said Darius, pointing at the Sergeant.

"Just as good, just as good," nodded the Sergeant.

"Just one more thing I've been meaning to ask," said the Chief, slightly uncomfortably. Darius waited. The Chief looked at the Sergeant who grimaced slightly, then back at his desk while he aimlessly rearranged some papers, his pen and a wooden carving of a dragon. "You... haven't got another alias have you Inspector?"

Darius froze, "What do you mean?"

"I mean you don't go by any other names than Inspector Perr-eel? That's what I mean."

Darius suddenly felt hot, then icy cold, then hot again. Certain he was sweating he inadvertently touched his forehead, a signal that caused the Chief to react slightly and glance at the Sergeant who nodded that he'd seen it. "Um.. no, of course not, why do you ask?"

"Only we've been trying to ascertain the identity of someone who goes by the name of Sir Hillman."

At this Darius was able to give them an emphatic denial: "No. I absolutely do not go by the name Sir Hillman and never have." The Chief looked at the Sergeant, in a pained way.

"No... I'm... not... sure... Nope, none the wiser!" said the Chief, "Might be, might not be. Couldn't expect to read a closed book like this one like um... an open book."

"Closed," said the Sergeant, doing the action as usual and making an elaborate creaking-closing noise. "Like a closed book with a lock on it and no way of peeking in between the pages. Just completely cuh-loh-zed!" This last elongated word was followed by random noises that may or may not be related to something closing, but which seemed to delight the Sergeant himself.

Darius tried a smile which looked more like trapped wind. "Thank you!" he said, waving the key. The Chief mimed slipping it into a pocket which Darius did, pleasing the Chief, then leaned across the desk to shake hands with them both. It was a normal handshake but they each treated it as something amazing, making impressed noises and waving their hands about.

Darius waited for one of them to say *I'll never wash it again!* But the Chief just said, "Bye then!" and so Darius turned to leave and the Chief said, "Oh Mr, Purr-eel..." Darius turned and with a wink, the Chief said, "Give her a kiss from me, eh?" and chuckled. Darius smiled and pointed at the picture frame second from the end, but the Chief's face dropped and he said much less conspiratorially, "No, not her! The Mayor! This afternoon!" Darius was surprised by the idea, but gave a confirmatory nod, tipped his hat and left. The key to the castle was in his pocket.

Chapter the Tenth.
The Castle, The House of Rock &
The Traveller's Rest Inn
Just South Of Prague

In his cold, dark room Adalbert shivered. Through the arrow-slit window he could see a glimmer of light on the horizon as dawn broke. It was morning and he was hungry. He was half-way along one side of the room, sitting upright on the floor with his back against the wall, legs out straight in front of him. On his lap sat a friendly rat which he had taken to stroking. "Don't worry Ratty, no matter how hungry I get I will *never* eat you, never ever! You are my friend." The rat hopped down and another hopped up in its place. "Nor you, Other Ratty, I won't eat you either, you're my friend too, so cute and furry, you are just such lovely pets! Who knew!" The rat jumped down and a moment later Adalbert found he had a rat in his lap again, which he automatically stroked. "Hello Ratty!" he said then, "Wait! Are you Ratty or Other Ratty? Or are you another Ratty altogether? I think you must be Yet Another Ratty! And who are you with your adorable pinky ears? Why, you must be Pink Ears! Hello Pink Ears! Look at you! So, so cute, yes you are!" About 20 rats were scampering about being busy, climbing up and over Adalbert as if he were just furniture and all were enjoying his affectionate little finger-strokes. Their noses twitched and they blinked at him with their little eyes and Adalbert was certain he could feel them vibrating as he stroked. "Are you purring?

I think you are!" His stomach rumbled loudly, "Don't worry Ratties-all, daddy Adalbert won't eat you!" but still he looked around the room hoping to see something, anything, edible. Rats, cockroaches and spiders, he really couldn't imagine ever being hungry enough to eat any of them. "Honestly! What did you all eat before I arrived? Maybe the answer to our little dilemma is that in a week or so, I'll give you all the biggest, biggest treat ever! You'll have such a feast, 'Yum yum', you'll say, 'Thank you daddy, this is a *lovely* feast!' because I'll have starved to death and you can all eat me up!"

Then Adalbert heard footsteps and as they became clearer, he was certain he could hear someone humming. It sounded like Bad King Wenceslas. The footsteps and humming came closer until they stopped outside his room. Would Bad King Wenceslas be this jolly if he had come to throw Adalbert off the top of the tower? Throw him down a well? Stick him with a sword or pike, or do him in in some other ghastly way? Adalbert decided he certainly could be this jolly and do any of those things and more. He swallowed hard and held his breath. The rats scampered away to the darkest corners of the room. Two keys turned in the high and low door locks and the door swung open. There in the doorway stood King Wenceslas, hands on hips, a warm smile across his big face. "Morning Adalbert! Sleep well?"

"No, it was dashed cold!"

"That's a fine thank you for not chopping your head off last night! Still there's always today, eh?" replied the King.

"Well it wasn't that bad, I suppose I'll get used to it."

"Right! Hungry are we?" the King produced a little note pad with a pencil attached by a string. He dabbed the end of the pencil on his tongue and said, "What do you want?"

"You mean for breakfast?"

"Yes quickly now, I have to get the order in by seven."

"Can I have toast?"

"Toast," repeated the King at the slower speed at which he wrote the word down.

"Fried eggs?" he ventured.

"Fri-ed e-gg-s," said the King, "How d'ya like 'em?" Adalbert stared, the King listed his options, "Sunny side up? Poached, Florentine? Benedict?" he waved the pencil around as his suggestions flowed.

"Benedict! Benedict!" blurted Adalbert.

"Sausage?" Adalbert nodded and the King wrote it down. "Bacon?" and so it went, with the King offering more and more food and Adalbert, always one with an appetite nodded at it all. He felt that if it wasn't all some cruel trick and that if he was lucky enough to receive any of it, it might sustain him here in the locked room for long enough for something to happen, for someone to rescue him. Darius perhaps. Darius was taking on the form of a man increasingly heroic to Adalbert.

The list of food was extensive and complete but Adalbert had one more request, "Can I have potato wawfulls?" The King looked shocked, stared at him. "Please? They were so very, very good!"

The King broke into a broad smile and gestured towards Adalbert, poking at him with the pencil, "You see? Didn't I tell you, awfully wonderful! Once you've gone *reconstituted potato formed into portcullis shapes and fried*, you won't go back to other forms of potato! Except roasties, they are the kings of potatoes of course!"

"Hashbrowns are pretty nice," offered Adalbert.

"I'll give you that, but the shredded and baked version more so than the little triangles favoured by the buffet breakfasts at budget hotels, don't you think?"

"I do agree," said Adalbert, "Though I'm not averse to either."

"There's always a place for proper chips," mused the King.

"On their day," said Adalbert thoughtfully.

"On their day," echoed the King slowly, then enthusiastically, "It's got to be the right kind of meal, like ham, egg and chips, don't you think?"

"Oh I do!" agreed Adalbert, "Stop it, you're making me salivate! Ham, egg and chips!" he repeated dreamily.

"Scampi?" suggested the King inquisitively.

"Of yes, scampi definitely," agreed Adalbert. "Sausage, egg and chips?"

"Fair dos!" agreed the King generously, "But all you've done there is ditch a few slices of cold ham and add some hot sausages."

"Granted," confirmed Adalbert, "But it's a good swap don't you think?"

"Well then, depends on the sausage," said the King. "I'd say yes if it was a good Cumberland, bit o' spice, pepper and wot-not… hang on lad! We can't spend all morning comparing sausages, got to get this order in by seven!"

"Oh, beg-pardon, it's just that I think food is my favourite thing in the whole world. More than anything. More than music, more than playing outside, more than waving at one's subjects, definitely more than girls."

"Prefer a sausage do you?" chuckled the King.

"Deffo!" said Adalbert, "Even a Continental one, though it's anyone's guess what goes in 'em. Seems more like pâté than actual ground meat."

Bad King Wenceslas regarded Adalbert for a moment, then said, "Right-ho!" in a perfectly jolly tone, "It'll be a while, I put in the order and they deliver it to the castle gates at around eight, alright? Quite the appetite haven't you?!" and with that the King was gone, two door-locks locked, and him padding away down the stairs.

The rats returned and he stroked them each until he had most of them on his legs, shoulders and even the top of his head.

***

At the House of Rock, Mrs Wife put the finishing touches to Shoshama's make-up and said "Oh dear, oh deary me!" This had been her mantra for quite a while now, starting with when she had diligently wiped off Shoshama's Gosh! make-up to reveal her natural look. She said an especially loud *Oh dear!* when she saw the effects of the hair dye on her further-shortened hair and had continued to do so at regular intervals since.

"Well, I don't think this has helped very much at all my dear. True, you look unrecognisable compared to the Halloween thing you had going on when you arrived, so I believe no one who knew you before will automatically acknowledge you as one and the same young woman, but still, all and sundry _will_ look at you! I guarantee it. I simply cannot make you vanish into the crowd, even with you introducing yourself as Eliška, a normalising moniker does nothing to normalise your natural beauty, the genetics of your face will simply not cooperate!"

Shoshama pondered on the nature of the problem which Mrs Wife was struggling with until the older lady returned with a good-sized mirror and held it out in front of her. This was her first chance to see her new self, the third incarnation of the Princess Shoshama and well-mannered, multi-talented servant-girl Eliška in just a few days and instead of an amused 'Gosh!' this time she almost swore. She pulled the mirror in, turned her face, looked from all angles and blushed. This girl may be her, Princess Shoshama of Persia and a fair maiden (very fair, some might say) by any standards, but this girl looking back at her, with her hair the colour of a quality Pinotage wine, matching lipstick, a little eye shadow which was an almost indiscernible shade darker and redder than her naturally caramel-coloured skin, was a shock. She had never seen herself look so beautiful. It is vanity to admire yourself, but she was amazed by her appearance. Shoshama was very used to being well-regarded for her looks and had learned to utterly take them for granted. Not today, she stared as if she was staring at someone else, someone fabulously more lovely than she, someone she would like to be, or someone she might wish was her friend.

"What are we to do with you?" said Mrs Wife. "This hair colour is called Deep Purple on the box, more of a metallic dark maroon though wouldn't you say? Well it's all the rage, all the pretty girls are wearing it but none I think carry it off quite like you!" Shoshama felt her hair, styled like a bob and cut perfectly so it bounced, revealing her longer than average and delicate neck. She ran a fingernail on the smooth skin and noticed her nail varnish matched her hair and lips, all Deep Purple by name, Pinotage by shade. She placed a finger to her lips to compare the shades and as her lips parted, she felt an awkward shiver of self-admiration and whipped it away.

"I don't know what to say Mrs Wife. I hardly see her as me!" Shoshama pointed at the mirror and catching her reflection, was intrigued again, turned, blinked slowly. "Aagh!" she turned away from it.

"Are you alright dear?"

"I don't know who she is!" Shoshama jabbed a finger towards the mirror but wouldn't look at it again, it bothered her.

"Do you want me to take it off dear? I have a solution to get this out of your hair and all the make-up will be off in a jiffy."

"No!" Shoshama said, surprising herself with how rapidly and with such certainty it was said. "I just don't think I want to look at her…. at me. It's weird. It's like she's someone else."

"It's a transformation for sure. I wanted to make you blend in, to change from undeniably Shoshama to unremarkably Eliška, but you've gone from undead to unbelievable instead. I'm sorry dear!"

"No, no… it's fine really," and she caught herself staring at the mirror again. She broke away by force and asked Mrs Wife, "So, do you think I might be able to work?" Mrs Wife looked doubtful. "I would really like to get in the castle. I'd just like to get in there."

"Get in the castle? Well that's easy as pie. Might not be safe, but it's not difficult, not in the least."

Shoshama was stunned for the second time in a matter of minutes and felt a tingle of excitement which made her shiver.

***

In the finest bedroom of the Traveller's Rest inn, Chatty stood before the mirror on the dresser and doused his face with cold water. His chap lathered up a shaving brush and sitting Chatty down, commenced the morning shaving ritual. "Is everyone excited about Split?" Chatty asked.

"I am for one and most are, but if you don't mind me saying your Highness, and I promise you they aren't ungrateful, no not at all your Highness, but there's one or two who ain't up for a thousand kilometres more travel."

"I see. That's interesting." Said Chatty.

"Not speaking out of turn your Highness, not at all, they'd go anywhere you wanted 'em to and not one will say a word directly, but if you asked 'em honestly, stay here, go Split. Most would say, *'Split, sea, ice cream and candy floss'* and a few, a small few would say, *'Let me rest here awhile if you don't mind.'* That's my honest tuppence for what it's worth your Highness. Yes it is."

"I accept your price man," and Chatty gave him tuppence, then held up a shilling. "Tell me who they are and this is yours."

At breakfast, with all 17 assembled, bags packed and excited to go on the next leg of their journey south, Chatty stood and addressed them. "I have news for you. Some of you, _most_ of you will continue south to Split. I on the other hand will not." There was an audible gasp. "I have matters to attend to in Prague, hastily left undone yesterday and I intend to return to them today. I don't yet know quite what to do, but I no longer believe Split is the answer. It is a diversion, and while I am happy that you, my good servants can go there and have a spiffing time, I must redouble my efforts back in Prague to achieve the worthy goal I sincerely pledged with my friends in Vienna when we all high-foured!" The servants waited obediently, Prince Chatty was in one of his good moods but that didn't mean there wasn't a catch. To drum up a little more enthusiasm, Chatty high-foured by himself, flapping thin air and letting out a half-hearted "Yay!" It didn't help. They still looked more dutiful than excited.

"Anyhow, no matter, I need volunteers to stay with me and assist me on my quest and for missing out on the seaside, I will reward you half a crown. I also promise a seaside trip to anyone who forfeits the Split fun after we are all done with this business." Two hands went up, one a coachman, another a footman, making two of the three about whom he had been informed. He smiled to himself pleased with the result, then turned to his seamstress, "How about you?"

She looked at her father who was another of the coachmen and with a sad face said, "Daddy, do you mind?"

The older coachman looked at the younger coachman who had already volunteered to stay behind, then back at his daughter, "If His Highness is asking, then it is your duty to stay in any case."

Chatty raised his hand to interrupt things and looking at the seamstress said, "Your decision."

"Then I'll stay," she said and looked relieved. Chatty ordered the rest to Split and that they should write to him of their safe arrival and with details of their lodgings care of the Grand Velký Hotel. Depending upon the outcome of events in Prague, he would hope to join them there some time later, or they would all meet again for the long journey home. Hands were shaken, there were lots of bows and curt-seys and Prince Chatty rose a little in their estimation. The general consensus is that most Royals were nitwits, but that Chatty was after all and underneath, a pretty good one and that all-expenses paid holidays to Split were a dashed sight better than slaving down coalmines, tin mines, in slate pits, cotton factories, steel factories or pretty much anywhere else they could imagine. Working for royalty was better than working anywhere else... and quite possibly better than *being* royalty too.

As one solitary coach returned north to Prague, the other three rolled south and young Clifford started singing his little ditty about *going on a summer holiday* again. The others, surrendering to his gaiety, joined in with the lyrics they had been unable to avoid learning and sang along, waving their arms side to side in the air, in time with the music and with each other. Ah, you couldn't make it up!

Chapter the Eleventh.
The Town Hall

"What exactly is your interest in our King Inspector Perr-eel? Or should I say, Mr Per-eel, nought, nought and with an exotic, continental seven at the end?" The Lady Mayor, spun slowly around the raised flower beds in the back garden of the town hall. She was all faux-fur, faux pearls and a tweedy two-piece skirt and sort-of jerkin combo. Her thick, wobbly arms seemed to float as if she was in deep water, waving in the current like massive seaweed, while her eyes flashed and rolled. She was almost dancing.

Darius manoeuvred himself out of her path each time she waltzed towards him and spoke earnestly, "My country has no wish to meddle in the private affairs of your realm Lady Mayor, but intelligence sources suggest there may be a missing Princess by the name of Petra and since investigating her disappearance, the matter of forty or so children and a dragon….? I am, may I impress upon you most earnestly, here only to assist you in any way I can."

"Oh so masterful! And so, so handsome! A bit skinny perhaps?" she mused, then prodded his chest, squeezed his bicep, "Oh!" she looked a tad disappointed, "A bit… hard too, oh well, in every other aspect, rather wonderful aren't you! Are they all like you down there!" she said, rolling and willowy as if she was personally tidal.

"Down… where?"

"Where you come from, down south," she said, with a stating-the-obvious tone.

"All like me…?" he said, confused. She pointed a little pudgy index finger at him and making little circles with it, whistled in a way nearly identical to the Chief of Police. "No, we have as many different people as you'll find in any major conurbation. I am truly just one man and really nothing special…" he pointed at himself and attempted the whistle. He was lying of-course, he was the Prince of a great nation.

"Nothing special? Not from where I'm standing mister!" she twirled towards him, eyes flashing wide, arms undulating, he stepped out of her path as she spun past.

"As Mayor of Prague, is it not your civic duty to…" he was trying to get eye contact with the Mayor who was doing revolutions around the roses, "…to…" she spun faster, "…to… Madam the Mayor!" she was caught off guard by his little shout and spun into a heap on the ground. Darius quickly stepped towards the poor stricken woman and reached down to haul her up, but instead she grabbed his forearms and did her best to pull him down, giggling and making a variety of over-excited noises. Finally, he pulled away and she remained on the ground by the roses. "Is it not your duty as Mayor to do something about the King, the dragon, the missing Princess Petra and all the missing children?"

"Do what though? What can I do?" she whined.

"They are all at the castle, aren't they?" he asked. She shrugged. "Oh come on, it's obvious, the children are kidnapped, the Princess is held captive, the Dragon, whatever on Earth that's about because DRAGONS DON'T EXIST, and it's all because the King is, well…. eccentric."

She wasn't listening, she was trying to break off a rose,

waggling a 30-centimetre-long stem to make it snap. It wouldn't break off as it was bendy and compliant and instead, she pricked her finger, "Ouch! She whined and held up the finger like a child, "It hurts!" Darius stared at her.

"Well? The castle?"

"Kiss it better!" she remained on the ground on her bottom and jabbed her finger towards him."

"But, the castle...!"

"Kiss it first," she said with a sulky voice.

Darius leaned in and kissed her finger. There was no blood. The Mayor made a swipe for him which he ducked and stepped back. "The castle."

"Don't you want to kiss me?" she asked, all big-eyed and pouty. "The Chief said you would."

"Did he really! Can you help with the King and the castle?" Darius was being firm.

The Mayor waggled the rose and finally snapped it off the bush then held it in her teeth so the stem crossed sideways and the rose itself was sticking out a little way from her left cheek. She then rocked on her bottom, finding it difficult to get up. Darius reached a helping hand to her again, but instead she rolled onto her knees and from all fours looked up at him with the rose stem clenched between her teeth and said, "Oohaaffhookeeshneehhushtt!"

"Pardon?"

Still on all fours, she whipped the rose out of her mouth and said, "I said, you have to kiss me first!"

"Kiss you? But..."

"Oh come on! Just help me up then! The kiss is a formality, a ritual between a dignitary, me, and a visiting VIP from another nation, you!" She put the rose stem back between her teeth and waited. It took some effort, for she was a mighty woman who was obviously well fed, but he got her up. Now standing close with the rose in her teeth she began to sway and make those happy noises again. Darius took a couple of steps back.

"Pah!" she pulled the rose from her mouth and made efforts to spit out whatever remained on her lips and teeth, "Pah, pah! Blimey, you are _SUCH_ a bore! KISS ME!" He leaned in to give her a peck on the cheek and she turned politely to present it to him, then at the last moment, turned face-on and simultaneously grabbed him around the neck with both hands. A forceful snog followed with poor Darius squirming and unable to escape, his feet almost lifting off the ground. She finally let go looking excited and victorious, wiping her lips with a forearm and leaving the rose, tangled and stuck on the back of Darius's neck.

"There! Wasn't so bad was it?" Darius said nothing. "That's a sort of hello. Later, we will have the formal goodbye kiss, you and me, Mayor and visiting VIP..." she pointed at each of them for clarification, "it's _muuuuch_ longer, much longer," she repeated, to make sure he had definitely heard her. Darius looked scared. She sat down on the wall of a raised flowerbed with a considerable plop, adopted a far more business-like voice and spoke as if nothing of the previous few minutes had ever happened. "Alright, you want me to march up to the castle with you and ask him to release Princess Petra _if she's there_ and all the missing children _if they're there_ and that he must restrain Dragon, who's a nice boy and has just been a bit mistreated?" Darius's face showed further confusion. The Mayor held up a palm to stop him speaking, "I know people say he's a vicious beast who'd bite your head off and swallow it whole, but I'm not so sure, I think he's just misunderstood." She paused reflectively, stared into space and repeated more quietly, dreamlike, "He's just misunderstood."

The Mayor stood up with some effort and a puff and studied Darius closely. He suddenly felt like he was food, "He might just want someone to be nice to him." She took a step forward and pointed at him. "Maybe he wants a cuddle? Doesn't every living thing need a cuddle, Inspector?" She took another step which Darius matched by taking one backwards. "Maybe, after a really nice cuddle he'll be so soft and loving people will wonder how they ever managed all these years without him, obedient, loyal, devoted, loving, and *always* ready for cuddle! Jumping up excitedly when you get home, licking you all over your face," she took a step forward, Darius took one back, "jumping up on your lap and snuggling-in all-cosy while you stroke him," she stroked her own hair lasciviously, "nuzzling your neck…" she seemed fixated by Darius's neck.

"It's a DRAGON!" he said loudly, waking her out of her dream.

"What is?" she said, looking a bit confused.

"The dragon!"

She spoke normally again, "Well…. not really…"

"Will you go? Will you address the King as Mayor and get to the bottom of this?"

"Never! I am the King's Mayor. I serve the King. He pays for everything…" she swept her arm about, over dramatically as if she was about to start doing her spinny-willowy dancing again.

"*How* exactly does he pay for everything?" asked Darius.

"Easy. Tax collectors collect tax, lowest taxes anywhere here in Prague by the way don't you know, no standing army. Taxes arrive here at Town Hall, we pay the police, the tax collectors, me and my staff and all the castle bills. I have a spreadsheet and an abacus for each line on the accounts. I'll show you later!" she flashed her eyes at him.

"No, I believe you. What bills?"

"What bills?" she echoed.

"For the castle. What bills for the castle?" he persisted.

"Oh. Gregory's delivers food three times a day. The King has A LOT of food delivered! And Mr Wife organises the King's wine delivery once a week. The King has a A LOT of wine! Then there's all the raw steak for Dragon…"

"The dragon eats steak?"

The Mayor put her hand up to the side of her mouth and whispered, "It's just old horse steak to keep the cost down, but don't tell anyone. There are a few other things we pay for, repairs, new flag now and again, few sticks of furniture… he really is the most economical King imaginable, except for the food and wine, but this is nothing compared to the banquets of a few years ago, now they _were_ expensive. Taxes are at their lowest ever so whatever else he is, he's a judicious King when it comes to the state purse."

Darius frowned, "So people put up with the missing Princess…. okay, fair enough, but don't they rebel when it comes to the abducted children? What about the poor parents?"

"Well, that's the thing I suppose, none of the orphans' parents have ever complained." She rolled her eyes in a sarcastic manner.

"How about the ones who aren't orphans. They're not all orphans."

"She thought about it for a moment. "Bit of a question for the Chief, that one, but no… can't say any parents have ever complained as far as I know. Some have said _good riddance_ and _glad to see the back of the little terror_, but none have come begging for them to be returned." She paused in thought, "The only person who's ever tried to stir up any trouble is the wife of a man who used to supply the King's horses."

"Go on."

"She likes nothing more than to meddle in other peoples' affairs. Small-minded, bigoted, bored out of her mind so she dreams up ways of being a nuisance to everyone else."

"Can I talk to her?" Darius leaned forward.

"No."

"No? Whyever not?"

"Because she knows nothing and because her only aim in life is to interfere. She adds nothing to any situation but takes away a great deal. She sucks the fun out of people. The sun hides behind a cloud and the colour drains from streets as she passes. She turns everything a dull, light-absorbing grey." The Mayor looked deeply sullen.

"Really?" said Darius, aghast.

"No not really, but that's how it feels. You see!" she exclaimed, "You see what she did to my happiness just by coming into my mind? No, no, no. I wouldn't wish her upon you. I'll do what I can for you and I promise she is a dead end… an affliction she has passed on to her husband, or so I'm told."

"What, being joyless?"

"No, a dead end," she said mysteriously.

Darius had his pen poised over his pad, "Can I have her name?"

"No." she said very definitely, emphasising it with a flat hand, but there was a twitch in the corner of her mouth.

"No? Why not? You *really* don't want me to see her do you?"

"I'm not telling you because you don't need her for your enquiries and anyway, I can't mention her name or I'll need fresh knickers and that'll be all your fault!" Darius looked pained and confused, his mouth open but he didn't know what to say. She twitched, amusement playing on her lips and in her eyes. "No! I'm not saying it. If I say her name I'll start laughing and that's it, I won't be able to stop until, until," she wafted her hands downwards from her waist, "Until I need clean knickers. Do you want my wet knickers on your conscience Inspector? Do you?"

He shook his head. Darius could not frown more deeply if he tried. The Chief of Police was nuts, the Mayor was eccentric beyond measure and the whole business of the abductions was bizarre. There were parents who didn't want their children back and some mysteriously miserable woman who was of no use to his investigation, but the mention of whose name would cause the Mayor to wet herself. "Alright, alright. Let's return to the question of the missing children. Are you saying there's no point in rescuing them?"

She composed herself, which included the odd gesture of smoothing down her own bosoms and causing some motion. "On the basis we imagine they are still alive, which we do, well, it's not a straight-forward situation is it? It's like when people steal food from the bins behind Gregory's that's passed its best-before stamp: technically it's theft, but it's theft of rubbish, so I advise the Police Chief to ignore it. Gregory's put it in a special skip marked, *food for stealing* when they close every night and the poorest of people, plus a few rich people who like to act poor for the kudos of it, form a queue, first-come-first-theft, take no more than three things maximum, and Bongo! Everyone's happy."

"Bongo?" asked Darius.

"It's a game people play where they all throw numbered balls at a someone who calls them out at random. The last one holding onto a ball with a number that's never been called out, wins a cake or a box of biscuits or a tin of rice pudding."

Darius reflected on a little bit of sanity in a crazy city. "Bongo!" he said, in a voice which sounded one step short of insanity. "They play Bongo!"

Luckily, the Mayor moved the discussion on. "But in your mind, we march up to the castle and ask for the release of the children and suddenly we've got 40, 45 kids no one especially wants…. well, then what?"

Darius was back from the brink of a Bongo-bonkers breakdown. "It's not okay to keep them locked up just because they are orphans or because their dodgy parents didn't want them! We need to *tain* them. And what about the fabulously beautiful Princess Petra?"

"Hang on, one thing at a time? You said what?" asked the Mayor, her most serious yet.

"I said it's not okay, just because…"

"No after that,"

"…their dodgy parents…"

"No after, after!"

"We need to *tain* them…" Darius said, already regretting it.

"There! You said it again. What?"

"Oh, *tain*?"

"Yes, sorry, I don't speak…" she waggled her finger and did the whistle, "… whatever your language is, I only speak this language, the one we're speaking now, and suddenly you chuck in a foreign word."

"*Tain*, as in the opposite of de-*tain*."

It slowly dawned on her, "Oooohhh! Detain them. Tain them, detain them. That's a new one on me. You use that in your country?"

"Well…" Darius was non committal.

"And the other thing," the Mayor persisted, "you described Princess Petra as…"

"Oh, I'm not sure quite what I said."

"Really? I'll tell you: You said, *fabulously beautiful*. Where does that come from?"

"World famous fact?"

The Mayor reflected on it and nodded slightly. "Well, nice teeth and eyes and hair it's true, but *beautiful*? I wouldn't say so! Pretty face but," and she did something like a body-builder's muscle-flexing, pose with a grimace, "Hard, a bit like you and not a single sign of femininity. I know she was only 14 when we last saw her, but no spare tyre, no saddlebags, not an ounce of back fat, a complete lack of bongo-wings, that one solitary strong chin, oh dear no! No doubt her dear dad the King would be buying her cellulite injections for her sixteenth birthday, no wonder she got no offers, I mean, who wants that?"

Darius waited for the Mayor's memory-trance to pass. "Mrs The Mayor, three things. One is about your finances. As employees of the city, you are not at the mercy of the King. The tax collectors should collect tax for the city from which *you* pay them and the police department and anything else you see fit, meanwhile you allow the King an amount each year, or simply pay all bills as they arise, but the two things, state costs on one hand and royalty costs on the other, they ought to be separated. You set the level of tax to balance your own books, not the King!" she gasped a little and fell deep in thought again.

"Two! Let's go to Gregory's, purveyors to the royal household and look into what's being sent up there exactly. I know you have the bills and accounts, but I think Gregory's can fill in some blanks."

She nodded without hesitation, "Always up for a date who wants to invite me out for a nice meal!" she said, causing Darius to grimace slightly.

"And three!" he announced. She looked up, alert and compliant, "I need you to come to the castle in an official capacity and with the entire police department, to ask these important questions. I suggest you ask for an official audience on official business!"

She stared, "Soooo handsome! Soooo masterful!"

"Well? You'll do it?"

She giggled. "Let me just say I am thinking favourably about your proposal and after you thoroughly inspect my spreadsheets and check my various abacuses, abaci, yes all my abaci, AND if, and *only if* I am satisfied with the sincerity of your goodbye kiss, which is only a goodbye-for-now kiss obviously, not a…" she became highly dramatic with a wail to her voice, leaning back with a forearm across her brow, "*Goodbye! It's over between us, I have loved you as I have never loved before, nor ever will again, but though my heart is rendered in two, unmendable by even the best glue made from gorillas, I know it is my fate that I will never, ever see you again as long as I live!*" She returned to her normal tone, "Not *that* sort of goodbye, obviously, more *see ya! See ya later!* Or *see ya tommorrah babe!* More that sort of kiss, though just so you know, it's still pretty huge though. *Then* I'll give you my promise to do all those things you want. What were they?"

"I need you to come to the castle. That's the big one."

"Yes, yes, kissy-kiss," she pointed to her large pouty lips, extravagantly plastered with shiny pink lipstick, "and I'll ask the King for an audience."

"You promise?" Darius looked a little depressed. Resigned to the spreadsheets and abacuses and some sort of hideous, slobbery snog with the Mayor.

"It's gonna happen!" she said in the weirdly deep voice of someone trying, but largely failing, to hold themselves in check.

Chapter the Twelfth.
The Castle, The House of Rock,
The Town Hall &
The Grand Velky Hotel

Adalbert could hear the workings of a mechanism, chains clanking, ropes straining, wooden spars creaking. He pressed his ear against the door to hear it better. It stopped when he did so. With a "Humph!" he went back to his straw bed and sat down. A mischief of rats followed him from the door and joined him. His stomach rumbled loudly and several of them started with surprise, but being rats, got over it quickly and returned to sniffing, twitching and washing themselves instead.

Then came the humming and the footsteps and Adalbert jumped up in pleasure at the return of the King, then sat down again pensively, as if unsure how he should be upon the arrival of his captor. The locks were undone and the King pushed open the door, sliding in first one tray of plates covered by cloches, then a second, then a third. Even covered, the food smelled unbearably good. "Those two are yours, that one's mine. I'll join you in a few minutes if that's alright, got that lot to take care of first," he gestured upstairs with his index finger and raised his eyes like it was a chore. Then he reached in a pocket and making sucky-kissing noises with his lips, brought the rats cascading to him as he tossed a fistful of cheese chunks and berries. The food pieces danced and bounced across the hard stone floor, chased by the furry creatures as if it were a crazy game of football. Adalbert watched mesmerised and the door closed. The King climbed the stairs, humming in time with each step. The door wasn't locked.

Adalbert stared at it, waiting for the King to come pounding back and turn the keys. It didn't happen. Instead the noise of his departure faded to silence until somewhere high up and distant, he heard other keys turning and a door creaking open. Small voices cried out and the King could be heard faintly making firm but pacifying noises, but no words were distinct. Adalbert crossed quickly on tiptoe to the door and opened it slowly, cringing at the slight creaking noise it made, even when pulled very slowly. He stepped out onto the wide landing area, stone steps curved away up to the left and down to the right. It all looked so different in daylight compared to the previous evening. Pleasant almost. In the broad stone centre column, a half-sized wooden doorway was open to a shaft with a series of ropes and chains visible within: This was the dumb-waiter used by the King to bring up the food. Peering up the shaft he could see the platform was a considerable distance higher than he was right now. This was a very tall tower with many more levels. Faint noises of activity drifted down, but nothing discernible no matter how he strained his ears.

Adalbert crossed to the top of the staircase leading downwards and paused. This was his chance to make a dash for it. He winced, he paused, he jerked as if to go and paused again. "Oh come on Adalbert!" he whined, "Are you a man or a mouse?" then turned to see a few rats peering out the open cell door at him, noses and whiskers twitching." "Aw…" he said affectionately.

***

Mrs Wife escorted Shoshama to the sixth floor, one below her own bedroom and using a key she took from a nearby chest of drawers, unlocked a substantial door into a windowless room at the back of the house. It smelled of wine. Mrs Wife lit a pair of wall-mounted candles which spouted tall orange flames in the cool air. Smoke spiralled upwards, dragging the flames taller still. The darkness drew back revealing an astonishing scene for a terraced house.

The middle of the room was stacked with wooden crates while the walls were lined with wine racks from floor to ceiling. The crates were in all sizes containing a single bottle, two, three, six or twelve. The names of their illustrious vineyards burned, branded in fact, onto the border panels of every case. Shoshama couldn't admit it, but she knew these names, they were celebrated in royal circles, individual bottles cherished by sommeliers, crates like these purchased at great expense by the wealthiest families and the wealthiest families of all were the royal families. "This is his stock room," said Mrs Wife. "He loves wine. He loves everything about it. I mean he loves the vinification process from which it is born, the bottles, the labels, the business of buying and selling wine. Of course, he loves the drinking but perhaps most of all, it's the talking he values most. The encyclopaedic knowledge, the endless expertise required for something ever-expanding, shifting, where wines grow or wither in esteem. He is excited by differing opinions, adores reminiscing about wines past, is electrified by anticipating opening something which has been laid down for decades. I do my best dear, but I know he loves wine more than anything. More than anything. If I mention laying down," she winked, "he thinks of laying down wine!"

Shoshama laughed, but she also stared at the vast stock. She understood what Mrs Wife was saying about her husband and felt, excited… "What was that word?"

"Dear?"

"The way Mr Wife feels about opening a wine which has been laying down for decades," Shoshama reminded her.

"I say he is *electrified* by the prospect dear," she said, slightly suspiciously.

"What is that word? What is *electrified*?"

"Oh silly me! I'm probably misusing the word. Its origins are from *electron*, what the Greeks called amber and refers to the way that if you rub amber, things mysteriously adhere to it. There's a strange magic, a kind of tingle, a sharp tickle about it. It is this strange magic, tingle and tickle I think dear Mister feels at that moment of anticipation."

"Got it," Shoshama said, a little dumbstruck. "Learned a new word. Every day's a school day."

"Except Saturdays," said Mrs Wife, quietly.

"Saturdays?" asked Shoshama, even if the comment wasn't necessarily meant for her ears.

"Monday to Friday is for all the academic subjects at school, you know mythology, verse, philosophy, astronomy, mathematics, reading, scribing and learning to play flute, lyre, piano or electric guitar. Sunday is for the physical arts, discus, javelin, hula hoops and mud wrestling, though that's mostly for girls."

"The hula hoop?"

"No, the mud wrestling, a sport for athletic young women since time immemorial. I foretell a time when flat-roofed buildings near transit stations are devoted to the activity and mostly male audiences drink ale and admire the participants preparing for the next contest." Shoshama was lost, this was something the young women of Prague must do that was unknown to her in Persia. "They practice with vertical poles, *very, very* athletic. Some say this is an art in itself." Shoshama did her best to imagine what Mrs Wife was referring to, but her imagination fell far short.

"Mister has a _LOT_ of wine, House. This is his business you say." House nodded proudly. "Who are his customers?"

"Well that's the thing dear and it's why I have brought you here. Mister has a dozen or so customers about the city but his biggest customer by far is…" she hesitated.

"Who?" although Shoshama thought she knew.

"Oh, should I say dear?" Mrs Wife looked worried, "I do not want to disrupt anything. I sense your arrival may herald change and like most people, I fear change even though, if I look to my past, I understand it has been a continuous series of changes, many of which have been for the better."

"You mean the King don't you," said Shoshama flatly.

"It's funny. Constant change. Evolution even. The world moves on, children are born grow up and leave home, we age and find that suddenly we are older than our parents were at a point where as teenagers, we thought _they were absolutely ancient!_"

"I'm right though, aren't I? It's the King isn't it."

"Everything is in a constant state of flux." Mrs Wife was lost in her thoughts, talking as if to no one in particular. "The world spins at 1000 kilometres per hour at the equator, wherever that is and flies on its arc around the sun at 30 kilometres per second and looping our universe at 220 kilometres per second! Astonishing isn't it! You see I _did_ listen in astronomy classes!" Shoshama thought these were nothing like her own astronomy classes, which had focused on naming a few constellations. "It's all utterly incredible. It's moving, changing, evolving, growing and decaying, and yet we sit and stare at the glowing embers of a fire with a Cabernet Sauvignon in our fist and imagine it will go on like this forever. Everything the same tomorrow as today, next week as last week, next month like last month and years to come pretty much like these last few years we've had. It won't, it simply won't." She left the idea hanging in the air, then turned to Shoshama and clasped her by the shoulders, reaching up a little on account of being shorter, "But it will be alright. It will, I promise! Especially for you, goodness look at you, you're a Goddess. You'd make quite a mud wrestler Shoshama, or you could stick to exercising on the vertical poles if you didn't want to get all muddy."

"I'm right though aren't I?" Shoshama repeated.

"What? Oh yes, the King, yes. He's at the centre of it all, he is the main customer _and_ the main supplier in one go." Shoshama looked puzzled. "Follow me but be very quiet!" Mrs Wife led Shoshama to the back of the room and to a dark velour curtain she had not previously noticed hidden among the shadows. The stubby little woman gently pulled the curtain aside to reveal a door. Unlocking it delicately, she then opened it and to Shoshama's surprise, there wasn't simply some kind of cupboard, but a void of darkness without apparent limits. Mrs Wife peered inside and listened, and when satisfied there was no one there, she took one of the candles and led Shoshama in. There, Shoshama saw a vast chamber, long, wide and high and filled with wine. Filled so much as to make Mister's storeroom seem completely irrelevant. The candle could not light the far reaches, but it was clear this was a wine cellar to outclass any other in any kingdom. "This is the King's wine cellar. He trusts Mister to supply him and Mister has supplied all of this. He also trusts Mister to taste some for him and the bottles Mister sets aside to taste are next door in Mister's own stockroom. Mister also sells a few of his _taster bottles_ to add coins to our..." she was searching for the appropriate term.

"To your other coins," said Shoshama in the same quiet voice House had been using and House conceded the point nodding. "So Mister actually sells some of the wine twice," added Shoshama and Mrs Wife made a noise like that wasn't entirely right (though it _was_ entirely right) and shrugged to conclude her comment on the matter. Shoshama put on her business-like face and summarised, "Mister is a clever man and if the King is happy with the arrangement, then I think that's all that needs to be said about it."

"Nobody else's beeswax!" said House.

"They can mind their own biscuits!" said Shoshama and they both chuckled quietly.

"And this is your way into the castle," said Mrs Wife pointing into the far darkness. "Though why you want to go up in there baffles me." Shoshama stayed silent, her eyes groping with the far darkness, "And if you do go, for goodness' sake take care. The King is mercurial. He is kind and generous but prone to bouts of great anger. He is lavish with gifts just like his father but if you cross him, he will then lock you up never to be seen again." Shoshama continued to stare. Now she had a way in, she hesitated. "Plus of course, there's Dragon," House added. Shoshama gulped.

***

"Well! I certainly learned something from you today," said the Mayor, looking squarely at Darius.

"You did?" he enquired, politely, kindly.

"Yes. I have always thought that the best way to judge a book was by its cover and looking at you... not sure whether you noticed, but when you arrived I *did* have a bit of a look at you... but anyway, from my looking, and based on what the Chief of Police said to me in his message, I was certain, certain I tell you, that you would have been a good kisser!"

"Oh." Darius looked sheepish, he'd rather hoped she was going to drop the subject. They were walking slowly to the exit of the Town Hall.

"Maybe I should have known from your rather colourless clothing?" she pondered, pressing an index finger to her big, bright lips, then waggling up and down at him said, "What's all this... white about? Is it your official police inspector uniform? Don't they pay you enough to afford dyes down in the south there? Don't get me wrong, it sets off your suntan something wicked and you, you, oh you are the most gorgeous shade of tanned, but maybe that's it, maybe I was too busy imagining the you under all that white to realise all that nothing-nothing-and-nothing white was trying to tell me something!"

"Well I'm sorry about the kissing, it's just that..."

"You kiss like a fish!" the Mayor interrupted.

Darius laughed, "Kissed a lot of fishes have you?"

"Of course! Hasn't everyone?" she looked confused.

"When exactly do you kiss fishes?"

"Fish market!" she barked, then scoffing, "How else do you choose which fish you want for your tea without kissing it?" she shook her head in wonder at his lack of basic fish-shopping expertise.

"By looking at it?" he suggested.

"Well I can tell you've never bought a fish in your life!" Then she clasped her hands to her face in horror, "Oh no!"

"What?" he asked, concerned.

"Don't tell me I tried to... oh no!" her colour drained, she sat down in the nearest chair, which at this point was in the entry way to the Town Hall building having almost exited it.

"What? What is it?"

She pointed at him with her arm out completely straight. "The reason you don't buy fish is because..."

"Because...?"

"Because... Oh, I can't say it! But it explains everything, fish kisser my bottom! It's because..."

"Tell me! Because what?" he implored squatting down in front of the distressed woman and holding both her hands with his.

140

She pulled them away slowly and composed herself. Then in hushed whispery tones fired out a stream of words rapidly, almost hissing, "Because your wife does all the shopping! You're married!"

"I'm not!" he blurted laughing, then regretted it instantly, this would have been a fabulous cover.

She jumped up, "You're not?" she said much louder again. "Well then you truly cannot tell a book by its cover! Oh I'll never understand!" She proceeded to exit the building at a business-like pace, Darius sped up to keep with her. "You know I was planning to announce our engagement today, but obviously that's not going to happen." Darius's mouth fell open, now he really did look like a fish. "No, I'll tell people we're just friends, alright?" she looked at him sideways as they walked.

"Yes, absolutely, and I hope we can be."

"Don't know. The disappointment burns. You had my hopes up. *I* had my hopes up…. *Again!* Just wait until I see that Chief of Police! *…handsomest man he's ever seen… looks like… …perfect specimen… never seen the like… brain of a genius!*" she quoted, then waved a bit of paper at him. "You should see the things he wrote about you! Perhaps HE wants to kiss you!" Darius looked horrified at the idea.

The Mayor's walking pace was incredible and Darius was having to take the odd extra skippy-step to keep up. A gentleman tipped his hat at them, "Morning Mayor!"

"Police Inspector from a place a long way south. We're just friends! Kisses like a fish!" She barked as they passed the man by. Darius made to speak but instead just looked apologetically at the man.

"Good day Mayor!" said a woman, one of a pair walking together.

"Morning Mrs Mitching! Nothing to report here, he's not my lover! Kisses like a fish!" which received a sad frown from the two ladies and one offered an apology as they were left behind.

"I don't think you need to say that to everyone, you know," suggested Darius quietly.

"Oh yes I do! Get the facts out there to stem the scuttlebutt! If I hadn't been clear, they'd all be assuming the worst... I mean... the best." She gave him a sideways glance, sighed and pouted at him with an extra-disappointed face.

Without slowing, the Mayor swerved into a cobbled side street and few shops up they burst in to one which smelled scrumptious. A painted wooden sign swinging from an overhanging iron frame announced it to be Gregory's Delicious Sandwiches and Vegetarian Sausage Roll Emporium. "Morning Daisy! Is Gregory in? Mayoral business! Don't worry about him he's with me. Well, not *with* me, it's a work thing, we're just friends, colleagues really." Daisy nodded to each chunk of information and Darius was relieved at the more professional introduction. "Anyway, he might look beautiful but he kisses like an absolute fish!" Darius shoulders slumped a little.

A buxom woman appeared from the back, "Mayor! How lovely to see you!" she regarded Darius and her eyes widened.

"Gregory, meet Inspector Perr-eel from a long way south somewhere or other. Official business. Got some questions to ask you about official business type-matters."

"Gregory is a woman!" Darius observed, rather pointlessly.

"Police Inspector is he?" asked Gregory, "He'll go far. With that astute piece of discerning observation, he's already better than our lot."

"Of course she's a woman, what else!" said the Mayor looking as if it was the stupidest question imaginable.

"Well, a man? Could have been a man. Not that it matters..." he tailed off and it all became clear.

"This is Mrs Gregory, owner of the best sandwich shop *in the known world* and inventor of the most incredible vegetarian sausage roll ever! Oh go on then, you've talked me into it! I'll have one, hot, eat-in, dab of ketchup, dab of mayo please!" Mrs Gregory flapped a hand at Daisy who immediately got on with the order. "And get him one too, he needs it. Needs a bit of *get up and GO!*" she punctuated the last bit with what looked like a dance move, but which definitely finished with a hip thrust. Gregory laughed and Darius, uncomfortable in the extreme, was certain he could hear laughter from other quarters in the shop but didn't look around to see who the amused people might be.

Mrs Gregory continued to regard Darius with great interest. The Mayor followed her gaze and said, "Waste of time. We're just friends. Kisses like a fish!"

"Oh really? Just goes to show…"

"You actually can't judge a book by its cover!" they said together and laughed.

"I think he might have the wrong cover on!" said the Mayor. "I mean, what is it with all that white?"

"Get that cover off!" joked Mrs Gregory in the low growl everyone in Prague used as the alternative voice to their own, and they laughed again. "What kind of fish?"

"I was thinking about that," said the Mayor, "I was hoping for Suckermouth Catfish, but I got Ocellaris Clownfish! No offence," this last aside was to Darius himself.

"Oh I see," Mrs Gregory looked as disappointed as the Mayor. Darius noticed Daisy, who was clearly listening to every word, frown as she withdrew the sausage rolls from the little steel oven. People in the long queue for food muttered the quoted names of fish and shook their heads sadly.

The Mayor poked Mrs Gregory on the arm, "I was hoping he'd be more octopus!" they laughed.

"Didn't get any octopus ink squirted in your face then?"

said Mrs Gregory and they laughed even louder, as did Daisy and the entire queue.

"Look here, could we get on with…"

"Oh yes," said the Mayor, "Back orifice Gregory if you don't mind!" and they walked around the counter and through into the back towards the office. The laughter in the shop continued unabated.

***

Prince Chatty sipped cocoa and from the huge bay window of the morning room, watching the people of Prague pass in front of the hotel. Behind him, his three loyal servants, one coachman, one footman and one seamstress stood in a little V-shape, silently, patiently, aware they were on a mission but unaware of Prince Chatty's plan.

Someone else unaware of his plan was Prince Chatty himself, for as much as he pondered the problem, his mind remained silent on the matter. He kept posing the question to himself with new phrasing, *how to release the Princess from her father's chains, rescuing a damsel under duress, freeing a prisoner from a castle tower*, and even *'taining' someone who has been detained* but no matter how he worded it, his little mental search engine could find no results.

Just then, his seamstress tapped him on the arm and said, "Isn't that Prince Darius your Highness?"

"Where?" he said, his head turning from side to side as if scanning the entire street scene in front of him.

"There!" she pointed,

"Where?"

"There, right there with that um, large lady," she continued.

"Still can't see her."

"There, your Highness, there!" she said just a little

exasperated, "There, the only person in the whole street dressed from head to toe in white." The Prince moved his head one way and the other but entirely failed to follow the direction she was indicating. Puzzled, the seamstress leaned forward and around so she could look at the Prince better. "Your Highness, your eyes are closed."

"Golly! So they are. Oh, that's bright!" he said as he opened them. "I was thinking. Think best eyes closed. No wonder I couldn't see what you were telling me about, where are they now?"

She guided his elbow and pointed again, "Up the street, up there. All in white next to a larger lady."

"Oh, you're right," Chatty confirmed.

"Yes, I'm absolutely certain it's him," she said, satisfied.

"Well who knows? I can only see the back of some chap in white. Could be absolutely anyone! Except us, it's obviously not us. And not a child either, too tall by far."

"But you said I was right?"

"Yes. You. Are. Right" he said slowly, word by word. "She. Is. A. Larger. Lady!" he patted her on the head in the most patronising fashion, and the seamstress pulled a disgruntled face. "No idea who she's with though. Goodness me! You servant types are a bit dim between the ears aren't you. Lucky I'm here!"

"Your Royal Highness, that man in white is Prince Darius."

"Alright. Boy," he said to the young coachman, "You look like an absolute nobody, follow him and report back." The coachman tipped his hat and made to leave but Chatty shouted after him, "I say! If you get a chance to do a sneaky approach, tell him I'm here and want to help."

The coachman looked a bit confused, "But how do I...?"

"Hurry boy or he'll be gone and you'll never find him again!" Chatty shouted with desperation in his voice.

"Eh, he's actually the only really tanned man in a totally white suit," said the seamstress a bit sarcastically, "I reckon you'll be alright, Brian." Brian the coachmen nodded at her and with a little wink, strode briskly out the door and up the street. As he passed the bay window Chatty waved him faster up the street with a whippy-finger action, whereas the young seamstress blew him a dramatic kiss, pushing it towards him the way you might push a high drawer shut. Chatty looked at her aghast at her boldness. She looked up at Prince Chatty and with no deference at all and with the biggest beaming smile said, "What??? I love 'im!" The Prince was suddenly flushed with warm feelings, blushed and smiled and looking back up the street, found himself envious of her joy. Where was his somebody to love so?

Chapter the Thirteenth.
Breakfast with Wenceslas

He didn't know it but Prince Adalbert was frozen by something experts would later call cognitive dissonance. He stood rooted to the spot between the open door of his tower cell and the staircase which led to freedom. If his own father were here, he'd shake his head in despair and accuse Adalbert of being feeble minded, for as long as the young Prince could remember, he'd referred to him as Addled-Bert, even when introducing his son; the Prince of Egham. His mother would say it was because his star sign was Gemini, meaning he was often of two minds about a thing. "More likely no mind at all!" was his father's opinion.

For Adalbert in that crucial moment the certainty that he should try to escape now that he was presented with the opportunity, was conflicting with his wish to spend more time with King Wenceslas. The first was simple and clear, the second was unexpected but powerful enough to give him feet of lead. He could justify not trying to escape by his certainty that he would be caught by the strong and probably angry *Bad* King Wenceslas, or that by the heaving of some remote wooden lever, a series of ropes and pulleys would release the dragon into the courtyard to terminate his flight by munching on a breakfast called *sizzling, wriggling, live squelchy Adalbert.* Not being particularly brave where dragons were concerned (he had heard it growl yesterday and his bottom had burped in fear), he turned, his posture that of a prisoner, a victim, someone permanently bending to the will of others and shuffled back into the room and slumped on his straw and sackcloth bed. The rats returned to their feeding, seemingly happier that he wasn't leaving after all.

Adalbert had left the door completely open though, which caused the King to pause a moment on his return. He looked at Adalbert, hunched and dejected on the bed and once again at the door wide open. The King's single raised eyebrow of reflection was followed by him seeming to come to some sort of conclusion. Nodding to himself and entering the room, he too left it wide open.

He brought with him a small folding picnic table and chair set. The kind you might take in the trunk of your carriage on a picnic, or to some scenic location with the intention of spending some days travelling from one spot to another and avoiding hotels in favour of being outdoors. In that case you would also certainly take a canvas tent; the modern sort they called 'pop-up' which weighed in at a lowly 200 kilos and which a team of strong and well-practiced experts could erect in under three hours. Beds and bedding were essential, as was a quality carpet with wooden boards under it to keep the carpet dry. Other items needed for 'camping' included hanging oil lamps, a portable gramophone, the wicker hamper of bone China and silver cutlery, the mini-Aga and bags of coal for its consumption, clothes in large trunks, themselves simply clever travel wardrobes which lock tight but provide drawers for everything, space for all types of footwear and hanging space for every conceivable attire including hats and coats. Last of all was the portable commode and its own mini-tent. The tents, beds, trunks, floorboards, mini-Aga and commode necessitated a large second carriage for their transport and a number of servants to erect and arrange them and later to break them down again when it was determined they were a bit too far to the left. Servants were also required for the servicing of the portable commode which was considered a worse task than dealing with one's master's foul morning chamber pots. The number of servants needed for this kind of expedition also posed challenges regarding their own accommodation, meaning further tents and bales of straw for sleeping. All-in-all, this kind of touring in multiple carriages, collectively called a 'caravan' was a right-old flipping palaver which always resulted in getting back to the castle with everyone in a bad mood muttering, 'Never again!' However, the little folding table and chairs were useful around the garden. And of course, perfect if you needed to arrange a cheery breakfast a few hundred steps up a dark and dingy tower for a prisoner you were keeping there.

After neatly and efficiently arranging the cloches, silverware, serviettes, glasses and jug of ale and a pot of tea on the table, the King broke the silence by looking directly at Adalbert and asking, "Right boy! Are ya hungry?" Adalbert appreciated the King's willingness to extend his kindness and smiled sheepishly, nodding with boyish enthusiasm. Cloches were removed and the most glorious aroma of cooked breakfast steamed up into their delighted faces. Adalbert's nose told his brain to be happy and his mouth to start watering. "Tuck in!" said the King.

"I heard voices... up there," Adalbert indicated with his fork. The King, his mouth already full of breakfast simply nodded confirmation. "I realise you are keeping... people here but also that, well, you are keeping them *alive*." The King seemed to mull it over then waggled his head in a sort-of *I suppose so* way, still eating heartily. "I rather hope to remain so myself... with your good grace." The King looked him in the eye, chewing more slowly.

The King spoke, "There's much I regret. There's much in life which cannot be resolved with all parties satisfied. It seems that simply by being here," a place he identified by pausing momentarily and pointing to the ground, "Here," now he indicated the castle, "And here," he tapped his heart then repeated, "I feel that simply by being here we are continually presented with challenges, the solutions for which make it certain, some or all must suffer some consequence or other. Choosing the path which causes the least anguish only to find there are further unexpected consequences… and more pain to come, means you can reach the age of, what am I – 30-something?" Adalbert tried not to choke on that estimate, "And realise, "continued the King, "that the only way to avoid constant anguish and regret is to think nothing of anything!" he grinned but Adalbert frowned, not understanding at all. "I mean boy, if I were forced to attend to my conscience and accept responsibility for all the wrong, I would throw myself off the top of the east tower. That's this one. Then who'd feed that lot of scamps up there, eh?"

The King's mood had lowered slightly. In spite of claiming to be immune from regret, he looked like someone full of the stuff. "No, life can be a series of choices along the lines of, *'Sire, wouldst thou prefer I poke thy left bottom cheek with a sharp, yet barbed spike of rusty iron, or thy right bottom cheek with the very same?'*" He sighed deeply and looked down at the floor. "Fate seems little concerned that we might prefer neither and instead perhaps, happy times with one's dear wife in rude health and one's daughter still amused by childish things. Why must fate be such a…, such a…" he looked up to his breakfast companion and appeared moist eyed.

Adalbert felt for him. "Sir! Dear King, I want to help." He forked in some potato wawfull smothered with dippy-egg yolk and moaned a little with gustatory pleasure.

The King regained buoyancy. "Marvellous ain't it!" he said smiling warmly, though his eyes still that same moist.

"Wonderfully awful you mean," corrected Adalbert, with his mouth full and the King's smile stretched wider still, his look lingered on the ungainly Prince. "Can I ask something else?" asked Adalbert.

"You may as well. I find conversing with you a sincere affair," he said, his regard returning to his large plate of food.

"Why did they call your father *Good* King Wenceslas? Why, *Good*?"

"Because people are easily flummoxed. They think in narrow, short fragments, see only what they want to see, listen only to soundbites – not full explanations, hear what they want to hear – not the honest, painful truth and want good news, not real news. Some fools actually prefer their news fake even when they know it to be so. They don't want to be appraised of the compromises and hear who will certainly disagree with a thing, only that a matter is tied up neatly with a silk bow!" The king waved his fork around while talking and did so with such passion and vigour, that he found it necessary to take a large swig of ale and then another of tea at the finish. Adalbert continued to study the King, his head shaking slightly unable to comprehend what he might mean.

"My father!" he said loudly, his mouth actually devoid of breakfast now, "My father spent hours each day walking the streets and giving coin to poor folk. To crowds of them! He'd walk down alleyways and hand out money!" he cupped his hands, "Big handfuls of money! He especially liked sick folks, dirty little kids, the homeless, old soldiers who'd fought in his wars and were now hopeless sorry and broken, passing the day out of their wits on gin. He liked urchins, tramps and street-walking ladies, the dirtier the better!" His face dropped and he lowered his volume conspiratorially, "I don't mean the street-walking ladies were dirty like... that, I mean he liked people better if they were filthy with grime. He used to tell me they were *real people*. Dirty people are *real* people."

Adalbert nodded, it had been clear the first time that the ladies were grimy from being on the street and now he wondered what the possibility of confusion might allude to. With a little frown yet still bursting with enthusiasm, Adalbert confirmed the principle, "Yes! I believe I know what he means, dirty women are best!"

The King paused, and seeing nothing but simple accord on Adalbert's innocent face, smiled a smile that wrinkled not only his eyes, but also his nose and continued, "Anyway, where does all this money come from? Bags of the stuff EVERY day?"

"The King's purse," said Adalbert with a definitive nod.

"Correct! And emptied every day. And refilled how?" The King was intense, prodding at him with a lovely looking chunk of sausage on the end of his fork. Back and forth and quite close, like a game his mother played with him where his food was swooped around prior to him having *'just three more bites'* before story-time. Adalbert's eyes followed the sausage intensely, going crossed eyed where necessary in order to keep up. Then like a good boy, Adalbert pounced, mouth agape and with pursed lips, whipped the chunk of sausage off the King's fork. The King froze and stared at him amazed, dumbfounded, then burst into peals of laughter. "Oh my boy!" he said, quite merry indeed.

"Where was I? Yes, refilled how?" This Adalbert didn't know, so he shrugged, but not carelessly, he shrugged the way you do when you genuinely want to know. The King answered slowly, "The Treasury, itself filled by taxes, and taxes which might be spent on all manner of things, instead were directed towards the needy. It was the King's new passion, that no one should want."

"Hooray! Good for him!" cried Adalbert.

The King gave a kind of nod of acknowledgement, one where his head briefly tilted to one side, "Indeed and when the Treasury ran a little low, he would tax people a little more. I refer to anyone with any money at all, he'd increase the tax on sales, on purchases, on property and on inheritance in order to redistribute funds from those with plenty to those most in need."

"Ah!" exclaimed Adalbert with his mouth full of food and thoroughly impressed.

"Ah, if only it were that simple. You see the numbers in need soon grew, swelled by folks from further afield and by some whose need was feigned rather than genuine and my father even spotted among those with their hands out, merchants dressed in rags and with grubby faces and wince-inducing limps unable to recall to which leg they belonged, begging '*Sire! Sire!*' to be handed back the very coins collected from them by the Treasury just days before."

Adalbert banged his cutlery-filled fists on the wooden table, "The beastly blighters! The rotten cads! They would deceive the Good King into returning to them the coins legitimately taxed for generous redistribution of a small portion of the wealth they had accumulated through industry and commerce rather than see it go where it was needed most; namely those folks probably too poor to buy the nice things the merchants sold in their merchandising, um, emporiums of, um, retailing..." Adalbert flapped his hands struggling for the word.

"Their shops," said the King.

"Yes those! Where poor people go to buy poor-people things, but obviously not the *very* poor people with insufficient girth to their purse, *they* are condemned to gaping at the window displays of poor-people-stuff and wishing their leg lost in wartime might return so that they could earn money with it… somehow… and go shopping on it!"

"Ye-ess," confirmed the King, albeit cautiously.

"The taxes increased to meet the basic requirements of needy, but now there were crowds of them. Prague is a significant city with a population of thousands and so very many of them were gathering outside the castle here every day, plus more from the suburbs and beyond. For coins, people will travel, beg for extra, telling their story to prove their need. Some wrote their stories in the form of letters, thrusting them at the King so he might read them, take pity and send money to them."

"If they can read and write, they can earn a wage!" Adalbert thumped the table with a harumph.

The King acknowledge the point, pleased and then continued. "My father could no longer cope with them clawing at him, screaming in his face, trying to grab the money directly from his robes. If they were in the last frantic, gurgling, gasps of drowning and he were handing out air, they could not have assailed him more desperately." Adalbert looked overwhelmed, his eyes darting, his face contorted with anxiety and confusion, his fingers waving like submerged plants. "I think he was a man on a mission and past the point of no return, so instead of reflecting, taking stock, instead of a new solution to the problem, in fact, instead of listening to anyone else he took to tipping whole buckets of coins off the battlements."

"Oh…" Adalbert recognised this generosity could not have ended well. "Then what happened?"

"Soon the money was all gone, so he went to see the Mayor, a grim old chap was the Mayor and he showed my father the books and explained there was no more and that he doubted any more taxes could be gathered, the people were all taxed out! But my father refused to accept it and insisted, *'More taxes!'* and the Mayor refused, so he was sacked and then we had no Mayor. No civil servants were paid because there was no money and no Mayor and my father the King, the *Good* King, because of course his fame as a generous giver to the poor and needy had spread far and wide, was left atop the battlements waving an empty bucket to the crowds of needy folk." The King paused. "*Good* King Wenceslas, the famously good King, known far and wide for his unfailing generosity and good deeds. Loved so much, some people thought he could heal their ailments by the laying on of hands!" The King raised his eyes to the roof and shook his head despondently. "Meanwhile his vexatious taxation was a matter of quiet angry muttering and secret meetings of treasonous discussion. The *Good King* story was widespread and celebrated by the newspapers, while the underlying truth was a more secret and darker matter shared between folk gradually losing their assets."

Adalbert was engrossed and he surprised himself by keeping up, just about understanding the principles of the story. He was fascinated with the issue and realised his own father, the King at home, did not talk to him this way. Instead, he accused the boy he called Addled-Bert of being a dunderhead and shared nothing of his Kingly mind with his own fifth son. His four older brothers? Certainly, handsome, strong, athletic and charming. They were like a matching set while he was distinctly the odd one out, and not in a good way. His mother the Queen merely sighed and compared him less favourably with other Princes. Her usual comment when looking at him was to ask aloud where she went wrong and while Adalbert understood she was referring to him, imagined she might just be confiding in him some other unspecified disappointment because that idea hurt less. As bad as this story of Prague history he was now hearing might be, he was flushed with joy at being included, valued as a breakfast companion and he found himself wishing Bad King Wenceslas was his father instead. Adalbert broke the silence with a cautious, "Then what?" He was engrossed and on the edge of his seat. He hadn't eaten in these last minutes.

"The money was gone so the crowds grew angry and rebellious. It was a good thing gone bad, a simple wild-flower turned to a dreadful briar patch, a nutritious cake gone mouldy and wriggling with weevils. With the best of intentions, he'd unwittingly created a bigger problem than had existed prior."

"Oh, that's terrible. The poor King! But what did he do? What is there to do in such a quandary?"

"The *poor* King? Yes, he was actually poor. Well, first he insisted more coins be smelted so that he could give them out."

"How clever! What a genius idea!"

"But there was no more gold and silver in the vaults so gold sovereigns were melted down, blended with cheaper alloys to make more. This way one sovereign could be turned into three."

"Amazing! Problem solved then!" Adalbert exploded with joy at the happy outcome to the desperate story.

"No, I'm afraid not. The assayers, the bankers, the people who control such things, determined that one new sovereign had the worth of just one-third of an old one and suddenly, everything tripled in price so we were back to where we started. Worse in fact."

"The absolute cads!" said Adalbert loudly. "How dare they!"

"They dare because they were right dear boy. You cannot simply manufacture money with no consequences coming back on you further down the line." Adalbert was silent.

This was a concept (and resultant dilemma) beyond his comprehension but his trust in the King was utter, so he took his word on the matter.

"So what did Grandpa do? I mean, your dad, the other King Wenceslas the Firstest?" Adalbert was blabbing a bit because he was riding a wave of fascination, lifted to an unfamiliar level of happiness. He was being spoken to by a proper adult for more than a couple of minutes without a rebuke, a sneer or an impatient slap across what he had learned to understand was his 'stupid, ugly face!' He shrunk back a little lest one was coming. They were always out of the blue and whenever he was slapped, his face stung with pain, sorrow and shame, but he remained, appropriately, *none the wiser.*

"He hid in here and did nothing," said the King. "Taxation was crippling the honest folks of Prague, meanwhile the angry mob outside accused him of callously abandoning them in their time of need and threatened violence. They literally wanted his head on a spike."

"The ingrates! Off with *their* heads, I say! Call in the army!" Adalbert thumped the little card table causing food to fly skywards, tea and ale droplets to splatter and the table to wobble precariously.

The King grabbed it and laughed, "Goodness! Your blood is up for this story young Prince. Good. You must learn from the past, *'Experience is a dear school, but some fools will learn in no other.'*" He left the thought out there for Adalbert to absorb, then after a moment or two, continued with the history lesson. "There was no army as such. They were a rabble of abandoned men and boys who hadn't been fed or paid for weeks. They had heard word of the King tossing gold towards all and sundry willing to sit outside the castle and await his appearance, while they, who had fought and suffered for the realm, had received nothing. They were a short step from an insurrection." Adalbert looked puzzled. "Rising up in force and deposing the King themselves." Now the young Prince gasped and put a hand over his mouth in shock. "It didn't happen," the King assured him.

"Phew! That was a close thing, I thought he was a goner there for a moment!"

The King raised his eyebrows, "Well, a delegation approached the castle with a request for an audience. They were an institute of business owners, shopkeepers, mill owners, factory bosses and the like, a chamber of those in commerce, the investors and organisers and employers of the city and beyond."

"Golly, what did they want?" said Adalbert intrigued.

"They told him his generosity was ruining them, that the taxation had starved their businesses of cash, that they had laid off workers who had joined the throng outside the castle demanding a handout, causing the group to grow ever-larger."

"I am at a loss to know how this can end!" cried Adalbert. "It is an absolute mare! What happened, pray tell, do!"

"My father dropped dead on the spot," he said calmly, yet obviously with some sadness to him. Adalbert's mouth fell open and he went to speak but instead burst into noisy sobs. Thrusting his chair back, he dropped his chest to his knees and wrapping his long arms around his long legs, seemingly several times around they were so long, he bawled into his own thighs.

"No, no, no! Not dead! Not King Grandaddy the Good! I won't have it, he's not gooooooooone!" wailed Adalbert.

The King frowned deeply, stood and wiped his hands and mouth on a napkin, regarding the young Prince with an expression no casual observer could discern. After a long-ish pause, during which the Prince made extraordinary noises while taking vast gaspy breaths in and loud wailing, sobbing breaths out, quite the loudest crying the King had ever heard, or in fact anyone had ever heard. Finally, the King walked around to the table and patted him gently on his broad, yet flabby shoulders. "There, there young 'un. No need for this. You knew he was dead. You already knew it, did you not?"

Without raising his head from his knees Adalbert blubbed, "Yes but just now he was alive!"

"In my account."

"He was aliiiiiiiive," he wailed, "and now he's deaaaaaad!" he wailed some more.

"Yes, yes, he's dead, there, there, it's alright."

Adalbert looked up, blotchy and damp but instantly calmer, "It is? It's alright?"

"Well, sort of," the King shrugged, returning to his seat on the other side of the table.

"Why? Why? Why did he die?!" Adalbert moaned very poetically.

"One particular man, one who owned a chain of retail clothing outlets cut deeply with a comment," Adalbert took in a sharp breath and held it. "He said that my father the King had not been generous at all, he said he had been reckless and what's more, he had been reckless with money which was not his, but theirs. That he had used his power in law to steal money from the hardest working, most enterprising royal subjects, bleeding them dry until they collapsed in ruin and then he the King, who had done nothing to generate or earn a single coin of it, had tossed it away to mostly no good effect to anyone who made big eyes at him. He accused my father of creating a divided realm of the producers of wealth and an underclass who felt incapable of making their own way in the world. That he had directly expanded and created more poverty. He said that all the hard work of the innovative, inventive working population had bought gin, snuff, tobacco and wagers on card games, nothing of use or worth and that the King had destroyed an economy and with it, the lives of ordinary good people and the hopes of the nation. In that last accusation there was no more than a grain of truth. Some might have wasted the coins, but many people *were* poor, they *did* need food, clothes, basic things. His solution wasn't a solution. It was simple, it worked briefly like, like…" the King searched for a metaphor.

"Like telling mummy the Queen it wasn't me who left a big curly poo in her best chamber pot!" The King squinted, gaped and shook his head slightly confused. "Denying it doesn't do anything about the poo. It remains in situ." Adalbert, satisfied with the analogy and pleased with himself, waited for the King to continue. The King remained speechless, his eyes twitching and his head shaking fractionally. Adalbert raised his open hand and shielded his mouth from the side and in a loud whisper said, "It _was_ me, I was only young and I wanted to try out mummy the Queen's gold-rimmed potty!" he giggled and his eyes twinkled with glee.

The King nodded, smiled a sad smile and continued. "So there he was – my father – dead. I imagine he knew his accusers were right. He couldn't bear to see children go hungry. He thought that abandoned women deserved a meal, a roof, a bed. Old soldiers marked by war outside and inside warranted a pension. But while he might have been right in his sentiment, he was wrong in his means." Adalbert's twinkle was gone now. His delight over his chamber pot story had evaporated and the realities of Prague's recent royal history overwhelmed him once more. He swallowed hard and nosily.

After a long pause the King sighed and scrunching his napkin, dropped it on the table. "And it cost him his life."

On the very last word, there was a slight crack in the King's voice and it sent an empathetic shudder through Adalbert such that he thought he might not help himself but cry over the man's obvious grief. Adalbert looked at him closely. He seemed anything but a jailer or a kidnapper of Princesses. Adalbert was well used to being confused, to being the only one blatantly unaware of the consensus reality of a situation, but this was a whole new level of confusion. Here was an obviously good man known internationally as the infamous Bad King Wenceslas who was holding him and who knows else prisoner. His brain hurt.

Adalbert stared at the King. It wasn't just his brain that hurt, his ears hurt, his tummy hurt, everything hurt, but nothing hurt more than his pounding, aching heart. "Did.... you.... hear that man say those things that caused the King, your father, to drop to his um, deadness?" He fancied he already knew the answer.

"I was 15, almost a man to look at, but a boy in here," he tapped his head. My father clutched his arm, stood, sat down in agony, folded his arms across his chest like this," the King demonstrated and screwed up his face in what was surely a good example of the original, "and died right there and then!" Adalbert's lower lip quivered but he remained in control. "I ran to him of course, held him tightly and slowed his fall from the chair to the floor. I watched his face sag as his spirit exited his corporeal being and found myself alone and surrounded by these men."

Adalbert sucked in a big breath and with another thump of the table shouted, "The absolute scoundrels!"

The King nodded pensively before he spoke, "But you see, they were right," he said with a reluctant, sad smile.

"They were? But what about the grubby homeless children? What about the veteran soldier or the abandoned widow? Wasn't he right to give them money?"

"They should be given money, help, something of what they need to restart their lives, but not by the King. It is not the King's place. This was the wrong way to go about it."

"So what is the *right* way to go about it? To solve the problems of the needy without making everyone else furious?" asked Adalbert fascinated.

"Who knows? If you can find a way, tell the world. It seems we always arrive at the wrong compromise. "You can't please…"

"'… any of the people, any of the time!'" said Adalbert. "I know! My mother and father say it all the time!"

"*All* of the people *all* of the time," said the King, further confusing Adalbert, but making him think about it for a while.

"I think I should never be King. For the life of me, I don't understand the first thing about it," said Adalbert almost amused with the idea. "So what happened next?" The King stood and appeared like he was preparing to leave, supping the dregs of his tea and wiping his mouth once more. "Oh, please don't go! Please tell me what happened next. Please!" This last plea rang out heartrendingly.

The King looked at him with some warmth and with a small sigh, sat back down. "That day I became King at 15." Adalbert frowned a little joining the dots. *Good* King Wenceslas was dead and now here was *Bad* King Wenceslas. Where could this story go but down? Perhaps hearing it would lead to a bad place, a place where he was captive and at risk of meeting his own end here in this dingy room in this tall tower.

The King puffed noisily, smacked his strong thighs with his strong hands and looked Adalbert in the eye again, more seriously now than for most of the conversation up to this point. "The army was on the brink of revolution, the economy was close to collapse, the treasury had emptied its vaults and produced so much coin that inflation had destroyed the value of things and we had the largest crowd of hopeless beggars the city had ever seen." Adalbert clapped a hand over his mouth again and shook his head despairingly. He was a superb audience.

"I smelted down all coinage and reissued new pure coins with new names. There were fewer, but they were *real* money. I made peace with neighbouring Kings and Queens and loaned the army to the strongest of them on the agreement that they pay my soldiers as their own and use them to defend us both."

"They agreed to that?" asked Adalbert, like a proper student of politics.

"Not all did and we were taken advantage of here and there, the realm shrank a bit but not too much, but overall? Yes, it worked. You see soldiers are hard to raise. It was an arrangement that suited us both and so I effectively gave them away for good because we would not have an army here afterwards and none would want to come back to a place with no pay."

Adalbert was happy enough listening but felt inclined to ask questions in the hope this would keep the King engaged with him for longer. "Could you not just send the soldiers home?"

"Unpaid? To no jobs just their starving families? Many would become mercenaries, that is soldiers for hire by foreign nations and possibly used against us here. I used them and secured their income for them and a promise of our safety in the process."

"Golly, that's dashed clever!" said Adalbert, genuinely admiring the King.

The King shrugged, "As long as it works, it's good. But the realm was in deeply in debt and many people were poor. They remembered the good times when there was work and jobs to be had and wages, not generous wages, but a living of sorts, and along came the King and showered all who waited upon him with coins. They didn't realise that from the first handful, the doom of us all began to loom, to grow until it could not be prevented."

The young, gangly Prince shook his head despairingly, "So…?"

"I gave out no coins but lowered taxes just a little in the hope that businesses would not fail. I negotiated with many people, concessions, promises, loans, schemes, anything just to keep things going and often alienating two people in order to satisfy four or five, then a new deal to satisfy the two while angering another. I could not see the blessed tunnel, let alone the light at the end of it! Plus, I didn't know if I was helping, I only knew I was keeping things going for another day and a good day was when the realm had a few more coins in the vaults than the previous and when reports about city folk included more hope than doom. Years of hardship followed, a period of austerity where joys were hard to come by, yet commerce struggled along, surviving, just. Later I lowered taxes a little, then a little more."

"Bravo!" called Adalbert, "And the people loved you for it, I'm sure!"

He shook his head, "No, no, not at all. I had reigned over hardship, toil and something close to absolute poverty. I hadn't caused it, but I had taken over from fiscal mis-management and so the painful period was mine, while the people still remembered the joy of plenty, that being my father's time."

"But he… *Good* King Wenceslas, ruined things and you… er, the next King Wenceslas, were the one doing the right things to fix it all!" whined Adalbert.

The King nodded and stirred the remains of some break-fast, "*Bad* King Wenceslas. Most people prefer jam today," he said. "They aren't that bothered that the realm can't afford its own existence as long as they have jam today."

"So flippin' short-sighted!" said Adalbert, genuinely exasperated, "A kingdom surely must live within its current means!" This was said with the vigour of someone in actual authority. "There can only be jam if the realm has the prosperity for jam!"

The King smiled, "You might make a King yet young Adalbert!" and the Prince glowed with pride. This really was the best day of his entire life. The King stood and placed a firm hand on the younger man's soft shoulder.

Adalbert looked up at him adoringly and there they stayed for a moment until Adalbert asked, "What about Princess Petra?" and the hand was removed, not violently, but slowly and the King turned and walked to the door, pausing in the doorway.

"I'm not ready to talk about her," he said with some sadness in his voice. Adalbert was sad too. His new best friend was leaving and would lock him in again until who knows when. Leaving always introduced the possibility of never returning. "You got enough there to see you through lunchtime and on to dinner?" asked the King waggling a finger at all the food that was left.

Adalbert was overjoyed by the prospect of there being a dinner. "Absolutely, thank you dear King, dear *Good* King! For I now know, and I know that I know, not just in a fact like I've been given by someone else who purports to know, but by absorption of the information and proper appreciation of the actual essence of a thing, I know that _you_ are an extremely, a supremely *good* King."

The King regarded him for a moment, it wasn't clear whether Adalbert's comments had touched him for he remained largely inscrutable, yet there was a flicker of something akin to a benevolent expression. After a long moment's silence he looked at all the food and waggling his finger again, he gestured around the room to the little piles of scampering rats and said, "Give those little blighters a bit would you?" and left, shutting the door gently but not locking it. Rats looked towards the door and twitched, gathered around Adalbert and looked up at him, twitching some more. A few climbed on to his lap, one stretching up towards his face, looking at him and twitching one might say in curiosity and affection. He stroked it and smiled, tears rolling down his cheeks.

Chapter the Fourteenth.
Gregory's Delicious Sandwich and
Vegetarian Sausage Roll Emporium

The back office of Gregory's sandwich shop was larger than expected and included an outer room where two male clerks sat with stacks of paper piled on their large writing bureau, each with multiple ink wells filled with liquid of differing hues speared with quills, an array of many-stranded abacuses and rows of notebooks with writing on their spines. On the wall were a series of chalkboards with the most elaborate graphs and columns of data in a variety of chalk colours. "Sorry about the chaos, end of the month, lot to do, invoicing and final tallies for performance. We run all the shops from here."

"How many shops do you have?" asked Darius.

"Is that a police detective question? Will everything I say be taken down?" she asked in good humour. Then, after a short pause and before Darius could answer, she and the Mayor both shouted, "Knickers!" and laughed. The clerks paused in their work and making eye contact with one of them, Mrs Gregory asked, "Have you backed up all these figures yet? Pointing at the 19 chalkboards around the three walls.

"Yes Mrs Gregory," and unrolling a section of a large, fat roll of paper, it was possible to see a replica of what was on the wall.

"Anyway, Inspector, the answer is 19," Mrs Gregory said, "I thought a detective like you could have figured that out," she swept a hand around the boards and he nodded, regretting the oversight. "I'd dearly like more. We could have 90 all turning a profit but I open each new one with savings earned from the others and so it takes time. If I had more capital I could increase sales dramatically." She turned to one of the two clerks, "How are we? What are the results like?"

"All up between two percent and seven percent year on year..." he hesitated.

"Don't tell me, except Štěrboholy."

The clerk nodded. "Still tracking down, behind by nearly 15 percent compared to last year."

"And all till?" The clerk nodded again.

"Inspector," Mrs Gregory said formally. "Business is up everywhere across 18 shops but not at this one in Štěrboholy." She indicated a chalkboard. "Even there, the people who pay on a monthly account are..." she pointed at the clerk,

"Up four percent," he said squinting at the relevant chalkboard.

"So the reduction in business is entirely in cash sales at the till," she continued, "So..."

"Someone is stealing cash, probably a member of staff because the money never makes it through the till," said Darius. Mrs Gregory held her hands up in despair. "The data alone isn't actual evidence," he continued in a police tone, "You'd need to catch the individual in the act, pocketing the cash instead of ringing it up, and even then, what you have would be for a solitary crime, with only circumstantial evidence for the other losses, so you'd be relying on a magistrate to determine there was a level of certainty in what is otherwise just a likelihood."

"We don't use magistrates in our system, too many of

them are what we call, *soft-brained-idiots*!" said the Mayor. "There's so little actual crime, the Chief issues fines or sentencing on the spot, or the Crown Court judge, otherwise known as... *ME!...*" the Mayor pointed at herself, "listens to all the evidence prior to levying fines, or bucketing, or the most serious of sentences, we deport them."

"Really? Where to?" asked Darius.

"Can't tell you that, but let's just say it's not as nice as here, roads clogged with carriages, always raining, all the citizens moan constantly and you have to get there by boat because they haven't dug a tunnel in cooperation with Frankia yet." The Mayor tapped her nose indicating discretion. Darius was amazed at this piece of information and looking amazed prompted the Mayor to add, "Don't look at me like that! It's not just us, every realm I know of sends theirs there too."

"Anyway, I'll need to sort Štěrboholy," said Mrs Gregory. "Might need your services Mrs. Lady Chief Justice. You'd be handy too, Inspector." Darius pondered for a moment, mildly pleased by the notion and deciding on the spot that he would be inclined to accept the interesting assignment.

Just then Daisy came in with two plates for the Mayor and Darius, each with a sausage roll and generous blobs of ketchup and mayo. When she'd handed them over, she issued them with forks wrapped in elaborate paper napkins printed with a replica of the Gregory's swinging shop sign and a line drawing of the original shop frontage. "Dab!" commanded the Mayor, showing Darius he must dip his sausage roll in one of the condiments.

"In mayo? Really?"

"Yes, dab!" she ordered him again.

"I've never had one of these before," he said.

"What a veggie one?" asked the Mayor.

"No, I mean I've never even heard of a sausage roll." They

looked amazed and watched him take a bite. Exactly the right temperature, flaky pastry, airy yet somehow tacky, and the veggie meat substitute, beautiful consistency, peppery, slightly juicy but not at all soggy and with no trace of any of the chewy bits which sometimes compromise real sausages. He moaned with pleasure in an uninhibited way and the two ladies exchanged somewhat sensual glances of surprise with eyebrows raised. "It's, incredible! Oh my goodness, that's absolute nectar!"

"Thank you, Inspector. It's our best seller," said Mrs Gregory. "All my own work." Darius looked at her again with the most serious face, then putting his fork and plate down for a moment, reached out and shook her hand firmly.

"Well done!" he said, like she'd just won a baking competition. She looked delighted. Commercial success was not a greater reward than this most sincere adoration of her proudest achievement among food products.

"Can't believe you've never had one!" said the Mayor, earning a nod of agreement from Mrs Gregory.

"It's my new favourite!" he said, "Pushed pork pie into second!"

"What pie now?" asked Mrs Gregory.

"Pork. Pork pie," he said. She shook her head, no more enlightened. "I'll explain another time. Could be a business opportunity for you."

They moved through into an inner office and after sitting down, discussed the King's daily food orders, tracking back through files from previous months, then previous years. After some interim questions by Darius, Mrs Gregory led them out again to a room full of silver cloches sitting neatly on shelves covered with white cloth. "These are all the King's own," she said, "We use these daily to take him warm food. I have a veritable mini-army of maids who take food up twice each day, eight in the morning and seven at night. We collect his order at seven am and five pm, although it's often the same, or…" she lifted one such order from a pile, "*Thursday usual*, this one says. That's a Hawaiian pizza, side of onion rings and dips." Darius liked a pizza but had never heard of the Hawaiian variety. After seeing the cloches, dinner services and silverware and being told, "He does all his own washing up you know! It comes back sparklingly clean, it's a bit of a mystery how he manages it." They returned to Mrs Gregory's office and Darius continued to study the accounts for a while.

After referring to several books of accounts and flipping pages back and forth, he said, "It's obvious isn't it! After Princess Petra's birthday feast on August the 4th four years ago in '33, food orders kept falling and falling, which is when you say staff were being retired from the castle, until here in November, how many does this feed, three or four?"

"Or just the King and one other," confirmed Mr's Gregory.

"Then it steps up a little at regular intervals, the orders increase, more breakfasts, more snacky lunches, more dinners, more potato…?"

"Wawfulls," said Mr's Gregory.

"More and more meals under more and more cloches. I'm certain you'll find that these increases coincide with the child-kidnappings."

"And it went up today with three extra breakfasts and more dinner food too."

"Today?" asked both Darius and the Mayor, looking at each other in shock. "More kidnappings last night?" Darius asked the Mayor.

"Not that I've heard. I would normally expect to hear… people do report the absence of orphans, although we have very few in the city now anyway." The Mayor frowned, "Maybe he's got guests…?"

"Anyway, the King, the remarkably stunning Princess Petra, 40-plus children…"

"Oh!" interrupted the Mayor, "There would be no children at 40-plus, goodness no! Children are up to 13 years old here." Darius looked puzzled so she continued, "Fourteen is young adult, 18 is properly adult, thirty is proper old, 40 is flipping ancient, 50 is like, 'What are you still doing here?' and after that, we don't have an official category because that's the last one we've ever needed."

"Official category?"

"Yes, they are all official categories, so on a documentation, people have to tock one,"

"*Tock* one? You don't mean *tick* one, I take it?" interrupted Darius.

The Mayor laughed, "No of course not. Ticks are casual. In official business, we use tocks." Darius looked puzzled so she drew one of each in the air with her finger, a tock simply being a reversed tick with the tail slanting up to the left.

"This place is so… weird," he said to himself.

"Anyway," continued the Mayor, "they tock either *A) Child, B) Young Adult, C) Proper Adult, D) Proper Old, E) Flipping Ancient* and *F) Off.*" She had recounted them across her fingers.

"'F' is called, 'off'?" asked Darius confused.

"Yes, F) Off. It's an abbreviation of Officially cautioned regarding their reasons for still being here."

"But that's awful!" said an exasperated Darius, slightly louder than normal. "What about all the people who are actually over 50, unwanted, sanctioned by the state for being, what, middle-aged! They're only over 50, you must have lots of wonderful citizens in that category. I'm certain I've seen plenty!"

"None. Not one. None at all. All…." She ran a finger across her throat and made a noise like a duck snoring."

"YOU CUT THEIR…?" cried Darius, his face a picture of shock.

The two ladies looked confused. The Mayor interrupted, "Goodness no! They are all long gone through natural causes. We would never hurt an old person. What do you think we are?"

"I don't get it. Okay, hit me, how is it no one is over 50?" Darius, asked in a resigned tone.

The Mayor clasped Darius's hands in her own, "Because no one really wants to be over 30. They all want to be 21 or 22, or 23 or.." Mrs Gregory joined in now so they both said, "… 24 or, 25."

"Alright, alright, I get it, you don't have to recount every number up to whatever!" said Darius, a little tersely, for someone normally so charming.

"Actually, that was it," said the Mayor. "Twenty-five. We find most people would be happy with that. Not many say, *'Oh golly, I just can't wait to be 26!'* they prefer 25 by and large." Darius shook his head slightly, not really understanding. "So here in Prague, what we do is delay your 21st by a year so you stay 22 for two years and then that pattern stays in place through your twenties so you have two years of being every year in that decade of your life, you get 20 years of saying you're in your twenties!" Darius found himself smiling a little, he chuckled and shook his head in amazement. Prague was a most remarkable and unusual place. "Three years for each of your thirties and four years for every year in your forties. It's an understandable pattern, don't you agree, Inspector?"

He shook his head in a mixture of dismay and wonder but the last shake turned to a nod instead, "I have to say I do! So it means that for someone to hit 50, they are actually…" he was working it out.

"No, no, not *actually*," interrupted the Mayor, "they are

actually whatever age they are under Prague law. It's just that if they were unfortunate enough to be born somewhere else, a 50-year old would be classed as…"

Now it was Darius's turn to interrupt, "A hundred and ten!"

"Exactly."

"Well no wonder you don't have any!" The Mayor made a slightly pained face and looked at Mrs Gregory who reflected it. Darius frowned.

"We did have one lady in her forties, what was she?" asked the Mayor.

"Mrs Bevvy? Um, 49 and a couple of months."

"So…" Darius worked it out, "A hundred and six where I come from."

They nodded, "And to be honest, she was such a lovely lady, we were all a bit anxious about the prospect of her hitting 50 and having to classify her as *What are you still doing here, F) Off!*"

"She was already *Flipping Ancient* according to your system, didn't she mind that?"

"No, people tend to agree and anyway it's *tongue in vestibule*." This caused another bewildered look from Darius, causing both women to put their tongues in front of their bottom row of teeth and push out the area below their lower lip in the most bizarre and grotesque of fashions. "It means, we don't really mean it, it's a bit of a joke."

"Are you sure you don't mean *tongue in cheek*?" The ladies tried that manoeuvre with their tongues and ended up frowning deeply. "It's an expression we use which means the same thing."

"Except who talks like that?" the Mayor laughed with her tongue in her cheek.

"I could ask the same thing!" said Darius, his tongue in the vestibule of his mouth.

They laughed, "See it works, you made a sort-of joke and we understand that you weren't actually asking that question because it was just *tongue in vestibule*."

Darius gave up. "Anyway, what are we going to do? The castle, the adorably beautiful Princess Petra," the ladies pulled faces, "however many children under the age of 14, what are we going to do?"

"Do we have to rock the apple cart?" asked the Mayor.

"Rock the boat?"

"No coastline here. Some boats on the river but a lot more apple carts. Don't try to force your maritime terminology on landlocked peoples, alright?" Darius let it go.

"I think we should. I mean I think _you_ should with or without my help, but I am prepared to help." This was Darius at his most serious.

"Ooh you! Mr Bossypants! Got a little shiver up my spine then, did you Gregory?"

"*Lower* spinal area!" she confirmed grinning.

Darius waited. "Oh alright then. Me and the Chief and Tom, Dick, Harry and... um,"

"Jim," said Darius.

"Oh, get you! And JIM, will go up there tomorrow, crack of sparrow!" Darius went to speak but decided not to bother. Crack of sparrow? The world was a collection of nations sharing a common language but divided by their colloquialisms and idioms.

"And what's crack of sparrow here? Half past ten? Four am? Go on surprise me!" said Darius.

The Mayor frowned, "You are an out-of-towner aren't you! *Sparrow* is eight in the morning, *crack-of* means a quarter of an hour before that. I want to arrive with the Gregory's delivery maids because the King will open the gates."

Darius was pleased with the headway they were making.

They had a plan and he was pretty certain the morning would bring, if not a resolution, then some significant progress. He felt in his jacket pocket for the key to the castle's back door and found it: large, heavy and bronze. Before he could use it though, he needed something else, something he didn't feel he could ask for.

In the front part of the Můstek branch of Gregory's, Prince Chatty's young coachman, Brian looked at sandwiches and long flattish and unfamiliar pastries but having no coins on his person meant he could only window shop. The smell of freshly baked bread and especially the popular vegetarian sausage rolls (a combination of words which was new to him) set his mouth watering in the most excessive fashion and he hoped Prince Darius wouldn't be too long because teasing his tastebuds like this was torture.

Chapter the Fifteenth.
The House of Rock, The Castle, The Streets of Prague &
The Grand Velky Hotel

Mister returned home at dusk with a cheery greeting from the hallway below and some puffing and panting as he climbed the first flight of stairs to the parlour above. There he encountered Shoshama with House and addressing his wife, stopped in his tracks with dramatic theatricality. "Who's this? My goodness! But before you introduce me, please tell me what happened to the dark-haired, pale-faced maiden we took into our house just yesterday? You remember, the one who looked as if she'd seen a ghost? Just when I was getting to like her! Where's our charming guest House?"

"Where's our guesthouse?" asked House quizzically.

"I'm asking you, what happened to Eliška and who is this strikingly handsome young woman who appears to have taken her place?" he checked his watch, "At five after five."

"Mister! You'll embarrass the poor dear. I have simply changed her look to help her fit in a little more readily."

"And then what happened?"

"It turns out to be impossible in her case. You simply can't make a sow's ear out of a silk purse!"

"Can I say, and I don't mean any criticism here, but I think you may have forgotten your original task and instead, followed some other instinct." House looked a bit baffled as she stirred the tagliatelle pasta with one hand and the meatballs in carbonara sauce with the other. "Imagine the owner of a grand estate asked a stonemason to knock him up a plain pillar on which he could hang a gate and when he returned, he found the stonemason had not done as instructed, but instead had created a replica of the Venus de Milo. *'What happened?'* says the man who wanted a gatepost. *'Turned out to be a rather extraordinary block of stone.'* says the stonemason, *'I simply couldn't make a forgettable rectangular pillar out of it. This particular stone you provisioned for the purpose among many thousands of thousands you could have selected and while nearly all the other stones could aspire to be little more than a gatepost, the stone in question turned out to be special, unique, incredible. I could not prevent it becoming what it always was under its surface. It was destined to be a blissful work of art and no amount of artless, clumsy chiselling by me could make it less.'*

"Do I understand you consider my efforts to be *artless, clumsy chiselling?*"

"Not at all dear House. Is the Venus de Milo clumsy? But like all supreme talents unveiling what they know to be a work of art, no bold claims are necessary, their skill is exceeded only by their modesty."

House addressed Shoshama, "You see why I adore Mister so? It is as if we have attended the theatre!" and while Shoshama reeled at being the object of such an oration, House turned to Mister himself and asked, "Did sales go well?" Mister nodded, "Just how much *tasting* occurred? I'm guessing *quite a lot.*" She turned to Shoshama and confided, "The consumption of wine affects men differently. Some become idiotic, some mistakenly believe they are rendered attractive, some think they must fight a lamppost, some giggle like girls and I used to think the best ones simply fell asleep. Mister here tops them all by becoming excessively cheery and poetic. Except for those whose husbands sleep, most wives are made glum by their fellow's imbibing. Not I! He is the living epitome of the saying, *the more the merrier*!"

Mister didn't answer because he didn't need to. "Oh Carbonara! How I love thee! I will fetch Syrah to make our party a four!" and dashed upstairs inelegantly and stumbling somewhat every few steps.

Shoshama made to speak but House held up a hand, "He'll be fine, he won't fall. Well, he might fall up the stairs, but he'll come down very slowly as if carrying a baby... the wine!" Shoshama, made an *'Oh, I see'* face. She knew Syrah was a grape variety and so guessed he had shot off to fetch an expensive wine but had still wondered. More bizarre things happen in Prague all the time than there being someone called Syrah hidden upstairs. "Syrah is one of his many wines my dear and please don't think less of him for his passion, Mister talks of wines as if they are alive." House continued to look at Shoshama and paused in her stirring, "Gosh all Hemlock! Each time I see you anew I am floored by your aspects." House shook her head in marvel and Shoshama began to wonder what she might be able to make of her new look.

"I really do like this Deep Purple!" Shoshama said, twiddling some hair she'd pulled around in front of her eyes.

"Oh yes my dear, of course you do. Anyone with a bit of taste likes Deep Purple. Mister! She called out loudly. I'm serving up!" Cautious footsteps on the stairs preceded Mister reappearing greatly pleased with himself holding a pair of contrasting Syrahs high, as if in victory. Shoshama wondered if Mister always selected only from his own storeroom, or whether he ever had cause to pluck something from the vast wine cellar of the King. Either way she didn't mind a bit, the food smelled delightful and she was aware of something that had been growing in her these last days. She was very happy here. Now the only thing she needed was to find Princess Petra, for her to be as wonderful as everyone said and for the two of them to become firm friends. The notion made her so happy she tingled.

***

The King had not delivered trays of dinner on this second evening of Adalbert's incarceration, instead he called in upon him and led him to a small dining room on a lower floor of the castle. They had traversed internal stairs and corridors which left the Prince confused as to precisely his whereabouts, but the view through the large leaded windows showed they were perhaps 10 metres above ground level and enjoying a different aspect because the vista was new to him. Three courses of food sat under cloches, the plates being on table-top heaters which used stubby candles to keep it warm.

"What's this wonderful soup?" asked Adalbert, trying very hard to eat more slowly by copying the King. His Royal Highness made odd faces of concentration as he hooked on some half-rimmed spectacles and studied a piece of hand-scribed parchment, "Potato, mild red chillies, coconut milk, coriander and cumin," he read aloud, then peered over his glasses at Adalbert, "Like it?"

"I had the most wonderful soup in Vienna and this is absolutely it's equal. I'm beginning to think I've been missing out on some gastronomic delights during my years growing up at Egham Castle."

"And you do like your food boy, don't you! I consider that to be a positive quality in a man. Tell me about your growing up." Adalbert suddenly looked glum. "Come on! Can't be that bad, you're a Prince of the Kingdom of the Angles, Saxons and Celts across the sea from Frankia in the Realm of Eggs & Ham, across the river *Thames* from Saint Anus!

See? I looked at a map!" The King had pronounced Thames with the 'h' as if the word was *the* or *there*.

"Egham Castle overlooks the River *Thames*," he said carefully and politely, observing that the King did not mind being corrected about the pronunciation. Directly across the river lies *Staines*. I am the fifth son of my father the King of *Egham*. I am his least favoured and will never be King myself." Adalbert went on to explain a childhood of bullying by his brothers and some rather stern and cold parenting.

"Fifth in line? It could still happen!" said the King, moving onto the second course and handing Adalbert his plate.

"No, I think if some catastrophe befell three of my four brothers leaving me second in line, they'd quickly bump me off to nullify the risk. Either that or the King and Queen would hurry out another few brothers. I expect there's already some clause, some plan to that effect." The King ate slowly, watching Adalbert and thinking. He asked about many aspects of Adalbert's life and found in each explanation, inequities, unfairness, exclusion, and often cruel treatment. It appeared to affect his mood and if it weren't for the fact that Adalbert was a prisoner and the King was his captor, you'd believe they were dear friends.

Dinner ended and Adalbert hoped they could continue talking by the fireside and that perhaps he could learn the secret of Princess Petra and of the castle's other mysteries. Instead, the King ushered him back to his cell saying, "Tell me this, young man; does your door have to be locked? Can I have your word of honour that you will remain within until I call again?"

"Yes!" said Adalbert eagerly, thinking his reluctance to engender the King's disappointment and a deep fear of the dragon quite possibly roaming free were easily enough to keep him in there with his ratty friends. The spiders were tolerable, tending to create webs in high places and out of reach of the rodents while the last of the cockroaches had disappeared as rat-dinner not long ago. "Though why not just lock the door?"

"I am learning about you." He said this earnestly, but not with amusement for it seemed more serious and Adalbert worried that perhaps the test was to see whether he had courage and, in that moment, imagined the King, slapping him on the back with pride finding him free atop the battlements, or sitting calmly in some great chair. The trouble was, he really didn't have that kind of courage because he wasn't like his brothers. He was afraid and wanted the safer option, the path that caused least trouble. He'd rather be known truthfully as afraid than risk angering the King.

"I'd like something," said Adalbert and because the King appeared to be waiting calmly, continued. "Perhaps a book to pass the hours? And an extra candle or two and another blanket…"

There was a moment's silence while the King studied him. "Bathtub?"

"Pardon?"

"A more comfy chair?"

"Oh, well I…"

"A nice carpet perhaps?"

"No really, I shouldn't have mentioned it," said Adalbert, "Really, I'm fine."

"Well dinner is over. Follow me." And with that, the King stood and walked not back the way they had come, but in the opposite direction and up other stairs. After several flights he opened a door to a modest but pleasant bedroom and pointing to a bathtub mounted centrally in front of a large empty fireplace said, "Couldn't help noticing it's time for you to bathe," he said tapping his nose. "You'll find what you need to light a fire there," he said pointing, "And you'll need to pump and heat your own water, no servants here and so also that means you will need to wash your own clothes in the tub and dry them by the fire. Can you do all that?" Adalbert confirmed he could. He hadn't told the King that during all those days when his father went places with his older brothers, he'd spent the time with servants in preference to clinging to his mother. It was the staff who raised him while busily going about their chores for 12 to 16 hours each day and he found the labour both satisfying and instructional. Their spirits were always up, they had cheery banter and helped each other, and he enjoyed all of it. Accidentally encountering his mother during those better days reminded him of her ill-temper and snide remarks to both Adalbert and any of the servants who happened to be with him.

When the evening arrived and he was forced to dress for dinner, the return of his brothers and his father the King would bring great tales of derring-do and he loved to hear of their adventures, but if they turned to him, it would always be a team effort of exclusion, insult and ridicule. They would drive him to despair, to tears and then laugh in unison at their achievement. Heartbroken, Adalbert would make as if for his bed but instead take a second supper in the company of staff in the kitchen. As a lost boy, this was where he could have his head stroked by a kindly woman, lean into a warm bosom and fall sound asleep, waking in the morning in his own bed and thinking immediately, not of his cruel family, but of the kindly servants. The extra meals, the food he ate for comfort, became more than simply physical sustenance and combined with a lack of vigorous exercise, he took on a different physique as he grew in all the wrong directions. He added more blubber than muscle to his body, more kindness than spite to his brain. He treated his servants differently than most Princes and this included paying one young woman to administer affection. He especially missed her humming and stroking during his enforced isolation and found himself humming All Things Bright and Beautiful until he missed her touch all the more, so immediately stopped and changed the subject in his head.

Adalbert was bathing in the tub in front of a roaring fire when there was a knock on the door. Startled, he waited, only to hear a second knock. "Come!" he called out nervously. The King entered, clutching a small stack of books in one hand and waving a cloth bag around at knee height with the other.

"Come on!" he called behind him and as he walked in, a trail of rats followed, scampering, their noses twitching. "Bag of berries and cheese," he said putting it on the mantle. If you want them to stay, feed them. If you want them out, put it all in the corridor out there." At that he plopped the books on the bedside table and said, "Books. Bit of everything. Stay here until I call you for breakfast." Adalbert nodded. "I mean it. You're alright in here so don't even think about leaving!" Adalbert thought about leaving and decided he absolutely definitely wouldn't. And true to his word, he didn't.

***

When Darius emerged from the back office and into the front of the shop, the Mayor close behind, he saw Brian looking directly at him and a cold shiver ran through him. *'This man knows me,'* was his instinctive reaction to the direct eye contact he'd received and which they had both maintained longer than was normal. As they bid Gregory farewell and thanked her for the Vegetarian Sausage Rolls, Darius was also aware the young man was following them, though some paces behind. At the end of the street, the Mayor presented her cheek for a kiss and Darius cautiously leaned in to plant a little peck there, ready for her to rapidly swivel her head and grab his head in her vicelike grip again. She didn't and a little peck seemed to satisfy her. "My lips still throb with unfulfilled ambition!" she said, explaining her inaction. "I'm not disappointing them over you again."

"Oh, sorry," he said, a bit pathetically.

"You don't come my way, do you?" she asked. Darius looked confused. "You're going that way somewhere, aren't you?" she pointed left, "I'm this way," she pointed right, "See you at crack of sparrow!" she said and strode off.

"Crack of sparrow!" he said calling after her. "Thank you!" he added superfluously, for want of *something*. Then turning, he spied his pursuer and gestured him over.

"Prince Darius?" enquired the young man with the deference of a servant.

"Who wants to know?" replied Darius, sort-of giving himself away in any case.

"I work for Prince Charles. He is at the Grand Velký Hotel and wishes me to inform you of it."

"Chatty's back?" he said delighted.

"Yes and he wants to re-join you on your mission," said Brian.

"Does he? Oh right-ho! Listen, I don't think he and I should consort publicly, I'm sort-of incognito hereabouts, so tell him to meet me in the morning. I'll be at the Town Hall at sparr …, at a quarter before eight 'o clock. Can you do that?"

"Certainly, of course. A quarter of the hour in the hall, eight…. Um, Town Clock!" repeated Brian.

"Quarter of eight. Town Hall." Darius said more slowly.

"Sorry Your Highness! I did know it, just got my murds fuddled."

"So you did."

"It happens a lot when I get hungry Your Highness." Brian looked longingly back down the narrow cobbled side street to Gregory's and Darius reached into a pocket to produce a couple of coins, instructing him to try a vegetarian sausage roll, hot, with ketchup and mayo.

"Also, tell Prince Chatty I am planning that we will enter the castle tomorrow morning. We're going in. The rescue is *on*!" Brian registered the important fact with a firm nod and after bowing, thanked Darius for the coin by showing it to him again and strode off towards Gregory's with real purpose.

"Remember the message!" called Darius.

"Yes Your…" Brian began to call back but was frantically waved down by Darius before he said any more. "Er, yes I will sir. I'll remember the sausage!" He had an apologetic face as he turned and retraced his steps towards the shop. The wonderful aroma was already getting stronger, drawing him in. In his fist he had a pair of 12-sided thruppenny coins. He could buy two vegetarian sausage rolls and have money left over for an ale or three!

***

It had been a busy few hours for Chatty. No sooner had Brian left in pursuit of Prince Darius than the hotel manager approached and presented him with a calling card. It seemed that a Lord someone-or-other had heard of his presence in the hotel and had come to seek him out. It would be only proper to greet the fellow, so Chatty ordered wine and after a few polite exchanges, explained he was on a quest to ascertain the facts around the existence or otherwise, of the most extraordinarily beautiful Princess Petra. The Lord had no information which might help matters and Chatty was just pouring them both a second glass when the hotel manager returned with a second calling card, this time from a Duke and Duchess. They were invited into the salon, given wine and told by Chatty that he intended to visit the castle in search of the Princess. Hardly had he finished when further visitors arrived.

It seemed that Prague's gossip-mill was working on overdrive. The news that a visiting Prince was staying in the Grand Velky Hotel caused great interest and many of Prague's elite, expecting the Prince might possibly agree to meet them as the evening was still young, quickly dressed in their finest and hurried to the hotel in their carriages. The same rumour had circulated a few days previously, along with the less-believable suggestion that he was here to seek the long-lost Princess Petra's hand in marriage. While no one really believed that second bit, they had visited the hotel in the hope of meeting the Prince only to find he'd already left for Split. Apparently, that account had been erroneous, because he was back. "Oh yes, certainly back," they said, "Staff have reported the fact to their families, along with details of his flamboyant appearance and royal eccentricities." And so they flocked to the hotel once again hoping for better luck this time around.

Before long, Prince Chatty was surrounded by a throng of Prague's finest and wealthiest and having retold his purpose a dozen or more times, he was now stood precariously on a wobbly chair, a little worse for the quantity of wine he'd glugged and telling the assembled multitude that, "Tomorrow I might die for love! I will storm the castle, beating down its mighty oak doors with these two hands!" he looked at them, "With these three or four hands! And with my trusty sword – whose name is *Swordy*, yes, Swordy, my trusty, trusty sword, Swordy – I will fight anywin and anythong, *anything and anyone*, who DARES wanned in my stay, *stand in my way*, in especially-particularly, a dragon, if such a beast exists!" They nodded and a few called back to him that it certainly did exist, to which Chatty frowned and hiccupped.

"I don't wanna kill a dragon…" he said, looking sad, but then raised his fists and with much gusto, shouted, "but I jilly will well aff I hiv to!" People looked a bit perplexed. Chatty looked reflective. "I mean, I jolly well will have I if to. If I have to!" This they understood and he received some nods and 'ah's. At which point he slumped down safely in his chair, the wobbling finally stopped.

The seamstress let out a long breath of relief, "Crikey I thought you was going to have to catch him for a minute." His footman sighed, clearly disappointed that he hadn't fallen and told her that he would have made to catch him like a good servant should but had always fully intended to miss.

The throng had finally left having got more gossip than they had bargained for after which he ordered steak au poivre with quadruple-cooked chips (which always seemed like one cooking more than was absolutely necessary). The meal in front of him, he was overcome by the notion that this was a *last supper* and he stirred his food, eating only slowly. Realising they were still sitting quietly nearby, he dismissed the footman and seamstress for the evening, calling after them that they must attend him very early in the morning and that depending on the outcome of the day, it might be the for last time. His mood could not be described as upbeat or confident.

A while later, Brian returned with a whiff of ale on his breath and proudly announced his success at conversing with Prince Darius. "And he didn't say anything else at all?" Chatty asked Brian for the umpteenth time. Brian shook his head and confirmed that was all of it. "Quarter of eight, Town Hall and that we are going into the castle…" he gulped as he said the last bit to himself. He emptied the wine bottle into his glass and the glass into his mouth and stood up, immediately swaying, "Oops! Steady on Chatty!" he said to himself, slurring slightly and plopped back down in his chair.

"Is that all for tonight Your Highness?" Brian had an assignation to visit a certain young seamstress, daughter of another of Chatty's coachmen. Her father was currently and conveniently out of the way en-route to Split while Chatty's servants were all staying down the street in a guesthouse. She being the only female of the party, had her own room. For Brian, the planets had finally aligned.

"No, you can't go just yet. Got a feeling I'm going to need your help to manage the stairs in a bit." Brian sighed inwardly. "Bartender!" The bartender, busily writing notes about Chatty's morning-arrangements and quietly mouthing, *Town Hall, crack of sparrow,* looked over from behind the shiny wooden counter awaiting the expected order for more wine, was instead asked, "Is the bartender here?" by a chuckling Chatty, "Only there's a beaver that's getting very hungry!" and laughed at his own joke. The bartender stared at him confused. "Is the *bar tender?*" Chatty explained. "*Bar tender*, like bartender but two words instead of one with an alternate meaning because of it!" The bartender now understood, but the moment for surprised mirth had passed. "Hence the beaver!" added Chatty. "That's why I said there was a beaver getting very hungry! Get it?"

Brian stared wanly into space and thought about the girl he adored. *'A hungry beaver? Yes, there probably is,'* he said and sighed again.

One more bottle of wine later, Brian helped Chatty up to his bed and then as quickly as the task allowed, left him snoring heavily. A few short hours later Chatty awoke dizzy, dry-mouthed and with an awful headache. He reached across to the pitcher and glass Brian had left him and poured the first of three large glasses of water. "A badger has sneaked into my room, tangled up my bedding, wacked me on the head with a cricket bat and done a stinky poo in my mouth!" he muttered squinting while tipping back the third glass. He staggered out of bed and went to the window, sliding it up for additional fresh air and leaned out. Sucking in deep breaths, he winced at the pain in his head. The street was dimly lit by gas lamps and as he aimlessly and absentmindedly observed the scene beneath him, he suddenly squealed quietly at what had just entered his vision. A stocky man in a heavy coat and large hat was leading a dragon up the street on a long, stout leather lead. The dragon wasn't huge, perhaps four metres long from the tip of its horned nose to the end of its scaley barbed tail, but it was big enough and Chatty shivered at the sight of it. With his eyes almost bulging out of his head, the poor Prince leaned back into the room and gave himself a stout slap, then squeezed his eyes tight shut, shook his head like an animal emerging from a river and returned to the window. The dragon was still there, just a few yards further along. Chatty whimpered again.

Its wings appeared modest in size, for pulled in tight to the body, they didn't touch the ground as it walked. The spikes on its back looked vicious and sharp, its clawed feet were large but nearly silent and as it rounded the corner and vanished, Chatty squeezed his eyes shut to fix the image there. "Oh, by all that is Earthly – a dragon!" he whispered. "A dragon walks the streets of Prague!" His eyes were wide open with a mixture of shock and fear and his chin had fallen to a new low, almost resting on his chest and for someone all too able to look a bit dopey under normal circumstances, this was by far his most dimwitted of bearings.

Something caught his ear and he turned the other way to see a rider on horseback. The horse itself was dappled grey, rather large and to his eye, a particularly fine specimen with a leaning towards speed. The rider matched his horse, appearing tall and athletic, strong certainly, although exquisitely crafted armour – engraved in a fine pattern which suggested great wealth and gave it a dull, silky sheen – covered what appeared to be muscular limbs. On his head he wore a matching helmet with the visor up, though Chatty could not see any detail of the rider's face. His sword was sheathed on the right flank of the horse and Chatty recognised the whole as being something obvious to all, but rather rare, an actual and completely proper Knight. Not one of the plentiful Knights whose only qualification was by title, having been granted the moniker along with large estates as royal thanks for donating serfs and taxes to the King, but a proper one with strength and fighting skill and quite plainly, bravery in big bucketloads. He understood the Knight to be brave for Chatty was well aware of the obvious contrast between the two of them. While his teeth chattered with fear and his legs felt like jelly and he very much wanted to go to the toilet, the Knight was casually stalking the fearsome, fire-breathing beast. True, the Knight wasn't directly confronting it, at least not yet, but he was following it and staying far enough back not to attract the attention of either the beast itself or its keeper. True too that the dragon wasn't the giant house-sized monster of classical paintings, but it was big enough. Its claws were vicious enough to pluck out some royal ribs, the spikes on its back could slice a man in two, the barbs on its tail looked deadly enough to whip off a head with a swish and a crack and its teeth would be big enough to bite off a Prince's arm in one solitary chomp. And if that wasn't enough, it didn't take much in the way of fire to make the average Prince drop his sword and run away and anyway, how did you fight something that was longer than a very big cow and could fly around your head shooting flames at you from a safe, circular holding pattern? His tummy gurgled. The toilet beckoned more urgently. He belched in an ominous sickly way which tasted ghastly, then did a little squelchy bottom burp which threatened a pooey disaster and clenching everything in fear, felt a drop of wee emerge. He moaned as he shuffled towards the commode. Fighting the dragon tomorrow might not only end in his demise, but his reputation would be in tatters. *"Did you see the dragon kill that foreign Prince?"* one onlooker would say, *"Yes, just after he wet himself, pooed his pants and let out a giant liquid scream!"* another would answer.

After a while attending to the chamber pot he stumbled around the bed and plopping heavily down on it in a seated position, another shudder went through him causing him to let out a noise more commonly heard from small girls accidentally standing on a crunchy snail.

Gathering himself up, Chatty hauled himself to a standing position and swayed, then walked to the corner of the room and with difficulty, lifted the heavy broadsword he had placed there earlier. "In a few hours' time I will need you Swordy!" he sounded very drunk, even to himself. "All along I had hoped you would just be for show, but it seems you will be needed for actual mortal combat and I can't promise that my first real go at being a warrior won't end with me a charred and smouldering corpse..." He frowned, swayed, raised his eyebrows and breathed awkwardly like he wasn't sure how. "This is what you get for being so brave in front of people! For speaking such folly about what you were intending to do! Now you actually have to do it! Idiot with a big mouth!" He cursed himself and his false bravado and drew another big breath to steady his nerves. It worked. After visiting such misery upon the poor chamber pot and gulping great lungfuls of the cold night air, his brain was found some clarity.

He pondered about the brave Knight but found no solace. Chatty would be saved from a fiery death If the mystery Knight would slay the dragon for him, but then, where would be his own glory? Something else had overtaken him too; the idea that in slaying the dragon he must inevitably win the heart of the Princess. Surely this was his destiny? And no sooner had the notion planted itself, that it took root and became his all-consuming purpose. This was something about Chatty's character he did not recognise in himself but which all his friends knew well. He could suddenly have an idea and be certain it was the only thing in the whole world that mattered. Then the next day, he would have a new one, often quite different, sometimes entirely opposite to his last and there would be no sense of contradiction, no awareness that he'd shifted his position after being so single-minded. Tonight's new and all-consuming certainty was that his entire existence had solely been preparation for his arrival here in Prague, and that his purpose in life was to save, then marry, Princess Petra.

He swayed, the alcohol was back and still very drunk, he hiccupped and muttered, "I may be a pick bittled, a pit bickled, a pick pickled but I know what I must dooo." He pointed towards the window. "Slay that Princess and marry that dragon!" and because he wasn't listening to his actual words, he didn't feel obliged to correct himself.

He let out a harrumph and adopted a very grumpy face. There was a new and unexpected obstacle in his way. How could he hope to win Princess Petra's heart if this magnificent fellow was the hero instead? If the mysterious Knight slayed the dragon he might well save Chatty's life in the process but his thunder would be well and truly stolen! Sadness absorbed him, his moods at the mercy of what such a vast quantity of wine was doing to his brain. Maybe he wasn't made for thunderous deeds?

Chatty stood up again, leaving that miserable notion behind and shook himself to muster some determination. Taking several deep and painful breaths to clear his mind and concentrating, he addressed his sword, managing to sound less intoxicated again, "The very heart of a Princess is at stake here. And not just any Princess but the perplexingly stunning Princess Petra's heart. Her very life may rest in my hands – or possibly that other Knight fellow's – and as you and I have always known down deep, deep down – down, down, deeper and down… from the earliest contemplation, from the Viennese-ese-ese outset of this quest, it is what *I* was born to do!" he thumped his chest and coughed, wincing, having done it a bit hard. "Me and you Swordy! Not Mr Big-And-Beefy Knight carrying on like all of my annoying brothers and being good at everything all the time! It is you and I who must slay the dragon, no one else. My fate is to be the one who tries dying, I mean dies trying, or wins hair-maiden's fart, I mean wins fair-maiden's heart!" And having resolved himself to fight the dragon, he hurried to the chamber pot once more, whimpering, "Oh bladder, oh bowel, more warning please! How am I to fight with you two so set against me?"

Chapter the Sixteenth.
To the King!

Shoshama rose early and silently and lighting just one small stub of candle, began to dress in the near dark. She pulled on the trousers she wore for horse riding, then for her top half, a series of comfortable layers which wouldn't restrict her movement. The finished ensemble was boyish in style, but even with her hair wound up into a small woollen hat, she remained uncommonly girlish. She was a girl and she looked like one no matter what. For example, had she chosen to complicate her disguise with a theatrical moustache, her delicate face and smooth skin would make her look like young woman with a stick-on moustache, no one would be fooled. But her aim this morning was not to be someone else, merely to merge into the shadows and be able to creep silently and smoothly.

Opening her valise, she reached deep inside and unzipped a separate compartment from which she removed a sheathed dagger. She slid it out and regarded its blade glinting faintly next to the flickering little candle flame; fine on one side, serrated on the other. It looked vicious and biting her lip, she slid it back into its sheath and made to return it to her valise, paused and then pulling up her top layers of clothing, wound the long straps around her ribs and tummy to secure it in the small of her back. She checked she could reach it by quickly unsheathing it once more, then gingerly replaced it and lowered her loose clothing over it. Shoshama swivelled in front of the mirror and nodded to her shadowy reflection in approval. The dagger was hidden.

Tiptoeing across the floor she descended the stairs to the floor below her lodgings. The Wifes were fast asleep two floors below, the rumbling, gargling and snorting of House's snoring blending with that of Mister's contented, rhythmic hum. He sounded pleased during his sleep while House spent most of the night fighting for oxygen as if she was chewing a mixture of iron bars and large pebbles. Shoshama paused and satisfied herself neither had been disturbed by her movements. She placed her hands on the door to the wine cellar and as she'd expected, found it was locked. Reaching carefully into the nearby chest of drawers she then located the key in its usual place. As quietly as the old lock would allow, she opened the thick oak door and once ajar, returned the key to its home. She entered and lit a candle, negotiating her way past the stacks of wooden crates and crossing to the back of the room in silence, her soft-soled shoes perfect for the task. Pulling the curtain gently aside, she took hold of the large key in the door to the castle and paused, suddenly experiencing the sensation that she was being watched. The hairs on the back of her neck stood up and a shiver ran down her spine. She turned slowly to look behind her and seeing there was no one there, with a gasp, released the breath she'd been unaware she was holding. "Shoshama! Get a grip!" she hissed on the outbreath and followed it with some deep breaths in. "I'm not even in the castle and I'm already nearly wetting myself!" she whispered, smiling and releasing some of the tension. Shoshama had expected to see House or Mister or both standing in the landing doorway and watching her with concerned faces. She didn't expect they would stop her, but she wanted the extra certainty that her entry to the castle would not be prevented by any well-meaning concern for her safety or to be delayed while they cooked up some alternative plan to introduce her to the King in a week or two. "I'm going in!" she said quietly to the absent host and hostess. Uncertain quite what she was going to find on the other side of the door, she once again felt for the dagger under her top, running a finger from the pommel to the ferrule and wrapping her fingers around it tightly. Comforted by the purchase offered by the leather grip, she let go, withdrawing her hand from under her clothing and patting herself on her hard rump. "Okay Princess, let's get this show on the road!"

Grasping the large key, Shoshama twisted it and unlocked the door that connected the House of Rock to the castle. Then, raising the candle to her lips she blew it out as she didn't want to show a light in the wine cellar when she entered. She gently pulled the door ajar just enough to lithely curl around it, closed it slowly by small degrees and leaned back on it in like a kind of anchor in the pitch black. With her left hand on the hilt of her dagger once more, she strained her ears, searching for any sounds. Who might be here? What creature guarded so valuable a collection? How might her discovery by a mercurial-mannered King, famous for the worst of reasons, be treated? She swallowed hard. All she could hear was the frantic beating of her own heart, made worse by the woolly hat pulled down over her ears.

***

Adalbert peeled open bleary eyes and blinked. Shafts of light angled into the room as the door was pushed ajar. A head poked around it, but Adalbert's brain always took a few moments to engage first thing in the morning and for the time being, he had no idea where he was. Something akin to the wispy recollections of a dream lingered some-where in his consciousness and with it came an underlying realisation that everything about his topsy-turvy existence made even less sense than usual. He was aware that he was conflicted, pulled between happiness and its opposite but couldn't as of yet, remember quite why. "Breakfast order!" called out a voice as the figure strode across the dark room. Adalbert knew he liked the owner of the voice but in his murky, half-waking state, couldn't quite place him. Then the curtains were pulled back dislodging a couple of rats which tumbled to the carpet and scampered away and the King said, "And look at that sunshine! It's going to be a glo-rious day!" A rat peeked out from behind Adalbert's pillow and blinked at the bright light. Adalbert stretched his long arms out and yawned while the rat sniffed his ear. The King's beaming smile was every bit as glorious as the day he had heralded, and as Adalbert slowly came to his senses and recognised his companions and surroundings, he felt a great deal of joy. He was happier than he could ever remember.

***

Darius arrived a few minutes ahead of crack of sparrow expecting to be first. He wasn't. Instead, he was amazed to come upon a great throng of people. A crowd was alter-nately clapping and cheering some activity at their centre and to one side two carriages with painted signs on them announcing *Prague Daily Herald and Tribune* on the one and *The City Times* on the other, showed that the press was in attendance. Darius pressed through to find Prince Chatty at the centre in a costume which included a shiny breast-plate and stout gloves and boots. In his gloved fist he clutched a large sword and appeared to making a variety of courageous poses, each eliciting a cheer from the people in the crowd. He looked more comical than usual, the sword having been originally fashioned for some mighty warrior while Chatty was sufficiently shorter than average to warrant a smaller sword, not one twice the size and clearly too heavy for the compact Prince to handle deftly.

Two female newspaper reporters with tight clothes and big hair (both Deep Purple as was the fashion), were talking directly to their assistants who busily scribbled down every exaggerated description the young women could dream up, while an artist concentrated on painting Chatty in the best of the poses he adopted and having a limited variety of brave stances, it was one he returned to most frequently.

"Chatty?" called Darius as he burst into the centre of the crowd.

"Darius! Old friend! Today is the day! It has come!" cried Chatty, who hearing his own words, pulled a face of anguish.

"What on Earth are you doing? What is all this?" asked Darius, sweeping a hand around the crowd. The reporters were rapidly describing the arrival of the extremely handsome stranger with the most glorious of suntans and who was dressed in an expensive designer white suit with a mother of pearl sheen topped with a matching white hat (brown ribbon to match his tan) and white shoes made from some exotic, glistening snakeskin.

"I have no idea! I didn't tell a soul, honestly!" Chatty didn't look convincing so Darius maintained a kind of stern eye-contact and waited, "Well, actually I told a few people what I hoped to do today, you know, rescue Princess Petra, slay the dragon…" he waved his sword a little pathetically and suddenly looked a bit scared again. Darius groaned loudly with exasperation and Chatty jumped straight back in, "But honestly, I didn't mutter a word about where we were meeting, or when, or anything!" Chatty was unaware in his loud and intoxicated state, that he'd been overheard by the bartender in the Grand Velky Hotel. Darius stood hands on hips shaking his head. "In fact, I didn't mention you at all," said Chatty.

"No, that much I can believe," said Darius and just then a brass band started up and everyone looked around to see the arrival of the Mayor in the company of the Chief of Police, the Sergeant plus Tom, Dick, Harry and Jim. There was confusion on the Mayor's face but, true professional that she was, she greeted everyone by name and gave each a beaming smile and in between, just seemed more perplexed than anything else.

"Golly! Wh-who-who's that?" sputtered Chatty.

"That," he said, pointing the way someone might summon one of Mr Schindler's *Stairfree-People-Lifters* (which frightened nearly everyone who entered and all of whom agreed it needed a new name), is the entire Prague Police Department and the Mayor,"

"G-golly! Which one's the Mayor?" Chatty was oddly transfixed.

"I'll give you a clue; the one *not* wearing a Police uniform."

"Well, that I'd like to see!" said Chatty, making no sense at all – but not for the first time. The Prague Police Force had halted, while the Mayor continued her approach.

Chatty froze solid like a statue as the Mayor addressed Darius. "I see we are approaching the castle en-masse. Are you sure that will help our cause? And is this your hired Knight?" she waved a floppy wrist at Chatty, who took it and kissed it lavishly, with a *'Madam,'* which pleased her visibly.

"Oh!" she said, almost singing it.

Darius provided a formal introduction, "Mayor, meet Prince Charles of Egham, from the Kingdom of the Angles, Saxons and Celts across the sea from Frankia. Charles, allow me to introduce the Mayor of the great city of Prague. This fine lady has been very helpful in furthering our mutual cause of locating the inestimably beautiful Princess Petra along with the missing children."

Chatty bowed, slightly too far given the weight of the pieces of armour he was wearing about his chest and shoulders and Darius had to help him straighten back up. Returning to upright, he was bright red from the exertion and this time with something resembling a curtsy, he said, "It's the greatest imaginable honour to meet you oh great Mayor of..." he hesitated, did his dim look, "all this cityness over which you Mayorise with supreme... Mayorness! Your city is magnificent, as is your magnificence as a marvellous Mayorlady and I will remember it and you, for the rest of my days," he gulped, "Or day," he said, looking glumly thoughtful, "I mean the rest of today. Maybe just an hour or so in fact!" and went pale. "Anyway, call me Chatty for however many minutes we have left."

The Mayor leaned in close to Darius, "The Kingdom of the Angles, Saxons and Celts across the sea from Frankia?" Darius nodded, "You haven't told him about...?"

"The deportation of your criminals?" asked Darius, this time she nodded, "Not a word. Knowing what I do of Chatty's peoples, I think they are a rag-tag-bagatelle of eccentrics, geniuses and down-to-earth common folks with a taste for ale and a penchant for a punch-up. There's probably no one you could send who wouldn't blend in perfectly well."

The Mayor paused for a moment reflecting on what Darius had shared in such a casual manner and looked at Chatty with some curiosity. "Really?" she said, relieved. The Mayor mustered herself, "So what is the plan Inspector?" Her name for Prince Darius puzzled Chatty and he frowned, not out of confusion, but annoyed someone knew something he wasn't party to. "I expected a quiet approach of our delegation and a high-level request for the King's cooperation. Are we to threaten him now? A Prince from a foreign power going armed to meet our King?" she waved a limp wrist at Chatty which he grabbed once more and kissed as lavishly as the first time. The Mayor's eyes flashed with delight, she giggled quietly and her hips traced a little impromptu circle. Then, catching herself, she adopted something of an angry glare which she directed at Chatty, though even he could detect there was something contradictory in her eyes.

"Swordy is for the dragon only, not to endangerise the King, nor any other subjects of the realm of the son of Wood-King, Wing-Could, Gone King Senseless!" blurted Chatty panicking.

The Mayor led Darius to one side, leaving Chatty to pose for his portrait. There, Darius confirmed, "He means Good King Wenceslas."

"I had assumed so from the start," said the Mayor. "Why does nature so often bestow a person an asset but then deprive them of something else crucial? It's as if she can never finish a perfect pie without throwing a Brussel's sprout in the recipe to make everyone gag!" she regarded Darius like a pie for a moment and added, "Yours is your ache-making reticence." She continued to imagine eating Darius pie for a moment and then turned her hungry gaze on Chatty. "Is he always this way? Of course he isn't, what am I saying!"

"No, no. Actually, he mostly is!"

"So… which is he, eccentric, genius or down-to-earth common folk with a taste for ale and a penchant for a punch-up?" she scratched her head, wondering.

"Well, I'd say he's most of those and that he's a thoroughly well-meaning leap-before-you-look sort of chap." She raised her eyebrows and eyed Chatty further. Still striking poses, he swung his sword about and managed to hack himself with the flat of the blade. Chatty let out a loud ouch to which the assembled crowd laughed, believing he was playacting. Darius noticed that the Mayor made to step forward but then restrained herself. "I wouldn't allow your impression of Prince Chatty to influence you with regard to your opinion of an entire nation! You ought to meet Prince Adalbert before making your mind up," suggested Darius.

"How is that Prince any better than this one?" she asked. "Can he compose entire intelligible sentences?"

"Not really one of his strong points. He's more an alternative than someone directly superior I'd say."

"And is he here somewhere? Will I meet him?" she said, still staring at Chatty, who blushed even more if that was at all possible, in fact he was blushing so much, he looked like he might need to go to the toilet.

"Actually yes, Prince Adalbert is here... well, he's supposed to be, although I haven't heard from him. I also have a third friend hereabouts somewhere..." Darius's voice tailed off as he scanned the crowd. Could either Adalbert or Shoshama be here somewhere incognito?

The Mayor followed his gaze as he scanned the crowd, "What is your detectivy mind doing? I just see a mob comprised of those nosey-parker reporters and a load of Praguers, mostly of the upper orders."

"Upper orders, as in the most wealthy?"

"And often the most useless and lazy too. Not one of them could build a house or a bridge like Mr Mason could, or conjure up a wooden barrel to keep wine like Mr Cooper can, or turn some wood into a wheel like Mr Right, or make wonderful arrows like Mr Fletcher, all manner of everything black and iron like..."

"Mr Smith, by any chance?" interrupted Darius.

"You've met him? Wonderful man, if a little sooty and sweaty, but those are qualities I find oddly appealing in a man, don't ask me why…" and once again the Mayor was in a dreamworld and curiously, allowed her eyes to scan Chatty again, who immediately blushed. Darius frowned. Surely this could not be what it seemed.

Darius brought her back into the conversation with what he suspected might be a clever question, "Why does Mrs Gregory do the baking and not Mr Baker?"

"Oh, you'd have no way of knowing would you? Mr Baker died, that's her husband and so she had to take her maiden name again."

"Oh I see," nodded Darius slightly flabbergasted that his logical assumption had scored a bullseye.

"Who else have you met?"

"Oh no one really," he replied.

"Mr Woodward?" she offered, "The very handsome Edward himself!"

"Your forester perhaps?"

"Indeed, so you *have* met him! Mr Timothy Tapper?"

"Makes wine," said Darius smiling cautiously.

"Absolutely! Mr Wainwright and his son Wayne?"

"They make wagons and put Mr Wright's wheels on them." said Darius, feeling hopeful.

"Goodness! Mr Arkwright?"

"Wooden chests!" said Darius, with a confident flourish.

"Yes!" she said, "Oh and his daughter Jenny is such a wonderful ballet dancer!"

"Does Mr Goddard herd goats by any chance?" asked Darius.

"Well you obviously know he does so that's another one to you. When did you meet him? He lives several-plus-several kilometres out of the city except every first Monday of the month when it's market day!" Darius shrugged, having a little fun with the game. "In that case, have you also met Mr Shepherd?"

"Ha! Keeps sheep!"

"He does, but I dare say you met him with Lonny Goddard. Did you also meet Pat Coward?"

"Oh good old *Cow-Pat* Coward the cowman?" Darius guessed.

The Mayor was clearly flabbergasted, "You are a mysterious man Inspector! Just one more, someone you wouldn't want to meet and as he keeps very much to himself I'd be very surprised if you'll have the foggiest idea; Mr Kellogg?"

"Pork butcher!"

"In one!" she said loudly, her hands cupping her wide face. "Is there anyone you haven't met?"

"I haven't met Mr Brewer who makes ale."

"But clearly you've heard of the man," she interjected.

"And I've yet to encounter Mr Weaver who I imagine is involved in clothmaking." Darius was enjoying this game tremendously.

The Mayor, shook her head, "Nooo, maybe you're thinking of Mr Webber? He's our principal cloth manufacturer and Sunny is here somewhere, I've seen him with Nancy, his wife." This threw Darius completely and he silently repeated their names.

"Do they have a daughter named Wendy?"

"See? You _do_ know them!"

"Wendy Webber?" he asked. She nodded. "And Sunny Webber?" She nodded again, a little more confused. "And Nancy Webber?"

The Mayor stared. "Are you alright?" Darius shook his head laughing and confirmed he was very alright. "Anyway Inspector!" barked the Mayor and turning serious again, "This will never do. All these people cannot go to the castle." And with that she waved over the Chief of Police. He walked towards them with his hands clasped behind his back. Seeing him walk off, his Sergeant adopted the same posture and followed a few paces in his wake and one by one, Tom, Dick, Harry and Jim all waddled over in exactly the same manner and all equidistant from each other.

"Not much chance of a quiet or private approach now." said the Chief, officiously. "The press is here nosey-poking and blabberpraddling and then there are all these echer-up-palongs of society here too. They're not going away without some entertainment." Said the Chief.

"I'm sorry, I didn't keep up with all of that," said Darius,

The Chief raised an eyebrow, "Which bits?"

"Blabber….?"

"You don't know blabberpraddling? The Angles like inventing new words, Germanic folks just join all the words together to make them longer and we Praguers join them together and then abbreviate them. News reporters blabberpraddle because they blabber-press-twaddle. They don't speak the language as we know it. You, a normal person, might say you saw an old lady sneeze, news reporters say, *'Ancient mystery woman explodes in near-death gooey-snot-fest catastrophe shock!'* That's blabberpraddling."

Darius gave a begrudging nod of approval. Prague might be an odd place, but it seems a journalists had *blabberpraddling* in common the world over. "Would it really be so bad?" Darius asked, "I mean, if we all go up there… the press watching, these rich city folk with nothing to do all day, the entire police department with nothing to do all day…" The Chief coughed disapprovingly and Darius gave him an affectionate little slap on the shoulder, "…you Madam Mayor, and Chatty tucked away behind us so as to cause no offence, wouldn't it help things along a little… maybe just a bit?"

The Mayor was resolute, "No Inspector, I'm saying no. We can't afford to upset the King."

Now it was the Chief's turn, "Maybe people can do this

kind of thing where you come from all that way down south, but not here Inspector," he said, pointing in entirely the wrong direction, then compounding it by trying several others, "South, er, south, south!" omitting the only remaining direction which was actually south as identified by Darius with a discrete tummy-level point. "We have a law in Prague," continued the Chief, "And right now we are all in danger of breaking it. That's the Mayor and the whole police department all on the very cusp,"

"We're on the very precipice of having to arrest each other!" added the Sergeant.

"Or ourselves! Easier for the paperwork," said the Chief.

"I intended to arrest myself!" said the Sergeant, "Then resist arrest and say, '*You're only making things worse for yourself*' and '*Leave it out, I ain't done nuffing wrong!*' and '*Law number 15; lying to a Police officer. The charges are piling up Sonny Jim!*' and then, '*You got the wrong man! That's Jim over there!*' which would be my master-stroke enabling me to slip away in the crowd!" The group regarded him in confused wonder, except for Chatty who nodded enthusiastically at each step of the brilliant plan.

"What law?" asked Darius, breaking the fresh silence, "What law could we possibly be breaking by asking these simple questions? And what's the word you use here when the Police talk nonsense? *Jabbercoppiffle?*"

They all nodded solemnly, "Yes Inspector, but that's beside the point. It's law number 67, disturbing the Status Quo," said the Chief in his most officious voice.

"Disturbing the Status Quo" echoed the Police Sergeant.

"The Status Quo, " continued the Chief, "The very rock our entire society is founded upon. Without the Status Quo, all sorts of idiotic nonsense can take root. The Status Quo keeps us true, stops us falling for silly fads and fashions and Ewe-Chew-Sensations!"

"Falling for what sensations now?" said Darius, getting used to asking these sorts of questions.

"You're not familiar with Ewe-Chew-Sensations? It's what we call silly new fads because when fools talk rubbish, they look like lady-sheep chewing grass." The Chief attempted a strange little impression of a female sheep chewing grass. It wasn't convincing, but it did look pathetic enough to make sense of the intended insult.

Darius led Chatty away to confer for a moment. "Chatty dear chap," he said cheerily, then gritting his teeth and squinting with angry eyes and a fixed glare, he continued as politely as he could, "I'm afraid the arrangement I went to great lengths to make has been completely ruined by the arrival of all these voyeurs! My plans are wrecked!" Chatty, quite used to being blamed for spoiling things – mostly because he was the one who actually did spoil things in this way – adopted an exaggerated *oops* face, to which he added an exaggerated verbal *oops!* For effect. The Mayor and the Chief approached, giving Darius no time to speak to Chatty any further. "Thank you Chief! Thank you Mayor! Let's all go home shall we?" and as the Chief shouted through a wooden loudhailer that the party was over and there was nothing to see and that the crowd should disperse or he and his men would be forced to throw rabbit droppings at everyone to disband them, the crowd did indeed begin to drift away and after a polite bow to the Mayor and a *good day* style nod to the Chief, Darius once again led Chatty away with a firm grip on his arm.

The Mayor called after them, "Bye then," in a slightly forlorn tone and under her breath muttered, "Men! Promise a girl excitement and adventure and at the last minute, what do you get? Latency and disappointment." She stomped her feet a little as she walked and butterflies swirled as she disturbed the grass. Then loudly enough to cause the last few people, including the Princes, to turn, she shouted, "Fingerbuns!" and was happy again that she had plans for the morning after all. The reporters watched people disperse in various directions and looked lost but having consulted the *Reporters Handbook*, climbed aboard their wagons and headed off for an alcoholic breakfast.

As the grassy area cleared there was one odd moment when Chatty, still being tugged along briskly by Darius, turned to look behind him and saw the Mayor doing the same. She hooked a little finger in the corner of her mouth and gave him a stilted little wave. Had it been on film, it would have been rendered in slow-motion for the benefit of an equally slow audience.

Darius continued pulling Chatty along, the latter stumbling a little here and there. "Sorry Darius old bean!" said Chatty very apologetically, "I had no idea all those people were going to spoil things. Where are we going? This isn't the way back is it?" Having been marching away from the others at quite a pace for a while now, they finally stopped. Darius looked over his shoulder and satisfied that people were far enough out of sight, they changed course back up to the castle.

"Come on, we're still going, you and I. We're doing it with or without the batty Mayor and the double batty Prague Police Force." They were walking so fast Chatty had to take occasional skipping steps to keep up.

"Golly, the Mayor is something isn't she!" Darius looked at Chatty sideways, "What's the hurry my dear Prince Darius and what's all this *Inspector* business anyhoo?"

"I want to get there before the Gregory's ladies deliver breakfast and the *Inspector business* was my cover. And it worked by the way. Everything I've achieved has been through that guise. Until…"

"I know, until *I* turned up, silly old me again! Well I bally well ruin most things so it's all par for the course," he said glumly, his face showing his sadness. Then he beamed again and repeated himself, "Golly, the Mayor is something isn't she!" hoping for a better reaction from Darius.

"She'd eat you for *braahkfaahsht!*" he said, doing his best to adopt the strange local, guttural way these things were sometimes said.

"Would she?" asked Chatty excitedly, not reacting to Darius's odd voice at all, "Would she really? Do you think so?" Darius stopped and stood in front of him and looked at him with a *What-am-I-going-to-do-with-you?* face that Chatty recognised as something bad causing him to look very sad again. Darius gripped Chatty's shoulders and shaking him lightly as he said, "Oh for goodness' sake! Don't fret. I'm a bit angry that's all. Look, you weren't to know my plan, and maybe, if we can get ourselves in it'll be alright after all. Maybe you haven't spoiled anything."

"Really?" said Chatty looking up a little. "Oh I do hope so!"

"Well who knows how it would have turned out with the Mayor and the Chief. I swear they are all bonkers you know! This whole place is bonkers! It could still turn out fine." And with that, they hurried on again and soon caught sight of the Gregory's ladies and the big handcart being pulled by boys tethered like horses at its front. "Goodness!" said Darius at the sight.

"I say!" said Chatty, "Dashed odd."

"That's Prague for you," said Darius as he increased his pace to catch them.

Chapter the Seventeenth.
Convergence Part i

When she was certain she had waited long enough and was definitely alone, Shoshama lit one of her candles. She had stared into the pitch black sufficiently long to know there was no light at all in this vast cavern. Her eyes hadn't adjusted to the darkness one iota but straining them had produced odd flashes of colour in the nothing and combined with the tap-tapping of tiny rodent feet on flagstones she could bear it no longer. There before her was the dazzling glare of the flickering flame. She could also see the hand that held the candleholder at the end of her outstretched arm and looking around, Shoshama heard her own neck creak. There were the racks and barrels to either side while down below were the shiny flagstones and her feet in silent, comfortable shoes. Beyond that was an eery and pure kind of darkness which pulsated black as her own candle blinded her. She needed to know where the exit was and which way she should go and rooting herself to the spot meant she could see nothing beyond her immediate vicinity but would allow anyone else in the cellar to see her easily. It was time to unstick herself and get moving.

Aware of a wide walkway crossing left to right just ahead, she crept towards it lightly and casting her light this way and that, elected to go right, but not before memorising her current position lest she needed to retrace her steps. The rack to her right was marked *Thirteen* on the end in convenient wooden braille. She estimated the distance back to the door in case she had to do it in the dark, perhaps 15 metres. After a walk of perhaps 50 or 60 metres she passed a rack numbered *Twenty-Six* and reached a wall of dusty bottles in a wine rack which rose way above her head and far to each side. This was not the way out, rather it was a dead end. She turned and headed back down the walkway, passing *Thirteen* where she joined it and counting down to *one*. Beyond that first rack, she found a steep wooden staircase which climbed up and to the right, which she ascended slowly and quietly. It had a safety rail which she grasped once but which creaked loudly, so she let it go, concentrating on quietly stepping and counting. Reaching 39, she arrived at a wooden platform to the left side of which was a large door through the end wall of the huge cellar. If this was locked she would be stumped. She would have access to more wine than she thought existed in the whole known world, but her plan to enter the castle-proper would be at an end. The door had a large iron ring for a handle and twisting it she heard it clunk loudly and come free. She would be able to pull it open now, but instead she froze, waiting to hear if the noise had attracted attention.

Nothing.

Cracking the door a fraction, she peeked around and saw a corridor, dark but not completely so and this prompted Shoshama to blow out her candle. She opened the door a little more, just wide enough for her slender form to curl round and entered the corridor. There were stone walls, substantial wooden doors and another staircase at the end which doubled back around on itself. This still felt like the cellars and seemed thoroughly deserted so Shoshama headed to the stairs and climbed again. "Sixteen," she said silently, reassuring herself that she had mentally mapped her escape route.

At the top she froze, certain her ears had detected the first significant sounds. Somewhere in the distance she could just make out the incongruous noises of children laughing and shouting playfully. If these were the kidnapped orphans, they didn't sound too unhappy about it. She followed the sound cautiously along this next corridor, passing more doors left and right and recognising she was now two floors above the wine cellar. At the end was yet another door and it was through this one that the sounds were coming, yet still only very faintly – she didn't expect to find children on the other side – but she was getting closer. The same ornate twisted black iron ring was the door handle, perhaps 20 cm in diameter and lifting it and turning it, she opened the door. Again, it made a noise when lifting the latch but Shoshama felt confident that the children were still too far away to hear the clunk.

Here the light was better still because a small window, set high on the facing wall above a further door which led to the outside, cast angled bright shafts where specs of dust orbited. More stairs led up from the left and while her ears told her this was her route to the children, something else caught her eye. Hung on pegs to her right was the strangest costume. She stepped closer and touched it. A thick and shiny, heavily textured material was fashioned into a bizarre and unrecognisable shape. There were colours to it ranging from a dark metallic green to areas of glossy red. Soft triangles emerged here and there as did something resembling a leg... and a foot... with claws. She stretched it out and gasped, for it was suddenly, quite obviously, a dragon costume. Opening it released some odour and it was animal not human, for the shape was nothing a person might wear and as she quietly and gently stretched it this way and that, she wondered how it might be used and what manner of animal might wear it. This was surely the truth behind the sightings of the famous dragon and the children it had eaten were playing cheerily somewhere upstairs. Shoshama smiled, pleased with her sleuthing thus far.

Suddenly, a snort came from the other side of a door adjacent to the pegs on which the costume hung and as a chill went up her spine, every hair on her body stood on end. The noise was not human and whatever beast made the noise, it was just a metre or so away on the other side of the door. It snorted again, then made a more guttural sound and Shoshama, realising this thing, whatever it was, might be sniffing her right now, lowered the costume slowly to the floor and backed away towards the stairs. It snorted once more, coughed and then groaned, deeply and maybe even a little sadly. Shoshama took several more cautious steps backwards. Petrified it might come crashing through the door at any moment she kept her eyes fixed on it and felt for her dagger in the small of her back. Her hand gripped the hilt and as she stepped back again she reached the bottom of the steps with her heels. Now she would turn silently and climb the stairs, but before she could do so, she was grabbed roughly from behind. One strong hand grabbed her left wrist which was already behind her back and jerked it upwards while another arm reached around under her right armpit and clasped her mouth. Both her arms were thus immobilised and the hand over her mouth stifled Shoshama 's surprised cry. She felt a foot jab in behind her knee collapsing a leg and dropping her to the floor on her knees, her assailant standing on one of her calves to keep her down. She wriggled once but was completely overpowered. Shoshama whimpered with frustration and slumped. Her rescue mission was over.

***

The Gregory's' ladies looked nervously at each other and even though Darius assured them he and Chatty were on official business, this didn't seem to settle their discomfort. The cart was almost as big as a carriage for people but was racked out to hold a great many cloches all heated by oil burning safety lamps. The smell of bacon and eggs was almost overpowering and Darius reached in to lift a cloche, "No!" said one of the ladies, anxiously. It was Daisy.

Darius recognised her and a moment of embarrassment affected him caused him to pause as he remembered her tittering in the Sandwich Emporium. He looked at her and saw fear in her eyes. His hand over the little knob, "I was just going to look, that's all."

"This is the King's property, you mustn't touch it." She looked desperate and the other ladies nodded in agreement, all seemingly very worried and seeking each other's faces for what to do. "We must go. We cannot be late!"

"All this is for the King?" Darius waved at the vast number of cloches, "How much breakfast can one man eat?" No one answered, but they did look conspiratorial. Darius lifted the lid to see a breakfast.

"No!" cried Daisy again pleadingly. Darius looked at her. Something was amiss. "Please!" she said, her eyes big, she looked at the cart and following her line of sight he identified a single cloche set above the others.

"The King's?" he asked pointing and reaching for it.

"No!" she shouted louder, "Please, please!" more desperate still.

"Stand back," he commanded her, which she did, close to tears, "Look it's alright," and with that lifted the lid to find a breakfast like the other one. And a folded paper note. He looked at the woman and saw her heart sink. She looked at the other ladies and they all wore that same, *it's over* expression. Darius unfolded the paper and read the handwritten note.

Corner of Týnská by the art gallery,
small girl says she is 4 with boy,
not her brother, maybe 18 months but who she looks after.
Another boy of 8 at Rytířská and Perlová,
a runaway whose parents died and
who was taken in by relatives who treat him badly.

"What's this?" asked Darius of the lady seemingly in charge, waving it at her, "What *is* this?" but Daisy said nothing and in any case he'd figured it out. "The Mayor doesn't know?" she shook her head, "The police don't know?" She confirmed this too. "Does Mrs Gregory know?" she shook her head. "So this," he waved the paper once more, "Is all you?"

"And the King," she said, "And the Princess."

"The Princess!" blurted Darius and Chatty in unison.

"Please, we must hurry. We cannot be late!"

Darius replaced the note, "Go!" they hesitated, "Go! I think it is probably a good thing you are doing, certainly well intentioned. Go!"

The boys in harness, silent and shuffling their feet for the last two minutes were instructed to move with the conventional clicking noises understood by horses and the cart lurched forward. "But the Mayor and the police?" pleaded Daisy.

"I'll attend to that," he said. She looked only partially relieved. "Trust me, it will be alright, I promise." The ladies left, moving faster to make up lost time.

"Will it be alright Darius?" asked Chatty as they watched them go.

"I don't know. I hope so."

"Great. Anyway, what's going on old chap? Fill me in would you because I really don't have the first, foggiest idea!"

***

While the King poured each of them a generous mug of tea and a flagon of ale, Adalbert took it upon himself to take the cloche from the King's breakfast before his own, significantly participating this morning rather than sitting and waiting for the King to determine the passage of events. He wasn't nervous today, just happy. He wasn't waiting to be chided, slapped or ridiculed, instead he was about to have a glorious breakfast with a great man he admired immensely.

The room was the same as the one they used the previous day, a dining room that might seat perhaps 20, with dark oak panelling on the walls and on the cosily low ceiling. Blue velour curtains hung heavily to the sides of the extensive leaded windows along the back wall while the other walls were occupied by a grand fireplace in which crackled a pleasant log fire needed only to waken the room after a night of emptiness, paintings of ancestors, a coat of arms and some nice-looking tapestries. Sunshine flooded in through the windows, one of which was open a few centimetres. Underfoot was a thick carpet, spongy and comfortable that extended to within two metres of all the walls.

Beyond the only door somewhere, there was a great deal of chatter, young, excited voices coming and going, their rapid footsteps combined with sounds made by plates, cloches and crockery. "Are those the other... the other, er...?" said Adalbert, as casually as he dared, searching for the right word.

"Occupants of the castle?" asked the King, giving him a quick glance as he busily sorted out condiments and serviettes for them both. Adalbert nodded, trying to appear only mildly interested. "All the poor little orphans. They eat like horses! Growing big and strong courtesy of the Crown."

"Only, they don't sound like prisoners," said Adalbert causing the King to furrow his brow as he considered the point. "When I was locked up, you said that if I cried out I would only be heard by other prisoners..." Adalbert mumbled a bit, feeling awkward about asking.

The King stopped his labours and levelled his eyes upon Adalbert. For a moment, Adalbert tried to look busy, but with insufficient to do he gave up and stared back. The King looked somewhere between sad and loving, Adalbert was loving and apologetic. Each understood this was uncharted territory, but that somehow they were safe with the other. "They aren't locked up – as you can well tell – they have the run of the castle but are not to go out nor appear on the battlements. Some people suspect they might be here but as many people believe they have been eaten by the mythical dragon."

"Mythical!" interrupted Adalbert, "But I heard it!"

"Ah, yes... Dragon exists and I'll introduce you today, but he wouldn't eat a child, don't think he'd even venture a little nip, as much as he looks frightening and can absolutely deafen you with his infernal hullaballoo when he gets excited or agitated. You know I actually tried to make him more aggressive, but I suppose it's not in his nature and I quickly gave up on that idea." Adalbert looked a bit perplexed, so reluctantly the King expanded on the point, "I couldn't be cruel to him, I suppose that's *my* nature coming out. In the end, we can improve, fettle, fine-tune, but underneath in our fundamental nature, we are what we are." There was a pause. They had started eating but now the King stopped and simply chewed sausage. In his left hand he held his fork and while gently thrusting in Adalbert's direction, he spoke earnestly, his eyes on his breakfast guest. "It's all a ruse of course, and not a very good one if you look closely, but no one did until you lot came along, you and that little Prince Charles fellow from your neck of the woods – Kingdom of the Angles, Saxons and Celts across the sea from Frankia – he's a friend of yours I suppose?" Adalbert nodded and quietly apologised, "Oh don't fret dear boy, our plan here was never robust enough, aside from a general fear of there being a dragon up here, it relied on locals staying precariously balanced between mild concern about the missing orphans and suspecting they were safe here so not wanting to upset the boat."

"Upset the *applecart*?" suggested Adalbert, who'd been accused of doing it most days as a child.

"Sort-of the same thing, it's an old nautical term I heard from a Genoese explorer."

"Oh, *rock* the boat?"

"No, I think you'll find the correct term is *upset*. Mind you, the chap was an extravagant liar, claiming to have discovered everywhere imaginable when we all know it was the Vikings who got there first. I've always thought explorers require extraordinary motivation to leave the safety and comfort of home and risk everything for… what? What could be better than what we have here in Prague, eh? So, it's inevitable that it would be the Vikings who would take to the stormy seas to escape their desolate land of non-deciduous forests and perpetual snow-bound darkness in search of the mythical land they call *Ibiza*."

"I don't think I've heard of that myth," said Adalbert dipping half a hash brown into his fried egg.

"The mythology claims it is a place of two halves; paradise and purgatory," the King became dramatic in his description, fluctuating his voice and making sweeping motions with his hands. "A land where sunshine and an azure sea promise serenity and tranquillity, but evil demons employ sinister and mystical magic to take a person's mind and reduce it to that of a weed in a meadow!"

"Golly! How awful!"

"People are enticed into caves by near naked strumpets and goblins who make promises of magic potions to lift the spirits but once inside, their eyes are filled by the glare of many pulsating suns, their ears pounded into submission by the rhythmic din of a thousand monsters stamping their great elephantine feet and howling in such pain that all human intelligence is expunged and the forever-lost souls, now held tight in the grip of insanity can do no more than sway like tall weeds in a windy meadow!"

"Well then!" barked Adalbert with a mouthful of food, "Sounds absolutely ghastly and I jolly well shan't be book-ing my holidays there! But the silly Vikings actually set off in search of this dodgy island you say?"

"When your land sees no sunshine from one season to another and no crops will grow because, well, have you ever tried planting seeds on a glacier? And you have to dig your-self out of last night's snowdrift just to take a poo, behind a cold tree, in the dark! Wouldn't you want to go somewhere sunny?"

"I would! But I'd stop when encountering a near-naked strumpet and refuse their offers to take my mind from me."

"Adalbert, you say that, but born with free will as all men are, the demonic strumpet appears as a lovely nymph! She catches your eye, she pouts and beckons you hither, she has something for you and one small step later you are forever doomed. Nature saw to it that men are gifted with a mind capable of building great structures, of breath-taking art, of soul-touching poetry, of fantastic, scientific invention, yet one glimpse of a sultry maiden can render them as helpless as a fish without water, gasping, blinking, defenceless."

"You speak as if the maiden is at fault dear King," said Adalbert, fascinated.

"Not at all, nature is at fault, or rather *at cause*. Nature's will is greater than our own, for the sweet and innocent maiden herself is captured by a warm smile, rendered stupid by a glance, energised and distracted by some aspect of a male torso." Adalbert shook his head faintly as if not able to understand the inferences. The King continued, still gesturing with his fork while eating his hot and tasty breakfast. "She busies herself with her daily toil, a basket over her forearm and thinking of nothing except the list of groceries needed for her dear mother. But… she spies a man in fine health working a plough in the baking sun, his muscles straining with his labour and she forgets the eggs, milk and flour needed for crepes. Or she passes by the forge and blackened and sweaty, the blacksmith hammers hot iron fresh from the furnace and wipes his dripping, soot-stained brow and all thoughts of tomatoes and beetroot vanish. Or passing the jetty to the Vltava River she comes upon a boat-builder whose companion is his trusty, patient dog and she joins the scruffy mutt in gazing upon his master adoringly as he delicately sculpts his perfectly curved stern post. Or she's passing an impressive manor house in the suburbs and inexplicably a fine fellow walks fully-clothed and drenched from a pond and the poor maiden faints on the spot from the soulful elation and aesthetic vibration she experiences deep amidst her mysterious loins."

"She does?" asked Adalbert, his mouth open, food visible.

"Mouth boy," suggested the King, demonstrating how to clamp a jaw shut.

"Your wisdom overwhelms me dear King. I fancy I should have been schooled here as a small boy and my life thus far might *not* have been so filled with folly, guffs and tragic errors of judgement."

"Ah! It is a man's place to regularly fall flat on his face. The skill is in making half of these events look deliberate and the other half appear painless." Adalbert regarded the King as he wiped a mixture of brown sauce and egg yolk up with his bread and felt reverence and along with it, some awe too. Breakfast filled his belly, conversing with the King filled his heart while the King's wisdom fed his eager, child-like mind. There was a pause in the conversation while they ate, so Adalbert asked again about the little children in the castle.

"The children are safe here, a blessed sight safer than on the streets, happier than they were in the orphanages and the other ones; the poor little blighters who were being mistreated, we've gathered them up too, continue to do so whenever we hear of their plight."

"Why though?" asked Adalbert, "I mean, why you? And why here in the castle?"

"Oh… that all goes back to…" Adalbert waited. The King looked up and then stared through the leaded window to some distant horizon. "Life can change from one thing to the opposite in the blink of an eye. It is like mythical Ibiza, paradise on one side, utter bedlam on the other. My wife the Queen was a little weak at times, but her condition had been stable and doctors said she would be fine as long as she didn't overexert. The next thing was to find Petra a husband, but she became increasingly opposed to the idea. The Queen begged me to delay but I was certain that when she met the right fellow all that soulful elation would churn away in her Princessy loins and her mind would surrender to nature's cause."

"She would lose her reason to the cause of love," said Adalbert, managing to keep up this time.

"The heart knows reason, that reason knows nothing of," recited the King, from some poetry or prose he'd learned long ago. He looked wistful for a moment, then continued, "So on Petra's 14th birthday, we had her meet all these splendid Princes we'd invited from all over the known world, including two of your brothers if I recall."

Adalbert said he remembered, "They returned raving about her beauty but also that she…"

"That she was difficult? Impossible? Rude?"

"That she rode away on horseback. That some cavalry and assorted Princes rode after her but that she was simply too fast for them." Adalbert watched the King closely. They had been on good terms for a couple of days now and while he had feared angering the King when he was first incarcerated, now it would pain him much more if he were to hurt the great man's feelings. "Was she too young to contemplate marriage?"

"She wouldn't contemplate it at all. The more we spoke of it, the more she insisted she would never marry in all her days. She was as unreasonable and irrational as only a woman can be when conversing with a man. It wasn't a matter of age you know. She was close to her mother, true, but not because she was still a little girl."

Adalbert scratched his head theatrically; he was anything but suave. "Perhaps she still might meet the right man?"

"You think not one of the 40 most eligible young men in the world might be right?" The King seemed amused by the question.

"Don't girls go through phases? I've heard people say, 'She's just going through a phase' when talking about a younger sister so maybe it's just a phase." Adalbert was patently no expert.

"Hmm. We can expect it to pass in a few decades perhaps," said the King playing devil's advocate for Adalbert. "She was antagonistic to marriage because she was completely indifferent to men and she was indifferent to men because she didn't admire them as something superior to womanhood, she competed with them with the intention of being better than them. I tell you Adalbert, there's nothing more dangerous than a woman who possesses all nature's advantages of womanhood while acquiring those few advantages available to a man. What does she want a man for if she's already more man than they are? She hunted with a bow, joined in swordsmanship when my soldiers trained and I mean with a proper steel sword, none of this wafting a foil about like an aristocrat! She wasn't going to *touché*, she was going to chop your bloody head off!" He laughed and smiled until it faded but there was adoration amongst the sadness. Adalbert was about to ask another question, but the King continued, "She still does all those things... and of course she rides a horse like you've never seen. If she were any King's son, he could not be prouder."

"Yet as a daughter, is she not beautiful beyond others? Does she not make you proud as your daughter?"

The King hesitated and made to speak more than once. A moment passed while he formed his thoughts. "I am proud just to know her. I find it implausible she is somehow *from me* because she is simply so much better than me." The King stood and taking his flagon of ale, crossed to the window and gazed out to the city below. A wagtail sailed past and the King followed its trajectory as it settled on the grass three floors below, identifying the bird to Adalbert affectionately. Adalbert thought about standing and joining him, but with their breakfasts almost finished, he was worried it would signal the end of things. What he wanted to ask was *'What shall we do today, Dad?'* but feared the answer. He saw the King smile at the scene below the window, a small chuckle almost emerged, but was contained. Adalbert imagined the wagtail was being especially entertaining on the grass below.

Still watching the world outside, the King continued his

account. "When she returned… this was after we searched for her, searched and searched to no avail, half the Kingdom scouring the forests and mountains, producing random village girls in the hope we'd pay them the reward money – like we didn't know our own daughter, the Princess! – and after her dear mother died of the illness all those eminent doctors failed to diagnose, she rode in to the courtyard early one morning looking taller, stronger and more fierce than ever and I dropped to my knee and begged her forgiveness." The King revolved his flagon between his hands and turning, finally made eye contact with Adalbert, his eyes damp and glistening, but with something that might eventually be described as a Mona Lisa smile. He appeared to be searching his mind for something.

"What happened? What caused her to return?"

Deep in thought, the King turned back towards the window, but not so quickly that Adalbert missed the smile forming. "She said she had heard of her mother's passing and could not bear to think of me alone."

"Well that was jolly good of her, don't-cha think?" said Adalbert brightly.

"…but that she had terms. Terms by which she would stay or be gone again. This time forever."

"Oh golly," said Adalbert more deflated.

"I must not speak of marriage. I must give up any plans I had for her to marry," he turned away from the window to face Adalbert again, "And I could not expect she would produce any grandchildren." The King raised an eyebrow and sighed. He appeared to be more at ease with this incredible position than Adalbert might have anticipated.

"Oh! So what did you do?"

"What could I do? I wanted her home so I agreed to everything. In fact, I suggested she stop making a list of specific conditions and instead assume I would agree to all her wishes from that day forward. To stop telling me things she *would not* do and instead, devote her mind what she *would* do. Forget defending against the life she did not want and begin to design the one she did. I would support it as long as she lived it at home in the castle where she truly belonged." Adalbert was impressed with the King's wisdom and was predictably eager to know what happened next.

"What happened next?" he said, precisely as predicted and exhibiting too much excitement for the gravity of the topic.

"Oh my goodness!" said the King, his gaze back on the wagtail, "Look at them!" he muttered to himself, there were clearly two now. "She devoted herself to sport, we rode out at night in disguise to exercise the horses and give her riding free rein. She practiced her archery here in the courtyard – a thing she has uncanny natural ability for – and insisted we fight daily with the broadswords. She exercised like a hired fitchett, bounding up the stairs, climbing the walls, she favoured acrobatics and fighting over dance."

"A hired what?" asked Adalbert, frowning. It was one of those terms he'd heard but wasn't sure quite where.

"You have them in the Kingdom of the Angles, Saxons and Celts, across the sea from Frankia I guarantee it. They are mercenary soldiers, trained killers. I'm glad to say we have no use for such extreme individuals in Prague these days. Anyway, these are the activities that occupied Petra, fed her spirit and I was keen on the same things as a young man but was sorely out of practice. Still, she forced me to work at it because I was no match for her unless I improved." He tailed off, frowned and chuckled. Then looking back at Adalbert said, "It's a lesson. If ever you are so low in yourself as to wonder if life is worth living – wait. Just hold on. Nature may snatch away your life's meaning on a Tuesday, but return it on Thursday, washed and pressed and honking

226

of fabric softener. So, as we practiced with wooden swords, me; as good as I ever was in my youth, her; beating me easily by this time, I realised... well, I realised I was content again. These moments with her were pure joy. And just when I thought I would be happy to settle for that life, she suddenly made it much, much better."

"How? What did she do?" said Adalbert, like he was an infant with the King telling a fabulous new fairy tale for the very first time. The King resumed his wagtail vigil and frowned more deeply, shaking his head in mild disapproval. Adalbert was almost desperate to see what the birds were doing down there to cause the King such distraction.

"One evening, I told her over dinner of the plight of some child who had run away from an orphanage in the city. One of the girls who delivered food here to the castle had found the little chap and diligently taken him back only to hear he'd run away again. She told me that particular morning that she was out of her mind with worry that he might end up drowned in the Vltava. Anyway, Petra announced we must disguise ourselves and go out and find him after dark. I thought this was a hare-brained idea doomed to end in disappointment, but I kept my promise to accommodate her in everything and so agreed on the spot and that night we went out on horseback and collected him."

"You found him!" said Adalbert, greatly surprised.

"Yes, easy as iced buns, just like that!" Adalbert licked his lips at the gustatory allusion. "The little squirt emerged from a dark alleyway when Petra called his name, *'Zemislav! Zemislav!'* sweetly and kindly and out he came! We had spent less than an hour circling the area along both sides of the river, she calling, me watching, tipping our hats to the few people out late and asking if they'd seen the little mite, they all thinking we must be his family for we were disguised of course. Anyway, back he came and suddenly we were three. We fed him up and when he stopped shivering from the cold, he spoke of the unhappiness in the orphanage and that the place he'd run away from was no better in a previous one he'd been at. He told us of his sister who he hadn't seen for a year who was kept in a girl's institution somewhere and of the homeless children he'd encountered when he ran away. It was a right-old sorry tale and I felt responsible… my Kingdom, with all these waifs and strays, unhappy and homeless. Anyway, Petra looked at me with that steely determination and I knew what she planned." He turned and looked at Adalbert who waited for the next instalment. "So now they are all here!" he said almost flippantly. "All of them, and we keep getting more. We feed them, Petra educates them, mothers the entire litter she does. For a girl who swore she would never have children, she is the most incredible mother!"

Adalbert was amazed at what he heard and had a great many questions. He wanted to meet Princess Petra more than ever but felt certain he would be intruding on her world of industry and worthy purpose, that she would not find much to admire in someone as aimless and clumsy as he was. *'She'll think me a silly mooncalf,'* he thought to himself.

It was obvious the rescue mission they had jointly embarked upon was unnecessary in the extreme. Princess Petra would not be happy to be saved and there was every possibility their arrival into her life was an unwelcome intrusion. If he was to meet the Princess without causing annoyance on her part, he would need to follow the King's wisdom in such things and was just forming the first of many questions when the King, who was still preoccupied by the wagtails said, "What on earth are they doing? The blithering idiots will get themselves killed! Come over here and look at these two fools!" Adalbert sprang from his chair and joined the King at the window, "Are they with you?" Below and off to one side were Princes Chatty and Darius. These were the wagtails the King had been watching for five minutes and they were obviously in dire need of immediate assistance.

"Come on!" barked the King. And off they went to administer aid before tragedy struck.

Chapter the Eighteenth.
Convergence Part ii

A little while earlier, Darius had led Chatty around the rocky hill via a path cut into the hillside. The castle loomed large to their left, towering over them, a white monolith of impressive proportions. Down the steep grassy slope to their right lay the city perhaps half a kilometre away. Climbing the slope directly would be very difficult indeed, virtually impossible dressed in armour, out of the question on horseback and suicidal if under fire from the high battlements.

Their path ascended as it spiralled up anticlockwise, its stony surface uncomfortable to walk on and steep enough to be fairly exhausting. Darius wouldn't allow Chatty to stop to catch his breath no matter how many times he asked, so when they finally arrived at a series of steep steps at the rear, Chatty sat on the second step from the bottom, while Darius sprinted to the top. They were narrow and had no rail or hand holds and rose to a good ten metres before they met a heavy studded door which was more iron bracing than oak. "Come on!" hissed Darius, and obediently Chatty came up the steps, leaning harder into the wall to his left with every step until he was virtually trying to smear himself on it. "Come on Chatty, what are you doing? It looks like you are trying to squeeze through the cracks in the castle wall!"

"This is ridiculous! A person could fall to his death here, where's the safety rail?"

"It's supposed to be precarious in case of attack. Easily defendable, impossible to batter it down! It's not for children to play on!"

"It's *exactly* the sort of thing my mother used to encourage me to play on!" whined Chatty.

Darius produced the huge bronze key from his pocket and inserted it into the lock. Would it turn? He wondered. What were the chances of the Chief having the wrong key? Substantial he thought, then rubbing his hands together unnecessarily, he gave it a turn. It would not. Darius tried one way, then the other but it refused to budge. He wiggled it and realised it wasn't a great fit. Surely a key like this would rest snugly? Well, it didn't, it waggled too much to be a good fit. "I think it might be the wrong key!"

"Let me have a go," said Chatty, but Darius was in the way at the top of the steps and although they wiggled this way and that, it was simply not wide enough for them to swap positions. To an onlooker, their antics would have appeared precarious. To them, there were several moments where the sensation of nearly falling to their death on the rocky ground below caused strange feelings in their tummies and a disconcerting clenching of somewhere near their bottoms. A situation like this could induce vertigo in everyone but an inebriated trapeze artist.

"Lift a leg up!" said Chatty dropping to his knees, "Not that one, this one!" he said, preferring the one closest to the castle wall. He then proceeded to crawl through the gap.

"Careful! You'll tip me off the edge!" cried Darius, grasping nothing of any worth on the wall with one hand and handfuls of Chatty's clothing with the other. The steps were very steep and ridiculously narrow and the platform at the top was barely wider than a single step. They swayed and wobbled and looked constantly on the verge of falling off. Chatty was on his knees with the key in his hand and his eye to the keyhole while Darius was on one leg and wobbling precariously.

"I think it's blocked," said Chatty.

"What with?" asked Darius, extremely uncomfortable with the situation.

"I think perhaps there's a key in the other side. Hang on, I'll try to poke it through." And with that he put the key in gently and pushed, the reciprocal effect being to nudge Darius off balance and he slipped, fell two feet and grabbed Chatty's arm. Chatty would have fallen but had hold of the only thing possible up there; the key and for a moment, the only thing stopping the pair falling, was the key. Then it started to bend under the strain. "Quick Darius or it'll snap off!" Darius slid down one more step and was finally able to balance himself, uttering an oath. Chatty took his weight off the key but which was now bent past 45 degrees. "That was close!" He proceeded to wiggle it gently and then said, "I can't push it any further Darius!"

"Because of the key on the inside?"

"No, because it's bent!" He pulled it out and placed it on the stone step under his stout foot. Pressing down, it began to bend.

"Careful, not too much!" said Darius, "If it snaps it's all over!"

"How did you get this?" said Chatty, pushing a bit more and feeling it straighten a touch.

"The Police Chief gave it to me."

"Is it for this door?"

Darius paused, "Crikey old thing, I certainly hope so. How many back doors does a castle have?"

"But did he say it was for a door up a death-defying mountain of evil steps?" asked Chatty examining it lengthwise, like an arrow. Darius didn't speak, he was thinking hard. "Not bad, let's give it a go!" Chatty said as he slid it in. With a determined wiggle it went in a further couple of inches and he let out a little victorious cry. "I think the other key has dropped out." Next, he turned it first one way, then the other, "It's turning!" the lock gave an audible scraping, clicking, clunking noise and the key did a full and satisfying rotation. "Done it!" He pushed the door, but it wouldn't move. Pushed again, "Confound it! Maybe there are bolts too, it won't budge!" Chatty slumped a little, then wobbled and gulped, "I flipping well hate it up here! This isn't what I imagined when we were planning to rescue the fabulously delectable Princess Petra!" he whined.

Darius stared and finally said calmly, "Try pulling it."

"What?" said Chatty absentmindedly.

"You pushed the door. Try pulling it."

Chatty shrugged and because there was no door handle of any kind, pulled on the key. The door shifted a fraction, "Crikey it's heavy!" he pulled again, "It's really stiff! Also look!" He gestured to demonstrate how the door was going to open, sweeping him off the narrow steps as it did so, "There's no space to stand here! This is absolutely the stupidest design of a door anywhere ever!"

"Think about it Chatty, it's not meant for the benefit of entry. No one who is welcome enters this way, it's an exit. It's for slipping out the back in a hurry."

Chatty pulled again on the key and the door shifted a little, but it had still not revealed the entire thickness of the door and so not sufficient that he could get his fingers around it to pull properly. "Keep trying!" Chatty pulled on the key again. The door moved a fraction. He pulled again but this time the door remained fast and instead, with a loud click, the key snapped off in his hand sending Chatty backwards, his arms windmilling until he was at an impossible angle on the edge of the top of the steps some ten metres up the side of the castle. Darius had lunged for him and grabbed his tunic and as Chatty fell backwards and down, Darius was pulled with him, first crashing bodily into the staircase, then precariously to the edge.

Chatty hung there awkwardly, his sword fell out and clattered noisily to the ground below, spiralling sickeningly as it demonstrated their route to a rocky landing before slithering another hundred metres down the steep slope. "Swordy!" cried Chatty, seemingly oblivious to the possibility that he might be dead in a few seconds.

"Hang on Chatty, I've got you!" Darius said optimistically because he hadn't really got him at all. Chatty hung limp in his jacket like a cow being craned onto a ship and as Darius clung to the steps for his own life with one hand, Chatty was gradually sliding from the grasp of his other.

Chatty went limp, knowing the desperate gasps emanating from Darius and the loosening grip on his back spelled the end. "Chatty!" cried Darius, realising he was not going to be able to hold him and that he was faced with letting him fall to his death or being pulled down with him. Darius grunted with effort as he made one last effort to heave Chatty up. "Your armour! You're too heavy for me!"

"Let me drop old bean," said Chatty calmly. "Lucky I'm not Adalbert eh?" That Prince weighed twice as much as the modest-sized Chatty. Darius, fit and strong as he was, knew the game was up and prepared to do something he knew would haunt him for the rest of his days; to drop his friend to his death. Tears were in his eyes. Tears of effort, of frustration and despair.

"Hold on young 'uns! Help is at hand!" called the King from the battlements, his hands cupping his mouth. Darius jerked his head up and saw the King, he appeared amused by their precarious predicament but then threw down a rope which he'd clearly anchored.

"Grab it Chatty, quickly! I can't hold you much longer!" Darius pleaded. Chatty stretched for it but couldn't reach.

"Come on boy, make an effort!" bellowed the King laughing, but then swung the rope a bit so Chatty could grab hold. With both of Chatty's hands on the rope Darius was able to finally release his grip on the tunic which meant he was also safe on the steps. He gasped with relief, his wet face still flat on the cold stone. He panted, shaking after the exertion. This had been the most intense experience of his entire life. He knew himself to be especially intelligent, very athletic and a bit of a hit looks-wise, but today he had been tested to his limits and… and what? Had he failed by deciding to let Chatty fall, or succeeded by holding on long enough for help to arrive? Should a person persecute themselves over a possibility or celebrate the actuality of things? He went limp and found himself shivering. More tears dripped onto the hard dusty stone steps.

Chatty hung on the rope and tried to haul himself up but simply wasn't strong enough, possibly because of the extra weight of the breastplate and thick leather armour he was wearing. "Darius, I can't!" he wailed. Somewhat exhausted but glad of the opportunity to lift himself out of his existential and precipitous contemplation, Darius crawled up the last step and leaned over, grabbing the rope with one hand, at which point, the door behind him burst open with a flourish and swept Darius clean off the small platform. From inside the castle, Adalbert stepped out to find neither Prince, but just a taut rope stretched vertically in front of him. He grabbed hold of it to steady himself and looking up called out to ask where they had gone. Above, the King roared with laughter. Miraculously, Darius still had hold of the rope and now both men hung on it a metre or so below Adalbert's feet.

"Oh come on boys!" shouted the King, "Either pull the

silly sausages up Adalbert, or have them climb down. What are you doing hanging there? Waiting for Dragon to fly in and rescue you?" he bellowed at the dangling duo, his laughter booming until he started coughing a bit, "I'll fetch him if you like! Haha!" At this Adalbert started hauling up the rope while the two started sliding down at approximately the same rate. A few seconds later they were no further down but the rope was nearly at an end, causing the King into fresh paroxysms of hilarity which turned to howling and streaked his cheeks with tears.

***

"Why, you're a girl!" said the voice behind her, causing Shoshama to let out a little yelp of surprise because the voice itself also belonged to a girl. Her woollen hat had been pulled off and her Deep Purple hair had tumbled out. Her assailant pulled Shoshama's dagger from its hiding place, sheath and all. "Gosh, this is quite a thing!" she said, carefully sliding it out of its leather scabbard. "For what dastardly purpose were you intended?" she asked the dagger.

Shoshama was guided first to her feet by a tug upwards on the back of her outer layer and then to turn around by a gentle hand pulling on her left shoulder. She swivelled slowly and saw the young woman before her, tall, with very blonde hair the same length as her own, piercing silvery-blue eyes and a beauty that dazzled her. That she was beautiful was beyond question but she was also unconventionally so, comprising perhaps three parts exquisitely perfect Princess and one part dashingly handsome Prince. The latter aspect was possibly the consequence of slightly stronger facial features, marginally broader shoulders, a physique which tended slightly towards that of an athletic young man rather than a more conventionally delicate female.

236

Shoshama herself had sometimes been told she was too boyish, but this remarkable specimen was something else altogether, perhaps what Shoshama herself aspired to be. The statuesque young woman used the tip of the dagger to lift Shoshama's chin slightly higher than was natural, then to turn her head, first one way, then the other. A flicker of pleasure flashed across the taller Princess's face as she examined her prisoner. Her eyes widened, she looked surprised, as if she was realising something.

"Princess Petra?" Shoshama got the words out through clenched teeth even though she was trembling. She tried to calm herself but couldn't exert control over her own body. She felt a little drunk, or what she supposed it was to be drugged. It wasn't a bad feeling, quite the opposite, strangely euphoric, but disconcerting to find herself so paralysed, suspended, mesmerised, lost.

"It's you!" said the tall young woman, almost too quietly to hear.

"P-p-p-pardon?" spluttered Shoshama rather clumsily, to which she received a little happy laugh, not meant for her, for it was her captor's private amusement.

"Who is asking?" said Princess Petra, sheathing the dagger and now playfully prodded Shoshama with an index finger while looking her up and down. "Who are you?" she said pushing her a step backwards with a firm prod to her sternum, "Where are you from?" her electric eyes sparkled. Another prod, another step. "What are you doing here... in my castle?" and back into the wall on which were the empty pegs, the costume laying on the floor. "Oh, I see you found Dragon's get up," she said, casually as if nothing was odd about any of this.

Shoshama tried to control her breathing although her trembling had turned into visible shudders. "Don't worry sweetheart, I'm not going to hurt you!" but still she pinned

Shoshama to the wall and leaning in, sniffed her neck and hair and delighted said, "Oh wow, you really do smell like a *girl!*" Their faces were just a few centimetres apart and Shoshama, overcome by an irresistible urge, surrendered to it as if propelled by some force beyond her own mind and planted a kiss on the other's lips, causing her captor to jump back and wipe her mouth with her forearm. A gasp of amused surprise burst from Petra, her eyes wide. She made to speak but ended up just staring at Shoshama, shocked and amazed. Her eyes sparkled more vividly than ever.

"Um?" blabbed Shoshama, "Sorry I..." she couldn't believe her own actions. She didn't know where that had come from. Not from her, she hadn't thought to do it, she hadn't decided on a course of action, it was more like a sneeze, a blink or a yawn... *What just happened?* Nothing made sense. For someone as controlled and deliberate and cerebral as Shoshama, this was all entirely alien and she was in turmoil.

"Kiss a Princess without permission would you?" said Petra with a raise of her eyebrows and a long glare. Her expression softened and she touched her own lips with an index finger, "Yes," a smile returned, "I am Princess Petra. And I have been waiting for *you!*" the final word was given a great deal of emphasis.

"W-what? What do you mean waiting for me?" It was such an odd thing to say, but the taller Princess remained silent on the matter and just gazed at her. Shoshama gazed back. She took a deep breath to calm herself and breathed out slowly. Even so it came out with an audible shudder. "You are even more beautiful than the legend would have it," said Shoshama, not sure she should be vocalising her thoughts, then, "And I too am a Princess." *At last!* she thought, *the first sensible thing I've said.*

"Really? Who? Come on, now's the time to tell. I've told

you who I am so *play the game*," she said with emphasis, "Out with it."

"I am the Princess Shoshama of Persia." She felt herself blushing. It spread from her cheeks down her neck and she felt it rush like a wave down to her shoulders, chest, tummy and beyond into her slightly wobbly thighs. She was so hot it made her eyes water.

Petra stepped forward and prodded Shoshama again playfully. "I have heard of you Princess Shoshama, but no one told me you were..." she tousled Shoshama's hair, ran a finger under her chin, "... so incredibly beautiful! I should have put two and two together!" and now it was Petra's turn to give into an urge, but with her lips poised a fraction away from Shoshama's and with both Princesses' eyes closed and breath held, she grunted in frustration and withdrew. "WHAT are we doing! It's like we're 11 and having a silly sleepover!" She adopted a childish voice, *'I would kiss a Prince like this, mwaa, mwaa, now you be the Prince and kiss me!'*," she giggled. Shoshama found herself oddly disappointed that Princess Petra hadn't kissed her but the taller Princess was suddenly all business, "Come on, I'll show you the children. That's why you came isn't it?" After re-hanging the dragon costume, Petra grabbed her hand and led her away, mounting the first of the stairs.

"Well not really. I came with my friends... to find you."

"What friends?

"Friends from the big wedding in Vienna, Isabella and Rupert. The wedding *you* were supposed to be at but didn't show."

"Is one of your friends called Prince Adalbert?"

"Yes, how did you know?

"Tell you later. What about, what's his name... Prince Charles?"

"Chatty, yes! You know them? Have you seen them?" asked Shoshama, hoping to hear news.

"Sort of. Don't worry, Adalbert's fine and I'm sure the other one's alright too. I'll tell you later. I don't understand why you came from that wedding all the way here to find me? What do you want with _me_ of all people?"

"We each had a reason for looking forward to meeting you at the wedding, and I mean meeting *you* particularly, and then you weren't even there. That made us wonder and worry and so four of us came to er... *tain* you."

"Four of you? And what, you came to *what* me? Tain? What's that when it's at home?" they reached the top of the stairs to a much wider and carpeted hallway. Doors led off the corridor several of which were partly glazed and through one such door, Shoshama could see children running to and fro, playing catch and generally having a raucous time. The noise level had increased by a few decibels up here.

"Oh, it's just a word meaning to free you. We figured you were being held captive."

"Well I am in some ways, but well, not really, not in the way you're suggesting." She sighed, "No one knows whether I'm here or whether I've vanished, or dead, buried under the flagstones, living as a scullery maid in somewhere miserable and rainy like the Kingdom of the Angles, Saxons and Celts across the sea from Frankia, or quite what's become of me! And that's if they even care – which most of them probably don't... which is fine by the way."

Shoshama paused, staring at Petra the way a person might the first time they encounter a being from another planet. Then, "Isabella and Rupert sent you an invitation to which you replied in the affirmative. That would suggest you're not dead wouldn't it?"

"Daddy has done that to every invitation for four years and we've never been to a single thing!" she leaned in very close again and Shoshama braced herself, but Petra simply whispered in her ear, "I'm an enigma, a paradox. I mean, come on, look at me! What sort of Princess is this tall, has muscles like this?" she placed Shoshama's hand on her bicep and twitched it.

Shoshama yelped and whipped her hand off, then put it back on and squeezed. Her eyes flashed and she said quietly, "The perfect one." *Oh what am saying?* Petra studied Shoshama's face, as if to read her mind. "Why don't they know about you? Why are you such a big secret?"

"Because of this lot of scamps," she nodded towards the door. "Daddy thought we should keep all this on the downlow." Shoshama was aware that Petra was examining her closely, looking all over, not just boring into her eyes with those piercing, backlit, silvery blue ones of her own.

"Has anyone ever told you your eyes are…!"

"What?" Petra looked amused, "Piggy? Squinty?"

"Incredible! Are you actually human or some sort of goddess?"

"Oh, just you keep that up and see the trouble it gets you in!" Petra radiated some sort of cosmic energy and Shoshama took a breath to calm herself again.

"He's the King, can't he just decree something?" she said. "Instead there's this great mystery about what happened to you and what happened to all these children. Before Prague, I knew nothing of it, but you not turning up the wedding in Vienna is what brought me all the way here." said Shoshama.

"Well then!" said Petra, pleased.

"I mean, it's such a web of deceit instead of just… I don't know… why not just set up an orphanage?"

"Because of how it started." Petra's excited and happy smile faded. "Because I ran away and my mother died and everything went wrong." In a matter of seconds she had descended into deep sadness and Shoshama felt it bodily, already sorry she'd asked. "My father locked the gates, sent all the servants home on a pension. I came home eventually and we had a big heart-to-heart and this is the result." Petra nodded again towards the room of children, something of her joy drifting back into her now that she looked at her charges. "It's not an orphanage because they aren't all orphans. And have you any idea how difficult it is to remove an abused child from its home? No? Well it's hard, even for a King. Unless you ignore the law completely and you have a dragon, then it's easy."

"Do you have a dragon? All I saw was a dragon costume."

"Yes, that's Dragon's dragon costume," said Petra to which Shoshama shook her head, still confused. Petra smiled, which pleased Shoshama immensely. "Dragon is a particularly large Great Dane. P.O.O.C.H people say he's the biggest ever."

"Pooch people?" Shoshama giggled, but Petra was serious.

"Prague Organisation for Orderly Canine Hounddogs. They know everything about dogs and are trying to breed new varieties." Shoshama looked puzzled. "Their goal is something small enough to fit in your handbag and that shivers all day so you can feel it's still there." Shoshama's frown grew deeper and she shook her head in wonder. "I know right! My theory is that dogs give off some kind of pheromone that affects human judgement. Have you seen the way some people kiss their dog's mouths? She screwed up her face and made little spitting actions, "Pah! Anyway, around here a dog is a dog is a dog. *That...*" she pointed, "... is his costume and the tail and chunky feet make it all pretty effective at night. I tell you, people don't want to get too close so when they get told to hand over the child or else, they just do. Sometimes it takes a few more threats but people who can't look after children or don't actually want them in the first place don't take much persuading to give them up. Real parents would die first rather than part with them and that's the difference I suppose."

"Who? Who tells them to hand over the child?"

"My father. Dressed like a dragon handler. He tells them."

"What does a dragon handler dress like?"

"Sort of all black leather, sturdy boots and a big hat and one of my riding crops!" she laughed. "Who would know whether that's right or wrong?"

"A riding crop for a dragon? Ah, but you ride don't you."

"Yes, and I go with my father, at least I trail him and Dragon on horseback, keeping a discreet distance. It's amazing how people only have eyes for Dragon. I think the disguise is unnecessary and I could be naked and still no one would notice!" she laughed.

Shoshama found herself side-tracked by her imagination. The idea of Princess Petra naked on horseback intrigued her, but her own interest in such a thing was unexpected. She felt she might be losing her reason and clenched her fists to get a grip on herself. "You like to ride though?" she said hopefully.

"Love it! You?"

"Love it!" she said, unintentionally mimicking Petra. They stared at each other, warm smiles, happy eyes. Just then a child ran out of the room and with her eyes firmly fixed on Shoshama, reached up and threw her arms around Petra's waist.

"Breakfast's here Petra! Who's this lady?"

"This is the Princess Shoshama and she is my dear, dear friend."

"She's your friend?" asked the little girl, the way they do.

"Yes she is," said Petra staring deeply into Shoshama's darker blue eyes, "And I think she and I will be riding together later." Shoshama looked more than pleased, but letting her imagination fly, she found a giggle rising and bit her lip to hold it in. She had lost herself again. Something unexpected was taking over her rational mind and fighting it didn't seem to work. Petra coloured up and suppressing a bigger grin of her own, winked almost imperceptibly and looked away bashfully. Had Petra kept her gaze on her visitor, she would have seen her face suddenly drop. Catching herself unexpectedly excited, she projected forward to being alone with Petra and found she was a little frightened. She suddenly wasn't sure she was thinking clearly. But there was no time to straighten things out in her mind right now because Petra was pulling her towards the nearby room. "Come on little one! Come on Princess, we'll share some breakfast, there's always plenty!"

Chapter the Nineteenth.
Reunion of Princes & the Hearts of Princesses

"Lower the buggers down before they fall!" bellowed the King with just a bit of a laugh afterwards and Adalbert, hard-wired to do as he was told, started reeling out the rope. On the steep grass below the narrow stone staircase, Darius bent in exhaustion, rested his hands on his knees and sucked in mouthfuls of air, puffing them out noisily. Chatty lay on the grass, flat on his back and motionless, his feet nearer the castle wall so his torso and head were angled steeply downhill. Darius cautiously stepped down the slope and reached out a hand to him but Chatty instead spread his arms and legs into a star-shape and by closing them, propelled himself a little downhill, then again.

"Chatty!" called Darius, "Stop!"

"What's the silly sod doing?" called the King laughing loudly. Adalbert was on his way down the steps and he too called out to the armoured oddball Prince of Egham. Darius slid a step or so down the slope to reach him, but Chatty, supine and on his own mini-mission, did the starfish thing again and slid another few metres downhill.

"Chatty!" Darius cried out again. "Chatty, what are you doing? Chatty come back this way!"

"I'm fetching Swordy!" he said, pointing vaguely backwards beyond his head and propelling himself further down the slope. Adalbert reached the foot of the steps and stretching out his long slender arm, helped pull Darius back up the short distance he had descended. Chatty was still grass-swimming backwards and somehow managing to make it look almost artful.

"He's one of yours young Adalbert, isn't he?" The King called from far above. Adalbert looked up, shielding his eyes from the bright sky. "Kingdom of the Angles, Saxons and Celts across the sea etcetera, etcetera," he continued. Adalbert shouted back that he was. "Hahruhm!" said the King, suppressing some kind of humorous outburst though his eyes looked shiny with amusement. He untied his end of the rope and dropped it down to them. "Split didn't agree with him then! Bring the daft buggers in for potato waw-fulls and tea. I'll get it all going. We'll entertain in the small dining room." And with that, he peeled away from the battlements and vanished out of sight.

"Bad King Wenceslas doesn't seem so bad after all," said Darius watching the space he vacated.

"He's an absolutely smashing fellow." He had Darius's attention with that statement. "Honestly. Once you get to know him, you won't meet a nicer…"

"Child kidnapper?" interjected Darius.

"I was going to say, a nicer King, but then I thought, actually, you won't find a nicer man. Anyway, he's explained all of that child-kidnapping business – more a case of child-rescue." They watched Chatty, now with Swordy in hand, trying without success to claw himself up the steep, grassy slope while Adalbert explained all that he had so recently learned. In between watching Chatty repeatedly gain a few metres, only to slither back to his starting point, Darius looked closely at Adalbert, noticing a change in him, an improvement.

Chatty waved Swordy, desperately seeking help and

Adalbert was about to shout down to him when Darius quietly said, "No wait a minute," and waved back cheerily.

"Help me! I cannot rise from here. I am only going backwards!" shouted Chatty.

Darius waved and shook his head, cupped his ears and made exaggerated shrugging gestures. "Give him a few more moments to struggle. His foolish pride rather scuppered my carefully constructed plans this morning. I would have had us enter via the big door at the front. This ruddy escapade nearly killed us both!" he said gesturing towards the steep stone steps.

"Did he upset the boat?" asked Adalbert.

"Rocked the applecart," answered Darius and they gave each other a warm, knowing smile. "I *do* like Prague, don't you?"

"Me too. Never, ever been happier!" said Adalbert, who felt that the eye contact he'd just had with Darius had conveyed something fresh, as if their friendship was stronger, or perhaps more equal. His existence was being validated in unexpected ways and the King's shout that *'We will entertain…'* had made Adalbert feel as if for once, he was an insider, a part of what was good, instead of being the one clumsily intruding, unwelcome and surplus to requirements. He smiled, warm inside, "We will entertain in the dining room!" he said too quietly for Darius to hear.

Then with Chatty waving more frantically and in danger of sliding too far down for the rope to reach, he threw heavy coiled loops down to him and together and with rhythmical effort, they began hauling the exhausted Prince back up to them.

***

As the children's breakfast concluded, some manner of well-practiced pandemonium followed as various of the bigger children cleared tables while others began the especially noisy process of washing up. The smaller children were led through a set of connecting double doors to another large hall arranged at the front as a classroom with neat rows of desks and chairs and at the rear as a playroom. The walls were covered in blackboards, maps, charts, the alphabet and a great many examples of childish art ranging from some rather fine work to aimless splashes of colour in indiscernible shapes. In years to come, the young artist responsible for the latter would go on to have a successful career selling originals to wealthy fools and a great many printed reproductions to the kinds of hotels which wanted to fill their hanging space with something, but were past caring what it might be.

Every child appeared to know their duties and remained boisterously happy going about them and while they hurried in all directions seemingly helping anyone younger than themselves and with a great deal of well-meaning bossiness from the older girls, it was clear there was great joy here. Shoshama watched Princess Petra directing traffic, calling children by name and clapping her hands to attract attention over the incredible din. Children are happiest when they are simultaneously at their noisiest as if the concentration required to stem their natural cacophony of racket robs their minds of its natural, unfettered flow. Shoshama had never seen anything like it, but in particular, she had never seen anything like *her*. She was deeply aware something was happening and was torn between spontaneously embracing the Princess and finding somewhere quiet to interrogate her own private emotions. Seeing her watching from across the room, Petra smiled and sashayed over between the tables and the children criss-crossing her path in hurried arcs.

"Is all this driving you crazy?" she asked Shoshama.

Something was indeed driving her crazy, but it wasn't *all*

this. "Not at all! I am flabbergasted by what you have done here. They all seem so... well, so perfectly happy."

"Children need to be constantly occupied so I keep them busy. Have you noticed how having nothing to do can put a smile on a grown man's face as he reclines in a chair in front of the fire, but children despise it as boredom and will cry in frustration, *'I've got nothing to do!'* they wail, as if it's the worst imaginable torture! They don't mind work if they can have a say in how it's organised, they like learning in small chunks and they especially enjoy a bit of responsibility so all the charts next door show who's in charge of what and when. Everyone has their thing to do each day, usually as part of a team." At this point a little boy started crying and a bigger girl came to report that he thought it was his turn to hand out the bean bags. Petra took the girl by the hand and collected the crying boy along the way, tugging him briskly by his hand so he had to trot to a wall chart. "What day is it today Crispin?" He said he didn't know, at which Petra slapped her hands on her hips, dramatically aghast at the idea. When asked, the girl identified the day as Saturday and Petra had the boy find his name on the chart on the line allocated for bean bag distribution. Tracing it upwards to the list of days across the top, she spelled out S-U-N-D-A-Y and they agreed his turn came every week but tomorrow, not today and that today, it was indeed Wolf's turn. Teary acceptance followed and order returned, as did Petra. "There's a lot of that kind of thing," she said, puffing her cheeks. "If someone else has a longer bit of blue chalk it's the end of the world for a little one."

"You are so, so good at it though. I wouldn't know where to start."

"I think it's just in us. I'm sure you'd be great. Anyway, later this morning it's ball games outside and after lunch a rather well-paid nurse comes for their weekly check-up, which is great because there are always plenty of scrapes and bruises. It seems boys are mostly interested in knocking smaller children over and as they get bigger, they need syphoning off to knock each other over instead of the toddlers. Father has them playing something called Rugger-bee and also teaches them wrestling. One and the same if you ask me!"

"Goodness Petra, this place is amazing for them. I'm inclined to believe these... poor unfortunates are actually the luckiest children imaginable." Just then, a stack of cloches tumbled to the floor and clattered about with an incredible din. Calm and unperturbed, Petra called instructions about who should help and how, then seamlessly returned to the conversation.

"Children adapt and cope better than adults sometimes, but they still have their stuff," she tapped her head. "We do stories at night and some of their questions about families, mums and dads, brothers and sisters, would break your heart. Also, there's meaning in a lot of this art," she pointed at the walls. "If you just followed your first reaction to the things they say and do, instead of keeping them here you'd probably decide to send them back to the same drunk daddy who beat them black and blue, punched their mother to the ground, took her purse – empty save for the few coins she had earned working in the pub – so he could buy ale from the very same place! You have to get past the fact that quite often, they actually miss their abuser." Shoshama remained silent, this was something about which she had no experience. Perhaps she would have delivered them back to the anger and misery the first time they asked to go home. "They start to understand the rights and wrongs of the situation at around eight years old. Anytime after six, but normally more like eight to ten."

"That's awfully young to have to grow up like that. And so harsh for them."

Petra raised her eyebrows and nodded, "Then you get the three-year-olds who talk like they are already adults, that completely freaks me out!" she pulled a scared face which made Shoshama laugh and blush again, "No really! Some kids just aren't children. You know how you get boys who at ten or eleven are still just overgrown toddlers?"

Shoshama shrugged, "I know some Princes twice that age who are just like that."

"Well once in a while, you'll find there's some little madam who looks right through you and says things, wise things, intuitive things they have no right knowing. I swear Maselina thinks she's my mother, and she is only four." Shoshama laughed again and had to suppress an urge to kiss the Princess. From the extended eye contact through the pause that followed, she knew Petra had the same idea. Shoshama turned her attention back to the children and felt a surge of emotion wash over her. She wondered what was happening to her and whether it was real, or whether she was blithely walking into a situation from which it would be hard to escape. Sometimes, while peering over the edge of high places, she felt a crazy urge to jump. She realised, this was exactly like that.

***

"Oh my goodness! I am in absolute bliss!" said Chatty with a mouthful of potato wawfull and egg yolk.

"Don't they have just the best food ever?" said Adalbert with so much excitement, he couldn't sit still.

Darius observed the King and noted how pleased he was to play host. "Your Royal Highness, you haven't had much in the way of visitors for quite a while I imagine."

The King looked at him, "I recognise you, young man. How are your parents? How is your... family?" He stared hard at Darius.

"Things took a while to settle down, but they are fine now, thank you sir."

"I am very pleased to hear it. Truly, I am. The only thing, the *only* thing that matters in this life is happiness. Speaking of which, are you married?" Darius confirmed he wasn't. "Nor is young Adalbert here, how about you Prince Chatty?" Chatty chewed slowly and shook his head, which was hung quite low as he answered. "Goodness! What's wrong with you all?"

"Ask my father!" said Chatty at exactly the same time as Adalbert said, "Ask my mother!" so they were entirely synchronised except for the mo-fa bit near the end. Darius blushed and said nothing while the King regarded them each in turn.

"Surely…" he gestured at them with his hands open as if he were holding a beach ball at chest height. "Surely some Princess would…"

"Maybe they are all a bit choosy," said Darius, "Like Princess Petra perhaps."

The King continued to look at them. "Humph!" hands on hips and nodding to himself as he thought deeply. "Forget the Princesses, half of them are your distant relations in any case and that's a bit of a dead-end for the gene pool. Too much cousin-on-cousin action and everyone ends up looking like a teenager who skipped several years of school and crawled out of bed in the middle of the afternoon looking for a Muckquaggy breakfast. No, no, find yourselves some handsome wenches from the upper echelons of society."

"What's a Muckquaggy breakfast?" asked Adalbert.

"A recycling business which the Mayor closed down on advice of the city's chief nutritionist. They made food for teenagers that mostly consisted of sawdust, carpet sweepings, chiropodist waste, shower plug gunge, bits from coat pockets and the bottom layer of old ladies' handbags."

"Sounds vile!" said Chatty. Darius looked queasy, Adalbert was thoroughly confused and made odd mouth shapes as he imagined the ghastly ingredients.

"Who…? Why?…" sputtered Adalbert, in an effort to resolve the confusion.

"Little bit of tomato paste, big scoop of sugar and a big scoop of salt, squish it into ball shapes and hey presto! A tasty yet disgusting meal with no nutritional value whatsoever," explained the King.

"Why would anyone in their right mind eat such a concoction?" asked Darius drily.

"It's called Marketing, which is now illegal courtesy of a new law, 77, *It is illegal to swindle and pimp a member of the public or for a business to trick someone into spending monies (or a greater sum of monies than deemed sensible) than they would have spent of their own volition.* Good one, eh? I helped draft it! Anyway, daft as brooms like most of 'em are, youngsters would squish two balls together so they looked like bum-cheeks and boobs. Pretty soon Muckquaggy was selling them in pairs like that and calling them Muckfarties and Muckboobies. It was bedlam I tell you, queues around the block, parents handing over precious coinage for their darling children to fill their bellies with Muck-nothing and all it did was make them bad tempered, fart like trumpets and look increasingly pasty and lank-haired!" The Princes made a variety of noises from *tut* to *yuk*. "Point being, the same effect of empty-headed, bad-tempered, lank-haired, farting-pastiness can be achieved by cousin-coupling."

"Good to know the city has a chief nutritionist," said Darius.

"Marvellous woman. Nothing she doesn't know about sweetmeats and good honest grub. Supplied all this!" said the King, indicating the scattered array of empty breakfast things. "And packed lunches and back again for dinner each night. Adalbert's sampled the fayre, right Adalbert?"

"You are referring to Mrs Gregory," said Darius in his detective inspector way.

"Mrs Gregory?" said Adalbert aloud, somewhat fascinated.

"The very same. I do so admire someone expert in their chosen field!" said the King, pleased with himself.

"It's a lady who makes all this fabulous food?" The king confirmed it dismissively, reminding Adalbert that the potato wawfulls were his own personal, Kingly invention.

"She makes potato wawfulls?" said Adalbert dreamily, as if he'd lost his reason to some quaalude-style narcotic.

"Anyhow, might be best to leave the Royal-Family progression to the brothers and sisters who don't have any choice in marrying kith and kin, and for you lot to strike out into the richer pastures of hard-working folks possessing a full set of everything nature intended!"

"How's that going to happen?" asked Darius.

"Why are you looking at me?" asked the King, flatly.

"I thought you might be leading up to something."

"Something…?" the King revolved a hand urging Darius to continue.

"I don't know. It just seemed you had an idea everyone should be married off and that perhaps you had an idea about how to do it."

"Like a ball!" said Chatty.

"Do you three realise the situation here?" asked the King with an entirely fresh and forthright manner. They waited attentively. "For four years I've been here merrily ticking along with my darling daughter, the fabulously beautiful Princess Petra and an increasing brood of ruddy-cheeked little chirrens, perfectly happy that there was no one out there who was even sure if she still existed, or where the lost children might be or what on earth might be going on, and suddenly you lot burst in and want me to hold a ball so you find yourselves some top totty!"

"Really, I'm in no particular hurry. Don't fret on my account," said Darius, except no one was listening because Chatty and Adalbert were making all the enthusiastic merry noises of little kids who've just been asked if they'd like a giant bowl of ice cream.

The King held up a hand to calm them, "Now Adalbert, I've been meaning to say something to you." Adalbert gulped slightly, he figured he knew what was coming and he wasn't looking forward to it. He'd enjoyed the last few days with the King and realised that the arrival of Princes Chatty and Darius changed everything. Their cosy and quiet little chats had been the happiest times of his whole life, but even this brief breakfast showed how fragile such perfection could be. He'd felt comfortable with the King in a way which he would have liked to continue forever, but with his friends in attendance, what had been intimate now felt like some sort of invasion. The King was going to suggest he leaves with them, apologise for his initial imprisonment and request that things go back to how they were before.

"Firstly, please accept my apologies for initially imprison-ing you," commenced the King in warm, after-dinner-style speech mode, *here we go then*, thought Adalbert. "It was wrong of me and I just put a long-held plan into action of frightening the Muckfarty out of anyone foolish enough to come nosing around. Petra and I have feared this day, but what we expected was an assault, someone out to do us and the little ones mischief, not some doe-eyed dope from the Kingdom of the Angles, Saxons and Celts across the sea from Frankia!"

"Hey!" said Chatty, at the reference, but Adalbert just looked misty-eyed and a happy kind of sad. Sad at what was coming, happy to be the centre of attention. Being called a dope was kinder than almost anything his own, actual, real, biological, registered at the register office father, had ever called him. In fact, he mused to himself that this King could call him any number of names and he'd still adore him.

"Anyway, I'm glad to say I saw sense and had you out of there and into proper guest quarters pretty sharpish." Adalbert nodded like a someone heading for the Prague guillotine...

...perhaps that requires some further explanation. In Prague, the death penalty is seldom administered, but on those rare occasions when it is, by interviewing everyone from family members to victims of his crimes and the arresting Police Officer, Chief Guillotine-Lever-Wrencher Andrew Eamons would collate details of the miscreant's life into a sturdy bound volume. Prior to resting his soon-to-be-detached head on the block, Andrew would read excerpts from the book to the criminal himself and the crowd assembled around the guillotine, relating the circumstances of his birth, infancy and growing up into an adulthood which would culminate in some heinous wrongdoing (like animal cruelty) and his eventual arrest. Slamming the book shut to great applause, Andrew Eamons would shout, "Pavlov Escortbar," or whatever his particular name was, for that was just the most recent example five years back, "This Is Your Death!" the same legend being embossed large on the front cover of the big book. At this point the sentence would be carried out, the criminal's bloody, dead handprint would be pressed on the inside front cover and the book given to the library, joining the others of its ilk being the most read reference books in the institution's possession. It seems everyone loves the cautionary tale of how someone strays from the path of good citizen and ends up sans-tete.

So, Adalbert was attentive yet pale with foreboding as the King continued. "I'm a busy man what with one thing and another, but in spite of myself I found that I enjoyed our meals together and looking forward to the next one," Adalbert attempted to say, *Me too*, but it caught in his throat and instead a little tear rolled very slowly from his saddest eye. "Now I'm not saying the Prince was going to challenge any of the great philosophers…"

"No, I try not to challenge anyone!" managed Adalbert with some squeaky effort.

"Yes… case in point I think… but anyway, simple as those conversations might have been, I enjoyed them tremendously and Adalbert," he looked directly and affectionately at the Prince in question, "I found I liked you very much indeed! I was not kind in the first instance, but you were so quick to forgive, so appreciative for what small charities I showed, that you gave me cause to stop and think. I have been happy enough here for these past four years with my wonderful, wonderful daughter and a growing band of pesky poppets, but well, that ain't enough. Your arrival made me realise something. You made something awaken in me that I haven't felt for quite a long time."

Darius had the oddest expression on his face as if he was holding down a scream, while Adalbert was becoming increasingly beetroot in colour, Chatty had almost dropped out, the way he did when any period longer than 30 seconds failed to include him directly.

"Adalbert, I have to thank you from the bottom of my heart…" continued the King.

"Or the heart of your bottom perhaps?" whispered Darius to himself.

"For making me realise… I do, I am, I do…" He simply petered out and silence ensued. If someone had possessed a pin, now would have been the time to drop it, except it would have ruined the incredible suspense. The King had paused mid-flow, and it was increasingly imperative that he speak, or several people would die of oxygen starvation.

"I do need a friend to share my days and especially my nights. I need one now. Even... no, especially at my time of life. You see, I'm not too old to want a companion, a friend, a trusty confederate, a consort, a match, a mate and at night, oh those lonely, lonely nights, yes a cuddle. A lover's squeeze!" Darius, who had just taken a bite of cold breakfast, spat it out again and with such force that it was lost forever in Chatty's spiky mass of ridiculously yellow hair, which had been made far wilder by the morning's antics. Adalbert's mouth was wide open now as the implications of the King's words sunk into his synaptic-sparse mind.

"Oh, well, I, um..." Even now, Adalbert was weighing the pros and cons of the situation and recognising the hesitation for what it was caused Darius to laugh out loud.

The King turned his attention to Darius but continued in the same vein. "Which is why I've come to a decision I thought I would never make, one which will no doubt disturb Petra and might not be what my dear, late wife the Queen would have expected of her husband. Nevertheless, I feel I must be true to my heart." Adalbert had seemingly resolved himself to what was coming and had taken on the same dreamy doe-eyed look which had become his thing around the King. "Therefore, and without undue further ado or delay, I propose to find myself a woman, a wife, and to remarry!"

Adalbert fainted, falling headlong backwards off his chair, Darius groaned like he'd heard a disappointing end to a long-drawn-out pun and Chatty looked up and said, "Huh?" which meant, *What have I missed?*

***

"These are the breaks I get throughout the day. The bigger children running the things we've organised and for the moment at least, no mishaps." Petra and Shoshama sat side by side and hand in hand at roof height overlooking the inner courtyard. Petra had taken Shoshama's hand into her own while talking and had then failed to let it go, keeping it gently in her lap. Shoshama wasn't sure what to do, recognising that the gesture was innocent enough in itself, but really not so innocent in its portent on this occasion. It was also true that she liked it, was thrilled by the skin contact and House's reference to the tingle known as *electricity* was a new description for what she was feeling. Even so, she remained fearful that her compliance might be taken as complete when in actuality it was time-bound. She was like a passenger on a mystery coach tour who asked how she was enjoying it today would answer, *'Tremendously!'* but who could not commit to tomorrow's review until tomorrow had happened. She fretted that Petra had made broader assumptions. Petra knew the itinerary; she had journeyed this way before.

This part grass and part stone paved area of the castle was behind and to the side of the front courtyard, and bounded by single-storey buildings, two towers and a high wall so it was completely shielded from the frontal approach of the castle. The noise was raucously happy and Shoshama, who had never been a big fan of children, felt herself slightly better disposed to them. She turned to look at Petra, having to lean away slightly because she was so close, and wondered whether her pleasant feelings about all these little humans was actually just the halo-effect of her confusing attraction to the Princess.

"Well this is all most unexpected," she said, vocalising her thoughts. Without looking at her, Petra gave her hand a squeeze. "I think I might be dreaming. Maybe I'm going to wake up and feel like an idiot."

"There are a few idiots in the city. If you want one, I'll get one for you."

"You know what I mean!" said Shoshama with mock frustration.

Petra nodded, then after a moment said, "When things get confusing, we feel obliged to think. And think and think and think and think and think, as if the answer to everything must surely be somewhere in there instantly available." She traced circles on the back of Shoshama's hand with her free index finger. "So, we get frustrated and exasperated and crazy with worry if we don't get one – an answer I mean." Down in the courtyard, a disturbance was causing a ripple of excitement through the children and like water, they flowed towards a corner of the yard, babbling cries of joy floated up to their ears. Shoshama was about to ask the cause when she saw it, a dog the size of a pony – and not a small pony by the way – was being led out by a boy of perhaps ten whose shoulders reached a similar height. It was almost entirely one colour, a dark, shiny gunmetal, with just a small patch of white on his chest.

"Oh my!" gasped Shoshama, a little bit fearfully, "Is that alright? Is that Dragon? He's absolutely…"

"Lovely!" Petra filled in for her. "He's about to get a hundred and something hands petting him, then he'll bound around the other courtyard for half an hour chasing a leather ball and all the crows, which I'm certain torment him for the sheer sport of it, and after that he'll get fed a huge bowl of scraps from Mr Kellogg." She waggled a finger towards the city. Shoshama waited, "The pork butcher. He started sending it up to my father after the first child went missing with a note saying that perhaps if we left the scraps out for the dragon, it might keep away from the city's waifs and strays." Dragon the enormous Great Dane, was turning in circles amidst a crowd of pressing children all reaching out to stroke, pat and hug the same ferocious beast whose mythological winged assaults terrorised the city-folk. Smaller children passed underneath him as if he were a bridge and no amount of boisterous mobbing seemed too much for him as he licked as many faces as he could reach, an act of affection which knocked some of the little ones onto their bottoms.

Little hands were thrust into the air and there was a great deal of jumping up and down accompanied by shouts of, "Me, me, me!" but a girl with spectacles read a name aloud from a list and one child of about four years old was lifted onto Dragon's back and off he walked, a bigger youngster each side holding her hands until she shook them off and they grabbed a leg each to steady her instead. The throng followed in Dragon's wake, greatly excited and calling after the rider advice that they remembered from when it had been their turn to ride.

"And this is the fire-breathing monster that you say terrorises the city and eats children alive!" said Shoshama.

"Well look at him! He probably could," laughed Petra. "Though maybe not, because although he's soooo big, he's not a puppy anymore. He's six years old, that's past middle-age for his breed and sometimes I think he prefers his stable to anywhere else." Shoshama looked and waited for Petra to explain. "It's big, it's a proper comfy bed with a nice wool mattress, he's got food and water and there's even a poop area tucked away around a wall." Shoshama smiled at the level of care expressed for Dragon, but otherwise couldn't understand the appeal. Now horses were another thing altogether! "He had his own door but he didn't like it."

"Didn't like it?"

"It was a big flap a metre square but he just used to stare at it and growl under his stinky dog-breath!" Shoshama frowned confused. "We think something came in and he didn't like it after that."

"Like what? Because whatever it was would have to be *inside* the castle."

Petra shrugged, "Don't know. Lynx maybe? Burglar?"

"Crikey, that would have been a shock, creeping through a big flap and coming face-to-face with Dragon!" They laughed. "Mind you, how stupid would you have to be to deliberately crawl through the world's biggest dog-flap?"

"I'm voting Lynx!" they both said in unison and laughed again. "Well, they do say a cat can look at a King," added Shoshama, turning away from the courtyard to look at Petra instead, her heart fluttering, her tummy tingling, an involuntary shiver running through her which must have been visible because Petra gave her hand a long and especially tight squeeze. "It'll be alright. Don't think, just be at peace, relax," she said soothingly.

"Relax? I feel sick! And anyway, what are you, some kind of expert? A witch? A possessor of souls? Why are you so calm when I am... urgh!" Shoshama made a guttural cry of frustration and tears came to her eyes.

"I've known for a long time. Unlike you I'm not having some kind of awakening, a reincarnation. You are a butterfly emerging from a chrysalis and you're wondering what happened to your slimy blob-self and *What the blazes am I supposed to do with these delicate wings?*"

"I am a slimy blob!" said Shoshama laughing and Petra stroked away a tear first, and a strand of Deep Purple hair second. Shoshama blew her hair away from her eyes and laughed again, leaned into kiss but found an index finger blocking her lips, "The children. Save it for later." Shoshama smiled conspiratorially and nodded. Her rational mind may be lagging behind, but her heart knew what *it* wanted. This was one thing about which she was certain.

"I've already saved about a hundred kisses... Oh my goodness, listen to me! My mother would... Oh I don't even want to think about that!"

"One step at a time young lady. We met like, two hours

ago and you're panicking over introducing me to your mother as your *lover.*" Petra added emphasis to the last word and Shoshama's gasp of excitement, disbelief about the situation and amused horror at the thought of explaining her feelings to her mother burst from her as a gasping bark accompanied by a little snot and spittle. She shrieked in embarrassment and shaking off Petra's hand reached for her handkerchief, but was beaten to it by Petra, dabbing here and there, peering into her eyes.

Shoshama leaned back, "Look seriously!" Petra paused, still smiling as Shoshama asked, "Is this actually happening? Have I gone mad? How long have I known you? I just don't understand how I can feel so, so…"

"In love. I know. I have known you for years Shoshama. I didn't know your name, I didn't know when you were coming for me, I didn't know how long I would have to wait, but I could have described you, painted you exactly as you are. Some nights I would lay awake and feel you across the skies, oceans and continents. I knew you existed and the moment I looked into your eyes down there this morning I understood it was *you.* I wanted to shout *You're here! You've finally come! I love you, I've always loved you!* but I figured that might freak you out."

"Yep, just a bit! Might definitely have freaked me out," laughed Shoshama. "But I know what you mean. I do feel like I've known you longer than just today and okay, I know we've been looking for you and I was *really* looking forward to meeting you in Vienna and I was *sooo* disappointed that you didn't show…"

"Why?"

"Why what?"

"Why were you so, so disappointed that I wasn't there? You didn't know me, we've never met, so why?"

"That's a good question," Shoshama thought about it,

stroking a pretend beard and smiling so much her face was beginning to ache from it. "Right, right, right, you're absolutely right! I didn't know it but I think I knew it all along without knowing it!"

"Er… good?"

"Look, I was excited to meet you because the things I'd heard you liked; horse riding, archery, weaponry, you know – boyish pursuits, well I like them all too, so I was fixated on meeting the one girl in the world who liked the same things as me." She had both of Petra's hands in hers now.

"Uh-huh," said Petra, appreciating the progression of thought.

"But that's dumb isn't it!"

"Because…"

"Because I was surrounded by men who did all those things all the time. If I just wanted a friend I was spoiled for choice. I came here with three friends and I didn't want any of them."

"No. You didn't *want* them." Petra squeezed hands.

"And why did it matter to me that you were so outrageously beautiful?"

"Oh dear, I'm not!" Petra laughed.

"Shut up! You are perfect! Too perfect, look at you, it's ridiculous!"

"Stop it! I'm not. But you are dear Shoshama, I don't think I've ever seen anyone look as sweetly lovely as you." They laughed, joyfully and a bit embarrassed by the mutual compliments. "Well that's a good sign; we aren't repulsed by the look of each other!" And now another ripple passed through the children below and they began filtering from the courtyard and into the building. "That's odd," said Petra seriously, pulling her hands from Shoshama's grip.

"What is?" asked Shoshama, "What is it?" She didn't want anything to break this spell. A boy of perhaps 11 was signalling from a far wall. Even though he was one of the bigger boys he could barely see over the huge battlements, but he used a kind of sign-language to which Petra responded in kind.

"Someone is coming," and when Shoshama still looked blank she repeated, "Three people are approaching the castle. The Mayor, the Chief of Police and someone else. Come on, we'll go inside with the children," and with that Petra led Princess Shoshama away by the hand. Looking down at her hand in Petra's she felt another warm shiver. She was perfectly capable of following someone into a building without being led like a child and she wondered; was this a consequence of Petra's time as a Governess of so many children, or some need; an unwillingness to let go of her new love? Shoshama shared that intense desire to be close, to take each and every opportunity to touch Petra. This was a craving like nothing she had ever felt, her hand was tingling as if electrified and as soon as that appreciation entered her consciousness, the sensation swept through her entire body causing her to gasp and bringing tears to her eyes. Still pulling her along briskly, Princess Petra turned (and let's imagine this in slow motion too, shall we?) and her expression changed from grimly determined to the briefest moment of mild distress as she saw Shoshama's tears, then realising their true meaning, to a deep and overwhelming adoration. For her, the approach of the people from the city carried with it some level of foreboding but she would allow nothing, not them nor anyone else, obstruct what she now knew was her destiny.

Skipping to keep up with Petra's long strides, Shoshama laughed as the tears rolled down her caramel cheeks. This was it. Bliss. Ecstasy. A love so fuelled with endorphins that giving a transfusion to a hamster would cause it to flap its little front legs and fly around the castle grounds singing with hamster-excitement. Best not then, because the world wasn't ready for flying, singing hamsters.

The thrill she had just experienced looking at Shoshama's face, adorably dishevelled, lips swollen with passion and cheeks streaked with tears of joy almost made Petra's long and athletic legs turn to jelly. This was already the happiest day of her life and it portended to be the beginning of a life so wonderfully fulfilled that everything that passed before was reduced to biding one's time in preparation. Even so, the arrival of outside forces boded badly and were a real and present threat to her happiness. As they ducked inside the small door from the rooftop terrace and back into the cool stone-walled corridor of the castle, Princess Petra's mind was drawn to her Greek Mythology classes from school. Their convoluted explanations of how life's mysterious twists and turns might be explained by the whims of Gods had always appealed to her and in her case, Aphrodite was clearly involved in guiding Shoshama to her door but perhaps Eris, the Goddess of jealousy was angered by the sudden intensity of their love and intended to throw some porridge in the works. Through clenched and perfect teeth, Petra muttered quietly to herself, her jaw determined, her eyes alive with happiness and excitement, "Back off Eris, or I swear you are going down, bitch!"

Chapter the Twentieth.
Visitors

"Well blow me if that ain't the doorbell!" said the King, as the echoes of the cheery two-tone chime rolled down the corridor outside the dining room. "Who the blazes can that be?" Darius shrugged while Adalbert remained in a state of minor post-trauma stress.

Chatty appeared bothered by the intrusion but then piped up perkily with, "Are you expecting a delivery? Have you ordered anything?"

"No, not until much, much later when the ladies bring dinner," said the King. Adalbert brightened up at the thought, his darker moods never lasting longer than his ability to focus his mind on a thing, so normally just a matter of moments.

"Perhaps it's for me?" said Chatty brightly.

"Have *you* ordered anything?" asked Adalbert while Darius opened his mouth to speak but just closed it and frowned instead, Chatty shook his head, no, he hadn't ordered anything. "Do many people know you're here?" Chatty gave a vague shrug. "Well, I suppose we should go and see, shouldn't we. Come on!" he said, addressing Chatty cheerily. As all three Princes rose, Darius was the only one of the trio looking remotely serious. Walking briskly down the corridor, they soon caught up with the King.

"Do you know much about the adoption process in Prague?" asked Adalbert, pondering his future. As it happened, The King did, being involved as he was with such legal matters, but his mind was on this latest disturbance and he didn't answer. Adalbert looked glum for a few paces, then seemingly found something to smile about and just as the glum spell had caused his gait to alter and his shoulders to slump, so his smile animated his whole, near two-metre lanky frame. Adalbert walked like it was a dance he was still learning and for whom dancing wasn't a natural gift. Chatty marched, adding a level of pomposity to it which looked out of sorts with his minimal height and so between them, they made Darius look cat-like and agile, when actually, all he was doing was walking. The King had it down too, with added shoulders-back regality. Noticing the King's style, Adalbert modified his gait but got it wrong and almost tripped over his own feet. Darius reached out to catch him lest he fall on the King and being so tall, drag him to the floor, though it wasn't needed because he regained himself in a couple of steps while Chatty, who was closer to the near mishap was oblivious, stomping along and making his short legs achieve the extra-long strides of someone important. Apparently, this required him to concentrate on his feet, meaning anything else passed his notice. To be fair, his little feet were closer to his head than for most adults.

They navigated a veritable maze of corridors and stairways in a seemingly random sequence until spilling out onto the battlements close to the front entrance. Once above it, the King called out "Coming!" in a slightly accented and higher-pitched voice which he used for such occasions and slipped on a breastplate and helmet before leaning over the battlements. "Yes?" he enquired. There below, he recognised the Mayor, whom he liked and admired, the Chief of Police whom he liked, and a woman he knew well enough and who made his heart sink, "Oh, massive piles of doggy-do, what does that harpy, heinous hag want?" he said under his breath but loud enough for the crouching Princes to hear.

"Who is it? Who is the heapy, harmless hog?" asked Adalbert.

"Please tell the King that the Mayor, the Chief of Police and Mrs Tickle-Krackedarse are here to see him!" the Mayor called up, her voice powered by capacious lungs booming around the courtyard.

"Ooh! The Mayor!" said Chatty excitedly and made to jump up and have a look, but Darius had a firm grip on him, so he found himself unable to move. He looked imploringly at his restrainer who shook his head firmly.

"Do you have an appoinkment?" asked the King, knowing full-well they didn't.

"I'm sorry we do not, but please tell the King it is imperative we see him on a matter of the utmost State-Legal-Administrative-Garbage," called up the Mayor.

"S.L.A.G.!" shouted up the Chief.

"She has the vocal power of an operatic virtuoso!" said Chatty to himself, causing Adalbert and Darius to look at him with concern.

"No appoinkment, but it's a matter of SLAG," confirmed the King in his soldier-voice. "I'll see if he's in!"

At ground level, Mrs Tickle-Krackedarse said, "That soldier looks so much like the King himself, I wonder if they might be related. There's much that goes on with the royal family which decent folk would shudder to know." Getting no response from the Mayor and the Chief she added, "Don't you think he looked like the King?" to which the other two still didn't comment, but instead exchanged knowing glances.

"I think we can say the King is *definitely* in," confirmed the Mayor.

"It is impolite to jump to any conclusions about the King or his household," said the Chief solemnly. "We will enquire about the matter in hand…"

"SLAG!" barked the Mayor looking directly at the middle-aged woman. The two were polar opposites, the Mayor being a woman of ample proportions who put a great deal of time, effort and care into making the most of her appearance, the result being grand, voluptuous and (to most) frighteningly overdone, while Mrs Tickle-Krackedarse might be made pretty with some days or weeks of expert makeover, if it weren't for the fact that she had spent a lifetime minimising nature's modest, natural virtues. Her hair was pulled back so severely into a bun that it stretched her bony face into a death-mask grimace, while her clothing appeared to be designed to resemble a gravestone in style and hue and the only skin on show was pallid and had never once been approached by jewellery, makeup or any adornment whatsoever. It was as if her mission was to demonstrate how men might be encouraged to ignore nature's primary call and to quietly allow the human race to peter out. Mysteriously, she was mother to two grown-up children of her own.

The King slumped onto his bottom behind the battlements depressed. "Oh bucket me now, for there is no circumstance on earth that that woman has brought us anything but trouble!"

"Not the marvellous Mayor!" exclaimed Chatty, his palms flat on his cheeks in shock.

"No Polly Tickle-Krackedarse! She is joy-sucking, miserable and loathsome and nothing she does is for any good."

"And her name is *Polly Tickle-Krackedarse*?" said Darius laughing, which caused Adalbert to look confused, while Chatty remained in some sort of private trance-like reverie while he muttered words like *operatic* and *marvellous* to himself repeatedly.

"Haha! Because her name is suggestive of tickling her bottom crack!" said Adalbert a bit too loudly, at which point, the King covered Adalbert's mouth with the flat of his substantial and meaty hand and Darius made a desperate shushing noise, his finger at his own lips.

Adalbert liked the King's hand resting across is mouth, so he leaned into it fractionally, smiled and mumbled, "Smmurree!" as best as his squashed face would allow.

"I'm going to have to let them in. You three can attend but say nothing unless I ask you directly." They nodded agreement and followed the King down the steps to ground level. "Prince Adalbert take Princes Chatty and Darius to the hall where I first met you. Can you remember how to get there?"

"Yes," said Adalbert, "We walk to the large door in the far right-hand corner which is up three steps. Enter that door, then the one in front, then up five more steps, although you weren't sure how many steps you have, I can tell you it is definitely five, then through a wide pair of doors which will be already open and into the Great Hall there in front of us." The King gave a bemused smile as Adalbert recounted the instructions from several days ago.

"Well then, that's it. Arrange the table and chairs so we four sit opposite the three out there will you?" he said gesticulating to the main castle entrance as he slipped off the helmet and breast plate. "A King and three Princes. It's a lot of purple blood for regular folks to address. Should keep the evil hag suitably polite."

"You don't mean the Mayor!" said Chatty, hurt.

"No! That repulsive Tickle-Krackedarse woman!"

"The one who wants her bottom-crack tickled!" laughed Adalbert.

"I can promise you she does not!" said the King emphatically.

"Adalbert, have you never heard the phrase *political correctness*?" said Darius.

"Yes. *Annoying or what!* What's that got to do with this? Am I being *politically uncorrect* or something? Of course! Can't say boo to a goose these days without the goose complaining to *Human Remains*!"

"Tickle-Krackedarse?" Darius said slowly. "Get it?"

"Yes! Be more polite to annoying people! My mother used to ask me instead of using a shoe cupboard, why I didn't just keep all my shoes in my mouth because that's where my feet were most of the time!"

Darius gave up with a little helpless head shake. "Right, crack on!" said the King.

"How many? Five hundred?" Adalbert asked him.

"Five hundred what?"

"Count to 500?" asked Adalbert shrugging.

"No, that was just last time. Go!" and off they went on the double, the sight of Adalbert's enthusiastic walk, and Chatty marching along with extra elbow-power giving the King a reason to smile for the first time since the doorbell had rung.

***

Having organised the children into their various indoor activities, Princess Petra led her visitor to a bay window overlooking the main castle courtyard. There, she settled Shoshama into a seat more than big enough for one, but a little tight for two as she proved by wriggling herself in snugly. With their thighs pressing firmly and Petra's arm around Shoshama's shoulders, she breathed into her ear, "My father the King," unrolling her hand as she gestured toward him down in the courtyard below. He lifted a huge iron latch from its bracket and swung open the passenger door within the big castle gates. First in was the Mayor, greeted warmly by the King, then a second woman stepped through causing the King to take a short step back and bow. "Oh, save us from that mean and miserable gorgon!" said Petra. The third through the door was the Chief of Police, with whom the King shook hands.

"Who is she?"

"Her name is Polly Tickle-Krackedarse and she hates me," said Petra a little depressed by her presence. "The rounded lady is the Mayor; she's lovely, that man is the Chief of Police and he's absolutely fine and I promise you that skinny crone is behind whatever mischief brings them here." The group of four walked across the yard slowly in conversation, the King notably most distant from the Tickle-Krackedarse woman.

"What's her name again? Polly Tickle-Arsewhatnow?"

"Polly Tickle-Krackedarse," said Petra, enjoying the moment.

"And why does she hate you?"

Petra squirmed and groaned, "Oh… "

"What?" asked Shoshama, smiling and shaking the other's knee impatiently.

"I suppose I have to tell you…"

"Tell me what?" laughed Shoshama. They were facing each other, eyes locked, pupils dilated.

"When I was 14, I mean, on my actual 14th birthday, my father arranged a…, how can I put it?"

Petra seemed genuinely sad and Shoshama was moved to assist her, "Oh, I know about the parade of potential suitors and that none were to your liking, but how is that Polly woman connected?"

"She had long held an ambition for her son to be my husband, but that was never going to happen because, while he was a perfectly nice boy, he simply wasn't royal."

"Not blue-blood enough for you eh?" Teased Shoshama.

"Oh I didn't give a fig about that! Don't you get it? I didn't want a husband. I didn't want a man of any kind for anything."

"Yes, of course. You wanted a wife!" she flashed her eyes.

"Well I hadn't quite reached that notion at 14, but I figured it out eventually and about that time I started dreaming about you. She waggled a finger towards Shoshama. "A lot happened to me while I was away from here hiding out, but that's a story for another time."

"Ooh!" said Shoshama dramatically, "I'd like to hear all about it!" dragging the 'all' out to an impossible length. "Anyway, you didn't dream of me exactly, just of meeting a girl you liked you mean," she squinted at Petra as if to discern some secret truth to the matter.

"Uh-uh," Petra said, shaking her head, "I saw you in my mind and I had no idea where you were going to come from because no one around here had your skin tone, your particular look, but when I saw you earlier today, oh!" she gasped and widened her eyes.

Shoshama laughed and blushed. After a pause she said, "So that woman hates you because you rejected her son? But you rejected what was it, 40 sons?"

"I didn't reject him. He wasn't even invited to present himself, which may have been a bit of a snub, but I made it worse at my party by saying I would prefer his sister, Elena."

"Prefer her to her brother?"

"No, I would prefer her to all the young men," said Petra. Shoshama shook her head and made as if to speak but wasn't sure what to ask. "Elena had been my friend since we were little because her Aunt Faye taught me piano and Elena's father supplied our royal horses. She was my best friend and really, at that time, I was suggesting I would rather have her companionship than that of a husband. I told the King and

Queen and the King told me I was being childish and the Queen…"

"What? What did she say?"

"I think she was coming around to the idea. I've often wondered whether she knew, you know, knew more about me than I did." Shoshama nodded. Mums are wise.

"Anyway, I did a lot of thinking while I was in hiding – a lot happened to me and I grew up I suppose – and by the time I came back, I absolutely knew my future was with you."

"Me!" Shoshama scoffed, shaking her head but enjoying Petra's insistence.

"I keep telling you. You, you, you! It was always you!" she leaned in and kissed Shoshama more slowly, more passionately and lingering longer than before, groaning slightly as she peeled their lips apart. Shoshama kept her eyes closed and relished the tingling.

"You didn't know me! We'd never met," whispered Shoshama, licking her lips, then biting the lower one.

"Doesn't matter. I saw you. You formed. I felt you, I knew you. I loved you. I have loved you for an entire four years." Shoshama frowned but happily, shaking her head in confusion. "When did you get your first idea that you might not be into boys?" asked Petra.

"Er…" Shoshama thought dramatically, her head tilted to her right, her eyes to the ceiling and an index finger to her open mouth, "Let me see… today, I suppose?"

"No, I don't mean…" Petra waggled a finger between them, "This crazy, amazing, uber-crush-excitement sparking between us, I just mean when did you realise you weren't the same as other girls, you know, by not chasing after boys all the time?"

Shoshama frowned, a small lock of hair had found its way into the corner of her mouth and Petra gently brushed it aside with a delicate middle finger, catching Shoshama by surprise. Her face came alive at the touch, reminding her of her first taste of champagne; the bubbles startling her tongue with their unexpected dancing. Petra was champagne and everywhere she touched jumped for joy. A deep frown began to furrow Shoshama's forehead but her eyes shone with happiness. Her head shook almost imperceptibly as she bit her lower lip once more.

"What? You mean..?" Petra was shocked, leaning away a little to see more of her.

"It's okay. I'm just getting my head around it. I've never had a proper boyfriend and I always thought I was waiting for Mr Right, for a man to appear who took my breath away and none ever did. In fact, even those who other girls oozed over just left me cold. I'd look at them and think, *What am I missing here? What am I supposed to be feeling because I'm getting nothing! Why am I always the odd one out?* Then today, something happened." Shoshama half closed her eyes and presented herself for another one of those heart-fluttering Petra kisses. It didn't come.

Petra placed an index finger against Shoshama's breastbone. "I'm worried! I'm worried I've rushed you into something. I *know* you are the one for me but you didn't even know you were... my way." She wasn't joking, her face gave away the depths of her concern.

"I know it's sudden but Petra, Petra look at me! I _am_ certain, honestly." She wasn't certain at all, but saying she was didn't feel like a complete lie. "When I said I was getting my head around it, I don't mean I wasn't sure, I mean I was only just beginning to understand my feelings. I have never, never, never, ever felt anything like this. It is real and I want it to last forever." This was completely true and she was pleased to hear her own passionate proclamation, it eased the tension that had been building up in her.

Petra looked a little emotional, like someone exhausted by the intensity of their own feelings. "Me too my darling," and now Shoshama got her next, longer kiss, with lips that felt softer and warmer than ever. They parted before hearts burst, though both felt dizzy and laughed about it while fanning themselves. "What's that woman's name? Polly Arsecrack – something?"

"Her maiden name was Polly Krackedarse." Shoshama laughed again. "She married Dick Tickle." Shoshama laughed louder, causing Petra to laugh with her, "And they kept both names, did the double-barrelled hyphenated thing, so he became Dick Tickle-Krackedarse," the laughter became hysterical and through her snorts, Petra managed; "So she became Polly Tickle-Krackedarse!" She held up a finger. "One more; my piano teacher, the Aunt Faye." Shoshama nodded laughing still. "Faye…" she was laughing so much she couldn't get it out, Shoshama was waiting expectantly and still laughing, "Faye Slica-Krackedarse!"

"Oh, you are absolutely making this up!" gasped Shoshama, her eyes wide in amazement and her hands pressed against her cheeks. Petra, her face red with delight, pursed her lips tight and shook her head in wide arcs of dramatic denial. The silence was broken when they exploded with convulsive laughter, tears running down their cheeks as they rested in each other's arms.

"Are you alright your Highness?" asked a little voice. And they turned together to see a dozen little faces immediately behind them looking deeply concerned and very innocently at the two Princesses. The sight of the little ones caused momentary discomfort then the two young women burst out laughing again.

"How long have you been here?" Petra asked, pulling the little questioner in for a hug with her free arm and kissed her head. "I am fine Lucie. *We* are fine! I have never been better.

Go and play now," and releasing her, she blew kisses at the others and watched them bounce away down the corridor.

***

As the King followed the small party into the Great Hall, what he saw pleased him immensely. In a matter of a few minutes, the Princes had arranged the long black oak table sideways the far end of the hall and cleared away the other furniture to the edges. Taking centre stage on the far side was a huge, carved, throne-like seat, ready and empty for the King. To the left sat Adalbert with Darius and Chatty on the right. The three Princes looked uncharacteristically stately, serious and imposing. On the nearer side of the table were three, smaller, lower seats waiting for the guests. But the final element which gave the King his broadest smile was that instead of a painting of the usual Good King Wenceslas looking down from behind the King's chair, the guests would be faced with a huge piece of Greek art borrowed from a side corridor and rapidly hung in its place. The depiction was a cloud scene of 14 intertwined Greek gods and goddesses in a state of unashamed undress. It was a fine, if unusual piece, but one well-judged to unsettle the guests.

As the King strode around to his place of prominence, the wide oak boards creaked under his weight and the guests fragmented. The Chief marched directly towards Darius and seated himself opposite him, reaching across the broad table and shaking hands enthusiastically, "So, so pleased to see you again Inspector Purile!" he said, pronouncing it correctly, "I see you both continued with your undertaking after we parted at crack of sparrow," and with that, he reached across to Chatty and shook his hand too. He then turned to Adalbert, "We haven't met," and stretched his hand towards Adalbert. Darius quickly introduced the third Prince, who did an unusually fine job of appearing both large and stately.

"I am a good friend of the King," Adalbert said in a mature manner none of his friends recognised. A brief flicker of amusement flashed across the King's face.

Meanwhile, the Mayor was gathering her copious skirts and settling into a seat directly opposite Chatty, the latter having stood and indicated the position with an open hand. Once she was comfortable, he reached for her hand and pulling her firmly towards him so she was hauled up against the table, kissed it as if he was trying to suck her skin off. It was improperly extravagant, but while Chatty peered up into her face, he knew he had found a willing recipient and the Mayor made appreciative noises while swaying snake-like as she hovered over her chair. When he finally released her hand, she sighed deeply and settled back as if satiated by a 12-course meal.

The remaining vacant seat was across from the King and Mrs Tickle-Krackedarse approached it reluctantly, her eyes on the manifold unspeakable parts of the human anatomy in the painting which hung a few short metres from her seat. "I don't recall *that*... that *thing*! Why...?"

The King turned in his chair, "Oh, you mean my Polybanksos? A gift from the Queen of Athens. Some people have suggested it contains a message for me. Do you think they might be right?"

"I think it ought to be covered with a tarpaulin," she said sniffing as she lowered herself vertically until she sat primly with her hands in her lap.

The King continued to admire the painting, "I still don't know why she sent it," he said, almost to himself as his mind drifted back to the sender. They had each attended the other's wedding and gotten along very well, but then he had also gotten along nicely with her husband, the rotund and heavy-drinking King of Athens. He remembered those times as lighter-hearted, uncomplicated and worry-free. The purse was tight courtesy of his late father's over generosity, but they were happy. He had a sense of himself being more alive, more vibrant, probably more interesting. "Well, I suppose I do know why she sent it, it was because my dear Queen had died. But why did she send… that Polybanksos specifically? So… filled with energy, with joy…" The king spoke quietly still staring at it.

"Because it was an unpleasant eyesore and she wanted rid of it!" snapped Mrs Tickle-Krackedarse loudly and without apparent sympathy. Then changing the subject, she wafted a hand at the assembled Princes, and with her nose high said, "I don't believe I know these young men."

The King turned and noting the Princes as if anew, smiled. "Ah my dear friends from various corners of the world, Prince Chatty…"

"Inspector Purile," said Darius flatly before the King could say anything and which left the older man momentarily agape.

"And Prince Adalbert," said Adalbert, "A very good friend of the dear, great King," he added, amusing the King again, though while he smiled to himself, his attention was on Darius in search of clarification about his double identity. Darius glanced at him for a fraction of a second, conveying enough for the King to relent and turn back to his guests.

The Mayor and Chief were both studying the painting closely from their vantage point and while the latter appeared to be appreciating it happily in a general, sweeping sort of way, the Mayor was wide-eyed and emotionally stirred, making new faces to each individual figure as she examined them in turn, her head jerking like a chicken. Chatty had leaned forward and rested his face in his palms while he blatantly stared at her and whether she was red from what she was looking at or because of what was looking at her, was difficult to know. When she appeared to finish her detailed scan, the King broke the silence by addressing her directly, "My dearest Mayor, what brings you to my home?"

"I'm sorry to say it is official business," she said, composing herself.

"Why be sorry, I am always available for you," he answered warmly. The Mayor looked towards the Chief for assistance.

"We come enquiring about the missing children," said the Chief.

"I see," said the King, "And how might I help with that matter?"

"We have to ask you what you know of their whereabouts," said the Mayor.

"You do? Why so?" enquired the King smiling.

"Because there has been a direct and legally binding notice," said the Chief grinding his teeth as he looked directly at the woman seated between them.

Mrs Tickle-Krackedarse cleared her throat and spoke, "I have brought this notice and it compels them to act. Something they have omitted to do with regard to this situation," she said, referring to the Mayor and Police Chief. The King remained silent.

The Chief continued, "No one has ever complained about a missing child, so while reports have arisen, there has never – until now – been a specific need to open an enquiry." The chief leaned back, crossing his arms. He was not pleased to be put in this situation and had no sympathy for the vindictive Mrs Tickle-Krackedarse. Meanwhile, the Mayor was discretely scribbling a note which she slipped across to Prince Chatty. Chatty lowered it to his lap and read;

Dear King,
I'm so sorry, we tried everything, including money.
She is determined to cause trouble.

— — — — — — — — — — — — — — — — — *Chatty. Tear here*

Prince Chatty: I must have you

Chatty read the note in his lap, choking when he reached the last line. He brought it up ridiculously close to his face and studied it carefully, looked puzzled and lowered it to his lap again, stifling yet more coughs. Though the others would never know it, he had been scrutinising the note for the droplet which she had alluded had fallen from her tear duct and onto the note paper. This, he presumed, was a womanly device intended to show passion and he was troubled over it, thinking that not finding any trace of the tear in question was a failing on his part. His diaphragm in spasms, he then looked directly at the Mayor with his face red and coughs of increasing magnitude suppressed in his chest and throat. Meanwhile, she was attending the King, prim and proper, but a brief glance at Chatty included a flash of a smile and a wink, causing the poor Prince to cough again and grab a jug of ale on the table. This he tried to imbibe while still coughing, causing it to erupt and spray over the Mayor directly opposite who jumped up with her arms aloft. "I'm so… cough, cough, sorry, cough, cough!" sputtered Chatty.

"No matter!" she said, "come with me before your heart arrests!" and with that she grabbed his wrist and pulled him around the end of the table, but not before he slapped the note into Darius's lap, who read it, raised his eyebrows as high as they could possibly go and passed it to the King. He read it below table level and reaching the last line, laughed like a roaring bull. Darius watched the pair leave and mouthed a big slow *oops*.

The King called out, "Do your best to save the poor lad lady Mayor, he's much too young to die!" She hurried Chatty out, still pulling on his wrist as he stumbled along just behind her.

"And back to business," said the King as he forced himself to stop laughing and regain a straight face. "So, what is the new imperative in the matter?"

"As I say, when no parent complains, there is no cause to investigate, but now someone has," said the Chief his regret and frustration showing.

"And as *I* say, that person is me," said Mrs Tickle-Krackedarse.

"Are you a parent to a missing child?" asked the King, suspecting he knew the answer.

"She has lodged adoption papers for a missing child… with the permission of the mother – there's no record of the father – and as such, she has become the first person to prompt an official investigation. Consequently, I need your full compliance on the matter." The Chief relayed all this like a man who suddenly hated his job. The King watched him closely, understood and thanked him for the professionalism with which he applied himself to his station.

"This child's name?"

"Does it matter? If you have the children here, you have him," sneered the vindictive woman.

"That doesn't follow at all. Whether we had one child or a thousand children here, it doesn't mean one automatically has to be the boy in question. What's the little fellow's name? Let's see if we can resolve this here and now."

"If I give you his name and you simply deny it, that won't be sufficient. I will need evidence!" she was raising her voice and the King's face darkened.

"His name madam!" barked the King. No one would ever win a contest of volume with him, not even the Mayor and Mrs Tickle-Krackedarse jumped back. She was a misandrist and believing the worst of all men, was inclined to assume shouting was only a short step from violence.

The Chief coughed, "If I may..." the King nodded towards him, his face softening in accordance with his feelings since his annoyance was directed exclusively at the grisly woman. "First we need to know *if* there are any of these missing children being cared for here at the castle."

"For the sake of exploring the proprieties of your investigation into the matter, let's imagine for a moment there are," said the King.

"The King obfuscates!" hissed Mrs Tickle-Krackedarse. The King clenched his teeth and the Chief held up a hand to her.

"A moment madam, you forget yourself." Then turning back to the King, "The difficulty here is, that if indeed there are children here, unless you produce young Libor, I'm going to need to interview all of the children in search of him. Perhaps no one knows his name, perhaps he has forgotten his name. I will need to spend some time to make certain there is no child of that name here. Unfortunately, the presence of the children, whom I am obliged to interview, will probably result in a determination about each of their futures too. By seeking one child, we may be forced to alter the fate of every child... here. *If* they are here."

"He's here. Of course he's here!" sneered Mrs Tickle-Krackedarse, "Locked away somewhere at the behest of that rathe-ripe Princess no doubt." The King stood, his face a darkening red.

"And what if Libor doesn't want to leave?" came a voice from the back of the hall. And turning, Mrs Tickle-Krackerarse and the Chief saw the missing Princess Petra, now grown up, 18 years old, athletic and imposing, taller than both of them, taller than the King, in fact at 1.8m she was taller than everyone except Adalbert. Next to her stood the Princess Shoshama, another stranger to the three visitors.

"I knew it! I knew you would be behind it. You always did take after your mother, more quean than Queen!"

"Madam!" bellowed the King so loudly she ducked as it echoed around the Great Hall. "You may be used to having your way with your pitiable husband, it is *he* who needs rescuing, no one here and certainly not by you!" She had now insulted both the Princess and the late Queen.

"I am a mother! She is not!" she screamed, pointing a bony shaking finger at Petra. "There is no mother here. And your record as a father is questionable. She has never been brought to heel and see what comes of free will!" She waggled a finger at the pair of young women, for loathe her all they may, she was astute. This caused some silence as the others began to absorb the inference.

Petra grasped Shoshama's hand and walked slowly forward, addressing Mrs Tickle-Krackedarse and the Chief in turn, "What if Libor *is* here but says he doesn't want to leave with this heartless hag?" Mrs Tickle-Krackedarse gasped and went to speak but was beaten to it. "What if he clings to the King as he begs to be allowed to stay?" She continued to walk forward, closing the gap. "What if he says *this* is his home and if you try to take him away he will simply escape and return? Would you force him Chief? Would you take legal steps to knowingly ruin a happy childhood?"

Mrs Tickle-Krackedarse looked furious but it was the Chief who spoke, "Well, technically the law says…"

"The law says we will ask the boy himself and there will be no one but the Chief and I present to influence him, and when we hear from him his wishes will be taken into account." This came from the Mayor who had appeared at the entrance to the Great Hall, she looked like someone who had just run a marathon and been hastily dressed by a band of blind monkeys. She still dragged Chatty behind her and he seemed to be sleepwalking on jelly legs, taking small jerky steps while being wide-eyed yet trancelike.

"You!" hissed Mrs Tickle-Krackedarse, "Look at you! Our disgrace of a Mayor, a nightmare more like! You trespass on decency with your eagerness to tantivy and debauch. Look at this silly boy you have swallowed whole. You are a fizgig, a Magdalen!"

There was a little high-pitched gasp from Adalbert, but otherwise the room was almost silent. Petra stood hand in hand with Shoshama about four metres from the group and while the King silently raged, the Mayor approached them with a calm and steely determination which caused Darius to see her in a new light. Apparently, she was flighty and scatter-brained when in need of a companion, but a different woman when recently satiated. "Princess Petra, I am utterly delighted to find you well." The Mayor gave a little curtsey, "My, my how you have grown, you look marvellously well. Your dear mother," at this point she turned to Mrs Tickle-Krackedarse and raised her voice, "*Our most wonderful and precious Queen!*" then turned back to Petra and softened her voice, "Would have been so very proud." Petra nodded demurely to accept the compliment but was a little red at the mention of her mother. "I don't believe we have met," the Mayor continued, addressing Shoshama.

"I have the honour to introduce my dear friend, the Princess Shoshama of Persia!" The Mayor curtseyed again.

"Disgusting!" muttered Mrs Tickle-Krackedarse. The King's jaw tightened and his fists clenched as he stared at her with contempt. She glanced at him repeatedly, her eyes twitching nervously. It had never occurred to her that had she not been a woman, verbal assaults like this would culminate in a beating. Protected by her gender, she spoke with the authority of someone powered by indestructible self-righteousness, "Let me remind you, the law…"

"Let *me* remind you, the law is the King… and I, we, write it. The Chief enforces it. It is written to be fair. The child's wishes will be taken into account and lest he mistakes the offer of a home to be somewhere warm and cosy, I will need to appraise him of just who it is who proposes to be his… his *mother*!"

Mrs Tickle-Krackedarse stood. She wasn't tall and appeared mostly skin and bone under her grim clothing, but her chilling presence still made her imposing. Even so, she knew she had met her match here today. Everyone was against her. "This is preposterous. There will be no justice here. But let me remind you, I am a mother. I am married. I have a husband. I have a son and a daughter. My husband works for a living. We are normal people and I know plenty of other normal people who want to know what has *really* happened to the children and what's more, who want that dragon slaughtered. Look at you all," she indicated them in turn. "A sex-mad strumpet for a Mayor, a deviant freak of nature for a daughter, an idiot for a Chief of Police, a do-nothing for a King and some empty-headed royal detritus blown in on an ill wind!"

Darius had been quiet throughout, but now he stood and addressed Mrs Tickle-Krackedarse directly. "You madam, have been very free here with your insults. It seems you have a fine mind yet it is long poisoned with hate. I would happily insult you for the next hour but it would be a waste of my time and effort, for nothing offensive could be said about you that you would not already know to be true." Mrs Tickle-Krackedarse gasped with indignation while broad smiles appeared on various faces and the King nodded in appreciation. "I may have been blown in on the wind and my initial purpose may have been fulfilled, but you have given me a new one; to oppose you with every fraction of my intellect, every ounce of my strength and to my very last breath. Until I met you, I was certain Prague was the best place on Earth, all yin and no yang and for all its attractions, I now see there is one solitary counterbalance; your foul *STENCH*!" He shouted the last word and his friends looked shocked. They had never, ever seen him angry.

"Who cares about the ravings of a blackamoor?" They gasped in unison and the King leapt to his feet.

"Fuck off out of my castle you evil bitch or I'll have your miserable head on a spike!" She shrieked and cowered once more, glancing briefly at the Chief of Police but finding no succour there, hurried away. At the door, she turned.

"I have influence in this city and so does my husband. We will be back in our hundreds, in our thousands as a unified people to dethrone you," she pointed at them in turn, "And remove these puppets from office. Make the most of your final days because it's all about to unravel."

With that the King stood and moaned, "Oh, that'll do! Did you misunderstand the fuck off as optional?" then marched off to the side of the Great Hall and heaved a broad sword off the wall with a dramatic flourish and the accompanying sound of metal sliding against metal. The woman screamed and ran. "Faster you nithing hag!" he bellowed, stamping his feet to mimic the sound she might hear if being chased. She screamed again and bounded down the stairs and hearing the doors crash at the bottom, the King began to laugh heartily. When his laughter died down, it was replaced by a deep frown and turning to Darius he said, "No guest of mine will ever be insulted that way without recompense."

Darius shrugged, "As a Prince, I mostly escape such

comments, but it is of no consequence to me, she may as well attempt to insult a horse by identifying it as Chestnut. Her problem is that she doesn't like what I said and when people exhaust their own intellect, they take to petty observational insults like fat or short, or in my case that I am unique here in being dark skinned."

"Which we all envy and adore, by the way," said Shoshama.

"Well, it's alright for you with your beautiful caramel tan!" said Adalbert. "Try being this pale. We all look ill when we are near anyone with a bit of pigmentation!"

"Whatever the situation, a person is marked out by what they do, the things that make them who they are, not by the hair colour they were born with, their height which is immutable after childhood, by their ears or their noses or their feet or the colour of their skin. I won't stand for it in my house and I will not accept it in my Kingdom." Darius smiled and accepted the firm handshake he was offered. "Whatever next? Are we to mock people for being ginger?" They laughed at the silliness of the idea.

"Don't you think it rather ironic that the only person with an issue about my skin colour is someone called *Polly Tickle-Krackedarse*?" said Darius and they all laughed again. All except Adalbert who frowned deeply and Chatty who stared into space like he was witnessing the origins of the universe.

"Have you ever noticed how often people who profess a thing to extremes, this idea or that belief, frequently turn out to be the worst hypocrites? Most of us live in moderation and make compromises. Their balance is often to scream one thing from the rooftops while secretly practicing the exact opposite."

"Do you think she has a dozen secret lovers?" asked Adalbert. "Or a secret basement filled with kidnapped children, all miserable?"

"Well, the silly misguided thing always was a bit spikey, but she's certainly got a hornet up her vice-tight bottom!" said the King, musing over the dilemma.

"She hates men because she wishes she was one," said Darius. "She overestimates her own mind, busies herself dismantling everything good with her fanatical theories and can only keep all these mental plates spinning if everybody else is wrong." The others watched and listened. There was something extra in Petra's face, but the King nodded as he absorbed Darius's assessment of the twisted, angry woman's psyche. "Life must be a constant mental strain for her. If she were an uncomfortable pair of boots, I would have the cobbler remove all the glue and stitches and remake her from scratch."

"A sort of reboot?" enquired Shoshama.

"Exactly," Darius confirmed.

"You wouldn't just throw her in the garbage?" asked Petra.

"No, not all," the Prince from India continued. "Did you notice? She is fine-featured and well-formed. The leather is of good quality but needs some serious buffing! She is tight in all the wrong places!" Darius smiled at his own allusion and the others mirrored him, chuckling at the idea. "Her sole is warped, so I say, heat up her glue and carefully resole her so she fits better."

"You are more generous than I," said the King. "But then you've had a quarter of one hour with her and I've known her for several decades."

"Was she always like this?" Darius asked.

"No, I've seen her sweet. But she lacks humour so I imagine this… this vinegar was always in her. She's definitely gone off the edge." He waved his hands and puffed, "This, this bitter bile, this explosion, it was a new low, even for her. The way she spoke to you…" Darius flapped a hand, dismissing it.

"I know what she needs!" said the Mayor with a devilish grin. They guffawed. "Any volunteers?" They turned to each other in turn, provoking violent head shakes and frightened noises.

"The poor, poor, woman!" said the King quietly.

"She's given us a real headache," said the Chief seriously. "A mighty temporal throbbing. And some nausea. She brings the kind of terrible hangover which is made worse by their being no recollection of a party."

"We will need to deal with it, that much is true," said the King. There was silence for a moment and then he spoke again, turning to his daughter he asked, "Where did this remarkable young lady come from?" Petra, who had latterly been staring at Darius with a look of sadness on her face, came out of her daydream and introduced Shoshama with a beaming smile returning to her face, at which point Adalbert stepped in to explain she was in their party.

The group now gathered in one throng and continued bowing, shaking and kissing hands and bonding after the drama that had just unfolded. Chatty had yet to speak and still appeared somewhat zombie-like though the Mayor made efforts to revive him by rubbing his back, pinching his cheeks and earlobes and crushing him to her firmly enough to have him constantly unbalanced so that he rocked this way and that and needed continually steadying by her so as to not collapse. He was a puppy and she was a toddler intent on demonstrating her affection by squeezing the very essence of life out of him.

"Does that woman have the influence she claims?" asked Darius, once everyone was past introductions. Most people seemed to have their eyes on Shoshama, who, in spite of her Ninja garb, had never looked more beautiful, more radiant, or more happy. Petra couldn't help but stare at Darius, and he knowing she was doing it, gave her a reassuring look. To the trained observer, there was something of an apology to it. This done, she returned her attention to the wider group.

"What has happened to you? You seem different?" asked Adalbert addressing Shoshama.

"My hair! It used to be brown silly," she answered tousling it and tilting her head shyly as she did so. Adalbert just said oh but knew there was more and it was probably to do with the adoring way Princess Petra looked at her and how their hands appeared glued together.

The Chief did his little throat clearing thing and said, "Inspector, I'm sorry to say she does. Not that people like her, but she will pick up support from a latent desire to know what happened to the children. The parents in question are dead or gone in the main and those who remain simply do not care, or are unfit to cope, but the good people of the city have always maintained an interest. She can easily muster support. I'm afraid we have left it too long – allowed matters to get to a point where we have work to do to maintain the Status Quo."

"Can I write into law that she is offensive and must be beheaded?" suggested the King with a grim laugh. The Mayor and Chief of Police agreed he could not. "Does it matter that she's a mother, a wife… all of that *normality – woman of the people* bunkum? Are we in the wrong because we are royalty and there is no Queen, no Mother of State?"

"Oh, no one thinks of her as a good wife and mother," said the Mayor. "The rumour among the people of the city is that she has two children because she has only ever had two lovers, on two entirely separate occasions." The group laughed. "And that she was fast asleep both times." More laughter, "And that they were paid by her husband because he'd rather not… perform his husbandly duty!"

"No!" they gasped, "Surely not!" They laughed, shocked by the idea but were reassured she was not some focus of virtue and popularity in the city.

"She's not well liked, but I'm afraid the Chief is right, she, and especially her husband if he is of a mind to, can muster support. I think we can expect trouble."

There was a long period of silence and reflection when each considered speaking but seeing the King, his head so low, refrained and instead cast glances to each other. Petra squeezed Shoshama's hand while she watched her father intently. The grip was especially firm and pained Shoshama a little, but she preferred it to being let go.

Finally, the King looked up, his face downcast and somewhat resigned, "We have so much to lose. So many little ones depend on us." The Chief and Mayor exchanged a look, their faces mirroring the King. "I feel we are on the cusp of something. Just when we seem to have everything we need to make a better life, it may all be slipping into the abyss. Dark forces are gathering and will soon cast a long shadow on our happiness."

"If Polly wants to bring darkness to our door, then we must shine a light for our people to illuminate the goodness in what we have done here. We will stave off her negative publicity with our own positive campaign," said Petra. "I have a plan to that effect and another in mind for her personally… but that one needs a bit more thinking about."

"Don't do anything rash sweetheart," said the King and she looked at him, squinting slightly as she tried to interpret his inference.

"No father, of course not." He sighed visibly and stood up. The others followed his lead and with that they joined the children for lunch and organised their defence of the Realm and the rock on which everything good was founded, the magnificent Status Quo.

Chapter the Twenty-First.
Memories

As the King slipped away from the lunch preparations, he looked back into the bustle of the kitchen and realised he had spent the last four years in limbo. It was the worst kind of coincidence that his dear wife, the Queen had died at the same time he was at loggerheads with Petra over her future. His guilt had made him withdraw and while he remained the King in name and – upon her return – a supportive father to Petra, the Princess found solace in a worthy cause. It was the children who gave them both purpose but standing in the doorway and watching the fabulously organised chaos, he knew that some very important things had been missing; the three Princes and the one Princess patting heads, bending to talk to the little ones, and bantering back and forth with one another added a layer of young adults to their little society which Princess Petra desperately needed. And seeing her happy and laughing like she was – and in spite of the recent shadow cast by the poisonous Mrs Tickle-Krackedarse – he realised she was happier than at any time since long before that fateful 14th birthday party.

It was also obvious that she was head over heels in love.

With a Princess!

In one fell swoop it explained everything and though he was happy for her, he was also fearful of how difficult her future might be. On one hand he hoped this was as real, as definite and as deep as it seemed, but that being the case, how many more Mrs Tickle-Krackedarses might they have to contend with in their life together? Bitter, jealous, angry and disappointed with themselves and their lot, rather than take responsibility for their own personal misery and failure, they point a craggy, accusing finger at everyone else and deem them wrong. They become convinced that their pious, fragile and narrow-minded sensibility is the only legitimate worldview. No matter that it narrows as it becomes constrained with innumerable *should* and *should not* rules which eradicate human nature, because in their angry, moralising minds they are *right*. They replace purity with guilt, joyful spontaneity with dour ritual and they come to consider all that is natural in people as somehow *unnatural*. These haters with small, black hearts, litanies of blame for all they think is wrong and sadly unfulfilled love lives, would flock to accuse the Princesses for finding the very things they could not, for being happy when they were not, for loving deeply when they had long ago missed their chances and now refused to open themselves to anyone else.

The vultures would gather and trusting that fairness would prevail, that love would conquer all, that the goodness in people's hearts would ensure no harm would come to the people closest to him was naïve. He must be ready to react. If necessary, he would be willing to overreact. The King knew the time had come for change. His glazed look washed away and the noise of busy, happy children being partially marshalled by young adults flooded back into his ears. He nodded, almost as if it were a tic, smiled and surveyed the joyful pandemonium around him.

Two things he knew: Lunch would soon be ready and Petra had a plan.

It was true, foodwise, everything was in hand and it

wouldn't be long now until they could serve up. Meanwhile Petra had her mind on all the things which needed doing to save the situation but she was aware Darius was trying to attract her attention without distracting others. They needed to talk. So, when the moment was right, she grabbed Shoshama's hand and signalled to Darius to follow them. Wiping his foody fingers on a cloth, he left the kitchen but aware the number of people over 1.4 m tall was rapidly diminishing, Adalbert called after them, "Where's everyone going?" This alerted Chatty to the situation and he paused his work of stacking serving bowls on hostess trolleys and before long all activity had come to a halt and everyone was looking towards Darius in the doorway.

He bowed, "The Princesses have business with the King. I have a need to *powder my nose*," this caused some of the children to laugh and that started the others off. "And I'm wondering now whether you can manage without us? Should I stay?" he said theatrically. The children called to him to go. "Adalbert? Chatty? Will you be alright for a few minutes?" The children laughed again and the two Princes agreed they could cope. "Children, can you look after the Princes? They haven't prepared many lunches before and need your guidance." This prompted a few of bossy 11-year-olds to cluster to them, at which point Darius slipped away.

Darius saw the Princesses down the corridor and Petra indicated he should follow. They entered an especially large bedroom and sat in comfortable chairs next to an unlit fire-place. Shoshama immediately liked the décor and wondered if this might be a guest room. At the far end was a four-poster bed so high it looked as if a person might need to take a running jump to mount it while to one side was a very large picture window which offered anyone in the bed the prospect of lazily gazing out over the city. Heavy curtains beautifully embroidered with turquoise and teal gave the room a feminine charm while in the centre and raised up on four ornate feet, was a large, deep bath big enough for two. The fireplace had the usual contrivance for heating the large amounts of water needed for bathing in style and above the mantle hung a large painting of the King and Queen, younger and not grim faced as so many monarchs are in such portraits but young, happy and in love. The Queen bore an uncanny resemblance to Petra, although a touch older, late twenties perhaps and slighter in build, for Petra had some of her father's strength. Did the Queen have slightly more delicate features, or did the artist simply flatter her that way? Opposite the fireplace and so directly behind where she sat, Shoshama finally noticed an open door to an anteroom in which were hung a great many clothes. These were surely Petra's clothes and so she surmised this must be the Princess's room. The happy realisation lit up her face and as she retraced her gaze in reverse, arcing back around to the other two, Shoshama became aware that Petra was gauging her reaction. She looked into Petra's eyes and wondered where she herself might sleep tonight and regardless of how much Petra might be able to mindread, Petra rubbed Shoshama's hand affectionately, smiling a smile that melted her heart.

Darius sat patiently, straightening the elements of his all-white suit and scratching the tip of his sleek nose. Princess Petra was first to speak. "When I first saw you I thought you were..."

"My brother Razi?"

"Yes... You are so alike. At least, to my memory, it is such a long time ago."

He smiled, "Are you sure you don't mean we all look alike?"

Petra feigned indignation, "You look much more like him than you look like anyone else I have ever met!" she said and laughed briefly. "He caused quite a sensation here when he came to my birthday party."

Shoshama watched in silence at her side, their hands still clasped together. She had come to a decision to stop thinking too much about what everything *meant* and just go with the flow – *her* own flow. She'd been briefly alarmed that she had fallen into Petra's life-plan, not her own and that the attraction of being so wanted was sufficiently intoxicating not to pay too much attention to who wanted her so much and why. But she soon determined that wasn't what was happening at all. Her feelings were genuine, at least, they were as genuine as any feelings can be when the heart is in charge, and *'Oh my* goodness' she thought, how her heart was singing today! It felt too right to be wrong and true, she may have only known Petra for a few hours but she was where she was meant to be and now that she was here she knew she would make any sacrifice, give up everything else she possessed, do anything it took to keep the younger but oh-so grown up, Princess Petra her by her side. She wasn't worried about Mrs Tickle-Krackedarse stirring up trouble with the people of Prague, for frankly, if need be, she'd whisk Petra home to Persia, but right now, in this particular moment, she looked sternly at Darius, hoping that whatever he was about to say wouldn't spoil things for them.

Darius held up his hands and looked at the backs of them for a moment. Reacquainting himself with his own shade of skin. "I've been west to the Kingdom of the Astruias, I've met Basques in their homeland and their kin the Celts, but I've never encountered a paler group of people than you are here this far east, with your translucent hair and translucent skin!" Petra laughed, regarded him for a moment, squeezed Shoshama's hand then stared into the fireplace. The smile faded to a sad frown. She wore her heart on her sleeve, uninhibited in revealing her feelings towards a companion and allied to the directness of her speech, it revealed a kind of perfect honesty.

"How is Razi?" she asked.

"He gave me a message for you." Darius had his eyes fixed on hers.

She shrugged, "Do I even want it?" her voice was raised a little, emotion was rising. "His last words to me were not kind!" She remained fixed on the empty fireplace.

Darius leaned forward and tapping her knee so that she brought her gaze back upon him, then nodding while he spoke said, "Perhaps his message may help to explain."

Petra turned to Shoshama and grabbed her other free hand so she held both, "You look worried, no need, it's okay I promise. But I do want to tell you about that day." She turned to Darius, "So wait Razi... I mean Darius! I'm sorry!" she laughed, deeply embarrassed by the Freudian error. Darius smiled and shrugged and the Princesses laughed, but Shoshama *was* worried. It was inconvenient that her new love should have a past. Why couldn't lovers arrive fully-formed but without any history, or at least without complications?

Petra began to tell the story, mostly oriented towards Shoshama but staring off around the room as she remembered the details and occasionally looking at Darius when referring to Razi. And so her mind pulled her back to that day, it was her 14th birthday and she really did not want to go there. Until Darius had forced the issue, she had avoided opening any of the myriad doors to that sad and troubled time. Daily, spurred by a random event or comment, to which her mind vindictively attached some tenuous connection to those months she spent in exile and another clawing hand would stretch out from her past and try to pull her back, to drown her again, in the guilt of abandoning her dying mother, of selfishly leaving her soon to be bereaved father to face the loss alone, in the shame of running from her betrothal party as if to illustrate to an entire nation, just how spoiled and ungrateful a Princess could be if she set her mind to it, and to gag and choke on the bitter pain of rejection. Petra wanted to stay here in the present enjoying the excitement of recent events, but like some psychological whirlpool, the presence of Darius and his mission to convey a message from Razi had sucked her into its depths and she was there again, on the castle lawn. It was the fourth of August '33.

Like a fortune teller in some kind of trance, she described the day; the sunshine was so hot it was baking the grass, stiffening and bleaching the heavy canvas of the marquees and forcing the many people who attended the momentous royal event to hide under parasols fanning themselves and drinking copious fluids. She was deeply unhappy because she did not want to be betrothed, could not imagine a worse fate and had begged her father to spare her for just another year. "Don't fret, you won't be married for at least two more years my dear!" he kept saying, "It's just a match, a promise to your future husband."

"Can't we leave it one more year my darling?" asked her mother cautiously, and not for the first time.

"No. It's all arranged. They are all here. Each one is a useful match for the Realm." He wasn't to be budged. "Forty!" he exclaimed, "I have found you 40 potential husbands and you must choose just one, one! Any one of them who you like," and when she looked angrily back at him, "Petra! There *has* to be one among them you will accept! Most girls in the Kingdom would wander blindfolded among them and be delighted with the first one she might stumble into." She folded her arms, petulant and stubborn. "Normally Princesses in your shoes have a choice of three, six at most. Many are given no choice, promised to a match of political convenience at six or seven years old, even younger sometimes and married off at 11 or 12 to produce an heir!" She didn't budge. The King turned to the Queen and jabbed an angry finger close to her face. "This is your doing! She is spoiled, difficult beyond reason, disobedient… Why if I had disobeyed my father…"

"I'm sorry Petra," interrupted the Queen, "Your father is right. You are infinitely more fortunate than most young women in your position. You must choose one young man." Then more softly, almost imploringly, she said, "You can still be yourself. You can still have friends. Choose yourself a companion. Have five if you like! But go out there, find one young man, tell him he is to be your husband and then bring him back to us. That's all you have to do."

But Petra was petulant and with wild eyes and clenched fists she shouted, "In which case I'll just choose the worst for the realm. I'll choose the one you would hate as a son-in-law!" and as she finished, she actually stamped her feet.

"They are all acceptable to me," said the King nonchalantly eating dried pineapple, a particular favourite nibble of his, "I may have personal preferences, but out of kindness, I have not befuddled you with them. That's true isn't it? So all you have to do is toddle off out there and choose one." He said this last bit like he was talking to a child of four not 14, waggling a finger in the direction of 'outside' and paying more attention to the bowl of dried pineapple than to her. Petra remained stock still, arms tightly folded, face down and pouting. He finished chewing and turned to her. Then suddenly bellowed, "CHOOSE ONE!!" making Petra and the Queen almost jump out of their skins.

The teenaged Princess burst into anguished tears and ran from the tent, into the dazzling bright sunshine and bounded off between some tents towards the castle. A dozen strides later she collided heavily with Prince Razi, knocking him to the floor. Petra may have been just 14, but horse riding, archery and a great deal of practicing with a sword had given her muscle most girls simply didn't have and the muscle weighed hard and heavy on her strong, milk-fed bones. His surprise turned to dismay when he saw her face streaked with tears and jumping up, he immediately led her away from the onlookers and out of sight among the many smaller awnings. "Whatever can be the matter? A beautiful Princess on her birthday! The world assembled to offer their admiration and compete for your hand! Why, if ever a Princess ought to be happy, today is the day!" He was taller, though not substantially, but at 21 years of age and as a consequence of his encouragement and care he seemed fraternal, paternal almost. He held her hands lightly and sat down on a wooden chest, but she would not, instead, she remained standing in front of the Prince.

"They do not want me!"

"Whyever would you say such a thing?" he said, looking up into her face.

"I have heard them, *'She looks like a man!' 'I fear she would beat me in a contest of strength!' 'She reminds me of that spider that might kill and eat her lover!'*" she mimicked.

"Oh!" he laughed, "they repartee with each other this way to put each other off and to soften the disappointment of not being chosen, for their individual chances are slim indeed. They all wish fervently for your hand, yet few believe you might stoop so low as to choose them." She looked him in the eye and a slight smile began to appear. "So, who is in the lead? Who do you favour? Tell me and it will be our secret!" They paused as the King passed by on one of the thoroughfares calling her name. She could tell he was still angry, but at least he cared enough to look for her.

When he was out of earshot, she answered Razi in a quiet confiding voice "I want none of them."

"So you think they do not want you, but in any case, you do not want them..."

Razi looked confused so she continued, "I do not wish to marry now or ever. I have no interest in being a wife and I certainly do not want to be *somebody's*. I want to remain my own. I am *mine*, I cannot be given away because I am not a gift. I refuse to be possessed."

Razi was taken aback, but also mildly impressed, "My, you have spirit!" She looked from side to side, while he remained fixed on her face. As her head turned she would catch his eye, linger a moment, then continue to turn the other way. She also rocked slightly to and fro and as she did so, she softened. "I'm guessing your father the King has his mind made up?" he swept an arm, "And that all this is not for nothing?" Petra nodded, a look of regret hanging on her like an invisible weight with a dark shadow. She sighed heavily and gently, unknowingly, stamped a foot. "You'll have to choose *someone*..." he said.

"I WILL NOT!" she shouted, causing Razi to jerk back slightly.

"But Princess, you _must_! I do not think this day can end without such a resolution. It is expected. The King expects it. The press is in attendance with the big-haired reporter ladies waiting to alter all the facts to suit the preferences of their slice of readership, the world awaits their columns and hand-drawn illustrations, its breath is held in fascination and excitement."

Petra stamped her feet again and grunted in passionate frustration. Tears appeared and ran down her cheeks once more. "But, but I do not want to, I do not, I do not!"

Razi shook her hands as if to rid her of this unresourceful emotional state and stood up, now looking down slightly. "Who is your choice? Who is... the least awful of all of these dreadful, ugly, ineligible Princes?"

She fixed her jaw firmly and with steely determination said, "I choose no one. That is my decision and if I am forced, I will vanish, I will die, I will fling myself from a cliff, I will ride my horse over the edge and she and I will die together!" She looked wild, bordering on violence, her muscles were tense and Razi was aware she was no ordinary girl.

Calmly, slowly, he said, "And yet, if you did have to choose, if you were to make your own choice, if you chose life, and if that life could allow you sufficient freedom to be yourself, to *not* be a possession, but a woman in your own right, a Queen, and not just a Queen, but a Queen with power, with a mind, with her own life, her own ways, her own choices. Then who?" and with her eyes fixed on him and a new expression of something dangerous beginning to form, Razi took a slight step back. She began to grin and there was something slightly manic about it, impish. "Oh, no, I mean er..."

"You!" she said with a laugh, "I choose no one! I choose me! But if I have to choose some ridiculous and annoying man, then the least infuriating, the least exasperating," she laughed, a bubble of snot appeared and was sniffed away again, she pushed him backwards and he fell back to a seated position, "The least repulsive! The least disgusting! The least stupid! The least pathetic!" she continued to push him with both hands with every accusation, so that he rocked forward and back again under her gentle assault. "The least likely to waste MY life while they aimlessly drift through their own pointless existence... that man is YOU Prince Razi! Decision made! Thank you so much for coming everyone!" she wafted a hand skyward and waved it regally, laughing at herself and sniffing the persistent snot bubble up again. Her face was red and blotchy with tears, but she smiled. Razi stared. She was beautiful when she cried, but outshone all nature when she smiled. After all the sadness, frustration and fear of these recent weeks, the Princess saw that there was a way out. Razi would make it alright. He would respect her and not just expect her to behave like a mute and obedient lapdog… with a belly permanently and grotesquely swollen by a parasitic series of heirs, one after another with barely a gap between them and the cycle only ending when she would die in childbirth. He would not expect that.

When the decision to marry Petra off had been announced, her life had taken a sudden and dramatic turn. She had gone from utter contentedness to abject misery and could no longer imagine her own future without detesting the prospect. If not for Razi that is. From being a vixen snared in a cruel steel trap, driven mad by captivity and prepared to chew off its own leg to win her freedom, a solitary means of escape had appeared which left her almost intact. One chance that it might just be alright after all. Her relief was palpable, almost overwhelming. She would be eternally grateful to Razi. With a bit of effort and application, she might even learn to love him for this, because he was a good man. Whatever his other qualities, he was nice, something so easily overlooked and yet so, so important in a person's character; being nice, the way he was being right now, as a first reaction to a situation. Decent, kind and nice. He could be worse, like so many of the proud, strutting peacocks or pampering poodles who spent too much time in front of a mirror. Most couldn't even fight.

She sat astride him in a most improper manner, her forearms resting on his shoulders as she laughed temptingly. Razi stood up, lifting her to a standing position in the process and to stop her pushing him anymore, held her wrists tightly and low by their waists. They were pulled closely together. Her smile was victorious and for the first time in weeks, she was almost happy. She stretched her neck slightly and half closed her eyes. He took a half step back shaking his head and quietly, so quietly it was almost inaudible said, "No." He let go of her, said "No," again, then "No, no, no!" turned and left her alone in the tent. Stunned, abandoned, appalled, confused, explosive.

Minutes later, the assembled throng gasped, some even screamed as they were forced to dive out of the way of the charging dappled grey mare as it cut through them at great speed with Princess Petra at the reins, clods of earth and clouds of dust exploding from its thundering hooves as it bolted past. The crowd stared in awe at the magnitude of what was happening and at the power she exhibited through galloping so hard and so fast. None had ever ridden at such a pace, few had ever seen it done. More screams erupted as she reached a distant hedge higher than the horse itself for all were certain a calamity was about to occur, but the horse rose as if flying and the Princess sailed over and out of sight. She was gone and the crowd stared in silence. The King stared with them, his head shaking almost imperceptibly. The Queen's eyes were not on the horizon though, she had turned towards her husband and standing very close, had fixed upon him such a glare of intense anger as could scarcely be believed. His face burning, he turned to her and began to speak, "I... I..." he was at his most broken, suddenly desperately sorry but his demeanour changed as the Queen's eyes rose to the sky and glazed while she simultaneously crumpled into the vast heap of her elaborate dresses.

Her physician would soon announce that the Queen had suffered a brain embolism, that she was very weak and slipping in and out of consciousness. He suspected she had been ill for some time and had been bravely hiding the fact in order to avoid overshadowing the occasion. He expected she would not last the night. She did, but not the next. Hanging on in the hope her daughter might return, but tragically, they were never to see each other again, for it was nearly three months before Petra was ready to venture home and explain the conditions she felt she must insist on, if she were to stay. This was a simpler matter than she had expected because having lost both his wife and daughter, he had sunk into deep despair and longed for their return. His wife was gone and could never come back and so all his hopes were fixed on Petra and he swore nightly while clutching small paintings of both, that if she returned, he would devote himself to her happiness, that all else could be set aside. And when she finally rode back into the castle one sunrise, she found it empty of staff, quiet save for the whimpered greetings of Dragon and the echoing, greeting caws of crows on the battlements. As her faithful mare shuffled on the familiar smelling cobbles, she looked around and hoped she could stay for, aside from the last few months, this was the only home she had ever known. It had been raining hard and the air was heavy with ozone. Heavy droplets of water fell from high battlements and splatted on hard stone which was always so bright when dry and slick and dark when wet like this. The place looked sad and almost lifeless and while it was her home, she understood it had no actual power over her. Unlike her father who she missed so much it hurt her heart. Cawing crows, rain sodden stone, and the high towers dripping tears for her mother, cruelly taken far too soon. It was such a contrast from the blazing hot and sunny day on which she had galloped away.

The story had been told and Petra looked deeply and longingly at Shoshama who pulled her in and hugged her warmly and at length, feeling her relax and breathe out as they pressed together. The account had affected her deeply and Shoshama delicately wiped tears away from the lower of her eyelids and dabbed her red and blotchy cheeks. She desperately wanted to kiss Petra to show her affection and although the kiss would be sororal, she felt she could not while Darius observed them so closely. Strange, because on any other occasion and with anyone else, she wouldn't have hesitated. For his part, Darius waited patiently while Princess Petra leaned back on the sofa deep in thought until finally she looked up and asked, "What is his message? What can Razi possibly say that would explain his actions that day? I was 14, he was a man! I thought that he might save me, instead he threw me to the wolves and my world collapsed. In 48 hours my mother was dead. In a week, the castle, *this* castle was all but empty. The Kingdom was frozen, leaderless, treading water, suspended in time. So, Darius, What – Is – His – Message?"

He took a deep breath, "When he returned, he spoke of how you rode away that day, the speed, the power and the way you jumped the highest hedge he had ever seen attempted by horse and rider. He said no warrior, no equestrian showman could ride like you. You amazed Razi!" Petra shrugged, although she was not impervious to the compliment.

"But he also had something else to say. He was sent here by my father, the King of our country in the hope of winning your favour and tying our two realms, and when he returned, we were all anxious to hear the news. At first there was joy when he admitted you had chosen him and then dismay when he told us that he had turned you down. In the shouting that followed he said he loved another, a common girl from the village who was already with-child by him and that he intended to marry her. My father demanded he give her up. He said he would have the peasant girl marry someone else who would look after her, that she would receive a pension, she would be fine and that she didn't need a Prince and that Razi would forget her in a month." Darius paused and sighed deeply, then allowed the smallest chuckles.

"Ah my brother! Razi refused to listen. They raved at each other," said Darius, smiling in his amazement at the drama he witnessed as a boy and waving his arms in a very un-Darius-like way. "Anyway, my father finished the argument by throwing him out and saying he was no longer a Prince." He delivered the conclusion like the bombshell it was. The Princesses mouths fell open.

"That left me as the heir." The Princesses were rapt. "I visited Razi, he lived well enough in the village and gradually, bit by bit and as the months passed, he was allowed to draw upon some of what used to be his wealth to establish himself as a farmer and landowner, so during that period, there was at least peace in the family because you see, not only was the girl from the village a total delight, but she bore them a son and suddenly my parents were doting grandparents. That's when I saw my chance." Shoshama and Petra both looked puzzled. "I said I did not wish to be King." Petra gasped, putting a hand to her mouth and Shoshama let out a cheeky *oops*, "And before I could suggest my nephew take the role of first-in-line to the throne, my father was ahead of me and already announcing it to all who would listen. So, there we are. My father is in very good health and this little boy is growing up to be the next King of my country."

"Is that the message? He wanted me to know he is married to a girl who is an utter, total delight and has a son who will be King?"

"No, no!" Darius, held up a hand in apology, "I wanted to give you the background. The message follows. Perhaps I am at fault for over-flowering things." Petra and Shoshama both shook their heads at the same speed, patiently looking earnestly at Darius and waiting for the next flowery instalment of his explanation. Shoshama remained worried, would there yet be something to cause the two lovers a problem. She was feeling uncharacteristically jealous, knew what it was, didn't like it but had no idea how to not feel it. She resented Darius being in Petra's bedroom and wanted the Princess to say, *Oh I don't care, I have everything I want right here.*

"He wanted you to know that he was sorry…" continued the Prince.

Petra threw her hands up, "Oh that's fine then. I may have been emotionally destroyed by the careless, ill-mannered way he cast me aside, but if he's sorry, everything is fine!" she was getting louder with every sentence, "Shall I send him a gift? Perhaps a bag of horse manure!" she shouted. Shoshama laughed, but did her best to pull Petra in, to stop her raging or perhaps storming off.

Darius spoke more calmly, "He said that he fell in love with you right there and then, on the spot, in an instant, but that the girl he was to marry was already pregnant with his child and although no one knew, and being a Prince he probably could have made all of that go away, he wouldn't do that to this simple girl and to the unborn child." Petra was charged with so many emotions from the day's events and now found herself welling up. Her high emotion finding an outlet and as she sniffled, a tear fell and as soon as it did, Shoshama's tears fell too. This symbiosis that had so quickly tied them together had made emotional mirrors of them. "He was _so_ sorry. He didn't reject you, he didn't want to say no, he was actually falling in love with you but honour kept him on the path he was already treading."

At this point, Chatty knocked on the door and called out to them but Shoshama shouted back that he should go away.

"Oh sorry!" he said a bit pathetically, "Only lunch is ready. We couldn't find you. The King is there. Have you got Darius in there? Is Princess Petra there?"

"Yes, yes. It's alright Chatty, we'll be there in a minute," she said more kindly.

"What are you all doing? Can I come in?" Chatty hated being left out of anything and goodness knows what he might be thinking. Actually, his head was empty for his imagination could come up with nothing that might be going on and that's why he was desperate to come in and see what he might be missing.

"Chatty?" called Petra, wiping away a tear.

"Yes Princess?"

"We'll be there in a minute darling. Off you go now." And with that he seemed content all was well, said *'Alright then'* and paced away.

Shoshama smiled, "I think the blood is returning to his head. He seems to be back to..."

"Were you going to say normal?" said Darius laughing.

"Well, normal for Chatty. You know what I mean!" said Shoshama. They laughed a little as Petra wiped away her tears with her sleeve, relenting when Shoshama took over and attended her with a kerchief.

"It's alright, really, it's alright," said Petra. "I thought I might like him enough for him to be the one, but I didn't run away simply because he rejected me, I ran away from the whole stupid day! I was 14! I didn't want to be married to a man and I still don't. It was never his fault and I would never have made such a good wife as this girl he has married. He has a son, you have a nephew, your father has an heir. I wouldn't want to be responsible for producing any of that! What happened to me wasn't Razi's fault. I don't even blame my father because he was just following custom..." she sighed deeply, shifted her posture. "I'm just... different I suppose. Some people will think there's something wrong with me, but I know exactly what I want!" and with that she pulled Shoshama closer. "I suppose I always have known it, even if I didn't know I knew it."

"Yeah that makes sense," said Shoshama as she was pulled

and squeezed and Darius smiled, loving his Shoshama like an old friend, feeling delighted for her and greatly admiring his new friend. Darius appeared to be happy for them but Shoshama still hesitated when it came to kissing her new love.

"Come on, we'd better go," said Petra. They stood and she leaned over to give Darius a hug and thanked him, then turned to Shoshama and gave her the mightiest squeeze and kissed her head several times with accompanying *mwaa* sound effects.

Now Adalbert bounced into the room, humming loudly and cheerily. Petra turned and both she and Shoshama shouted, "Alright Adalbert, we are coming!" together and exactly in time. Flummoxed, but not offended, he swivelled theatrically and left as quickly as he had arrived.

Darius paused and looked at her closely, "Allow me to say it Princess Petra, there is nothing at all wrong with you. You are more than special. You, my dear, dear Princess can have anything you set your mind to, or anyone you set your sights upon." He looked at Shoshama and smiled. He continued, "You are a remarkable woman like no other I have ever met. Well, that's not quite true because the more I think about it, the more I realise that perhaps you are a lot like Shoshama, but no one else I've ever met." The Princesses laughed and side by side, pulled each other in at the hips.

The two young women walked to the window where sunshine had broken through the clouds and was flooding into the room in golden, dusty shafts. Darius watched and there was an elongated pause while the two Princesses studied each other. Shoshama allowed a flicker across her lips and eyes, Petra's face changed from milky pale to a pinker shade. "No more broken hearts," Princess Petra said, "Mine races and swells fit to burst." Synchronised they smiled at Darius, then turned to gaze at each other and Darius, amazed yet joyful, cried with happiness for them.

Chapter the Twenty-Second.
Party Planners

"The plan!" said Petra at lunch, "Is to announce a Royal Garden Party for the people of the city. A feast, music and dancing. And at which we will reveal the good work we have been doing with the children. At the same time, we will introduce Dragon to the people." The King puffed out his cheeks, his immediate reaction made him appear unconvinced. "Father, they are coming after us. All these things are going to be revealed whether we like it or not. This way we do it on our terms, we are in control. Dragon is a harmless Great Dane, he doesn't look harmless I grant you that, but he certainly is. And the children, well... we just have to think about how to do it right, we have to orchestrate it so it's obvious they are fine here or we will lose them."

The room was boisterously noisy with 90 children eating, talking, laughing, occasionally one would cry and receive attention from an older child, be put back on the bench from where they had fallen, or have the soup replaced they had flipped into their own face, or be led to the bathroom for a major clean-up after what was known in the castle as an SPI (an equally major Surprise-Poo-Incident) and if it was bad enough a *Pootastrophe* which might be described as *Pootastrophic*. This chaos was their normality and they were safe, warm, well-fed and loved. They occupied a place in their own society and they were receiving an education. "You have to show them this," said Darius pointing. "Create a tour. We will prepare the older children to do group tours all day. People can see academic and physical education classes, the excellent facilities you provide, this great diet they receive and they can talk to the children themselves. We just need to structure it, manage it, brief the children so they understand."

"Well volunteered young Darius!" barked the King, "Next!" Darius threw up his hands in surprise but accepted the role and laughed about being caught like that. "Prince Adalbert, you are in charge of catering. We'll have a thousand here every day for each of the three days. Get yourself down to Mrs Gregory's Delicious Sandwich and Vegetarian Sausage Roll Emporium and plan it with her."

Adalbert looked petrified at the prospect so Princess Petra jumped in, "Don't worry, she's amazing. You just tell her the numbers and she'll take care of everything." He wiped his brow with mock-phewness.

"But you'll be her man so to speak," added the King, "You and she are in charge of food."

"Well, I *do* like food, it's true…" mused Adalbert, thinking about it.

"Do you really my boy?" laughed the King, "I can't say I noticed!" he said and laughed some more.

"Chatty?" Petra said addressing the last Prince, "Do you know anything of music and dance?" Shoshama and the other two Princes laughed, because while he was expert on very little, these were things close to his heart.

"A bit," he said, unsure whether the laughter was supportive, but then they explained it was absolutely his thing and he was given the task of recruiting musicians to play through the day and the arrangement of a dance to be held on the evening of the third and final day in the Great Hall for selected guests.

"I was rather hoping I might have a job which included the Mayor," he said meekly.

"Including disappearing up the Mayor's dresses, you mean!" laughed the King. "Don't fret boy, she'll have you on a leash before you can say hoot to an owl! You'll need *Swordy* if you ever want to fight her off and even then, I wouldn't give you good odds!" They all laughed, including Darius, who understood better than most. "No, no lad, you sort out all the *Shimmy-Fandango-Boogie-Woogie*!"

"We'll have dancing outside each day," said Chatty, his face alive with enthusiasm. "Competitions, lessons, displays and demonstrations!" he was already in his element and they all agreed it would be marvellous.

"We," said Petra, indicating the King and Shoshama, "will meet with the Mayor and the Chief of Police." There was silence as Petra contemplated the difficult meeting and pleading their case. A lot hung on the cooperation of the main city officials.

"They are with us, don't you worry my pet," said the King, "But we must be quick enough to prevent that Krackedarse woman from gaining support."

"I have a separate plan for that miserable, self-righteous, poo-stirring, harpy hag but it's risky." They looked at her, waiting for it but her response made it clear she wasn't ready to share just yet.

"Reading between the lines, do I detect a mild dislike for the woman?" said the King, breaking the silence and making everybody laugh again.

"Meanwhile, there's a mountain of publicity needed to win popular support. We need posters, invitations, tickets, it all needs organising."

"On it," said Shoshama raising a hand. "And how about stalls? Local traders, marketeers, vendors? Let's bring the life of the city to the castle grounds?" They cheered and agreed. "And we're not just trying to save the school here… is it a school? An orphanage?" Petra shrugged and agreed a school would do, "Let's go big. Let's propose to expand it for day-pupils. There will be more classes, from more teachers, state funded education for every child! We will be the first realm in the world to offer such a thing!"

"We…" said Petra nudging her and enjoying Shoshama's adoption of Prague.

"What? I love it here!" said Shoshama, and the Princes all joined in with similar sentiments. "While I'm on a roll, Mr and Mrs Wife will supply the wine I presume?" She addressed this to the King.

"Of course!" said the King, "You know House and Mister?" she confirmed with a happy nod. "Yes, yes, no one knows wine like Mister. Come to think of it, we are going to need staff up here again."

"Oh I rather think they have settled into retirement somewhat and I was rather hoping they could be guests."

"No need to ever retire from tasting wine!" laughed the King, "No, no, we'll get new kitchen staff and they can carry on as they are. Yes, they can be guests, two of my favourite people!"

Darius spoke up again, "I rather think you have the makings of your next wave of kitchen staff right here amongst the young ones. All they need is a little adult supervision and training." The King agreed and added there were all sorts of skillsets being developed and that the school ought to be recognised as a place of development for the city's future commercial, agricultural and industrial specialists.

"Now then, when?" said the King and all reasonable suggestions were rejected until he finally announced, "Next weekend. It has to be. Posters must go out today. We cannot wait so come on you lot get busy!" They finished up their plates and tipped back the ale from their glasses and stood up from the table, energised, focused and motivated. One by one, the King hugged each of them and thanked them personally, calling them *my son* until Shoshama, who he led aside and said quietly, "Thank you young lady for bringing my daughter's spirit back. I have never, ever seen her so happy. If it lasts a day, a week or a lifetime, it will still have been worth waiting four years to see."

"Would it be very silly to say I hope it will last a lifetime?" asked the Princess peering up into his broad face.

"Yes," he said laughing, "For we never know what will happen in the future, we only know our intentions in the present. But don't let my cynicism deflate your zeal because our intentions matter even more than our actions." He squeezed her arms and shook her slightly and Shoshama smiled, amused by the way men naturally showed affection.

Petra joined them and put her arms around both, "The two people I love most in the world!" she was squeezed back by her father and the Princess. "And mummy of course."

"Of course," said the King.

After what seemed like an eternity in the midst of this group hug Shoshama spoke, her voice slightly muffled, "They do?" asked Shoshama.

"They do what dear?" asked the King, leaning back.

"Intentions matter more than actions? I know actions speak bolder than words, but do intentions speak bolder than actions?"

"You've got a thinker here Petra. I do like a thinker! Keep musing and sometime, we'll have a chat if you haven't figured it out by then?" he said rubbing her back with his big hand.

"You can't just tell me now?" she asked.

"No, no! It's far better if you use your brain. I'll just fill in the blanks. Eventually."

"It's what he does," said Petra, still looking at her father.

"He is the best King a Princess could ever have as a father and I love him so." And with that they squeezed once more and parted. There was a great deal of work to do if the Status Quo was to be maintained.

Chapter the Last.
Afterglow & Mirrorball

After the busiest week of their lives spent in preparation and four very long days of Prague's public amassing in the grounds of the castle, the royals and guests settled into their assigned seats in the Great Hall, in readiness for what Chatty had named, the Great Prague Ball. Though somewhat exhausted, they were euphoric, for all-in-all, the extravagant events could not have gone better and now, with the hard work behind them, they were free to relax among friends, drink and be truly merry.

Such had been the clamour for tickets that the proposed one 1000 guests per day for three days swelled to 1200 per day and extended into a fourth. What's more, so many additional Praguers made the trek up the long and winding road to the castle just to get a glimpse of proceedings, that low fences were erected and areas cordoned off for those without tickets to sit with their families, have a picnic and observe at least some of the excitement from a short distance. This necessitated moving some stalls and traders to line the outer wall of the castle to unobstruct the view of the various daily activities.

The Mayor made the most tremendous speeches to open and close each day's proceedings, establishing the Queen Angelika Děti Škola as Prague's new school, those last two words being old language for children and school. State funding was a simple matter, for in consultation with the Mayor, it became apparent that a healthy city economy which had been greatly boosted over the last couple of years by the low taxation, had provided more than sufficient revenues. Without a military to support, and with a very economical realm and King, the state and royal bank accounts were delightfully full and land had been earmarked between the city and the castle for the creation of a fabulous new facility for education, including full-time residency for any children who needed its sanctuary. Funds were further boosted by the commercial sponsorship, first of classrooms, then of entire wings as volunteers lined up to offer the Mayor money if their family name and crest could adorn some aspect of the buildings. This had turned into something of a competition when Mr and Mrs Wife had the Mayor make a public announcement that they would be sponsoring the construction of a School of Oenology as part of the new facility. There, youngsters would learn the art of winemaking for commercial enterprise. It was this announcement that started the rush of donations, as other Praguers decided that if people living in modest Castlerock Street could afford to assist then so could they and all manner of lump sums followed.

Tours of the existing school facilities resulted in hundreds of adults blowing their noses and dabbing their adoring teary eyes as they were waved out of the castle exit after a 30 excursion through the premises allocated to the children within the castle. Darius had arranged examples of all the various activities of which the children regularly partook, plus the school kitchen where food was either being prepared or served as well as the exercise courtyard and kitchen garden. Adorable toddlers explained how happy they were and the older children spoke of the practicalities of their good fortune to have been rescued. Brief accounts of their former misery brought gasps of shock and horror from the public who had little experience of that now extinguished aspect of society. Each afternoon, when the Mayor spoke of the achievements of the school from child rescue to providing a safe environment and an education for a future outside of the facility when the oldest completed their tenure at 13, she could barely string more than a couple of sentences together without the crowd applauding enthusiastically, causing her to pause and wait for them to quieten down. But the loudest cheers were when the Mayor brought the King on stage followed by a further increase in volume when Princess Petra climbed the steps, introduced as the architect of the present school and the mother to the city's abandoned and maltreated children. As the pair of royals bowed to their subjects, the Whoop-Whoops! grew ever louder and most people couldn't decide whether to wipe their happy tears from their cheeks, blow their drippy noses or just keep clapping from sheer, unbounded admiration.

Music and dancing provided a delightful backing track to each day's event, the former being delivered by a variety of talented musical acts. The posters all claimed *Daily Melodious Musical Acts* and Chatty spent the entire week trying to get Adalbert to pronounce the word. He was stuck on *malodorous* and no amount of practice or repetition was able to shift him.

"Melodious," said Chatty.

"Malodorous," replied Adalbert.

"Melodious!" repeated Chatty,

"Malodorous!" replied Adalbert with extra enthusiasm.

"No! MELODIOUS!" exclaimed Chatty with extra zest in the form of volume.

"MALODOROUS!" replied Adalbert, just as loudly.

"Adalbert listen!" pleaded Chatty with desperation. Adalbert concentrated. "Mel."

"Mel," replied Adalbert carefully.

"Odi," said Chatty, hopeful.

"Odi" said Adalbert.

"Uss!" said Chatty pleased.

"Uss!" shouted Adalbert, proudly.

"That's it! Now put it together, "Mel-odi-uss, melodious!"

"Malodorous!" barked Adalbert, delighted with himself. Chatty looked like he might cry, gave a feeble smile and walked off. "You're not introducing any of the acts Adalbert," he said, moodily over his shoulder.

"Can if you want me to!" answered Adalbert cheerily, "Anything to help!" It hadn't been necessary.

The daily dancing competitions Chatty had promised presented an opportunity for he and the Mayor to take to the temporary wooden floor to give demonstrations and they probably would have won prizes had they not ruled themselves ineligible, for it seems this was something they both had a deep passion for. Of course, the other thing they both had a deep passion for was each other and this required frequent visits to seek privacy within the castle. By Day Four, people were beginning to comment that the pair needed to eat some more of Mrs Gregory's delicious vegetarian sausage rolls because it looked as if all the dancing was making them lose weight. "There'll be nothing left of you!" said Mrs Gregory to the Mayor.

"You'll be chamfered to a fine point!" laughed the King to young Chatty.

There were so many dancing lessons offered by local talented experts that it resulted in an agreement to establish a School of Dance within the new Děti Škola and such was the interest in the art of the musicians, that this was supplemented by a School of Music whose teachers would include the various visiting sons of Mister and House, who between them were virtuosos on most stringed instruments, keyboards and percussion. Of course, Shoshama was an accomplished pianist in her own right and performed twice daily at the events and added her promise to give lessons at the new music school. Excited young men lined up for her autograph, spluttering out admiration for her playing and afterwards agreeing amongst themselves that she was a goddess and claiming they felt they had made a special connection with her in the few seconds of her company in which all manner of exaggerated glances and reciprocal compliments were invented for the purposes of boasting. And dreaming, and wishing, and maybe even hoping.

Adalbert and Mrs Gregory outdid themselves, providing such a feast that the city had never seen its like, even in the great days of the dear, late Queen. In the week leading up to the events, Mrs Gregory had run her baking facility 24 hours a day with three shifts, rapidly employing and training new staff. While the 4800 ticket holders ate heartily, the young waiters and waitresses took food to the boundary and gave delicious sandwiches and even more delicious hot vegetarian sausage rolls to the crowd beyond the low fence. Joining them on occasion in dishing out the ample food were Mrs Gregory herself, well known to many city folk but also the Mayor, the Princes, the King and Princesses Petra and Shoshama. These generous interactions did a great deal to make the royal family the subject of popular adulation and many were heard speaking of the outstanding beauty of Princess Shoshama with her contemporary Deep Purple hairstyle and of the handsomest of Princes ever seen, that being Darius. Such was his popularity with the women of Prague, that along with some letters (including proposals) and bouquets of flowers for the two Princesses, his personal fan mail arrived by the sack full.

One notable thing was that Adalbert had taken literally the King's command that he be Mrs Gregory's *man*. When he introduced himself to her in her fabulous emporium on the very same day plans had been laid out, he bowed, kissed her hand and said, "The King has sent me to you and says, *I am to be your man*," which seemed to get them off to a particularly good start. Now perhaps Mrs Gregory wasn't quite as wildly abandoned with her lust as the Mayor, but the well fed widow had been without a man for several years now and wasn't too reticent to allow nature to take its course. Adalbert had never met anyone with such culinary skills and she had never encountered anyone quite so genuinely generous with their praise for what she could achieve in the kitchen. And in other rooms of her various properties, if so minded.

After the first day of the event, Mrs Tickle-Krackedarse arrived at the castle gates hand-in-hand with young Libor. Two days previously, Petra had taken fate into her hands by taking him to the very stately Tickle-Krackedarse mansion in the Malá Strana district of the city. While the older woman stood silently fierce and tight-lipped, Petra told the boy, "Libor, this is the nice lady I told you about," and after explaining at great length all of the boy's preferences, likes and dislikes, habits and hobbies, encouraged the shuffling mite to shake hands.

Mrs Tickle-Krackedarse was clearly taken aback by the depth of personal detail she was expected to absorb and said to the boy, "Well young man, you can tell me all about it over a cup of tea and a custard cream. Do you like custard creams? I also have ginger nuts." He gave an embarrassed little nod and after a firm nudge from Petra, said boldly, "Yes thank you, I do like custard creams *and* ginger nuts!" and this was further confirmed by Petra smiling and saying, he loved all biscuits, cakes and sweet things in general, but that he was a good little boy who would eat most things presented to him.

Petra received a long look from the older woman and read in it some conflict and when Libor momentarily resisted letting go of Petra's hand, she looked slightly pained, guilty even and promised him they could visit the castle soon, phrasing it as a question and looking at Petra for confirmation. The Princess stooped and hugged him and said, "Of course darling Libor, anytime!" then looking at Mrs Tickle-Krackedarse said, "Anytime at all, for absolutely anything at all," then, "Go on Libor," at which he walked into the substantial house, peering over his shoulder with a slightly sad expression and a long, awkward wave.

And now he was back and when Petra asked whether he had come to visit, the older lady said that if it was alright with the Princess, that he should re-join his friends, from whom the parting had caused him to cry himself to sleep on both the two nights prior, but that the invitation to live with she and her husband remained forever open. Petra scooped him up and immediately he gripped hold like a monkey, with his arms about her neck and his legs clasped above her hips, his face pressed firmly against hers. Then looking deeply into Mrs Tickle-Krackedarse's eyes, said, "Thank you. This is very, very good of you."

She looked uncomfortably contrite though her tone remained somewhat aloof and sniffy as she said, "Yes, well, we all want what's best for the children don't we?" flopping a pair of gloves over the free hand which rested on her handbag.

"We do. Please visit Libor again soon," and although she wondered whether the older lady ever would, was pleasantly surprised to hear that arrangements had been made to take him out for the day the following week and that he could select up to three friends for the outing, followed by her asking,

"If that's alright with you, your Royal Highness?" to which Petra said, she thought it was a splendid idea and encouraged Libor to give her benefactor a hug farewell-for-now.

And so, a bridge had been built to the person who had brought so much trouble to their door, but in so doing had caused a very beneficial revolution at the castle. None of the present, extraordinary activities would have happened had it not been for her and so out of fear and strife came resolution. Their world was a better place because the extremely annoying Mrs Tickle-Krackedarse had challenged it. She may have been wrong, but inadvertently she had helped improve the lives of all the people she claimed to despise.

Because of Mrs Tickle-Krackedarse's challenge, many thousands of Praguers had reason to celebrate their great city, its forward-thinking achievements and its extraordinary royals. They saw the orphanage, the school, were entertained by music and dance and treated to a right-royal feast. But there was still more. Extra to the billing on the posters and mail-pieces deposited through every letter box in the realm, was the surprise arrival of an unnamed, unannounced mysterious figure. Once each day, a masked warrior dressed in loose, comfortable clothing of an Eastern style, appeared and put on a demonstration of fighting skills with a variety of weapons as well as unarmed combat. His opponents included Tom, Dick, Harry and Jim and a few invited locals who were either skilled swordsmen, or those adept at fighting with a staff. They were abetted by strong-looking boxers and wrestlers each taking their turn to pit their skills against the masked warrior. While no one was going to be injured in these demonstrations, it was clear that the mystery man outfought them all in their chosen fields, particularly the poor policemen, who though trained in basic fighting skills, were repeatedly thrown on to the soft mattresses or spun around, flipped upside down or made to trip over their own feet. As people shook their heads in wonder, the Chief of Police circulated the crowd identifying who this clearly wasn't, for whoever the masked combatant was, he couldn't be simultaneously performing and watching himself. Many girls and women determined this must surely be the handsome Prince Darius, but the Chief was certain the masked man was taller and, in any case, found Darius watching with fascinated interest on more than one occasion.

"You have organised all this Darius, so who is he?" asked the Chief.

"We each organised one aspect Chief. I don't know who arranged this bit of entertainment and I have absolutely no idea who the masked man is. I'm just glad he's on our side." Looking closely at Darius and knowing him to be a foreign agent with fighting skills, the Chief wondered, but was inclined to believe him. One thing the Chief was sure of was that whoever he was, the masked fighting machine was more popularly known about the city as Sir Hillman, an elusive vigilante who had eradicated a few lowlifes from Prague over the years. When one of the performances ended, the Chief followed him, but watched in awe as he scaled the castle walls like some kind of spider-acrobat and disappeared over the battlements.

One particular man in the ticketed audience had aroused the chief's curiosity on the first day because of his strikingly foreign appearance. His skin colour matched Princess Shoshama's and his black facial hair included a moustache with Fu Manchu tails and longish beard that spread barely wider than his mouth. He was certainly not local and added to his own mystique by being among the last to leave and then arriving with the earliest members of the public the next day, and the next. Since members of the public were allowed only a single ticket each, this was already odd. On the third day, the Chief was so concerned he sent Dick to keep an eye on him, but the constable returned five minutes later saying, "It's alright, he's Princess Shoshama's bodyguard."

"What? You didn't ask him, did you? You were just supposed to watch him!"

"I know and the first time I took my eyes off him he vanished and the next thing I know he's tapping me on the shoulder and telling me I should tell you not to worry, he's here because her dad the King sent him on the trip to Vienna and she doesn't know he's here because she thinks she sent him home from the wedding with her ladies."

The Chief just said "Oh," it all ringing true and on the fourth and final day, he received a nod of acknowledgement from the man when he personally swept the audience and found him in his usual seat which was near the back and without an especially good view. The Chief nodded back awkwardly and decided to tell the King. The King told Shoshama and she plucked him out of the departing crowd and had him take up quarters in the castle. Apparently, he had purchased lodgings opposite Mister and House's home in Castlerock Street, somewhat alarming his hosts by turfing them out of their front bedroom but paying so handsomely, they moved out of the house entirely. He'd then spent several days and nights denying himself sleep and watching the front door opposite waiting for Shoshama's departure. When his hosts unexpectedly returned and told him all about the exciting fayres to be held at the castle and of the visiting Princess he bought tickets at many times their face value and attended daily, content that she was safe and happy, but beside himself that he'd obviously nodded off and missed her leaving her lodgings.

Like the Chief, the bodyguard had been fascinated by the masked man doing the combat demonstrations. His own skill was with a pair of curved blades and while he felt skilled beyond all others in their deadly art, he watched in awe and admiration as the performance unfolded each day. The speed, the agility, the combination of four deadly limbs would have been humiliating to a man whose sole purpose was royal protection, if he wasn't instead overcome by a kind of hero-worship.

The highlight of each day was the final event on the schedule and was carefully staged at twilight for the greatest drama. Smoke was generated around the castle gates and fires were lit which spouted and flared while a fanfare of trumpets built tension and 20 deep bass drums beat out a rhythm that started slow, but gradually grew to a crescendo. This cacophony was joined by more and more percussion instruments and finally a brace of electric guitars played by the Wife boys, Jimi, Ozzy, Sammy, Bruce, Lemmy and with Sting on bass.

Then, from the smoke appeared the dragon and people variously gasped and shrieked. The King held him on a lead and made it appear that the dragon was straining, although to the careful observer, he clearly wasn't. The sense of danger was created by the smoke and music, a phrase that would soon after take root in Prague culture so that people would say, "Oh it's all smoke and music!" when referring to something that seemed grand but was really nothing of the sort, more a show for effect than reality. And this was the case with the dragon because as the smoke and flames billowed and electric guitars wailed as their strings were bent and hammered, a small, lone child appeared from the sidelines and approached the dragon. The King pulled back on the dragon's lead and signalled for the child to go back, the crowd shrieked and screamed and called to the child, and some brave souls sought ways of scaling the tall safety fence erected in the area of the castle gates, but realised it wasn't possible and the one passenger gate was temporarily pad-locked for safety. There was panic, mothers cried, fathers banged the fence and people reached fingers through the gaps in desperation.

The little girl was soon in range of the dragon's fiery breath, then closer until the beast might leap forward and bite off her curly-topped head and just as the crowd shrieked its loudest, fearing the best day of their lives might be ruined by infanticide, the child climbed upon the dragon's back. The King released the dragon's leash, the gate was unlocked and the little girl rode it into the main arena to the gasps of the 1200 guests and thousands more gathered in the cheap (well, free actually) seats.

A crowd of 90 children mobbed the dragon and while the monster became virtually invisible amongst them, it was clear he was being hugged and patted and then the oddest thing happened. As the King entered the crowd of little ones, they began to hold up what looked like pieces of the dragon, as if they had torn him apart. The crowd gasped when they saw his tail and again when his skin was held up by several children, his fat legs floppy and lifeless, then they screamed as his fierce head was pushed aloft by older boys. And then the crowd of children parted leaving the King standing next to the biggest dog anyone had ever seen. The shocking, frightening performance, which had invoked near heart attacks in some and temporary loss of bladder control in others ended with the music and flames fading and one man standing with an especially docile dog. The same, original, curly-locked little girl reappeared and after receiving a slobbery lick on the face from Dragon, once more was assisted onto his back, and grabbing him by the scruff, and giving his flanks a light kick, she walked him around the periphery of the arena. Other children followed, the bigger ones lifting the original child off and placing another on and then repeating the exchange over and over without Dragon breaking his stride. And now the crowd cheered and clapped in exhausted and emotional relief as the fearful legend was laid to rest.

And it was here at the close of the day's events that the Mayor would give her final speech, urging people to not spoil the surprises for the next day's guests and so to keep proceedings to themselves until it was all over, to be safe on their way home, to look after themselves and be kind to others, to praise their royal family, for who could ask for finer people to steer the realm? To sleep easy and safe in their beds knowing the Prague Police Force was almost entirely without work and that should anyone step out of line, they'd get their ass kicked by the masked mystery man, who most people agreed was surely Sir Hillman. "Thank you, dear citizens of Prague. You can be proud of yourselves and your city for who can think of a finer place? I can tell you true, there is none! Thank you all, with your help and support, we will continue to strengthen the rock on which our nation is founded, the Magnificent Status Quo! Goodnight, we love you!" and with the loudest cheers and standing ovation imaginable, all the musicians assembled to deliver some especially rousing (and very loud considering it would be a while before Prague scientific genius Jim Marshall would invent amplification), twelve bar blues in E major.

On this fourth and final day, an August Monday that happened to be Petra's 18th birthday and would be established as August Bank Holiday Monday from this day forward, 130 special guests filed in and took their seats in the Great Hall, for the Prague Great Ball.

In the school, newly hired help along with a host of volunteer mums and older girls were laying on a mini ball for the children, their number already boosted by the wider population of Prague no longer hesitating to bring waifs and strays to the Castle. They had food and music and balloons and entertainment in the form of a glove puppet show which told the story of two Princesses, three Princes and a dragon, although the dragon turned out to be pretty mild mannered by the end. This was their first time without either the King or the Princess involved with them and as a portent of times to come, it went tremendously well.

In the Great Hall, the King dressed in all his royal finery had pride of place with Princesses Petra and Shoshama to his right, each in elaborate and exquisite dresses of magenta and gold respectively. Adalbert and the Mayor opposite, Chatty and Mrs Gregory next to them, while Mr Mister Wife and Mrs House Wife had seats reserved for them right next to Shoshama at her special request. Darius was two seats away from the King to his left and, since he had elected not to bring a guest, was seated by the Chief of Police and his wife. Everyone was dressed to impress in their Royal-Ball-Best.

Seated elsewhere among the esteemed and special guests were all the most eminent people of the city, including the Big-Haired Exaggerators of the Press (all paid-up members of BHEP, an organisation devoted to generating income by giving people something to read and whose motto was, *No fact is too crucial to ignore or replace with an alternative*, and who learned the new 'high-fouring' thing and added a drinking cry *'cash over accuracy!'* which, by repetition, got them very drunk indeed).

On one table earmarked for people who needed forgiving and bringing back into the fold were, among others Mr and Mrs Tickle-Krackedarse, their daughter Elena and her new boyfriend. Elena's father, who had spent a lifetime supplying expensive horses to the Royal Household, including the fine specimen ridden by Princess Petra, was glad his wife's animosity to his former employers was at an end and after a week of particular upheaval with the arrival and subsequent departure of young Libor, paraphrased her directly by asking, "Are you settled now? Satisfied they aren't doing the devil's work and fouling the city?"

"Why didn't they tell us? Why did they have to keep it all such a big secret?"

"I don't know my dear. Could it be that some people are a bit quick to jump on their tall cow and become meddlesome nosey-parkering fuckwits?" he said, giving her a gentle and uncharacteristically affectionate pinch on her bony nose.

"I'm very sorry to say, I was entirely wrong on the matter. The King is a thoroughly good man and ignoring the Princess's complete lack of interest in finding herself a suitable mate, I see she is a remarkable woman. Perhaps in devoting herself to these children she has foregone desires of a carnal nature entirely." Mr Tickle-Krackedarse, who, unknown to his wife, owned the biggest mud wrestling club in the city, almost choked on his wine and had to feign a cough as she dabbed at him with her handkerchief. His wife's warped ideas about human nature never ceased to surprise him. "I shall direct my future nosey-parkering at others whose own nosey-parkering will bring no good. Except for that, I feel it is a redundant pastime." Mr Tickle-Krackerarse felt this was substantial progress and smiled like a husband might when slowly learning to admire his wife once again. At the ball, the couple appeared happy.

"They look like their old selves again," said the King to the Mayor. "This is how they were when they were first married, then they started to drift apart and she turned into a right battle-axe. I think Petra's high-risk strategy with young Libor was a master stroke."

"I would like to think I too oiled certain wheels your Majesty," said the Mayor, looking smug. The King appeared more than curious. "I explained that the pair of them had come close to receiving a visit from Sir Hillman and that I had no power to stop their assassination once they'd established themselves as enemies of Prague."

"Enemies of Prague? That's a rather strong verdict on them, especially him, he's been…"

"It was an empty threat, I have no power, no knowledge even, of Sir Hillman's intentions, but it wouldn't have surprised me had they vanished *on holiday*, never to return. He begged me to intervene on their behalf and promised he would try to control her."

The King looked doubtful that was possible, "How would any man do that?"

"I told him, I absolutely ordered him, to attend to her in the manner a husband should, that it was his duty," the King looked anguished and turned from the Mayor to regard the couple across the Great Hall.

"Rather him than me!" he said. "And it appears to have helped. Between you, you have worked a miracle, for I would have wagered she was beyond redemption, when all he needed was some advice about his husbandly responsibilities. So simple!"

"Not really, I also threatened him that I would make him ambassador to the Kingdom of the Scotts and send them both to the wild and woolly highlands where men wear skirts even though the weather is permanently gloomy because it rains even more than in other parts of Britain, where the sun rises late in the morning and sets again just after lunch and the local's favourite food is a load of animal organs encased in the stomach of a sheep and cooked with their version of spice. *'No more Gregory's?'* he asked and that seemed to do it. I think he's been reconnecting regularly with her ever since and using vegetarian sausage rolls as a source of motivation."

"Well it's an end that justified any means necessary," said the King surveying the Great Hall and feeling delighted with the happiness which filled it. To his right, Petra was engrossed in the conversation Shoshama was having with Mr and Mrs Wife. With Shoshama turned slightly to her right and Petra leaning on her to listen in, she was able to enjoy some illicit physical contact amidst this well-behaved ball.

"Beware prying eyes and the tittle-tattle hungry press," said her father to Petra earlier that evening.

"You'll need to try to keep your lips away from hers for a few hours," suggested Darius to Shoshama, causing her to blush and so far, each had taken the advice.

"So we had a foreign Princess under our…" said House smiling and pointing upwards.

"Roof?" offered Shoshama.

"No. We haven't got a roof, it's all just part of the same rock we are standing on."

"Under your rock then," she said smiling. "And thank you so much for those lovely meals and with your help getting me into the castle."

"Mission accomplished eh?"

"I came in search of a missing Princess," said Shoshama.

"And I'm very glad she came!" added Petra. The Wifes bowed slightly while Petra winked at Shoshama.

"It is we who should thank you," said Mister. "The King has told us you requested we be here like this."

"Such an honour," said House.

"Such an honour," said Mister, "And it's ten after eight," he said glancing at his pocket watch the way he did and apropos nothing. "And on top of that, that we should be allowed to continue our wine supply and tasting business in the manner to which it has become accustomed to be after all this time of being." House tutted at his sentence construction.

"Yes, I feel he is happy with the arrangement," said Shoshama.

"And you have given generously to the Děti Škola. You are sponsoring the School of Oenology I hear."

"We are donating a portion, plus our time and expertise, but the King is funding the main part." Petra looked surprised. She recalled the announcement and understood it to be the Wife's enterprise.

House leaned in, "Your father the King wanted to make the announcement of our donation knowing that once it was made, other traders and folks in the echer-uppalongs would all follow suit."

"Which of course they did," said Shoshama while Petra allowed a noise indicating it was all pretty clever.

"Which of course they did," repeated House. After which Mister said it again too. As well.

"You two friends then?" asked House waggling a finger between them.

"We are indeed!" confirmed Petra.

"What licky, licky and all that?" she asked without batting an eyelid.

Petra yelped and Shoshama gasped, "House! We are just friends, really!" said Shoshama, "What would people say if they thought that? Or if you said that to people who hadn't thought that until you said it and then it was in their minds?"

"What's that dear?" asked Mister.

"Nothing Mister, go back to your wine. This is girl talk and I'm not blind, but you two are the loveliest of girls. I've known you all your life," she said addressing Petra, "And I couldn't love you more if you were my own and I was heartbroken to hear you were gone and then buried all that pain, tried not to think of it too often. And this Angel of the East arrived at our door and I thought, hello, what have we got here? And all she could think about was how to get in the castle. Now we know it was because she wanted to find you. Like a cat scratching at the door where all the rabbits are hung she was, eager's not the word for it. Anyway, here you are, looking like the cats got the cream, all milky lips and purring your hearts out!" and again the Princesses gasped and laughed. "Anyway, good luck to you and come visit. Come for breakfast tomorrow, we got your favourites, Biscowheats and you can have I might on your crumpets too."

"We will," said Shoshama and meant it.

Petra leaned on her father the King and sighed happily. He patted her arm and then frowned as he looked the empty seat to his left. "I say, Petra dear, what's all this about?" he said wafting his hand around the empty place, "Homage to your dear departed mother? Not saying I don't approve but…"

Petra looked at him with a lively expression and excited eyes, something that would have seemed unusual to him had it not been near-permanent since Shoshama arrived. "Oh!" she said frowning suddenly, "Weren't you supposed to be finding a wife?"

"Oh, good grief girl, I've been far too busy these past days for that. Anyway, I'm not rushing into it at my age. Sort of thing takes time. Needs thinking about. Not a spring chicken. Heart needs warming." He was almost muttering to himself but it all made Shoshama just laugh harder, which confused him.

"We have one more guest," and with that loud announcement, the curtains parted at one side of the Great Hall and from the back corridor which had originally housed the large and unapologetic Greek painting, emerged the lady who sent it, the Queen of Athens herself. Her hair was spiralled, copious and black, hanging past her bare shoulders, while her tanned skin was set off by a wraparound white dress in the style of ancient Greece and which could have been borrowed directly from any of the naked goddesses in the picture which still hung above the King this evening. A great deal of gold jewellery festooned her wrists and hung about her neck and from her ears. She was about halfway between the skinniness of the young Princesses and the ample plumpness of the Mayor and to the King's eye, which benefitted greatly from her low-cut dress, she was just about perfect.

The King was on his feet and bowing, "My dear Queen, how lovely of you to attend, but how…?"

"Princess Petra invited me," she purred in her adorable Greek accent.

"But how was there time? Why a messenger would still be on his way to you!"

Petra jumped in at this point, "No father, when the painting arrived and you liked it so much that you wrote to thank her, I also wrote to the Queen suggesting she come and visit Prague and I did so because I was certain you would not go to Athens." The King meekly agreed he wouldn't have gone. "So I begged her to make the trip and told her how beautiful Prague was and that you would be delighted to see her and whatever happened beyond that, I'd show her the sights. So…. she wrote back and said she would come for my 18th birthday! She's been here at the Grande Velky Hotel since Wednesday. Just in time!"

"Well!" he said, "I am dumbstruck!" which wasn't quite true and as he pulled out her seat and helped her push into the table, a ripple of applause began which grew into something of a standing ovation and glasses were raised and a succession of toasts proposed to the King, the Princess, the Queen of Athens, the Queen Angelika Děti Škola, the Mayor, the Chief, the visiting Princes and Princess Shoshama. The King responded with an impromptu speech where he thanked his guests, the Mayor, the Chief, Mrs

Gregory, the Princes and Princess Shoshama, the Queen of Athens for gracing them all with her presence and most of all, Princess Petra for being a truly incredible daughter, a statement which was so heartfelt it brought tears to his eyes and made the words catch in his throat.

"Did you like the gift?" said the Greek Queen, leaning close to the King for privacy.

"Absolutely! I wrote and told you so!"

"Pah!" she waved a dismissive hand, "You could have hated it and still sent a letter of thanks. But you really liked it eh?"

"Who wouldn't want their own Polybanksos? And yes, I find the... subject precisely to my taste." She raised her eyebrows to this admission, "What I mean is, I've never thought the human form to be anything other than nature's perfection personified. Think of a big cat, a bird of prey, a shark even, a fine stallion, all fabulous designs that amaze and intrigue, but none as much as our own species." The Queen nodded slowly, studying him, but still seemed dissatisfied with his answer. The King took a forkful of food and between chewing said, "And you know what I like best about it?"

"Go on."

"That some people don't know how to respond to it. I like their discomfort, their shock and even for some uptight twits, their disapproval."

"THAT'S why I sent it!" she exclaimed.

"They look at a little harmless patch of fur, the nipples for baby meals, the bits nature gave us to um... carry on with and they are absolutely appalled and yet under their clothing, they have all the same doings and wotnot!"

"Ha! Doings and wotnot." She winked, her big brown eyes and long, long eyelashes exaggerating the gesture. "I knew you would like it but I also knew you would enjoy rubbing all the doings and wotnot, the tits and bums in stupid people's faces!" He laughed warmly, looked at her and frowned as the laughter petered out. "You miss your wife?" He nodded sadly. "I loved her too. I loved my husband, he died, I loved your wife, she died, I loved you, you didn't die, so here I am."

"I'm sorry about the King."

"Why? He died of too much living. If he'd lived a bit slower or a bit less, he would probably have lived longer, but he crammed it in to 42 years and went. If he'd had it explained to him in a contract he would have signed it."

"Forty-two though, that's just your third year of being 30 here. So young…"

"Forget him now. On his deathbed he suggested you."

"He did? Me?"

"Yes, of course. So tell me, have I wasted my journey?"

"Not at all. It's just a bit of a surprise that's all. It's been quite a week!"

"The Princess told me all about it. But you've been in limbo for the last four years. I hope my gift stopped you forgetting what doings and wotnot are for or you'll never find a new wife."

"They say you never forget how to ride a bike."

"As a Queen, I've received better compliments," she said smiling, to which the King, realising what he'd said started panicking, "That's better. I'm flustering you. It is a good sign!" and gave his thigh a squeeze.

With her, the Queen had brought a letter from the new, young King and Queen of Vienna, who had stopped off at the Palace in Athens while on their honeymoon and upon hearing where the Queen was bound, each wrote to Petra. Johann to say they had sorely missed her at their wedding and that they hoped to visit on their return loop to Vienna in a few weeks' time and Isabella to say that several people had been seeking her out at the wedding and that she hoped all was well with the missing and consequently, mysterious Princess. Petra anticipated their visit anxiously. Should she be candid about her love for Shoshama or ought they to be included in the vast span of people for whom ignorance was the safer option?

While Petra mused over her letter, Chatty had been reading a piece of card delivered by a newly appointed castle footman. "What do you have there my little darling?" asked the Mayor.

"A card from my staff at Split. On one side is an illustration of people enjoying the beach with a slogan, *Wish You Were Here* on it and on the other a brief note of thanks signed by each of them. It's kind and they are asking if they should come here, return to Wolverhampton or if I might go there."

"And what would you like them to do?" she asked.

"I don't know..." he said, slightly flustered and looking at her. "What do you think?"

"We will go to Split together," she said, in the decisive way he adored and appreciated in her. "A honeymoon!" she added, giggling and wriggling. Chatty stared into space, a little frightened but certainly happy.

Dancing commenced after food and once again, the two of them showed everyone how to turn a pleasant pastime into an impressive artform and folks wondered just how a lady of such generous (although firm to the touch) proportions could be so light on her feet. There were gasps of happy surprise and raucous applause when later in the evening, the music was silenced to announce the engagement of the dancing duo and the scene repeated itself when Mrs Gregory announced she and Prince Adalbert were also engaged. Petra leaned into Shoshama and whispered that she was sorry convention meant they couldn't do anything dramatic and public like that and that she was proud of her, but even more so herself, for acting with such propriety when all she wanted was for the two of them to kiss. Then to her horror, Shoshama stood and said, "Let's see shall we?"

She tapped her wine glass and for the third time in the evening, the band petered out and peoples' attention was drawn to the action-packed top table. "Ladies and Gentlemen, Lords and Ladies, King Wenceslas and the Queen of Athens, Princess Petra and the Princes. It is my greatest honour and pleasure to have come to know these people and to spend these last few weeks in the magnificent city of Prague." This caused applause. "Firstly, may I congratulate Prince Chatty and the Mayor and Prince Adalbert and Mrs Gregory on their engagements," more cheering and applause. "And now I would like to draw your attention once more to everyone's heroine, the incredibly beautiful, incredibly talented, incredibly good-hearted and well, just incredible Princess Petra!" and so much applause, cheering and foot-stamping followed that people shook their heads and laughed at the unparalleled wave of adoration the Princess now inspired in people. "Like you all, I love her deeply and so.." The King watched intently, a feint frown appearing on his face, while Darius wore a similar expression of concern and hesitancy and a sideways glance at Petra herself showed her to be shaking her head and looking a little panicked. "And so…"continued Shoshama, "Please raise a glass with me and wish the Princess a happy 18th birthday!" The room stood and sang her birthday wishes and when it was over, Princess Petra curtseyed gracefully and sank to her seat, her legs a feeling unsteady.

"You! Oh my goodness I thought you were going to…"

Shoshama leaned in and hugged her tightly. "Happy birthday darling. I love you," receiving the tightest hug back and a repeated refrain of *I love you, I love you, I love you* in her ear.

The dancing recommenced for the fourth time and the two Princesses danced with the King, with the Princes and with each other. On one of the occasions when Petra danced with Shoshama, the latter said, "There's a piece of your past I want to know about."

"Go on," said Petra, their dresses so large at the hem that they were pressing two circles into one as they danced.

"The three months you were away from here. Where did you go? What did you do?"

"Oh gosh, that's a story. I promise to tell you, it's not a secret, but not now, not here." Shoshama was satisfied and looked forward to hearing of her lover's adventure.

During an excuse me, Adalbert swapped Mrs Gregory with Chatty who graciously introduced the Mayor to his friend. Both were suffering from an unfamiliar form of exhaustion which included jelly legs among its many symptoms. "My goodness, these Prague ladies, Chatty!" said Adalbert.

Chatty widened his eyes and puffed his cheeks in reply. "I'm riding a wave of bliss dear chap. A beautiful floaty wave of the utmost bliss!"

And as they were pulled into each other's fiancée's bosom, Adalbert called out, "But mine comes with extra servings of food!"

And as they spun around past each other the next time, Chatty said, "Whereas mine just comes with extra servings!"

Darius mostly watched from the table, looking serene and content. He had congratulated each of his friends on their engagements and taken the opportunity to ask Chatty if he knew his fiancée's name. "Yes of course!" said Chatty, "It's Mary."

"Really?" asked Darius bemused, "Are you sure?"

"Yes Mary, why?"

"Mary or Mayor-y?"

"Mary or Mary? What are you asking?"

"Mary or Mayor-eeee? Mary the Mayor or the merry Mayory Mayor?"

Chatty squeezed Darius's elbow and uncharacteristically for him just said, "Don't care which it is Darius. That's how we differ I suppose. Let me know if you ever get to the bottom of it though!" and giving him an affectionate slap on the back walked back to where Mary or Mayory was seated. Seeing him approach she waved him in and presented a lap for him to sit on.

With Chatty comfortably wrapped up in her arms, she then waved Darius over to them and offered him a chair between her and the Chief. Once Darius was seated the policeman said, "So, are you a Prince *and* a detective, or just a Prince?"

"Until coming to Prague, just a Prince."

"I don't believe it!" said the Chief, "You have always been more than that."

"Which is why we want to offer you a position here," said the Mayor, to which Darius enquired what type of position that might be. "We don't know, but something in security,"

"You know I don't need a wage don't you? That I *am* actually a Prince and not in need of any earnings."

"Yes, which is why the offer includes an apartment in the city and all your expenses, but no actual salary, "said the Mayor.

"I'll think about it," said Darius.

"Please do Inspector, er Darius, I mean Prince Darius. We need you," said the Chief.

"Oh I don't know that you do, but I promise I'll think about it. I do like it here, I mean it."

"Can I ask, is any part of your name Purile," asked the Chief, taking care to pronounce Purile, Perr-eel, "Or was that just a cover?"

"No, no that's my actual name. I am Prince Darius Purile.

Not much of a cover using my real name was it? The only bit that was made up was Inspector." The Chief looked at him in admiration while the Mayor planted a series of kisses on Chatty's head as he sat comfortably on her lap. Chatty looked like he'd just been given the loveliest gift imaginable and beamed his affection back up at her.

Elsewhere, Adalbert and Mrs Gregory were now doing a slow dance and held each other tight, rocking from side to side and having to steer out of the path of Mr and Mrs Tickle-Krackedarse who were just as tightly embraced but equally aware of the other couple's proximity. Just days before, these two had been on opposite sides of a table, their horns locked in a bitter battle. While Adalbert had not been the subject of her personal bile, she recognised that to him, she might still be the enemy. As they passed, Adalbert caught Polly's eye and she looked deeply sorry and apologetic and Adalbert, being the big, friendly chap he was, and without a bad bone in his body, just gave her one of his wide, dopey smiles and watched as her face cracked, a tear fell as she blubbed once and mouthed, 'Sorry' to him once more before she was spun away in the slow dance. Adalbert took bigger steps and positioned himself once again behind her so that he was able to give her a gentle little pinch in a delicate area suggested by her name. She gave a little squeak and leap and turning to see who her tweaker was, saw Adalbert's grinning face and laughed good humouredly. This was perhaps the first spontaneous and good-humoured thing she had done in several years and she was not unaware of how it made her little dry heart sing. In that moment, it turned from dull grey to a faint shade of pink, and what's more, it grew fractionally bigger. She was on her way. The couples parted with Mrs Tickle-Krackedarse and Adalbert each telling their partners what had just happened and all to great, mutual amusement.

The King spent the evening in happy conversation with the Queen of Athens, and Petra was delighted to see them laughing repeatedly. They had spent some time standing before the big painting she had sent him just four years ago and while she couldn't hear what they were saying, she did note that her father's hand was around the Queen's waist. It was clear they were getting on, she a widow, he a widower and although the King was a decade older, that didn't seem to matter at all.

Seated once again and deep in conversation, the King topped up the Queen's wine glass, she laughed and slid the glass back across to him, now he laughed, downed it in one and refilling it once more, slid it back to her. She laughed with more delight than ever and took a modest sip, then leaned her head on his shoulder. Petra watched and it warmed her heart. The other thing that warmed her heart was that whenever she looked around for Shoshama, whether she found her in conversation with someone or dancing with a guest, she always seemed to know Petra was looking and smile right back at her across the void. It was as if they could feel each other's gaze and knew when it was upon them. Petra learned she could not see Shoshama's eyes upon her without it lighting a fire within.

At about 2 am, the King helped the Queen of Athens to her feet and said he would show her to her quarters and then retire himself, and they left together, waving over their shoulders to the polite applause of the crowd. This was the signal that others might leave if they were ready. Usually, such a move preceded a mass exodus but not tonight. As time passed, a few coats were brought by the new footmen and couples and fours said their farewells and went to their carriages, some drunk, all merry and all proud to have been at this uniquely Great Prague Ball where so many momentous things had occurred. All in all it was a much slower

Geoffrey Fitchett

trickle of weary revellers, taking their time to bid all and sundry goodbye, with promises to meet in the days to come and unqualified praise for all that occurred to bring them together. It was universally agreed that the good times were here once again.

Among those receiving hats and coats were the Chief and his wife who dutifully circulated to say they were leaving. When he reached Petra, the Chief asked, "Princess, I wonder if you have any notion about the masked mystery man, the one who folk are now saying was Sir Hillman?"

"Sir Hillman?" Petra responded with a face suggesting ignorance.

"Yes, the individual with such athleticism and fighting skills as to make him seem almost superhuman. Tall yet lithe," he looked her up and down, aware this was improper, yet his manner was supremely deferential, and she knew him to be a loyal royalist. "*Someone* invited him. I mean *someone* must know him, must know *who* he is. He *is* someone. I wonder do you know anything about him?"

"I'm sorry I do not. Sir Hillman, you say?" She pondered as if thinking deeply about the question.

"Yes, Sir Hillman Avenger, he's something of a vigilante. He has removed a few undesirables from Prague society over the years and so while his operations are not entirely condoned by the state, there is no appetite to obstruct his efforts. He could even be considered something of a hero, after all he is clearly a force for good." The Chief watched her reaction closely and Shoshama was also deeply interested in the discussion. Petra just shook her head and said she couldn't help as she didn't know anything about the man.

"Well of course we're all assuming it's a man because it would take a very special kind of woman to possess those fighting skills. Wouldn't seem possible." Shoshama took a

347

sharp intake of breath as the realisation of what was being suggested dawned on her. "For the sake of the city, I hope he continues to look after us, that we can rely on his rare but incisive visits," concluded the Chief.

"Come on George, don't monopolise the Princess, it's time to go home," said the Chief's wife.

"It's alright Mrs Dixon, your husband could never out-stay his welcome and we all appreciate the superb work he does for the city," said Petra.

"We are only just learning about how much you have done for Prague, Princess and I think people only know the half of it even now, so thank *you*!" said the Chief, shaking her hand and bowing with genuine admiration and sincerity.

The Great Hall continued to empty, but faster now and Petra took Shoshama by the hand and said, "Ready?"

"Gosh I'm so tired! Was the Chief of Police saying what I think he was saying?"

"What, that I know who Sir Hillman Avenger is?"

"Petra darling, I think he was intimating more than that?"

Petra gave a non committal shrug, "What would I know about him?" said Petra with a twinkle in her eye.

"What indeed? As if I needed any more reasons to love you!" she said laughing.

"And my darling Shoshama, I certainly do not need any more reasons to love you." Her face adopted the visage of sheer adoration, the former amusement giving way to passion.

Shoshama grinned. "You may not need one, but I still intend to give you one!" Petra gasped and punched her on the arm, "What? I mean a reason to love me more, I was thinking a nice cup of hot chocolate, why, what did you think I meant?" to which Petra punched her again.

"Ow! That hurt! Who are you, Sir Hillman Avenger or something?" and the sound of their laughter faded as they mounted the stairs together.

Darius watched them leave and smiled, happy for everyone including himself. He had decided. He would not be staying in Prague because he needed to go home. There was business to attend to and affairs to settle, matters to sort. He was eager to leave because once all those things were done, he would be free to return and start his new life, for he too intended to make Prague his home. Where else could a man find so many of his best friends? And where else could he get a vegetarian sausage roll as good as Mrs Gregory's?

The end

Acknowledgements

Thank you to whoever misquoted Somerset Maugham
A little research suggests that the earliest and closest version of *everyone has a book in them* is probably Somerset Maugham, who in his 1938 memoir *The Summing Up* wrote, *'There is an impression abroad that everyone has it in him to write one book; but if by this is implied a good book the impression is false.'* Perhaps it's a good thing that until recently, the second part was unknown to me because propelled by the idea that surely, we do all have a story to tell, I started mine a decade ago.

Writing, or at least *attempting* to write, had a dramatic effect on how I read other peoples' work and I began to ascribe opinions like, poetic, dull, contrived, lazy, genius, overreaching and incisive to what glowed forth from my Kindle each night. Reflecting on the worst ones, I was compelled to believe I could do better and on the best ones, that I didn't belong in their company. And these two competing positions remain securely rooted, collecting evidence to support their claims and ready to offer (respectively) support or a derogatory sneer whenever the opportunity arose.

More than a decade ago I began *the book*. A part-fact but mostly fictional historical novel set towards the end of WWII featuring my father – who was a serving sergeant in the British 7th Armoured Division and my wife's grandfather, a Sherman tank commander in the 749th Tank Battalion in Patton's 3rd Army. It was and remains a momentous struggle to create the story, research the historical detail and the geography of the setting and even the basic stuff of a writer's day-to-day work, to know who said what a few chapters earlier. Along the way it stalled, it lurched forward, it reversed into a ditch, it emerged muddy but ready to go again, then conked out once more. It contained commendable parts but it was so, so hard! Well, I'm not a writer am I. And yet everyone has a book in them and maybe this is mine… One notion compelled me to keep going, the other, that what I was experiencing was proof that it wasn't meant to be. By nature, I may be a bit of a pessimist, but something has kept me writing it.

Thank you for the idea for The Rescuists

Then, in a period where the big novel was sitting uncared-for up to its axels in mud, *The Rescuists* happened. Explained more fully in the foreword, it was six-year-old Mila's little story of the Princess and The Knight (spelled Nit) that set my mind to work and The Rescuists flew from my fingers and into the digital files of my laptop at a pace with which I was entirely unfamiliar. For that, thank you Mila.

Thank you for keeping me writing

At first I handed each chapter to my wife Jennifer. She had formed frown-lines over the other book and had been forced to find a wider and wider variety of ways to tell me she didn't like/didn't understand/was bored by/ confused by/thought I should change what I'd given her, was now saying, *"I like it, it's really good."* This was a surprise. We were in unfamiliar territory. As it progressed, I farmed it out further, seeking honest feedback from two more people I believed would not

mince their words and what I received was copious enthusiastic encouragement along with notification of typos and
continuity errors. Greer and Jo, thank you, because if it
hadn't passed your muster, it would have gone no further.
Expecting a rather different response, I then gave it to Paul,
a business associate of mine dating back to the late 1980s, a
bastion of grammar, someone who wrote a corporate email
to all 60 of our employees explaining the proper use of the
apostrophe. The world needs gatekeepers for these things or
we'll all be talking like we're auditioning for Eastenders or
a job on Radio 1. I figured Paul would be the one to instil
some reality, he could bring me back down to Earth, burst
the bubble with his pragmatic common sense, politely end
the dream with one of his infamous personal assessments.
I expected, *"Well… it's a bit of fun I suppose. I'm not sure
who's going to like it… someone somewhere perhaps."* But what
I got was more praise. He liked it and reported that he'd
laughed out loud, a rarity when it comes to reading he told
me. Jennifer, Greer, Jo and Paul were the ones who kept me
on it, pushed me to finish it and made me return to it and
make it better once I thought it was done.

Thank you for solving the near-impossible task of getting The Rescuists published

Paul's unexpectedly enthusiastic support was the extra piece
of motivation needed for me to take the next step; farming
it out to publishing agents, a stage every budding author
faces and at which so very many come unstuck. The advice
is to send your manuscript along with a series of carefully
worded begging letters designed to fit the agent's specific
and diverse criteria. If the agents banded together and
jointly conspired to thwart all future publications, the way
they go about their business wouldn't be much different.
The problem for agents is that so few new books sell in any

quantities, partly because they are simply not commercial enough and partly because the market is so crowded. That statistic works against the new author for her or his chances of having written something commercially viable are pretty slim. It might be good but that doesn't mean it will sell. On the other hand, it might be tripe, but that doesn't mean it won't.

In this the world of books is no different to so many other commercial enterprises. New businesses mostly fail. New restaurants rarely last beyond a year. Most budding recording artists don't make it anywhere near the charts. Most motorsports competitors spend a lifetime involved in local, club events and never cast a shadow on the grid for the big national or international race events. They may all dream of the big time but the majority of personal enterprises, endeavours and stories will remain mired in the small time. We hear the success stories from all disciplines and walks of life because they get the airtime, but there are many, many more attempts that end in disappointment.

Projecting my own thoughts for a moment, I expect there are quite a few writers who don't really expect their book to occupy Waterstones window display but would be happy to have a boxful to distribute among friends. That it should just see the light of day in print, conventionally bound and adorning a smattering of people's bookshelves rather than curl up forgotten, a stack of yellowing printed sheets (accidentally shuffled out of sequence and with a few key pages missing) loosely stacked in a shoe box on top of the spare bedroom wardrobe, or unlikely ever to be seen again, saved – but only ironically – in an innocuously titled file in the depths of the author's desktop computer.

Self-publishing might be the answer, but the stats suggest otherwise. Like a housewife deciding it's time she learned to drive and after failing to engage with a local driving instructor, she enters herself and her dinky Fiat 500 into a British Touring Car Championship race at Silverstone. It probably won't end well, she's keen to have a go with or without the help of the experts and insiders but frankly, she doesn't really know what she's doing and is just hoping her talent will carry her through. It's pretty crowded and competitive out there, but without help at the grassroots level what choice did she really have, what else was she to do? And with self-publishing there have been success stories so just like big winners on the lottery, there's always a chance, right? No matter how small, she can hope?

That's where Gareth Howard of Authoright came in. I thank him for spotting enough of something worthwhile in the Rescuists to be prepared to support me in investing in its future, giving it life, getting it out my laptop and into your hands.

Thank you for the wonderful cover art
Indianapolis artist Katie Deveau produced the cover and the drawing of Darius for the inside of the book and we had a great many Transatlantic video calls nailing down the detail. To understand the task she insisted on reading the manuscript and I was concerned that the uninhibited Britishness of the humour might not entirely work with her. I need not have worried because she liked it a lot and even read passages out to her chap while the two of them laughed together. What more could I ask? She also said that she absent-mindedly hit 'play' on a podcast on her morning commute and then spent a few minutes trying to identify why she was experiencing disappointment. Finally, she realised she was wishing the Audible story was *The Rescuists* instead of the other, already published work she had downloaded and was working her way through each day. That little bonus anecdote was the icing on the cake. Thank you

for the artwork Katie and for liking the book, something I might have hoped for but would have been arrogant to expect.

It seems that a journalist took Maugham's witty line and made it funnier by saying, *"Everyone has a book in them, and that, in most cases, is where it should stay."* I hope more people agree this is one of those which deserved to come out. If you agree, I save my final thanks for you. Thank you dear reader!